BRIGHT SHINING
AS THE SUN

BRIGHT SHINING AS THE SUN

An Émile Cinq-Mars Novel

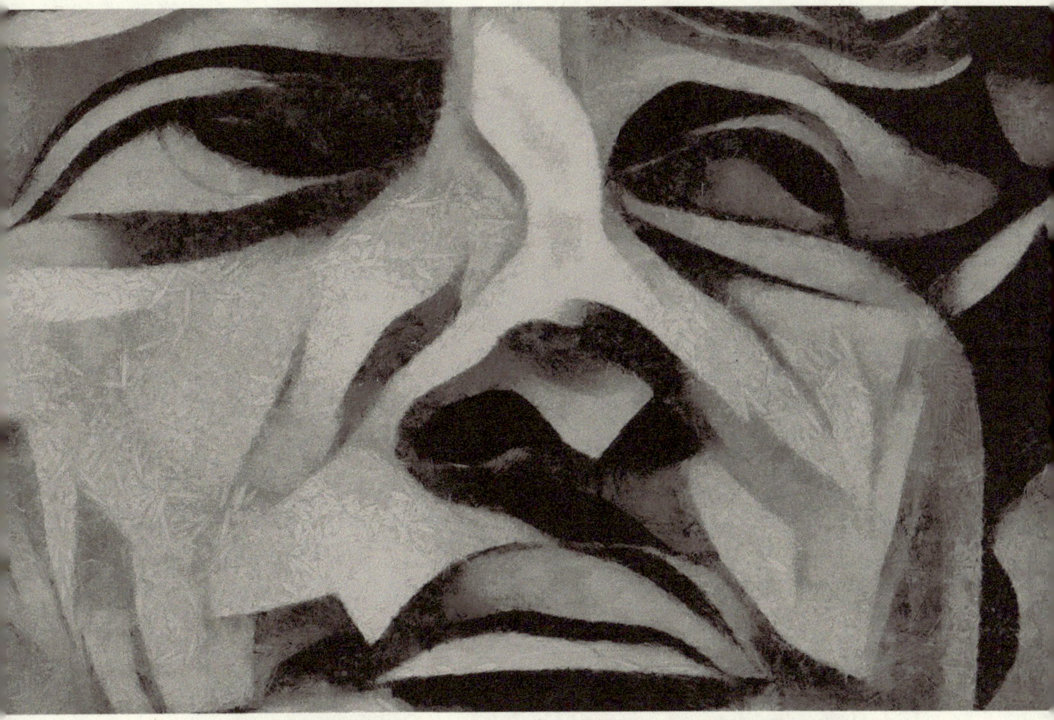

JOHN FARROW

EXILE editions

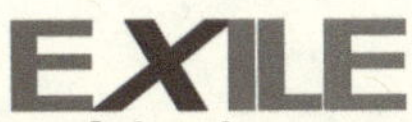

singular fiction, poetry, nonfiction, translation, drama, and graphic books

Library and Archives Canada Cataloguing in Publication

Title: Bright shining as the sun / John Farrow.
Names: Farrow, John, 1947- author
Series: Farrow, John, 1947- Émile Cinq-Mars thrillers.
Description: Series statement: An Émile Cinq-Mars novel
Identifiers: Canadiana (print) 20240424530 | Canadiana (ebook) 20240424565 | ISBN 9781990773303 (softcover) | ISBN 9781990773334 (PDF) | ISBN 9781990773310 (EPUB) | ISBN 9781990773327 (Kindle)
Subjects: LCGFT: Thrillers (Fiction) | LCGFT: Detective and mystery fiction. | LCGFT: Novels.
Classification: LCC PS8561.A785 B75 2025 | DDC C813/.54—dc23

Book and cover designed by Michael Callaghan
Cover image by breakermaximus/shutterstock
Typeset in Fairfield font at Moons of Jupiter Studios
Printed and Bound in Canada by Gauvin

Published by Exile Editions ~ www.ExileEditions.com
144483 Southgate Road 14, Holstein, Ontario, N0G 2A0

Canada ONTARIO CREATES

We gratefully acknowledge the Government of Canada and Ontario Creates for their financial support toward our publishing activities.

Canadian sales representation: The Canadian Manda Group, 664 Annette Street, Toronto ON M6S 2C8 www.mandagroup.com 416 516 0911

North American and international distribution, and U.S. sales: Independent Publishers Group, 814 North Franklin Street, Chicago IL 60610 www.ipgbook.com toll free: 1 800 888 4741

To the greats:
To my great-nephew Rundle,
and my great-niece Inga,
and my great-nephew Erik.
If not for now, then someday.

PART ONE

CATCH AND PITCH

PART TWO

FOUND AND LOST

Part Three

RUN AND HIT

Part Four

ENTER AND BREAK

PART ONE

CATCH AND PITCH

1. Punishment and Crime

A slurry of truths, lies, and reminiscences.

Sombre facts float on a sea of wild fictions. Montreal Sergeant-Detective Émile Cinq-Mars, retired and yet recovering from a gunshot wound, declines to interrupt the spiel. He must discern what part of the rigmarole is invention, which observations chronicle the facts, what's a falsehood right on the spot and for what reason, and which tales reflect reasonable assumptions. In a litany of contradictions from the lips of the ageing, wounded hoodlum, he must decipher what's true, what's false.

Says Sykes:

A thing we say: *If you can't do the time, don't do the crime.* We're like a chorus. We say: *I can do five years standing on my head with my head in a bucket. Touch the ceiling with my toes. Entertain myself that way, walking on the ceiling.* We say those things horsing around, figuring life out. The ups. The goddamn downs.

Some say six years. Some substitute seven. A guy brags he can do six-to-eight standing on his head, his head in a bucket, the bucket full of ice. You know how braggarts get. But there's a cut-off. Comes in at around eight years, nine. I've done the calculations. Nobody in their right mind gets into double digits. Nobody brags he can do 10 years standing on his head even if his head is *not* in a bucket. A whole decade upside down in or out of ice water, yeah, that's too much for any man alive to bear. For starters, it's hard to think of yourself 10 years down the road, picking up where you left off like nothing's changed. Wherever you leave off from, 10 years later nothing exists. It might *look* like something's still there – not so. Everything got different on you. You can't find your way back to what's not there no more. That's how the honest wretchedness in life passes you by when you pull steady time. One way or another, Émile, we all pull steady time. For me, that's the one real certainty I know that I know.

The ex-con takes a pause. Cinq-Mars waits and says nothing.

Says Sykes:

Everything, when you're looking down the barrel of 10 years, moves on without you.

What once was, was. What was is no more.

There's no present. The past you're living in got took away by the future. Folks call it the present but it's not that. Not for you. You're not there yet.

Lucky for me, all my long stretches got cut in half. Released for good behaviour. I thought of you those times. You'd be proud.

Like I tell anybody who wants to listen, on the inside the sun don't shine. Or it comes up grimmer than the night is dark. Time does not pass on the inside. We know it can't stand still. Time just gets took away from you. It moves on without you, then leaves you behind.

Says Sykes:

Fact is, I been falsely accused as much as I been guilty of some charges. People don't believe me when I tell them I feel no deep resentment about those false accusations. They think I'm trying to sell them a stale loaf. Why is it that I don't cry in my sleep or weep in my morning porridge? Folks who are well-meaning ask me that. Like the shrinks in the can. *You must be angry, Douglas*, that's something they say. *Deep inside*, they say. Drawing me out. *If you think you're so innocent, you must be pissed off.* See, people don't get the difference. To be falsely accused does not make me an innocent man. In my head, to be falsely accused for this or that crime, all that does is make up for the crimes where I was never caught. Where I was never the accused or where I slipped the rap. A wash.

A little anger. I'm human. But no lingering bitterness. It's all a wash.

Until now, yeah.

Now is different.

This one charge is too big a charge to pin on me.

Never mind 10 years, I could get 20. Twenty-five! Which in my case means life. *My* life. No way can I do that standing on my head. Or sleeping in bed. Or sitting up in a chair. *This*, this here is not a wash, Émile. It's a goddamn ice bucket. I might deserve something for, well, you know, for whatever, for something nobody's thought to accuse me of yet. Nothing like this.

Not saying I'm innocent. Who is? I *am* saying that I have been falsely maligned.

Émile Cinq-Mars is brought up short, remembering how this man can use a word such as *maligned*, that he possesses a vocabulary outside the norm. He wasn't always destined to be a low-life criminal. He possessed aspirations before that day on the railway tracks. Sykes was a mere boy in his teens when they first met. In those days, the boy read books. He studied. He imagined a future. He was going to make something of himself.

All that went wrong.

Says Sykes:

Émile, this time is nothing like those other times. I had my complicity back then. I know. We know. This time, I'm fighting for my life.

Call me arrogant, I happen to believe my life is worth fighting for. Ain't that a switch from the golden olden days, hey? Imagine that. Me, thinking I'm worth something.

I could go down for second degree and you might think to yourself that that is a justified decree, whether I did the deed or not, because murder got me in trouble in the first place, right? We met over a killing, you and me. I didn't do the time back then for that one on the railway tracks. Not in the ordinary sense.

Then there was that other time. I know you know what I'm talking about. Yeah, the worms. The worms. Listen. Get your head around this. We try to forget the past, don't we? We try, right? Still, you must know, and I have found out, it's not entirely possible. Everybody fails that test, right?

See, you're all I got, Émile. You. All I got. I can forgive the past, but I can't forget it. I'm calling on you in the here and now.

I figure you know why. Tell me I'm not dead wrong.

You're not saying much, Émile. You're like one of them shrinks in the can who never say peep. They stare down their noses at me. And you, you've got the biggest one in the country. Nose, I mean. You know it, too, don't ya? What a honker.

Keep staring. See if I care.

Émile. That one time you saved my life. Then twice. You did it twice! Don't you want to see if you can do it again? You don't want those first two times to go down in vain, right?

Think of it as a challenge, Émile.

I sure want to see if you can do it again.

I'm depending on it.

Look, I'm sorry about the nose crack. I didn't mean no insult. Joshing you is all.

You're not saying much. Why so silent?

Émile, come on. I can't do the time. That's the point here. Trust me on this one: I did not do the crime. Okay?

2. Out and In

Dare to compare. In Montreal, Park Avenue is never so grand as boulevards sharing the name in other cities. Neglect tends to the street's facade, intertwined with insipid development. As the street slopes uphill at its south end, office windows are indelibly smudged by airborne grease and grime, stale exhaust soot. Salesmen at a car dealership stand with their hands in their pockets. Glumly gaze. Absent-mindedly fondle themselves and think about grabbing a coffee. Former rooming houses are now martial arts studios or dance studios or questionable import-export firms. Needle-trade factories have heard the last of their wretched machines spin silent, the business shunted to China, Bangladesh, Turkey. Fur companies persevere since animals providing the fur off their backs still shit in the woods up north and not in Asia. On the sidewalks, various muddles of pedestrians clomp uphill alongside the blunt of traffic, which is one-way down as if seeking bottom. As this is Montreal, they pass a church. Men in suits. Men with briefcases. As this is Montreal, they pass an empty lot. Women in suits. Wearing flats. They know it's true, that New York begs the comparison, that alongside the grandeur of Park Avenue in New York City, *avenue du Parc* in Montreal commences the day as depleted and shabby.

Like their lives. The people on the streets suspect that that's true, too.

The avenue commences with a further ignominy, fixed as it is through its early stretch with the dull name *Bleury*.

Above *avenue des Pins* – in English, mistranslated into the singular: Pine Avenue – the roadway expands into a six-lane thoroughfare, acquires its appellation and brooks the Big Apple comparison. *Parc* lances the grand playground of Mount Royal, the broad grasses and forested hilltop, famous for vistas, ponds, walking trails, and proudly sharing its architect, Frederick Law Olmsted, with New York's more renowned Central Park. Northbound, narrowing again, the boulevard returns to being congested, chock-a-block through a perpetual clash of cultures, immigrants and Hasidim, French and long-standing Portuguese, a potpourri of nations and students, merchants and shoppers, Haitian, Italian, Indian, Arab, the generations commingling. Exterior staircases spiral to second and third stories. Above the thrum of buses and trucks, cars and childhood racket, residents inhale a cooler breath or smoke on their balconies. The narrative of the street dulls down through blocks of warehouses and factories on the verge of being gentrified, buildings claimed for the interim by musicians to bang their drums loudly, by visual artists to throw paint on canvas or chisel stone, and by students and other drug users before the street ducks below a set of railway tracks then rises into a community that draws its name from the avenue's abrupt conclusion: Park Extension/*Extension du Parc*.

It's here, after a tedious drive north in the heat, that a man locates a legal spot to nudge his beat-up Corolla into an endless coil of automobiles. He's on *avenue de l'Épée*, the Street of the Sword, the name confiscated from Paris, some say. Covertly, it's here that he extracts a weapon from his trunk.

No sword. For him, a plebeian pistol.

Hunched over, to block his enterprise from prying eyes, the man switches out the standard magazine. Always an issue: concealment or more capacity? The new magazine of the ported M&P Shield extends the handle and gives him an extra couple of rounds, which he might need. He hopes not. He does not want to get into a goddamn gunfight.

Get in, get out. Kill. Maim. Hear the screams. Jump ship. That's the plan.

Only a scant few know why he has arrived on a muggy summer's day to inflict his damage. He intends to both kill and refuse to kill. Reasons for his choices wander across the continent and wend through time, eventually coming home to roost. He alone knows why he does what he does or how he goes about his business.

He alone knows why he will shoot to kill some and shoot to merely wound another.

It's complicated.

Set, he tucks the Smith & Wesson M&P Shield under his belt, tugs his windbreaker over the jut of the grip and the magazine, then slams the trunk's lid. Not long ago he was rear-ended – he says, although, drinking, he may have backed into a pole, the details elude him – so he needs to bang hard to get the latch to click.

It clicks.

Hot out. Blistering. Feels that way to him. He's the only man in the neighbourhood wearing a jacket. His bald scalp sweats. The long and stringy hair at the back of his neck is damp. For some, it's a fine day that's a tad warm and humid. To him it feels hotter.

He wears the symbol for infinity tattooed on a protuberant nub above his left eyebrow. He remembers to return to the car for his ball cap, to conceal both his telltale baldness and the tattoo while he's entering the premises nearby and again when he comes back out.

If— if – he comes back out.

3. Peace and War

On his left, two cops are in a squad car waiting for the light. On his right, a cop is ticketing pedestrians. Law enforcement has come to this. Ticketing jaywalkers. People once were free to walk these streets with impunity and dodge cars at their own risk. Now the city comes down heavy against jaywalkers. Sharpie thinks so and the problem is the government. Any level. Why the hell does a government constantly need more money? Are they in business? No wonder a guy turns to drugs to earn an honest living these days, taxes what they are.

Only crime pays for the ordinary citizen.

His Tahoe towers over the squad car. He'd like to dust the cops right through the intersection. Force them to give chase. Spill their coffee. Trouble is, this pair might want him to do that.

He taps down on the accelerator like a citizen as the light turns green.

A call comes in over the car's speaker. Fucking Bluetooth is amazing.

He takes it. "Yeah?"

"Need you back at the gym."

"I told you I'm taking the rest of the day off. You don't listen when I talk?"

"We got people down."

A good enough reason to call. He can't fault the guy for that.

"Talk to me."

"No count yet. Two, three. Cops are there now."

"Christ. What is this? A joke? Some kind of war?"

"Sharpie, they hit the bank in Park Ex."

A bank counts drug cash as it arrives by the truckload. Not likely a war, but still no joke. He'll be dealing with brain-dead punks who thought ripping off a gang's private accounts was a stellar idea. Floating corpses by midnight.

"How much?"

"Quarter mil, give or take."

Hell to pay. His own skin might feel the heat.

"Coming in."

Sharpie steps on the gas pedal, cop car be damned. A uniform can run the plates, find out who he is, then leave him alone. He can handle *flics*. Bigger trouble lies ahead.

4. Taxes and Death

Called to the scene of a triple homicide, Sergeant-Detective William Ralph Mathers is mystified. He doesn't do homicide. The shooting took place in Park Extension, a neighbourhood where he's lived for decades. That could be the impetus behind the order. He might be expected to dispense local knowledge, identify a victim, or rundown a list of urchins and other prominent scuzz-buckets. That may be the thinking but given that he lives in the relative anonymity of a high-rise and rarely interacts with people on the streets – his friends dwell elsewhere – he expects to be a disappointment.

If he's not on hand to dispense local knowledge, the murders could connect to criminal activity where he's knowledgeable. The victims might be thieves, swindlers, or fraud artists – this sad end to their lives predicted from the dawn of time. Though what he overheard sounds like a crack house. Not his bailiwick. Does some clown assume he knows about that stuff merely because he lives nearby?

He goes with his first thought. He must have had a run-in with the dead. Booked one or two for petty larceny, and now his name pops up on their sheets. Whatever this roll of the dice is about, Sergeant-Detective Bill Mathers is baffled.

Folks are out on the street or perched on their balconies when he arrives. They revel in the thrill of squad cars flashing cherries, and of an ambulance moving over to make way for a morgue's van. TV trucks squeeze in. Cameras roll. News of the murders hit the airwaves and folks with radios become oracles to the rest. Kids flock to the scene, on foot, on bikes, on skateboards. On the run. Older men adjust their afternoon strolls to permit a detour, then stand around to rue modern-day life. *Kids these days.* Generations, races, languages intermingling. Street party time. A whiff of marijuana on the air. Perfectly in sync, a pair of beer bottle caps roll in advance of Bill Mathers's stride, tinkle into the gutter. He walks through the cop maze, flashing his badge when necessary, and enters a skinny triplex through the street-level door. He mounts the interior stairs. A uniform guides him with a jut of his chin to the upper floor.

Where it all went down.

The scent from one apartment as he goes up is pungent, of fish. From the next, curry. The door at the top floor opens on the acrid aroma of death and money.

And he *sees* death, and money, in a glance.

"Who're you?"

The detective asking the question is in homicide. Mathers recognizes the face, although it takes the context of a crime scene to prompt the memory. He doesn't bother trying to pull up his name.

"Sergeant-Detective Mathers." They'll both speak French. He offers a glimpse of his badge. "*Sud.*"

This guy is north. *Nord*. "You're what, lost? You need directions?"

"Got a call. Doucet?"

The detective eyes him up and down. Mathers ignores the ad hoc inspection and hunts deeper into the room. From the doorway he spots a couple of bodies, as expected, and stacks of cash, which is a major surprise. Who bothers to raid a gang's bank, which is what this must be, commit three murders, so the story goes, then leave the loot behind?

A helluva lot of currency is out on display.

The two officers study each other some more. "In back," the guard dog lets him know.

"Thanks." Mathers heads in that direction.

"Hey," the gatekeeper calls out.

Mathers stops, turns.

"My job today? Make sure nobody helps themselves."

"Who keeps an eye on you? Or is that my job, why I'm here?"

He can see that he's caught the man off-guard. He doesn't wait for a comeback. He carries on down the hall, stepping over a blood trace circle in chalk, and into the kitchen. Sergeant-Detective Léon Doucet is not a man he knows, either. He realizes he's seen him around more often than the first guy. They've spoken in the past. He's not going to remember why now.

Even here, in the kitchen, cash is piled on countertops and on the floor. He has a quick glance around. The blood trail goes out the back door, open to a balcony and exterior stairs.

He identifies himself. "Mathers. You're Doucet? You called me in?" On the job he usually speaks French and does so now.

"*Ça va*?" How's it going?

"Not bad. You?" He scratches the back of his scalp as if investing in a serious thought.

"No complaints." The man's lower lip is large. Unlovely. Otherwise, he looks good for a middle-aged guy in a stressful job. He has an admirable head of thick grey hair. He's wide across the shoulders and chest, fit for a man of his size and years. More fit than Mathers is. That bothers him. He's got to start working out again, stop blaming the kids. He's getting pudgy. Doucet says, "I'll give you the royal tour."

"Sure. Why am I here, Sergeant? Does this relate to something of mine?"

"Let me walk you through it. That might flick a switch."

He consents with a nod and follows Doucet into a small space, one that normal tenants use as an extra bedroom or a sewing room or a kid's den. The current inhabitants utilize the space to count drug money, with a bill-counting machine set on a small table in the middle of the floor. A ledger lies on the table also, along with a half-finished bottle of Molson Ex next to a pair of empties. The Ex stands for Export, which Mathers has never understood, given that it's a run-of-the-mill domestic brew.

Beery scent to the room. Way too stuffy. The window out to the back lane is shut. Dark curtains have been pulled aside to let light in, although the foliage of a maple up against the glass keeps the atmosphere gloomy.

"Not used to this much cash lying around," Mathers remarks. "Not outside my dreams anyway. You?"

"Never worked at the mint, no. Up to $70 grand in this room. Another $120 or $140 in the kitchen. Best guess from a look at their ledger. Our people haven't counted yet. The rest of the house, all told, another $90, I say. My partner imagines it's $150. He might be more right than me. Or he has bigger eyeballs. Small bills, all street deals. Imagine, just imagine, the germs in this room. The grubby hands of how many addicts and perverts smeared these bills?"

"Wear a gas mask."

"Good thought. I'll take you up on that. We need to get an accurate count soon, otherwise half what's here gets lost along the way."

"It's tempting."

"If you're bent that way. If you have no scruples."

He causes the statement to sound like a question.

"You didn't invite me in to discuss my scruples. I hope you don't expect me to count."

"Right you are. Twice around. Recognize this guy?" Doucet inquires.

A body is on the floor. The dead man is small, five-three or four. Slim build. Thick black hair with the sides trimmed bare in a punkish style. Caucasian. Olive complexion. Italian is Mathers's first thought, although he could be of generic Mediterranean extraction. Anywhere from Spain to Morocco to Israel to Greece. Or, back to his first thought, Italian.

The man's ankles are crossed as though he made himself comfortable on the floor after being shot through the temple. Brain tissue floats in a thickened pool of blood captured by a depression in the floorboards. A chair is shoved under the table with the money-counting machine, so if nothing's been moved then the victim was shot while he was on his feet. Mathers sees the blood-spatter on the opposite wall in the narrow room. The stain goes above the man's height then in drying rivulets back down. Whoever shot him was somehow beside him when the weapon was fired. The killer didn't come in blazing. If he'd been shot from the doorway, through the temple, he'd have landed differently, most likely on his face, not on his back like this. No, the shooter was next to him, the range so point-blank the muzzle grazed his skin. Blown back slightly, then he crumpled, the life gone out of him that fast.

Surely Doucet knows all this and doesn't require his opinion.

Still, Mathers tells him, "Killed this one first."

Doucet gives him a look. He made that determination, although not from evidence in this room. "Why say that?"

"The shooter was standing right beside him. If the others had already been shot, he's not just standing here, is he? Practically in the middle of the room? He'd hide or cower or duck or run or attack – something."

"So, you don't know him?" Doucet asks.

"Should I? No. I don't. No recognition at all. Do you have a name?"

"Bardi. He's called Frank on some sheets. Francis on others. Could be he was giving himself a second identity to hide his full rap sheet. Sad, if it worked. Clerical error is also possible. Equally sad. Under either name, he's a low-level grunt. Not known for his intellectual capacity. We used to have words for somebody like him that we're not allowed to use anymore."

"Got you," Mathers says.

They return to the hall. Bedrooms are off it on one side, the adjoined dining and living rooms are on the other. The dining room resembles a messy lunch counter; money is stacked in the living space next to a machine that packages the bills for shipment. Finished bundles are ready to be sent to the dry cleaners.

The money counters who worked here felt safe. Not much security beyond the intense locks on the doors. Was it the secrecy of the place that allowed them to drop their guard or was it confidence in their ability to provoke fear throughout the known universe?

The two bodies Mathers saw when he arrived interest him again.

A man and a woman.

Mid-50s.

The woman gave tattoos a bad rep. A mess of them are visible without any discernible design or aesthetic virtue. She's blonde but not at the roots. She might have been considered attractive in her day; in death, she looks no worse than she might have in life, which is bedraggled, beaten down, defeated. Angry. She's plump and buxom, emphasised by a tight-fitting, yellow T-shirt. Blue stretch pants show off an ample bottom. They're a mistake, the pants. Not much of a dresser.

The guy looks like the sort of loser who would wind up on an old brown carpet one day, caked solid with his own blood. Gel hair. A show-off tattoo on his neck and a scar that slices across the back of his jaw. A knife-fight souvenir. Earrings. A thick silvery necklace that Mathers calculates is not precious metal. The crack of his ass is exposed at the top of his chinos and it's not an accident of his fall. Typically, he walked down the street showing off his butt cleavage. Too old to be excused. In both cases, bullets hit the victims in their chests, although the woman was slammed twice, the guy only once that he can see. Good shooting though, since these two were on the run from the moment the first shot was fired in the back room. They didn't get far and the woman, in the end, sank to her knees. Mercy denied.

"The man tried to run," Mathers says. "Except that the door was locked. Half a dozen bolts on it would take too long to trip. He decides to stand and fight because he has no choice. Dude got out his gun."

"We saw that. The shooter didn't come from the front. He came from the rear."

"You knew all along the guy in the backroom was the first to go down."

"Among the bunch of us here we've got half a brain in total, give or take."

"Okay, then why the blood going out the back door?"

"This guy here with the gun? Got a round off."

"Hit the shooter?"

"Thigh."

"Thigh? How—"

"He ran out by the backstairs," Doucet explains. "Exactly why I don't know. Gunfire brings people onto their *front* balconies for a peek. Novel enough, doesn't happen *every* day. Or, wounded, he wanted to get out via the lane. Don't have that answer yet."

"Wait a minute," Mathers postulates.

"Yeah, I know, the coin is slowly working its way down."

"He left money behind. He's shot. He's a wounded shooter on the loose. That helps."

"Not what I thought you'd say."

"Then I'll ask the obvious. Why the thigh? Here's a better one: How do you know?"

"The shooter's in custody, Bill. May I call you Bill? That's how the first officers found out about this. Found him bleeding in the lane. The neighbours got nervous. Worried about their property values, I guess. They took a vote and called the cops. The first shots? They might have let that pass. But not some guy bleeding out their back doors. Anyhow, the shooter couldn't run. Every time he took a step he fell, then pulled himself upright using a fence-post. Then fell again. Dizzy, I guess. In pain. Our guys, when they arrived, followed his blood trail back through the lane and up here. Feel free to call me Léon, by the way."

Mathers takes a slow look around, absorbing the scene. "Three dead, the shooter in custody, and we can presume the bulk of the money is accounted for. This one, the woman, judging by her position was the last to go. She got down on her knees and begged. For that, she got nailed twice. That leaves only one question to answer."

Doucet both smiles and looks down at his feet at the same moment. He knows what question he means. "What's that, Bill?"

"Why the hell am I here, Léon? By the way, I don't know these two either, in case you thought otherwise for some strange reason."

The Investigating Officer signals him to walk away. Bill Mathers notices then that other officers and technicians are within earshot. The two men go into a side bedroom where there's a bed that looks as though people slept on it, or fooled around on it, and Doucet shuts the door. An assault rifle stands in a corner. So, some lethal security here, but not at the ready. Careless.

"We weren't too gentle on the shooter. When I say *we*, I don't mean *me*. One of our esteemed colleagues, nameless, who's not in the apartment as we speak, pressed down on his war wound and made him holler to the sun and to the moon and to the stars."

"Why?" Mathers asked.

"Why what? To get him to talk, of course. He didn't. And he won't."

"So torture's not the best option. No big surprise. Not to mention—"

"Try not to mention it. We know it's not kosher. That event didn't happen. The point is, he will talk on one condition. He has a condition. Can you believe it? Killers today. That condition, he'll only talk to one other person."

This is increasingly peculiar, and Mathers stares at him, waiting. Finally, losing patience, he says, "Not me."

"Not you. Too bad. That might've made it easy. I thought of you because the only person he'll talk to is your old partner and boss."

A quick run-through yields who he's talking about, as any recent boss still on the force could have been contacted directly.

"Émile Cinq-Mars," Mathers concludes out loud.

"Bingo. Since the old guy's retired – how's he doing, by the way? Heard he got shot. What kind of a retirement is that?"

"Recuperating," Mathers attests.

"Since the old guy's retired, since you were his long-standing partner, can you talk to this guy, the shooter? See if that works. If not..."

Doucet lets his voice trail off.

"If not?" Mathers probes.

"Talk to Cinq-Mars for us. See if he'll come in. Out of retirement and off his sick bed. We'll find out what our guy will say to the one and only Émile Cinq-Mars."

Nothing to turn down here, the requests are framed in a reasonable fashion. Mathers is stuck wondering what he's missing. Gut instinct, he feels there's something.

"The guy's not talking at all?"

There it is: The crack in Doucet's presentation. The man cocks his head slightly to one side, then pulls it back again, as though debating whether he should say what he knows he should say.

"Léon?" Mathers pushes him, having caught him out. "What is it?"

"The shooter. He's got his own version of events. They always do."

"Such as?"

"Says he was the fourth victim in the room. Except he got away. Says the shooter went out the front door."

"You're not buying it."

"Our suspect is not a money-counter. Higher profile than that, so why be here? And why didn't the shooter finish him off if he was hobbling away on a wounded leg? Wouldn't be difficult. No, that's a bullshit defence. We'll break it down."

"Did he say he recognized the shooter? If it wasn't him?"

"Says no. He also says he's only talking to Cinq-Mars about it. Only him."

"And the front door. The bolts tripped or not?"

"Tripped. He could have done that to make it look like a shooter went out that way."

"Really? With a wounded leg, he trips all those locks, then goes out the other way?"

"Changed his mind?"

"No blood around the door."

"His pants sopped it up at first, I'm thinking. What do you want from me?"

"What was he doing here, Léon? Does he explain that much, at least?"

"He'll only tell Cinq-Mars that."

"Didn't give any reason? Was this supposed to be a robbery? That should be obvious, except whoever did this left behind a ton of cash."

"The shooter left it all behind. We found almost no bills on our guy. Eighteen bucks in his wallet, which he says was his own and I believe him. Says he was a victim, and that he'll tell Cinq-Mars what he knows. Look. The guy's real stubborn. Stomping on the bullet in his thigh proves it. I called you in, Bill, to help us out. What do you say?"

No glory in it. He knows that. He's willing to help anyway. "I guess he noticed that somebody witnessed the thigh stomp? He won't file if we agree to get Cinq-Mars?"

"It came up."

Mathers sighs. Cops. "Sure. Lead me to him."

"Where are you on your shift?"

Mathers checks his watch. "Two hours and a bit."

"Same as me. Good. Time enough."

"Where's your guy?"

"PDQ 33."

Mathers figures that the English assignation to the letters, *Pretty Damn Quick*, could fit here. The station, *Poste de Quartier* 33, is practically next door, a block-and-a-half south. With any luck he'll finish his shift a touch early, be home in the blink of an eye – *pretty damn quick*. Surprise his wife and kids that way. Toss a ball around with his son and daughter in the lane before dinner.

"Not in a hospital?" Mathers asks.

"A flesh wound. He's making some bigger claim on misery but he's not the physician, is he? Anyway, they told us they had no bed available. I guess the next guy hit by a car sleeps in the street. We're supposed to bring him back tonight. If his vitals are good, they'll release him to us. Or not. For now, we own him."

"Cool."

"Go up there on your own, Bill. Bean-counters are on the way. I need to get them organized under sentence of death. I trust cops with money no more than I do thieves. Less, actually. At least I know what a thief will do. I'll make a call, get you a one-on-one. I'll pitch-in before you're done."

"What's his name, our boy?"

"Sykes. Doug."

"English?" These days, the gangs, if not Italian, or eastern European, or Jamaican, are French. The English have been shoved out of the lowly rackets. Except for a few recalcitrant Irish they've moved on to white-collar stuff, or they've gone to Toronto. They rarely appreciate getting their hands dirty.

"One of your kind, yeah. Even better, right?"

He has no qualms about speaking English on the job, although he's not had an opportunity lately. He tells Léon Doucet, in French, "Doesn't bother me. We'll see if I remember how."

That wins him a quick smile, and Mathers heads out the door. The gatekeeper makes a move to frisk his pockets, then breaks off his joke and lets him go.

5. Answered and Asked

PDQ 33 is located on *avenue Beaumont*, where *de l'Épée* terminates at the south end of Park Extension. Further south the street reconstitutes itself but is interrupted here by railway tracks and defunct factories. The *poste* shares a desolate complex with other community services, and Bill Mathers pulls into the police parking section in the rear of the building. He sticks his identifying tag on the dash, extracts his keys, clambers out, and locks up with the fob.

Work has been dull lately. He now has a murderer who claims to be a shooting victim to interrogate. Life is that good.

He's ushered into a vacant interrogation room. The officer offers coffee.

"Sounds good," Mathers says, "but, you know, hot coffee between a murderer and a detective might be a temptation too great for someone to resist. I won't say who."

"We use spill-proof mugs. Any fluid needs mopping up, it's blood."

Spill-proof mugs. What a concept.

He opts for water anyway and specifies paper cups.

He's reasonably sure the man was kidding about the blood.

The water is on the table and he's studying the rap sheet of the suspect when the man is brought in. "Water's cold," he offers in English.

"As long as it ain't the Kool-Aid."

The fellow rubs his wrists after his cuffs are removed. He gulps the water. Shot in the leg, operated on, and hauled in for questioning about a triple murder in which he's the prime suspect can build a thirst.

They're seated on opposite sides of a plain pine table and are left alone.

Mathers gives him time to squirm. He wants to access his experience with the process.

Except the man doesn't squirm. He's mute. He's not afraid to glance at Mathers and appears comfortable as he casts his eyes around the nondescript space. On occasion the detective has wished he could be in a room with bloodstains on the floor, as the other officer had intimated, if only to observe the reaction. He scares no one on his own. His old boss, Cinq-Mars, was fond of calling him a baby-face. Being in his middle years now has helped with that, but only modestly. Nor does he come down on the side of force or intimidation in his day-to-day. He recently heard a confirmed story out of the Middle East where prisoners had to piss on the faces of decomposing corpses, their eyeballs gouged out, ears missing, teeth extracted, noses obliterated, their rotting bodies piled in open toilet stalls and covered in the defecation of other prisoners. To relieve themselves, prisoners had no choice but piss and evacuate their bowels on that wretchedness, all the while accepting that their own bodies would soon resemble these and be placed on top of them, to be soiled by the next batch of torture victims. Learning of that dimension of horror, Mathers's reaction was to confirm his preference for respect and human kindness in breaking down a suspect's will to resist. Cinq-Mars had taught him in his early years as a detective, when he'd been a willing acolyte, to keep the gates to hell locked. That's one door you don't want to leave ajar.

He finishes perusing the rap sheet where he found no reference to his former partner as an arresting officer. Sykes was into small-time stuff, petty larceny, nuisance arrests, primarily across the continent in Vancouver. Only in his youth did he do short time in Quebec and otherwise only a couple of years here and there. What's apparent is that he kept rough company. Not a patch member of a biker gang or an affiliate and not probationary either, but aligned with the Hells Angels. An acolyte, then. A salesman of illicit goods and services. At worst, a pimp – out west he was employed in strip clubs – although he does not look mean enough.

"You're Doug," Mathers begins. "Sykes."

"Las," the man corrects him.

"Excuse me?"

"Doug-*las*. Douglas. I don't use Doug. Never have."

"*Dougie* is out of the question, I suppose."

"Broke a man's nose for that once."

"Funny. You don't look that tough. I'm Sergeant-Detective William Mathers."

"Didn't say I was tough. I'm fussy is all. For example, you're not the one I asked for. Saw that the second I stepped into the room. I can hardly contain my disappointment."

"Will you punch me in the nose for that? Who'd you ask for again?"

The man is older than Mathers, 60 or so. He checks the sheet – 56. Younger than he looks. Weathered skin, with a grey pallor as though from too many cigarettes. That he's endured a protracted illness is a possibility, rendering that yellowy death-warmed-over look. He has already winced twice, an indication that his painkillers from the bullet wound are wearing thin. His eyes are deeply set. As if famine or life's hardships have pulled the eye sockets back into the skull – a look that projects his very soul as trying to hide from life. Not only the bullet hole in his thigh has caused him grief. The world, generally, has done that. Other than the solemn eyes, he seems relatively nondescript to Mathers, somebody who'd pass by unnoticed in a down-market bar. He wouldn't scare anyone either. He'd look the part hanging around a pool hall or moseying up to a slot machine in a dive, although he *is* a man who'd set off alarm bells if he ventured up to Summit Circle, out for a stroll among the homes of the wealthy, or if he took too long to wander the perimeter of a bank. Not a scary disposition and visage, yet dispossessed, saddened, forlorn, potentially trouble on two legs: Mather's quick assessment.

"You don't know who I asked for? Then why are you even here?"

His eyebrows are rather untamed. His hair, grey and brown, falls over his ears and curls up at the back of his neck. "You shot three men, Douglas. That has an effect. You don't get to say where you go or who you talk to anymore."

"Number one, *I* got shot. Me. I was the fourth victim. Number two, I shot nobody. Number three, I asked for one cop specifically. I remember now. Wasn't you."

"Who then? Tell me his name."

"What's the point?"

"I might be the only person who can help with that. Could be why I'm here."

"On principle, and through long experience, I'm not inclined to believe what cops say."

"Tell me his name, then we'll see what I can do."

The man takes a moment to decide. He has nothing to lose, only his pride is holding him back. He doesn't like to repeat himself as he's already been through this.

"Fine," he concedes. "For what it's worth, it's Émile Cinq-Mars. You knew that already. Help me out here. I told those other cops. I'm only talking to him. Him only. That means not you."

"Let's see if we can make it happen. Tell me why first. Why him, specifically?"

"History."

"You have some history with the man?"

"I think I just said that."

"Did you hear? They have spill-proof mugs in this station."

"Sorry? What?"

"Spill-proof mugs. Fitting, no?"

Sykes can't find anything to say on the subject.

Mathers forges on. "Is he your long-lost brother from another mother?" Cinq-Mars taught him the technique. Keep your suspect baffled. Come at him from different angles so he's never sure what you mean or what you're saying. Confusion can work when a suspect fails to differentiate between what's pertinent and what's not. Something might escape then that he never intended to reveal. Also, if a bad guy concludes that the detective is incompetent or a bungler, he tends to lower his defences. "You happen to share a burger and a beer 10 years ago? What's the deal?"

"Are you out of your mind or only pretending?"

"My point is, Douglas, you may want to talk to Émile Cinq-Mars. He's retired. I presume you know that. What you might not know, like you, he got shot recently. The bullet a tick off his heart. Had it been your heart, with what we know about you, you might not have been revived. Who'd bother? The point is *you* want to talk to *him*. Why, though, give me a good reason, why *he* would agree to talk to *you*?"

"I'm sorry to hear about his trouble."

"Is that an answer? Do you think it is?"

"How do we know he won't talk to me until somebody asks?"

"And say what about why?"

"Tell him that Douglas M. Sykes is under suspicion for murder." His voice carries a subtle yet theatrical inflection. "A false accusation. Due to his long-standing and entirely justified distrust of police departments, Mr. Sykes will only speak to Émile Cinq-Mars. Otherwise, he's mute."

Some speech. Articulate and perfectly formed.

"M?" Mathers asks.

"I'd love to tell you that it stands for Montana. Or Mordecai. Or Montgomery. I'll take any of those names. Michigan or Manitoba.

The prophet Malachi will do. Sadly, it stands for nothing more than Michael."

"But not Mike, I bet."

"Never that."

"Or you'd break another guy's nose."

"If he was smaller than me and I didn't appreciate his tone, yeah. Seriously, would you call the Archangel Michael, Mike?"

"Are you an archangel?"

"Don't be ridiculous. But it's why I'm Douglas. Not Doug. To distinguish myself."

Mathers studies Douglas M. Sykes a moment. It's dawning on him that he is not dealing with a run-of-the-mill criminal intellect. The guy's sheet shows that he hasn't done much with his life, yet an intelligence underlying his expression tells him that he could have. He tells him, "I partnered with Cinq-Mars. I might do."

"You might." The man folds his arms across his chest, as though he's willing to take that into account. "I've been found guilty by association in my life when that was dead wrong. I understood it: People had no way to decide so they went by association. You want me to find you *worthy* by association. Like the judgement of those who put me away, that could be wrong."

Noticing that the suspect claims to have been falsely accused in the past, Mathers presumes it's a habit. Yet the man advanced no bitterness about the experience. He tells him, "I partnered with Cinq-Mars longer than anyone. The reason for that, he trusted me. Other partners, he ditched."

Sykes appears to accept the argument in a positive light; for a moment, Mathers expects him to come around. A notion soon dashed.

"You make a noble point," Sykes tells him. "I see the virtue in it. Like I said, I have no way of knowing. Until somebody makes my request known directly to Cinq-Mars, to the man himself, and

I hear him turn me down flat with my own ears, I won't be chatting about nothing pertinent to what went down today. Clam up and lawyer up. That'll be my mantra. You get nothing more than static out of me."

"Mantra. That's a word."

"Call me a mystic. People have said worse things."

"Pertinent. Another word."

Mathers resorts to the water, Sykes does the same, and they perform a gesture of tipping their paper glasses toward each other to toast the other's good health. The tribute doesn't work, as Sykes winces when pain from his thigh zings through him.

Pain, Mathers suspects, that may not be fleeting.

Hoarse, Sykes says, "Émile will talk to me."

"Why?"

"He can't resist."

Mathers stares him down again. The longish hair, his look: not hard to imagine him as a refugee from the hippie era. Or hippie-influenced era, as he's a touch young to have come of age in the '60s.

"Understand my hesitation, Douglas. If Émile Cinq-Mars is willing to talk to you, you will have to pay him a hospital visit. Today, you were patched up and dismissed lickety-split. The road to recovery for Sergeant-Detective Cinq-Mars requires time. He may not be healthy enough to talk. I'm not sure, as I haven't been to see him."

"Some partner you are."

That hits a nerve. He should have visited by now. His former partner resides in a hospital a fair distance out of town, and Mathers has a job to do. He has a family that demands his time, and he hasn't possessed his usual energy lately. Still, he ought to have taken the time to visit him.

Sykes cocks his head to one side. "I'll travel out his way even if you won't."

"Don't expect a limo. It's the rear of a paddy wagon for you."

"I've never travelled first class. Might not like it if I do."

"Chained down. Armed guards. If you expect your biker friends to break you out on the highway, think again."

"Mathers, is it? I suspect you don't know this: That's a real comical remark you said there. If my situation was not so dire, I might be laughing my head off right now."

"How so?"

"Trust me. I know bikers. No need to deny that. Not that I ride a Harley myself. A couple of those guys merit being called friends of mine, that's possible. Acquaintances, more accurate. Yet, I can tell you truthfully, I don't know a single biker, friend or otherwise, who'd lift his pinky to break me out of here or help me out with my tale of woe. They sure as hell won't be shooting up a cop convoy on a highway. The opposite may hold true. Hilarious, right?"

Mathers perks up. "The opposite? Meaning?"

"What happened today," Sykes points out, and lowers his voice. "What you, the police, wrongfully accuse me of doing – think about it carefully – breaking into a biker's bank, shooting the place up. I was there, I don't deny that part. No point when I left a cup of my best blood behind. One hundred proof DNA. Now, what happens if bikers have ears, as I believe they do, and they happen to accept what you guys put out there for John Q. Public to hear? I will not require an armed escort to stop somebody from breaking me loose. But I might need one to keep myself *alive* long enough to talk to Émile."

Something in the way he said his good friend and former partner's name, without the surname, simply *Émile*, wins Mathers over. No harm in asking. He'll find out if Cinq-Mars will talk to this guy.

"That's why I put up such a fuss," Sykes states.

"I didn't hear about a fuss."

"Not well-informed, are you? At the hospital, I told them I required two armed guards on the door, one more on the window. No way do I keep breathing only in the company of nurses. Plus, I don't want them cut down in the crossfire."

Somebody at the hospital, Mathers guesses, took the man's opinion under advisement. He wasn't denied entry or released early due to a chronic shortage of beds. They simply took his presence to be a risk they could do without. This, too, of course, could be a scam the man was flogging. He asks, "How far back do you go with him?"

"Cinq-Mars? Long ways."

"Nothing too recent?"

"Nope."

"You're sure he'll remember you?"

"Count on it."

A knock, and Sergeant-Detective Léon Doucet sticks his head in. Mathers waves him through.

"What you told me," Mathers continues with Sykes, not minding Doucet's presence, "is an incentive for you to proclaim your innocence. You're not concerned about the law. Or us. A gang's been harmed, its people killed. You fear retribution."

"You're catching fire, Detective. You're bursting into flames. That's what I'm saying. I won't deny it."

"Isn't that a reason to lie your way out of this?"

"Think like that if you want. I know better than to follow some false hope down the tracks. You get run over by a locomotive that way. Why I'm asking for Émile."

"I don't follow."

"If I tell you what happened, I don't expect you to believe me. If by some miracle you do, I don't trust you to do anything about it. And if you do try to help me out, how do I know you'll do it right? That's why I will only talk to Émile, or I won't talk at all."

"This bullshit about believing you," Doucet interjects. Mathers is surprised, although he has no reason to be, that the man's English is impeccable. No trace of an accent. Mathers's French is very good, but this guy's English is perfect. "Ballistics came through. What I expected. The shot that nicked you? Came from a dead guy's gun. The man you shot in the living room. You weren't the fourth victim at the shooting, Mr. Sykes, because you weren't shot by the killer's weapon. You were shot by a man defending himself against your incursion because you were the killer."

"I can explain that," Sykes contends.

"Be my guest."

"Only to Cinq-Mars."

"Oh really? We found where you ditched your piece. Near where we found you. Between that fence-post and the apartment, along your blood trail. So you won't think I'm bluffing, I'll tell you exactly where. On a garage roof. Thanks. Keeping it out of the hands of children, throwing it up there like that, it's appreciated. I'll remember to blow you a kiss when they send you up for life."

Sykes doesn't seem fazed in the slightest. "I'll explain that, too. Only to Cinq-Mars. But I wasn't *nicked*. I was fucking *shot*."

"You realize," Doucet reminds him, "that your ass is on the line here. Big time."

"More than you know. That's why it's only Cinq-Mars or the alternative."

"What alternative?" Doucet bites.

"Send in a priest."

"For what?"

"Last rites," Sykes explains. "What we used to call 'ass wipes,' but I'm not that vulgar anymore."

Mathers explains, "He's afraid bikers want his rear."

"Not the way priests do," Sykes says.

Doucet pulls a face. He has an idea. "Let them have him. Save us time and trouble."

"Funny," Sykes remarks. "You should play down at the Comedy Nest."

"Why'd you shoot those people?" Doucet wants to know. "Seriously, where was your head? Okay, for the money, not that you got away with any, but you know who you're up against. Were you on crystal meth? Out of your skull? Why'd you do it? Some stupid grievance? Help us out here."

Sykes tries to laugh him off, his grin suddenly ruptured by a jolt of pain. Then he argues, "There's one question to ask, one only, and it's not if I shot nobody. I didn't. It's why for the love of God did *I* get shot?"

"Self-defence, after you started gunning people down. If not that, then why weren't you killed like the rest?"

"Now we're up to two questions," Sykes notes. "Both valid. Why was I shot, and why wasn't I killed dead on the spot like the rest?"

Mathers can follow a portion of the suspect's logic. He understands how a man can believe that what he says in his own defence is less important than who he says it to. He can be right about that.

"Sykes, forget what you said before," Doucet intrudes. "You know, about the absence of cordite on your hands." He turns to Mathers for a second, to marvel. "That's the word he used. Him. Cordite." Then stares back at the prisoner. "We located your gloves. Your latex. You didn't toss them far from the scene. Did you think we wouldn't look? Goes to the crystal meth theory."

"I don't wear latex to shoot people," the man maintains, and pulls a straight face. "See? That proves I'm innocent."

He's trying not to offend anyone unnecessarily, although a wry smile begins to uplift the corners of his mouth.

"Who belongs at the Comedy Nest now?" Doucet remarks.

An odd silence ensues, as though the last question is worth consideration.

"I'll call Cinq-Mars," Mathers announces. "See where that leads."

"Fine." Doucet has been looking for that all along. He won't object. The prisoner has already demonstrated his stubbornness. Then he asks, "What's the matter with you?"

Sykes has shut his eyes. He's wincing in evident pain. His torso convulses an instant, as though a badass cop is standing on his wound again. He emerges from the spell slowly, paler than before. Ashen. "I'll need a shot, gents, if you be kind," he whispers. Immediately, he puts up his right hand, as though to halt the protest bound to rush back his way. "I'm no druggie. Whistle clean. A spliff now and then when the mood strikes. This is strictly a medicinal request."

"Yeah, like I'll take that at face value," Doucet tags on, although he has a dilemma. About four hours ago the man was shot. He's wondering if he should not return the suspect to the hospital, and asks Mathers, "How long before you find out?"

"Taking care of it right now. While you wait." Mathers pulls out his cell phone.

"For sure I can hang around for that," Sykes tells them, in a whisper, no less confident than before despite an involuntary gasp. "I got nowhere to go."

Mathers puts the call through to his former boss in his hospital room. It's answered promptly. Cinq-Mars must have been holding his phone on his lap, expecting a call, or merely hoping for one from anyone.

"Hello?"

"Hey, it's Bill. I hope you're doing okay, Émile. Listen, I want to hear about that, but first, I'm in a situation. You might find it entertaining, relieve the monotony of your day. Sorry I haven't been to see you. I will. Before we get to my apologies, something's come up."

"Bill who?" Cinq-Mars asks him.

"Come on," Mathers says.

"Oh, the guy who never visits. That guy. I'm too much out of his way now. That Bill. Go ahead. What's the favour you want to ask, and incidentally, good luck with that."

"How about I send flowers? Will that do?"

"A box of chocolates could put us back on the rails. Also, I'm looking for a whisky smuggler. For the good stuff. You're conscripted."

"Wise guy. Look, I've got something better than chocolates or whisky. I'm sitting straight across from a murder suspect."

"Since when do you do murder?"

"It's been an hour. You like peculiarities, Émile. Get this. The guy says he'll talk only to you. He says you two go back in time, into ancient history. If your Alzheimer's hasn't kicked in too deep, you might remember him."

"Who is it?" Cinq-Mars skips the repartee. He doesn't camouflage his interest.

"His name is Douglas Sykes. Never Doug."

Silence. His former partner might be trying to recall the name; or determine if he wants the conversation.

"Émile?" Mathers prompts him.

"Sure," Cinq-Mars answers quietly. "Set it up. I'm not supposed to travel. The trip in from New Hampshire was brutal. Idiots nearly killed me. I'm talking about the guys in the ambulance."

"I heard. Thanks, Émile. We'll go to you. I'll be in touch. You take care now."

"Hang on a sec'."

"Sure." To Mathers, it sounds as though the old guy is taking a drink of water. In a moment, he checks back with him. "You okay, Émile?"

“Bill, I added an infection to my trouble. It’s weakened me and the medics have Sandra in a tailspin. If you don’t mind, give her a buzz tonight. Remind her that I’m half-ox, half-brick. Lie, if necessary. Be convincing. This won’t pull me under. I sure as hell didn’t survive a bullet to die from a freaking blood infection. Help her to believe that.”

Mathers takes another minute to wind down the call. He should have visited. He should have called more than just the one time previously. His old boss and partner doesn’t sound right. He’s not his old self.

Neither Doucet nor Sykes know how Cinq-Mars answered the main question. Doucet waits expectantly. Sykes, though, sits back in his chair as a smile begins to glow across his visage, then breaks into a full-blown grin. “He’ll talk to me, won’t he? Won’t he?” He slaps the table hard, startling the other two men in the room. Ice cubes in the water cups tinkle. “Damn, yes!” he exclaims.

The sudden, ecstatic motion does him no good. He yelps and topples over, crashes down, staggered by a sudden pain in his thigh. He gasps, and writhes on the floor.

Doucet is up and stands over him again. In his judgement, the prisoner is not faking. “Hell, I’ll call an ambulance.” Looking back at Mathers, he explains, “Set up that conversation for another day.”

“Trust me, it’s not happening that fast.”

His old boss, he’s deduced, needs to improve. Cinq-Mars is no longer as invincible as he may have been, nor as strong as he thinks he still is. He’s no brick. Ox, neither.

6. Ladders and Snakes

"Some guys," Mittens mutters, "get bred clueless."

The guard passes him a beer.

A French-language tabloid proclaimed that the biker kingpin was living out his prison days in the lap of luxury. Readers could infer for themselves whether that meant he had a butler at the ready, a mistress in a side room, or exclusive shopping sprees down at the mall. In reply, the jailed biker wrote the hack a letter, asking if he wanted to trade places anytime real quick, and if so, for how long?

No threat was implicit, not from any close reading of the message, although direct contact from Fréderick "Mittens" Grégoire by itself was disconcerting. The reporter lost sleep. He dashed off a return note saying that he intended no slight. He preferred his life on the outside, he assured him, to the confinement Mittens so heroically endured.

In a subsequent column, he referred to him as a saint. "The patron saint of the people. A hero," he asserted, "for the masses. Like Robin Hood."

The biker had made his point. Yet the scribe also made his. If Mittens was not bunking at the Ritz – no wine locker, a paucity of conjugal visits – neither was he wearing a Guantanamo jumpsuit.

He did have a guard who served him beer in a plastic cup.

Hard time is one thing, the journalist noted. Hard time in the lap of luxury was a different price to pay. A steep discount off any life sentence.

If he enjoyed a few perks, Mittens argued, folks needed to understand the necessity. He had an empire to control, or did people want chaos on the streets, blood and gore on their sidewalks? He had responsibilities; side benefits came with that. A person under the demands and restraints of his businesses required a few hours of relaxation during the day, or all hell might break loose.

Pandemonium could erupt on penitentiary grounds, where few would notice and fewer care, or hellishness could bust loose in a public square. "One example, you know?"

Accommodations in exchange for peace on the sidewalks seemed equitable to many.

Having an image to cultivate, Mittens Grégoire continued to dispatch letters to misguided correspondents. One guy wrote that Mittens no longer wielded the power he once enjoyed. Talk of that nature needed to be cut off at the knees – a phrase he used in counselling the reporter. "Your false speculation needs to be cut off at the knees. Terminated, like that." No explicit threat, but the reporter did feel weak in the knees reading it. He reversed course in his next column, writing that "new developments demonstrate that Fréderick 'Mittens' Grégoire is not only firmly in control of Montreal crime syndicates but also outwardly across the province of Quebec and the rest of Canada. Authorities have recently concluded that he is a more powerful figure today than ever, despite his malicious confinement."

Anyone getting it into his head that the boss is no longer the boss, or broadcasting the view that he's vulnerable, compromised his security. Any miscreant who damages a gang leader's mystique needs to smarten up.

Managing how people perceive him has come into focus.

An assassination attempt occurred outside the weight room. A knife to his gullet. A slash across the biceps. Help from the gym arrived in a fury, the onslaught thwarted. The instigators were beaten to a pulp and stabbed with their own weapons before guards weighed into the melee. The attackers were then incarcerated elsewhere for their protection. Relocation merely delayed the inevitable.

Eventually, their innards spilled across a shower room's concrete floor.

As he explained to his daughter, Mélanie, "For one punk, they carried his guts out in a bucket. The other guy, most of him got hosed down the drain. *But*. Who did we get? The guys who did it, sure, but not the guys who gave the order. A failure to execute also has consequences."

Bad enough being knifed in a penitentiary he was reputed to control, but since then, he's endured worse.

His son breaking out of prison looked good for a time. He didn't escape in the traditional sense. He didn't jump a wall or dig a tunnel or get smuggled out in a body bag. A guard opened the front door and let him walk out. Luc 'The Needle' Grégoire stepped into a waiting taxi and the cabbie never bothered to switch on the meter. A manhunt ensued and the prison itself was turned inside out trying to unravel how this could happen in modern times.

As if it was a mystery. A bribe here, a compelling threat there. The Needle is free.

Getting him out for a week was imperative to take care of a matter, and his son successfully extended his trip for 20 days.

"Who keeps track how many times?" Luc told him on a call after his recapture. "Six different women. I kept track of who, not the number of fucks."

"Only six? You had three weeks!"

"Had to play it safe, Dad. I read that a hundred and twenty-two cops were assigned to find me. Not for that, I'd've done a dozen, easy."

That was his boy. A good kid. Sex with six different women over three weeks wasn't so bad, really, taking his plight into consideration. Mittens had hoped he'd play it smarter, though, escape to Florida and live on the lam for months or years. Sadly, The Needle had been nabbed – betrayed by one of his six lady friends, who knows? – and has now resumed life in a familiar, low-rent cell.

That depressed Mittens. Which is significant. He has to guard against depression. When it overwhelms him, he can sink like a stone.

With The Needle behind bars, and a little unfinished business coming up, Mittens was depending on his daughter. He didn't boast about family like Mafia mentors of old used to do, but he understood to keep a lid on certain things. While their planning was meticulous, their communications were compromised. Mittens learned that the job had fallen apart when four Sûreté du Québec officers visited him in his office. One cop whistled, impressed with his digs. Bounced his butt on the sofa. After a few minutes of mild suspense, the cops arrested him.

"Hey, fuckers! Are you blind? I'm in prison already. The fucking nerve you guys got."

"Fréderick Grégoire, you are under arrest on suspicion of conspiracy to commit murder."

"What're you gonna to do? Stick dynamite up my ass? Fucking SQ! I'm doing life in here. I got no more years to give."

"Mittens, it's the principle of the thing."

He knew how this was going to look in the tabloids. People would agree that he was vulnerable. That he controlled nothing. That sad song.

The cops concurred that he had no more years to give, but that did not deter their effort to snap his balls off. "Incidentally," the arresting officer told him, the grit of what he had come to say in person, "we arrested Mélanie, too. Yeah. Sorry to relay bad news. Conspiracy to commit. She's going down with you. Guess who's to blame for that?"

That was the deal, then. Take down his last family member. Portray him as vulnerable. Make him look impotent and let that be an invitation to anybody who thinks he has a pair to take another shot at rubbing him out on the inside, while his businesses come under siege on the outside. You'd almost think that the cops had chosen to play favourites and didn't count him among that group.

They tried to break his spirit, instigating the tailspin of depression.

Now this. His friend, the prison guard, came by to say that he was expected in the laundry room.

"Checks out?" Mittens inquires.

"Hard to evaluate. Your people, for sure. If they're still your people."

Never trust a living soul. Especially don't trust the people you're expected to trust. The guard himself could have switched horses. "Almost supper time. What's up?"

"Dunno. The look on their faces? Trouble. They have a concern."

He had to go, find out what tenement fire needed to be extinguished this time. Always a risk going to a meeting in a penitentiary when your own gang brother might betray you. This wasn't a day for that. He was informed that a drug bank on the outside, one of his own, had been slammed. Three dead. His guys were worried. The security guard at the bank was wounded and arrested by the cops. That guy had been the shooter.

"Who?"

"Douglas Sykes."

"What are you talking about? He's a punk. Like, from Vancouver, or something."

Everybody knew that.

They waited on him to give an order, to fix this. He was upset.

"Let it play out," Mittens told them. "Either he winds up in the can, so we whack him slowly on the inside, or he gets lucky and takes a walk around the block. That case, we nail the twit. What a punk. After what I did for him. I let Sykes retire in my city."

They were waiting for Mittens to ask the prickly question.

First, he wanted to know, "What was he doing there anyhow? He's not security. Is everything falling apart now? We got punks doing security?"

No one had answers. Everyone was baffled.

"How much we lose?"

A couple hundred grand was possible. Or more.

"Sykes took all that?"

Three men simultaneously shook their heads in the negative.

"The cops," Mittens was informed, "took the money. Sykes left empty-handed."

They figured he was more upset than he was willing to let on. Mittens said, "Let's make sure they spend it on *our* dope and *our* pussy. Collect most of it back that way."

In the laundry room, men recognized that the joke was feeble, the result unlikely. That was the worst part of the bad news filtering through to him lately. Folks were losing their trust in him and losing confidence in what he did for them. Who and what they controlled was unravelling at a pace Mittens seemed unable to abbreviate. How it looked. As if bad news, these days, possessed its own momentum.

The news was worse than the people who told it to him knew. Far worse.

This was serious.

When it looks like nothing is standing, shake the foundations. Reassert. Rebuild. Show not only the street, but the whole goddamn power structure, the wise guys and the cops, the gangs and the freelance punks, even the judiciary, the warden, the hacks – the public, too – show them who will rip their eyes out for looking at him crossways.

They're all punks. The whole fucking world.

You hire somebody to do a job, and he turns out to be a goddamn punk.

That night he woke up suddenly. The prison was nearly silent. No outside disturbance had interrupted his sleep although he could hear men snoring. Smelled the odour of their skins. Either that aroma or a premonition had snapped right through his subconscious and shaken him awake.

"Oh shit," Mittens Grégoire said to the wall of his prison cell. He looked up at the ceiling and spoke the man's name. "Sykes."

The guy knew things no man should know. The cops were holding him. He assumed he was going to keep quiet but if Sykes ever figured out who was gunning for him and why, he would most likely ask for a quotation on the value of his secret knowledge. What then? Trouble times 10. Mittens knew where Sykes had wandered in his travels and what he'd overheard. Shooting up his bank was a good enough reason to have him terminated in the mind of his gang, but Mittens had at first recommended *patience* with carrying out the act. That order had to be rescinded and replaced by one that promoted *speed burning fucking urgency*. Sykes knew stuff. He was sitting in police custody right now knowing stuff that he should never have been allowed to know and he was by nature a garrulous soul. A talker in his heart. Other gang members would accept that he was clearly off his nut doing what he did, shooting up a gang bank – *did he fall out of his treehouse? Did somebody kick him in the head? What's the explanation for that?* His gang would understand that Sykes could not be allowed to live but they would not comprehend the switch to urgency. They'd want to take their time, to be *careful*. And *smart*. Along the way, what Sykes spilled to the cops might get back to them, and that is where the urgency lay. The *flics* can be indiscreet with what they learn. Hell, they might call up a hack and have the news published. Where would he be then? Looking over his shoulder. Mittens has no time to be careful or smart. He cannot explain this to his people. In his sleep, he's already figured out what to do. Two birds, one stone. The man needs to vanish without a trace. Not in due course, as he previously let on. Immediately. *Now*. In police custody, if it has to be that way. The only man to do the job properly was the same man who botched it the first time.

Of course, no gang member could ever know that. He had to keep it to himself.

That part aside, the plan was brilliant. Fucking foolproof if it goes down properly.

At dawn, as the prison awoke, Mittens issued an urgently revised command. Half English. Half French. *Ghost Sykes tout de suite.* In French, he ordered who should do the solid. He emphasised, "Only him."

7. Tide and Time

Guilt goads Sergeant-Detective Bill Mathers into visiting his old partner in hospital. He drives out in the morning and finds his mentor cheerful, although his pallor is disconcerting. Émile Cinq-Mars looks as though he could use a bath, is grizzled, and his greyish hair needs weeding.

The most familiar aspect of his appearance is his gargantuan nose.

"Chipper," Émile Cinq-Mars replies to the standard query on how he's doing.

The younger man permits his scepticism to show.

"Seriously," the patient insists. "If you visited two days ago instead of sitting at home and watching TV, you'd have booked my hearse by now. I'm not sure that Sandra hasn't. If so, she'll need to cancel. I'm doing well."

"If you say so."

"Saying so. What's the scoop, Bill? You're not here to comfort an old friend or you'd have arrived weeks ago."

"Will you let up on that? Or do I put the recording on continuous loop?"

"Are there chocolates in that bag?"

"Whisky."

"Ah. All is forgiven. Show me."

The Balmoral meets with the man's approval. He immediately requests a paper cup from the bedside stand.

"Émile, it's morning."

"I'm deprived." Fingers enumerate his points. "There's no time like the present. I need a pick-me-up. Sandra isn't here yet. How many ways do I need to justify this? A cup, please. Join me?"

Mathers declines, although he's amused by his friend's enthusiasm for the spirit. "I assume it's not recommended, or Sandra would have supplied you."

"She's stingy about it. Takes the bottle home at night. How about hiding this one, before she arrives?"

Mathers finds a top shelf, way at the back.

"So, Bill, what's the verdict?" Cinq-Mars inquires.

Mathers brings him up to speed on the previous day's triple murder and recounts what Douglas Sykes has said for himself. "Who's he to you, Émile?"

"You didn't bring him with you?"

"I wasn't sure you'd be up for it, but he's not. Only a flesh wound, or a muscle wound, but it's set him back. I doubt he'll recommend the experience."

"Apparently, we're supposed to rest after being shot. Who knew?"

"How do you connect to him?"

"The old days," Cinq-Mars comments. Not much of an explanation.

"Your old days extend back to the Ark."

"Life before Bill," he clarifies, which still leaves eons.

"Your name's not on his arrest record," Mathers points out.

"I brought him in on a murder rap. He was a kid. Like him, I was starting out."

"Really? That doesn't show on his sheet."

"Expunged."

"Why? He was innocent?"

"A minor at the time. He was never convicted."

"So, innocent?" Mathers asks again.

Cinq-Mars won't agree to that. "Guilty as sin. A man was tied down to railway tracks. Sykes stood by while a freight train decapitated him. He collected the feet and set out to bury them. That's when I nabbed him. A cohort or two disposed of the head and hands."

Mathers wasn't expecting anything of that nature. "Holy shit."

"Nothing holy about it. A gruesome act. And like I said, still a teenager."

"You couldn't make the charge stick? A minor or not, he had to face the charge."

"It wasn't a question of making it stick."

"Seems like it to me. No witnesses?"

"You don't understand. I worked to get him off."

Mathers wasn't expecting that either. "Wait. What?"

"He wasn't a good guy, Bill. The dead man, I mean."

"How is that the point? A murder was committed."

The man under the hospital sheet and grey blanket rearranges the position of his posterior with some difficulty, then settles again. "A killing we couldn't prove. Do me a favour, Bill. Don't tell him that part. I believe he thinks otherwise."

"So, you worked to get him off because you couldn't prove he did it?"

"You make it sound so complicated."

"No. Actually. You do."

"Bill, we would not succeed in convicting him. No witnesses. No evidence. Except for the feet and he could talk his way through that. We never found the head. Down the tracks were these ghosts."

"Sorry? What are you on about?"

"Don't worry. They weren't real ghosts. No such thing, right? Bedsheets decorated up and hung in the trees. Waving around in the breeze. We couldn't explain them and at first nobody wanted to connect the ghosts to the dead man. If they were part of it, that made the murder way too elaborate for a 15-year-old. I was never convinced of his guilt myself, and he talked a good game. We had terrific conversations. He had a nice mother. He could have found the feet lying around anywhere. Although he freely admitted seeing the guy lose his head. Literally. No conviction on murder was likely, yet an outside chance of rehabilitation. Weigh the two together. He was 15 years old and had lived through a nightmare. In the circumstances, what would you do?"

"Do my job. Go after his accomplices until somebody broke."

"I forgot to mention his accomplices. He wouldn't give them up. I admired that."

"You're having me on. Still, I'd have gone for a conviction. Made damn sure that the charge, at least, if we didn't convict, stayed on his record."

"He was a minor!"

"I wouldn't have *expunged*. Leave a paper trail for the next cop to follow up on."

"Leave a paper trail and he'd be dead in short order. Real bad people involved. He had good reasons not to give anybody up. The main one being, he was scared shitless. With all your spit and vinegar, you'd see this boy into his grave?"

Mathers is sullen.

Cinq-Mars smiles. He understands the man's dilemma, not knowing the context. "You and me, we think differently sometimes. Rehabilitation. That's what I had in mind. That, and some form of payback to soothe your open wound."

"My open—. I'm not wounded. What kind of payback?"

"Ah. That's between me and him. Let's say that we got something out of it."

"Who's *we*?"

Cinq-Mars manages a shrug, and further deflects the question by jutting his chin to one side. "He's been helpful, Bill. Shown his gratitude. What's going on? You're accusing him of shooting up a biker's bank? That's not in his nature."

"We suspect his finger was on the trigger," Mathers says. "One curious thing, Émile: a couple hundred grand in small bills was left behind. Even with a wounded leg you'd think he'd stuff his pockets. Which corroborates his side of the story, that he was a victim, not the shooter. But then, why didn't the shooter – if it's not him – pack a bag with cash? Or did he ditch it somehow? Or forget to bring a bag to drag away? If there was another shooter, or an accomplice, he may have run off with folding money. Still, an awful lot of loot was left behind. If it was me, I'd still be there, filling my socks."

"I can see you pulling that dumbass move."

"Thanks, Émile. Glad to have you feeling chipper again."

They both share a smile, and Cinq-Mars adds, "It's the whisky talking."

"Was he a stoolie?" Mathers presses him.

"You know I don't like that term."

"I can't keep track of all your preferences."

"You know where it comes from, don't you?"

"Let me guess. You've told me."

"Short version," Émile Cinq-Mars starts in. "Folks catch a pigeon. Tie a tether on its ankle. Feed it crumbs on a stool. Other pigeons fly down to join in the feast. Then folks blast away. Of course, the *stool pigeon* gets cut down as well."

"What was the point of that?"

"Rid the world of pigeons. I don't like the term. It makes it sound like we take out anybody who helps us, along with the bad guys."

"Shit happens, Émile."

"On occasion. Doesn't mean we should celebrate the terminology. Calling someone a stool pigeon shouldn't doom the poor boy."

"Even though he is doomed."

"You're a pessimist in your old age, Bill."

"Your eternal optimism has been missing in my life."

"Sarcastic now, too. Do you know that pigeons are smart? They're crafty. Douglas Sykes is, too."

Mathers takes a slow stroll to the end of the patient's bed. "Okay," he digs in. "If he's not a stoolie, he's what? A fink? A snitch? A canary? A rat? What term do you prefer?"

"Let's call him an old acquaintance. Eventually, he explained the ghosts to me. That convinced me that he didn't do it. Everybody else began to think so, too, or at least doubt their ability to convict."

"What were the ghosts?"

"A decoy. To grab the attention of the engineer and the brakemen when they passed by in the locomotive. Distracted, they wouldn't notice a man knotted to the tracks up ahead, then stop in the nick of time like in a silent movie. I'm sorry, but a 15-year-old doesn't think ahead to do that, even a very smart one."

"Who does?"

"That's the thing. Had to be adults accustomed to killing and to figuring out what impediments might crop up. Plus, the dead guy was no saint. The kid was not our killer. I helped get him off. Now you're saying that he will only talk to me?"

"That's where we're at," Mathers confirms.

Cinq-Mars resorts to the whisky again. "He was always a smart cookie, our Douglas Sykes. Not surprised he wants to talk to me. Bill, what level of security is he under?"

"A uniform is on his door, I expect."

"You expect."

"I imagine."

"You *imagine*? That's nowhere near good enough."

"It's not my *poste*, Émile. Not my case. Should I make an inquiry?"

"One uniform standing guard can mean trouble for both of them."

"How do you mean, both?"

"The cop, too. What hospital?"

"The Jean Talon, I believe."

"That old dump? I'm surprised it's still standing. Hard to defend."

"What are we defending?"

"He's a marked man."

"Funny. Sykes said something like that himself."

"Did he? That's ominous."

"Meaning?"

"Even if he didn't do it, one biker gang or another will think otherwise. Aren't the really tough guys getting out of prison these days?"

"A bunch have. Not all, thank God."

"They won't be coming out in a friendly mood. Now somebody crosses them? Disrupts their system of high finance? Kills three of their own? Sykes needs a fully armed escort around the clock. Bill, pardon me for giving orders here, but for God's sake get him out of that hospital and into a secure facility. The sooner the better."

"You're right," Mathers says. "I'll ask about that."

"Bill!" Cinq-Mars shouts out. "Make it happen! Now! This is serious."

He finally jumps to it, pulls out his cell phone to make the call. While Mathers is asking his department for Sergeant-Detective Doucet's number, Sandra Cinq-Mars arrives with a fresh batch of fresh-cut flowers and the item that Bill forgot – chocolates. The two kiss, and Mathers can see for himself that Sandra is happy with her husband's progress. Less happy about the glass of whisky. He continues out to the corridor to give them time to catch up in private. He's told the number, dials, and prepares to fully convey the urgency to the Investigating Officer. He's hoping he can do that. Deliver the appropriate dose of passionate intensity.

"Yeah?" Doucet barks at his end.

No hard information to go on, a paucity of evidence. Nothing but hearsay that stems from a former member of the department who happens to be retired and was never much liked. Mathers takes a breath. "Léon," he makes plain, "we need to save lives. No delay."

"Okay. How? Whose?" the Investigating Officer replies in a flat voice. Even though the other guy is playing it cool, Mathers can sense that he's hooked his fish.

8. Easy and Quick

The symbol for infinity is tattooed on a lump above his left eyebrow. He wears it proud.

Jarred awake by a phone call, Raccoon is staring into his bathroom mirror. If not for the tattoo, he barely recognizes himself. He needs to find his bearings in space and time, between yesterday and the coming hour. Somewhere between this dump of an apartment and the sewer rat's gym where he's expected, he'd like to vanish.

His hands on the sink visibly tremble.

Getting the shakes is something new. He's been quivering for a day.

Killing three people bothers him less than the likelihood of their friends' retribution.

If they had friends. He's about to find that out, one way or the other.

Except that he can't get moving. He lacks motivation. He's stuck in place. Immobile. Just looking at himself. The dark rings under his eyes are perpetual. Why he's called Raccoon.

He addresses the tattoo above his left eye. Infinity, you dial my number? This it? Last day alive?

Dead in under an hour. Or worse. Begging to die. What went wrong?

Yesterday, everything went right.

Okay, stop. Get control of yourself, man.

Yesterday went right. You pulled it off. *I did good!*

Yeah, you know how to plan, how to execute.

So?

So?

Calm the fuck down.

He decides to shave. Might as well look half-decent if he dies today. Give the undertaker something to work from. He can take away his raccoon eyes if he's any good.

He still doesn't budge. He quivers. Fixated on his infinity tattoo.

The phone call that woke him told him to get his ass down to the gym. Two hours sleep, but nobody gives a damn about shit like that. He doesn't either.

Finally, Raccoon snaps out of his self-induced trance.

He shaves. His hand shakes. He cuts himself. Twice.

Dabs the blood.

He dresses well. Makes himself look half-decent. Enough to give the undertaker a clue.

The gym is a short car ride in his crumpled Corolla. On the way, he tries to determine if an invitation this early in the morning is a good thing or a death warrant. Either way, it's unprecedented. If the boys wanted to knock him off, they'd rap their knuckles on his door, ask him to take a drive into the pretty countryside or down by the river to enjoy the cool air, to beat the heat. How about riding in the trunk? Mind if we crack your head open first? *Why the hell* would they invite him to show up at the gym? To work out? As if they'd say, "Gone flabby, Rac. Break a sweat. Show us some muscle tone before we plant a bullet in your brain. If you have a brain. We got our own doubts about that."

None of this seems totally fair.

He should be allowed the time to stuff himself with the breakfast of champions: bacon and eggs and cheesecake. One final splurge.

No way. They wouldn't order him to get into shape if they plan to float his sack of bones down the St. Lawrence River. He shouldn't be so damned nervous. They'll worry if he's nervous. They might shoot him for looking like a worried man.

Stop!

He orders his nerves quiet. Tries to think positively. Nobody knocked on his door. Nobody dragged him down to the gym. He received a phone call. A polite invitation. Nobody is going to call up the guy they intend to kill. Too risky. Calls can be traced. Which means they intend for him to live through the day.

Difficult, though, stepping into the gym with a leather harness strapped around his nerves, binding them tight. Hard to play it cool that way. He'd like to tell somebody: *Go ahead. Off me. I'm cool with it.* Go down that way, be talked about as the coolest corpse alive. He'd have street cred then, if only from the grave.

He thinks all that but knows he can't pull it off.

The first guy he meets confirms it.

"What's eating you, Rac?" The guy's name is Chiclets. He had an assortment of teeth knocked out by blows from a baseball bat, then collected them when the fight concluded. His opponent lay on the floor bleeding out. He kept his teeth in case they could be implanted back in. No dentist was able or willing to do that. Instead, he settled for dentures and keeps his real teeth in a jar. He's threatened to turn them into a bracelet.

"Me?" Raccoon asks. Vital organs are leaping through his skin. "Nothing. Why?"

"You look jumpy."

"I'm not jumpy." His liver. A lung. Leaping out of his skin.

"Chill, man. Work to do. Quick and easy. Up your alley. Steady nerve, bro."

"I'm steady. What's the job?"

Cool, but jumpy. He might survive the day. He just needs to handle his paranoia.

"You packing?"

"Empty-handed. Pat my balls down tenderly, that's all I'm asking."

"Take your word on it. In back, bro. They're waiting."

He wasn't frisked. They trust him to enter the back room. Weird.

This could be a ploy. A man can still get shot in the back room. No one would hear a shot fired. A man can be carried out and dumped in a van and even the men doing the carrying would lose all memory of the experience.

The gym is empty as he walks through it. The weight room is still. Only Chiclets is behind him to guard the door. Later in the morning, body builders will show up, flexing their muscles, gazing at their asses in mirrors reflecting mirrors. Racing to nowhere on stationary bikes. Pumping iron like prison cons. But at this hour, no witnesses.

The guys in back don't notice his jumpiness. They hardly look up. They tell him about a job. He has a small part to play.

"What part?"

"The usual."

The usual is never a small part.

They'll support him, they say, with what he needs.

"What job?" he asks. His voice sounds right to him, almost as disinterested as they are.

"Mittens called it in." Mittens can be mentioned in this room. They scan for bugs on a regular basis. It's a sanctuary, a place where people can talk and nobody on the outside can listen in, but it doesn't look special. He's surprised by the dullness. Bare wood chairs. A beer fridge. A sofa for an afternoon screw or snooze. He likes the ceiling fan but overall he's not impressed.

"Mittens," Raccoon repeats.

High windows, too. Nobody sees in or out. He likes the ceiling fan but the carpet's regrettable. Nobody would know if they rolled him inside it, the hot dog in a bun, the pig in a blanket. He should have had breakfast. He's thinking of food.

"We picked you," one of the two men in the room tells him. Sharpie was named after the pen. He's known to be the brains of the organization. Others say he just knows how to take care of money. He doesn't say anything about that himself and everyone knows why. He doesn't want to offend Mittens. Whatever Mittens gives, he has the power to take away. Some doubt it but Sharpie does not.

Neither does Raccoon.

"That's cool," Raccoon says. "Picked me for what exactly?"

"You think on your feet, Rac. We always say, Rac can think on his feet. He's got brains in his heels. This needs to be done quick. No plan. You go in, do it, get out. That fast."

No plan means a high likelihood of failure. For the job, they've chosen a man they consider expendable. Nothing to do with his quick-thinking heels. They want somebody who doesn't know squat. Nobody they'd miss. Somebody they're having doubts about. Somebody who didn't get the job done yesterday, that kind of guy. "How quick?"

"Like it's done already."

"Immediate."

"You want help, you got it. Your call." They also offer him a choice of weapons. "We requisitioned a supply. Take what you need. Leave the rest."

Douglas Sykes, they tell him, is in the Jean Talon Hospital.

"Sykes."

"Shot three of our own yesterday."

"Sykes did that?"

"You weren't friends?"

"Barely knew the guy."

"We need this done by noon. Noonish."

"No problem."

"Not necessarily. I can think of one, Rac. There's a complication."

"Okay. There usually is."

"He's under police protection."

They are quiet in the room a while. The two men sitting across from Raccoon don't move. They stare back at him. Cigarette butts have been stubbed out in the ashtray between them; no one is smoking right now. Raccoon wouldn't mind lighting up, he's just not sure that he can do that without revealing how his hands shake. They quiver, which anyone who looks close can see. They might think he's scared. They might think he's hiding something. They might be right, too. Both ways.

Douglas Sykes being under police guard is more than a complication.

"What did you expect?" Sharpie asks. "He's in custody."

"I did not know that."

"Now you do," Sharpie points out.

"We got that one complication," the man who hasn't spoken previously remarks. He's broad and heavy and when he dons his biker colours he comes across as scary looking, tattooed up the wazoo and sporting a ring in every visible orifice. In here, he's wearing designer jeans and a soft pink pastel shirt, and the overall look is less menacing. His hair is slicked back tight against his scalp and tied in a ponytail. He wears less metal when dressed in regular clothes. He's an affluent man with a preference for elegant haberdashery that always includes pink. He's known as Pinkeye.

"A big fucking complication," Raccoon points out.

"We sent a guy down to check on things," says the man in the pastel shirt. "He says the cop is not airtight. Goes to the bathroom. Walks down the hall to the coffee machine in the visitor's lounge. Chats up the nurses. We see opportunity in his lack of attention. We'd saw his legs off if he was one of our own."

"I do him, too? A cop?"

"We recommend you don't," Sharpie says. "Your call."

"Major recommendation that you don't," Pinkeye underscores. He seems to be the one in charge of this operation, not the one who handles money.

"Need-to-kill basis," Sharpie confirms, picking up on Pinkeye's emphasis. "Otherwise, no. Course not. Who needs that shit?"

"Remember," the other man says, "Mittens wants this thing done."

"By noon," Raccoon frets. "Not much time to plan a hit."

"No time to plan. It'll be good for you, Rac. This is top down." Sharpie is overweight although his bone structure is slight, even delicate. Like Mittens, he has a reputation for both cruelty and brains. "I'm not saying it gets you a patch. I never make no promise like that. You been interested. Where there's a will, there's a fucking way, right? Even if you are English. Not local, someplace nearby. Like Ontario. The Maritimes. We're opening there. Prince Edward Island. There's opportunity. This could be a way in if you follow through. It's got the smell of primo opportunity, Rac."

Raccoon thinks. They watch him think. He's wondering what ever happened to Quaaludes. They used to be around, then they disappeared. Seems like every year there's a new drug of choice. He concludes, "No problem."

"You want a couple guys?"

"I work solo. Like that, nobody can say nothing later."

The other two men take a moment to check with each other.

Raccoon adds, "If I get there and change my mind, I'll call."

"Yeah," the smaller of the two agrees. "We'll give you a number. Watch what you say. Watch every fucking syllable comes out of your mouth. Know what a syllable is?"

"I won't give nothing up, Sharpie. You have a toolbox, you said?"

The two men check with each other again. The heavy guy rises from his chair. The motion requires a big push. "This way," he says.

Raccoon can't believe his good fortune. Everything is working out better than he could imagine. He's not jumpy anymore. Cucumber cool, he'd describe himself that way.

The heavy man offers a choice of five guns. There's also strangulation wire and a shiv. A candy store of lethal weaponry. This is so much better than having to explain why he's not packing himself, how come it is that he ditched his kill-piece. Yesterday, he tossed it onto a garage rooftop. He doubts the cops found it.

Sergeant-Detective Léon Doucet raps lightly on the open door to his boss's office and leans his shoulder against the jamb. He's decked out in a suave grey suit, a yellow shirt, blue tie. Self-conscious about his prominent underbite since birth, he compensates for the physical blemish with good grooming and distinctive togs.

Covering the mouthpiece on his phone, Lieutenant Gaston Tremblay, who doesn't dress well and has already slackened his tie, nods permission for him to speak.

"Intel on our suspect says we should go heavy on protection."

"What intel?" Tremblay asks.

"That's the whole message. You won't believe the source."

"Hang on," the lieutenant says into the phone. He presses a button to put his caller on hold. Then addresses Doucet. "Try me."

"Émile Cinq-Mars."

"Him? Is he out of retirement? First, the killer will only talk to him and now the old guy's giving orders?"

Doucet waits, rather than toss more fuel onto that fire.

"What's the detail right now?" Tremblay asks.

"One man on the door."

Lieutenant Tremblay presses down on the *hold* button without releasing it. "Suss it out for yourself. Take two uniforms. Find out from the medics how long before we return Sykes to holding. Decide for yourself the protection required." He lifts his finger from the *hold* button and speaks into the phone in a dispirited voice. "I'm back."

Doucet's expected his request to be met with more resistance. Not everybody reveres Émile Cinq-Mars, his boss being one of those who's never felt enamoured. When he was on the force, Cinq-Mars manoeuvred himself into a position where he answered to only a very few and not to the guys next up the chain of command. They had to be leapfrogged to find someone who'd give him an order. He carried that kind of weight. So, resentment. Doucet knows there's a difference between disliking someone and discounting that man's opinion. Doucet figures his boss is a decent cop, one willing to make the right choice even when he'd rather not.

The hospital is not far. He'll get the duty sergeant to assign a couple of uniforms; he'll stick them with guard duty, no matter his assessment of the situation. Better than having to take your good black suit to the cleaners.

Raccoon didn't depart the gym as quickly as the bikers handling him desired. They may have been buffing wax on the shine of his ego when they praised him for thinking on his feet, yet the man takes pride in his ability to plan, to anticipate and play the angles. He has analysed the downfalls, the slip-ups and sinkholes, that befall his peers. For a man who's committed at least one murder for every five years of his life, he's done remarkably little heavy time, four years here, three there, and never for significant crime. That's because he plans. And pays attention to detail. Even if this is a quick job, it still deserves advance thought. They might be hiring him because he's expendable, but he doesn't have to play into their expectation of the shooter being caught. They aren't going to look out for his skin once the job is done; he needs to do that beforehand.

He planned yesterday's operation in detail, and it went off without a hitch. So well that this bonus assignment has come his way. Those guys don't have a clue. They hired the man who killed three of their own the day before while helping the man they really wanted dead to escape.

Geniuses. He's outwitted them. He'll outwit them again.

Not that it's going to be easy.

For all his alleged quick mindedness, he thinks this one over slowly.

He does due diligence on the theory. To undermine the theory, you need to know what it is. He can, as Sharpie suggested, wait for the cop to slip away to the john, or go down the hall for a cup of joe or to chat up a nurse. That's the theory. Raccoon can then slip into the hospital room and with the aid of a silencer take care of business. That's the theory, not that he intends to carry it through. He has other intentions. He needs to get the plan down first, then figure out how to disrupt it. In theory, that plan is less messy than a knife, although he'll bring the shiv with him. He's willing to entertain the notion, to make it look like that was supposed to happen, if the circumstances worked like a charm. What he must do is find a way to make it *not* work.

The problem with the theory is that the hit happens regardless of whether the cop cooperates with respect to his movements and his inattention. Raccoon may have to take a chance, and that's where he has a problem. He doesn't believe in bad gambles and any gamble where he could wind up dead – or worse, incarcerated – is a bad gamble. Should the cop unexpectedly return, should a nurse notice the victim's heart stop on a monitor at her station, should she sound an alarm, or should the alarm be automatic, he'd then have an armed police officer between himself and freedom with a dead body at his back. His so-called partners don't care about such details. If there's a gunfight, if a cop is killed or if Raccoon himself is slain, that's not a worry for them. The only thing that counts is that Douglas Sykes is dead first.

That's how Mittens wants it.

If Rac dies, too, they'll consider it a bonus.

Any unintended consequence is merely trivial.

He's forced to figure out how it can all happen with none of it happening. That's a conundrum. A word he knows.

He's at risk no matter how this goes down. Raccoon feels differently about dying today than his so-called partners do. They don't give it a second thought. Their agenda is different. A way around his predicament is to avoid a gunfight, and the way to make certain that no gunfight takes place is to neutralize the cop immediately. Not to kill him. Or hurt him. Just remove him from the action. If everything goes south, the cop might thank him for sparing his life.

Okay, that can be his counter-theory. His upside-down, inside-out and backwards way of thinking. That's his starting point to figure out a way to explain himself.

He chose his tools wisely. The gun is small to make it invisible as he enters and departs the hospital. He accepted the silencer, although he'll need to carry it separately to keep it concealed. He decided on a briefcase, which Sharpie provided. He took the shiv, left the strangulation wire. And he wanted a wide-brimmed hat, to conceal his identity from the cameras that are bound to observe his entry and his exit. He didn't want a hat that anyone had seen him wear before, and so, not one of his own.

He was asked if he required extra ammunition in case things go bad.

Raccoon smiled. An extended gunfight would entail either his death or his endless imprisonment. Extra ammo would not help, and he had no intention of giving anyone the satisfaction, neither the cops nor his gung-ho confederates.

"I'm good," he announced, "as is."

He's already made up his mind to park by the Jean Talon Market, close enough to the hospital yet far enough away to be faceless among shoppers where his comings and goings will be ignored. If he has to depart the hospital on the run, the last thing he wants is to jump into a nearby car. In a crowded neighbourhood, he can lose his pursuers on foot along the congested streets and alleyways, circling back to his car undetected. That part of the plan, he hopes, won't be necessary. Still, always expect the worst.

Raccoon pauses a moment. He slumps down over the fender of his car. The weight of his choices falls upon him. Overwhelms him for a moment. Not the unreality he's been negotiating with himself, not the concoctions he's devising to explain himself later, but what confronts him, really. His only way out of this, for real, he figures, is to do that cop.

It's the only way to neutralize him. Take him out of the picture.

It's the only way to deal with the aftermath. It's the aftermath that he needs to plan.

He wishes he had more time. Life, he's thinking, is always the same fight. A no-holds-barred punch-up. He hates that it is that way. *With me, why is it always both ends against the middle?* He's asked himself the question before without receiving an answer.

He could just shoot his way in and shoot his way out, give it all up. Blow it all up. Shoot the target, kill the cop, go down himself in a shitstorm if it comes to that. The trouble is, all that he has, all that he can hold onto in life, all that he knows about himself, comes down to this one thing: The man he's been charged with killing, two days in a row now, is the one man on earth he will not kill. Period. End of sentence.

The cop? He might have to. But not the guy in bed. He can't. He won't. Not him. Not Douglas Sykes.

9. Seek and Hide

All piss and moan, Douglas Sykes had a rough night. His return to the hospital further aggravated his pain. Examined by a surgeon, an earlier miss came to light; an infinitesimal nick to the thigh bone created a microscopic splinter with a razor's sharpness. Tissue and a vein had abraded, causing internal bleeding while brutalizing a nerve.

"Nothing too serious," the physical assured him. "Killing you, I bet, right?"

The doctor did not appear to detect the irony inherent in his remark. Or his delivery was inscrutable.

Sykes was operated on a second time, with local anaesthetic, then confined to bed. A private room was commandeered so that a guard could be at his door. He awakens woozy with painkillers yet in need of more. Hollers for a nurse. Only as he pushes himself upright does he discover himself handcuffed to the bed's side rail. He spots a clicker. Presses it frantically. A nurse and the cop who's been trying to seduce her show up on the run. Bless their carnal hearts. Disoriented, panicky, he laments, "I'll die on you!"

Less a prediction than a threat.

Constable Angelo Matti sees the matter differently. "Hey, bud, you're doing okay. You woke up is all. I know what that's like, some days."

Sykes blinks, rubs his eyes. He figures out where he is and his current condition. Which isn't that bad, everything considered.

"What are you? My personal ninja turtle or something? I got a question for you, Ninja."

Officer Matti smiles. He has a naturally friendly disposition. "Go ahead."

"If you're supposed to be guarding me—"

"I am guarding you."

"Who's guarding you?"

The nurse finds that funny. She takes less kindly to Douglas Sykes trying to put his clothes on. He's stretching his free hand across to the locker by the head of the bed, and with difficulty is attempting to yank his duds off their hangers. "Mr. Sykes, you have not been released. Stop that. You're not going anywhere."

"Hate to break it to you there, bud," Matti supports her. "You're under arrest."

"What's your point?" He slides off the bed. The handcuffs keep him standing there. "Where're my socks? Goddamnit, what've you done with my socks?"

"You're not going anywhere," the nurse reiterates.

"Did you hear me say I was? Does it look like I got a plane ticket sticking out my arse? I simply refuse to die with my ass hanging out of this thing." He flips open the back of his hospital gown to shock her with a rear view.

The gallant Officer Matti jumps to her defence. "Prisoner Sykes! Cut that out!"

"Behave yourself," the nurse tacks on. Yet seems amused. "You're not dying."

"Nurse— What's your name again?"

"LeClair."

"Really? That's it? You don't have a first name?"

She considers the wisdom of a reply. The man is reputed to be a murderer. "Francine," she admits.

"Francine. I'm not dying – *at the moment*. Look at me. I'm standing on my own two feet. Couldn't say that when I arrived last night. Lovely name: Francine. Suits you. I'm not in that much pain compared to yesterday but I could use help in that regard. Franny, you get me? A little something? For the pain? Pretty please?"

"What's your problem," Matti interjects, "if you're not dying *at the moment*? You think you will? Paranoid, much?"

"Do you have a clue, Ninja? What's my situation? Why're these cuffs on me?"

Matti hasn't given it much thought. "Suspicion of murder?" he says, partly a question.

"Worse. Suspicion of killing three Hells Angels. Not patch members, nothing like that, or I wouldn't be vertical now. I killed their employees, though. I don't say that, but others do. Ask yourself. What's my life expectancy? What's yours, guarding the door?"

Officer Matti is suddenly cognisant of his circumstances. He'd thought his mission to be nothing more than babysitting a prisoner, not defending the Alamo.

"Look at him," Sykes points out to Nurse LeClair. "He's wetting himself."

"I'm not—"

"Ninja!" Sykes yells. "You owe me your balls! I could have walked out in the time you took to unhook her bra."

"I wasn't! How did you—"

"Good question. Did I wake up and catch you in the act? Did I hallucinate? Can't say. But lucky for you I didn't run. Your paycheque you owe me."

"Ah, dude. You're handcuffed to the bed. You were never going anywhere."

Sykes stares at his shackled wrist a moment. He'd forgotten. "Give me five minutes. I'll gnaw through bone. Then run."

"Gross," the nurse says.

"Sorry, I don't mean to offend your delicate sensibilities, Francine. Point is, this guy has a job to do. Looks to me like he's been guarding you more than me."

The nurse gives the young cop a look, conceding that he's got him there.

“All right,” Matti says.

“All right, what?”

“I’ll protect your sorry ass.”

“You and what army of whack jobs? Cowboy, you got to take this serious.”

Matti shares a glance with nurse LeClair, who seems to concur.

“Don’t sweat it,” the cop says. “I’ll be on the door.” He has a way of breathing in and inflating his chest, as though to indicate that he’s now suited in armour, as he steps from the room to take up his station.

“You,” the nurse instructs. “Bed.”

“Only with my clothes on. I’m not wearing this shit. Where’re my socks?”

She issues an exasperated sigh. “In your shoes.” She steps in front of him, bends over, and turns his shoes around on the closet floor so he can see his precious socks. She stands before him again, hands on hips. “Your clothes don’t leave the closet. You’re not really a murderer, are you? I look in your eyes. I don’t see that.”

He’s honestly stunned. “Wow. That’s as fine a compliment as I heard from anybody. From a cutie pie, too! Thank you, Nurse Francine. I might have a good cry for a minute or two. Hey, that’s another thing. Your new cop boyfriend should never be leaving you alone with a suspected killer. The man’s incompetent. You should be cross with him. Look, all he’s got going for him is being young. Me? Experience.”

“Now who’s flirting?”

“Showed you my ass. You’re on to me now. I got nothing left to hide.”

“Un-huh. I’ll bring you a Tylenol, Mr. Sykes. You missed breakfast. I’ll see what I can do about that, too.”

“My god, an angel in my midst. That’s a first.”

“I’ll be back in 10. I better find you in bed.”

“Or what?”

“Trust me, you don’t want to find that out.”

“*You* should guard the door. We’ll all be safer.”

She leaves him to his own devices. Underneath his gown, Sykes pulls on his underwear, going carefully over the bandaging that protects the incision in his leg. To him it looks as though they did a tidy job. Credible.

“No blood,” he says aloud after a cursory examination, and crawls back in the sack.

He fell asleep.

His eyes snap open the instant the door does. In a single motion he slides off the bed onto the floor, his right arm snared upright, his wrist cuffed to the side rail. The sound could have been anything. A careless orderly wheeling in a gurney, slamming the door against the wall. His angel-nurse Francine handling a spastic tray. Yet Douglas Sykes is wired differently. His nerve endings propel him to the floor. After the life he’s led, any sudden wicked noise means trouble.

From his position under the bed, he sees two sets of feet by the entrance. The cop’s, and an intruder’s, and the intruder forcefully whispers. “*Hands back! Now!*”

That he whispers is frightening.

“You don’t want to do this.” Matti’s voice. Quiet. Intent. Laced with fear.

“You want to fuckin’ tell me what I want to do? What I don’t want? *Hands!*”

Sykes hears the clink of handcuffs – he’d recognized the sound anywhere. He hates it. Then the cop is shoved into the john.

The door swings shut behind them both.

He doesn't know what's going on in there. The intruder is taking his time. Sykes pulls the bedsheet down, to make a tent for himself. He knows he looks pathetic now. He's nowhere close to being fully covered. The man comes out from the john. Sykes hears the main door being opened, and held open, and assumes the intruder is checking the hall. Then he returns to the room. "What the fuck?" the man murmurs.

Sykes assumes the empty bed prompted the remark.

The intruder is coming around to his side. Sykes awaits his fate. The man kicks one of his protruding feet. Sykes then sticks his head out from under the sheet, gives up the pretense of being hidden. The rest of his body is exposed, a lump.

He suddenly feels better about his chances. "You again," Sykes says. "What's going on? Change your mind?"

"Douglas," the man greets him, "what can I tell you? I got another call."

"Again? Twice?"

The man smiles. He finds it funny. "Your name keeps coming up. Man wants you so dead, bro. Deader than dead. He wants you dead even before I get to kill you. What did you do that was so wrong?"

Raccoon pulls the sheet off the patient on the floor, tosses it on the bed. He reaches out a free hand to help him up and Sykes makes it to his knees. The visitor has a distinctive look to him apart from the dark circles under his eyes, the hat covering his crown baldness, and the telltale tattoo. His cheeks sag into his jowls, his jowls double up. His eyebrows slope sharply to both sides completing the perfect hang-dog look. A girlfriend advocated for the infinity tattoo to elevate people's gaze from the lonesome sad sag of his look while concealing the ugly lump. She'd been studying make-up and hoping to get into film. A career nixed when her coke habit spun out of control. The last he heard she was in jail.

"Who sent you?" He pulls himself upright, handcuffed in place. Raccoon had taken that likelihood into account. One reason why he couldn't wait for the cop to be out of sight – he needed his keys.

"You don't know who? The Hells, Douglas. The Hells sent me."

"I figured *that*, but *who*? Who exactly?"

"You're not always this ignorant. Mittens wants you dead."

"Fuck me gently. What the hell did I ever do to Mittens? Does he even know me?"

"You tell me. That's *my* question. How'd you get his attention so bad?"

"That'll take some thinking about. Rac, what are we doing? Are we breaking out?" He shakes his manacled wrist. Raccoon counters with the key pilfered from the cop. "You're so kind. I hope I live to appreciate this."

"It's a tightrope, my Douglas. We've been jammed up before. This one? If I fail to kill you twice in two days, I don't want to know what's next."

"Got that. Me neither. For both of us. Out of the skillet straight into the flames. How are you playing this?"

"Me? Don't ask. I got my plan. You don't want to know it. You? It's run, my bro."

"That cop's okay? You didn't do nothing stupid?"

"When am I ever that stupid?" Raccoon cocks a hand to his ear. "Warned him to be quiet. He's behaving. Sorry, Douglas, short and sweet. No time to catch up."

"You planning on shooting me again?"

"Not today. But move fast, okay?"

Rac comes closer and works the key into the cuffs.

"Is that trouble for you?" Sykes massages his freed wrist and asks him about what they're hearing. A siren outside. A glance through the window eases their fret.

"We're in a hospital," Raccoon reminds him. "It's a fucking ambulance."

The man suddenly steps past Douglas Sykes, yanks open the closet door, and tosses clothes onto the bed.

"Get dressed," he commands. "This is a jailbreak. You're sprung."

Sykes moves quickly then. Flings on his pants and shirt. He doesn't take time for his socks but shoves them into a pocket and puts his bare feet into his shoes.

Quickly, he cinches his belt buckle.

"What's going on, hey? How does this play out?"

"It's complicated," Rac tells him. "Go. Now. On your own. Run. Beat it. Keep your head down. Get on a plane. A train. A bus. Hitch-hike. All that. Get the hell out of town." When Douglas Sykes still doesn't move, as though he's in shock, he tells him, "Move! *Go!*"

Sykes continues to stand his ground, as though he won't accept freedom unless it's explained to him first. "Who's doing this?"

"Who? I told you who, Douglas. The Hells. Straight from Mittens himself, the order. Now get the fuck out of here or I'll shoot you where you're standing until you're not."

"You're so kind overall. Just tell me why. What did I ever do to Mittens?"

"Oh, Christ, when did these rocks fall into your head? You think they'd tell me that? I'm setting you free, Douglas. Think of it like the old days. You're on the run again. Get going. I know you know how." The intruder pleads with him to comprehend his new circumstances, and quickly. "Douglas, this is a good day. Go. Get out of here. And no, we won't never see each other no more. That'd be fatal."

"Same as the old days."

"Same as. Go! Fuck!"

"Promise me, Rac. Nothing stupid."

"Me? Come on. Get real. Now go."

Finally, he runs. At the door, Sykes pauses to check the corridor, to make sure he's not being observed. Then scampers across the hall and takes a dogleg into a stairwell.

Behind him, the man with the infinity tattoo above his left eyebrow watches him go.

He puts his gun away in the briefcase he let fall by the door when he first barged in. The one with the silencer. Takes out the cop's pistol from his waistband. He goes over to the bed and grabs a fat pillow. Then returns to the john.

Angelo Matti is shackled to a pipe under the sink. He sees the door open; his attacker enter. He sees his own pistol in one of the man's hands, a pillow in the other. Very quietly, he says, "No." A plea for mercy. The heavy door behind his attacker closes on them. "Don't do this. Man, come on. Think about it first. I don't mean nothing to you. I hardly seen your face. I'm not looking now. I can't identify you. I'm not looking. Did you kill him? Sykes? Is he dead?"

"That means what to you?"

"I wanna know. Please. Don't do this. You don't need to do this. Christ, if he's not dead, you don't need to do this to me. If he is, I can't hurt you, right? I'm not looking at your face. I can't identify you. I can't!"

The man with the hang-dog face says, "I need a way out. Sorry, you're it. Douglas killed you first, see, before I got here. Then escaped. Nothing I could do. It's the only way out for me. He's taking the blame, see. Not me. He can escape. I can't. He escaped before I arrived. I came up empty. All I can do is tell you why."

The two doors are shut. Between the washroom and bedroom, and out to the corridor. Also, the pillow will help keep it quiet. He won't use the gun with the silencer. The bikers said he had brains in his heels. Okay, he'll show them what it means to think on the fly. He will use the cop's own gun. The cop is about to scream, a cry that would have gone unheard anyway, and Raccoon folds the pillow over the pistol and shoves it into the man's face and mouth and presses the pillow down hard above the man's chest and fires. The man's brains blast out under the sink behind him. Blood flows out from under his head where it's crashed to the floor.

It fell with a soft sound, his head, a muffled thud.

Raccoon hears it under the echoing muted blast. Strange, that sound.

He stands.

He checks his look in the mirror. He appears not to be stained in any way.

He puts the gun down on the countertop.

Washes his hands. Leaves the tap running. Selects a towel. Turns off the tap with the towel, then wipes the tap and the faucet down. Then he wipes his prints from the gun. Then he dries his hands. He hurries but he's sure to be thorough.

He wipes down the door handle. This one, then the one to the hall.

He returns to the washroom and folds the towel neatly. Puts it back in place.

He chooses a facecloth to take away with him. To open doors. Press elevator buttons. For now, he stuffs the cloth in a jacket pocket. Doing so, his fingers touch the handcuffs' key.

He'd forgotten. Now he rethinks. He decides.

Holding the key with his facecloth, he springs the handcuffs free of the cop's wrist. Then off the sink pipe. He folds the cuffs together and returns them to the cop's belt. Wipes them down. Then stands.

Good. He's done.

This is what you call thinking on your feet. I got brains in my heels.

He returns to the bedroom. He lets the bathroom door shunt shut behind him.

The man with the infinity tattoo cocks his fedora down over his eyes, then leaves the room. He looks at no one in the corridor. No one looks at him. He heads right, toward the elevators. One happens to come up quickly, and he exits the floor, heading down.

Across the hall, Douglas Sykes has left the door to the stairwell open a crack. He never ran far. He did nothing more than take cover. He sees Raccoon go. He exits the stairwell. Hidden, he watches the man enter the elevator. Then looks around. No one pays attention to him, all dressed up with nowhere to go, and he returns to the bedroom.

He stares inside the john. Then lets the door close and he just stands there. Stands there a while. Then he pushes the door open with his back and returns to the far side of the bed.

He takes his clothes off.

He's naked.

He hangs everything up in the closet again.

He puts on his hospital gown as best as he is able. The back goes untied.

Though it pains him to do so, he snaps the handcuffs on one wrist, so that he's manacled to the bed's side rail. As before.

He gets down on the floor.

Douglas Sykes stretches out, as far as he can stretch out, and covers himself with the sheet as he had done before, as if he's still hiding. He pulls down the wire that attaches to the alert button and flips it toward the other side of the bed. Out of his reach.

He hopes that the nurse he's met, Francine, will not be the first to arrive. What's to be viewed behind the bathroom door is not fit for anyone's eyes, and he hopes that she will never see the cop,

Matti, lying there, the man who was chatting her up, half his scalp blown off it looks like, the way his blood and brains are smeared.

He doesn't know all that's going on, but when all hell breaks loose, the last thing you want to do is obey the devil's own commands. A lesson he learned the hard way a long time ago when, at 15, his life was altered forever. That mistake, obeying the devil's command, is one he won't make twice. Yesterday, he had stalled his escape, hanging on a fence-post, repeatedly pulling himself up only to fall, bleeding in public until help arrived. Today, he still won't run.

He won't go down for this. At least, he'll try not to.

10. Tribulation and Trial

Sergeant-Detective Léon Doucet is pacing the floor in the interrogation room when Bill Mathers arrives. His jacket droops off the back of a chair; his shirt sleeves are rolled. His tie is cinched tight to his collar. He's visibly incensed.

"I heard," Mathers says.

"I was five minutes away. Bringing extra guards like you and Cinq-Mars said."

"Did you know our man?"

"To say 'Hi.' Super nice guy. Young. No wife, no kids, thank God." The man's large lower lip gives him a bulldog look that suits his mood. "Shouldn't say that. It's a shame he never had a wife and kids when he had the chance. He'll have a mother, though. A dad. Brothers. Sisters. Friends. Buddies in uniform."

Mathers releases a private sigh, then asks, "What do we have on the shooter? I just drove in from Ontario."

"Sykes shot him. Up close and personal."

Mathers is too stunned to speak.

"Officer Matti's own gun," Doucet tells him. "He says otherwise, of course. Sound familiar? He's the only one at the scene who's not dead."

"What's his 'otherwise?'" Mathers is not sceptical and that's evident in his tone. He's merely looking to be better informed.

"More kickass bullshit. From his rear to my ear. He's being processed downstairs. Be here in a minute. Sit in. Play the good cop. I don't have it in me."

"He's been around the block. He's seen that act before."

"Not after killing one of our own, he hasn't."

He has a point. "Okay. Fine by me, Léon. But – am I on this case?"

He hasn't been assigned. A *sud* cop and a *nord* cop; homicide and felony; usually, never the twain shall meet. "A cop's dead, Bill. These circumstances, the brass won't deny us anything."

"Okay. What bullshit has he dribbled so far?"

Doucet pulls his chair out, sits, and is waving a hand in the air – either to dismiss the question or to get started – when they're interrupted. Douglas Sykes is escorted into the interrogation room, wrists cuffed in front of him, ankles in chains. "Ask him yourself," Doucet replies for everyone to hear.

Sykes opens with a proclamation. "Either I tell the truth, or I shut my mouth." His prisoner's shuffle is augmented by a pronounced limp. Chain links clink on the floor. "Sorry about your officer. He seemed like a sweet guy. Him getting whacked had nothing to do with me."

"You were there."

"I didn't do it."

Sergeant-Detective Léon Doucet waits for the officer who brought the prisoner in to leave. Then heaves the table on its side and rams it against Douglas Sykes, against his knees, scraping it across the floor and driving him back to the wall. Sykes falls out of his chair, tries to get to his feet when Doucet redirects the table, ramming it forward, this time pinning him into a corner where he's tightly trapped. His eyes are frantic and wild and appealing for mercy. Doucet snarls, "A cop is dead! Don't fuck with me!"

The veins in his neck bulge.

"I'm sorry about that."

"Don't you fucking be sorry! Shut up, all right?"

"I can't be sorry?"

"You can't —." Doucet declines to finish his sentence. He grabs Sykes by the hair and slams his head back, once, twice, three times against the wall. Behind him, Mathers is on his feet, stunned himself and immobile. Suddenly he knows who stood on the prisoner's wounded leg yesterday, who learned firsthand that Sykes was stubborn beyond the norm. Mathers steps to the wall on his right and flicks the switch there to *On*. He speaks loudly enough for his voice to rise above the straining and panting in the room. Loud, yet calm. "You are being recorded. Sergeant-Detective Doucet and Sergeant-Detective Mathers are in the room. Tell the good people listening your name."

Shaking behind the barrier that Doucet has imposed, the man looks from one cop to the other "Sykes," he confirms. "Douglas M."

"Speak up. Louder." He's a long way from the ceiling mic.

Much louder, as though his safety depends on it: "Sykes. Douglas M."

Doucet steps back, stands fully upright. His perfectly taut tie is too tight to adjust, but he tries anyway. He then walks to the wall beside Mathers and puts a thumb on the recording switch. Turning to face Sykes, he makes sure he sees him flick it to *Off*.

"So much for that bullshit," Sergeant-Detective Doucet contends.

He doesn't move while Mathers crosses the room and pulls the upended table back onto its four legs. Sykes is left crouched in the corner. He has a shallow cut on his forehead. His long hair and ashen complexion contribute to his whipped dog look. Mathers flips the table upright, drags it back to the center of the room. Picks up the fallen chair and returns it to its proper place. Facing Sykes, he juts out his right hand with the palm facing upward, then flaps his fingers against the palm, urging the man on the floor to stand. Sykes, on tenterhooks, does so.

Mathers walks around to the far side of the table. He sits. Doucet won't, that's clear. The officer paces, all adrenaline and fury. Sykes eases himself down into his appointed chair again, wary of the man with the caged animal disposition.

"I know what this is," Sykes says.

"My advice? Say nothing unwise," Mathers warns him, again calmly. "If you think you know what's up or down, I'll point out that never before have you been accused of murdering a police officer. Am I right about that?"

Sykes agrees with a nod.

"What you think you know is no longer valid."

He nods again. "I told him I don't want a lawyer. Doesn't that show my cooperation?"

Mathers is inclined to say he's made a colossal blunder but keeps it to himself.

"You know why I don't want a lawyer, right? Because I want to talk to Cinq-Mars. Doucet, you could make that happen, you said."

"Give me an hour alone," Doucet states. He yanks back his own chair, then crosses the room and flicks the wall switch to restart the recording. In theory. He sits on the chair and effects a smouldering pose that nearly pulls a laugh out of Mathers. He's a volcano set to erupt again. Next time, Mathers won't be shocked if he blows his top.

Whether Doucet is putting it on or if it's for real, Douglas Sykes figures that it makes no difference to him. Either way, he'll bear the brunt.

"You talk," Doucet directs Mathers. "I'm too pissed. See what shit coughs out of his gorge."

"Same rules as yesterday," Sykes maintains, a smidgeon above a whisper. "I talk to Cinq-Mars, or I don't say peep."

The smouldering man stands again. Sykes looks up at him and holds on to the table, to push back this time. "Get the wall," Doucet says, and Mathers is on his feet. He goes over and flicks the switch off again. He doubts the machine was ever connected. Back at his own station they often are not. They rely on portable units there, not these unreliable, built-in, ancient affairs.

Doucet slows his movements. Each turn or step is meant to intimidate but Sykes won't look at him. The detective comes around to his side of the table and lifts him by his collar. Moves him to the back wall. He's methodical, he takes his time, and whales on him up against the wall, body blows, bruising his ribs, pounding the air out of his gut, a long pause between each assault. He leaves him in a lump on the floor, gasping.

Doucet goes back to the side wall and flicks the switch on again. Returns to his chair.

"Sit," Mathers says.

Crumpled over, Sykes rises slowly. Lurches to his chair. Sits.

In a low, unhurried voice, staring straight ahead at no one with a blank expression, Doucet reminds him: "A cop was murdered this morning. By you. You don't get to ask for your own private conversations. We're done with that."

Mathers allows time for the comment to sink in. Sykes is smart. What Doucet is saying will make sense to him in a moment. Today is not yesterday, and he needs to process what the difference means for him.

"I understand," Sykes states from his chair, quietly, humbly. "But I didn't do it."

"I'll crack your head open down the middle," Doucet warns him. Sykes is still not looking at him.

"I'm not lying."

"When have you ever not lied?"

"I want a lawyer now. That's your fault. For what you did."

"Tell me what happened," Mathers, the good cop, intercedes. He doesn't deny the request for counsel, he's simply deaf to it. He can always say he misheard.

"I told them already."

"I'm in the dark, Douglas. I haven't heard a thing. Explain it to me."

Sykes nods, squiggles around in his chair. "The door banged open."

"What door?"

"To my room. Banged open. I can't explain my reaction. I was half-asleep. I slid out of bed, landed on the floor, like in a split second. No place to hide. It's all I had."

"Then what?"

"I only saw their feet."

"Whose feet?"

"The cop's. And the guy who came in, his feet."

"You and feet," Mathers said.

Sykes looks at him curiously then.

"So, you didn't see their faces," Mathers continues.

"How could I?"

Doucet butts in. "That's fucking convenient." He clenches and unclenches his fists, his wrists at rest on the table.

Sykes checks the hands, then says, "I didn't see them."

Mathers nods to encourage him. "What did you hear?"

Sykes wets his lips. "The killer ordered the policeman – I met the kid, the cop, he was a good one – he was supposed to put his hands behind his back. Or give him his hands. I can't recall exactly. I heard handcuffs clink on. Once. Like it was only on one wrist."

Doucet bumps his chair forward and puts his elbows on the table. He folds his hands together. He argues that "No handcuffs were used."

Sykes hesitates. "Really?"

"Funny how you can hear a single clink but can't recall what was said."

"I'm telling you what I heard. Or thought I heard."

"Go on," Mathers says.

"I saw them – their feet, I mean – go into the john. They were in the can a while—"

"How long is a while?"

"Half a minute. Twenty seconds. Felt like eternity on hold. Like they pressed the pause button on the world."

"Poetic. Go on."

"The one guy came out. Not the cop. He came over to the bed."

"Why?"

"Saw later, I was missing a pillow."

Both policemen take a moment for further commiseration. They know what the pillow means. Even Mathers knows, and he hasn't heard the story. Doucet confirms it with a nod. Not that he believes the man's story. Even so, a pillow had been in play.

Mathers asks, "He didn't see you?"

"My feet stuck out."

"Pull them back in, why not?"

"Too scared. Too late for that. I didn't want to move."

"Go on," Mathers says.

"He went back to the john. Ten seconds later, I heard it. The gun going off. Behind the wall, you understand, he had that pillow, that heavy door was tight. I still heard it. I know that sound, man. I'm sorry about your guy but I was scared shitless at the time. I figured I'd be next. What else could happen? Nothing good."

"People been dying around you the last two days," Doucet pipes up. "Cause of death? Bullet holes. Wherever you go people get shot. How do you explain that?"

"I can't."

"You can't? So, you got nothing to tell Cinq-Mars even, is that what you're saying?"

"He knows the background. It's not like I don't want to cooperate. But it's hard to figure out what's going on. If anybody out there can help me, it's him."

"Because he's smart and we're as dumb as oyster crackers."

Sykes looks at him. Mathers does, too. "What's an oyster cracker? But anyway, that's not my implication, Detective. It's because he knows me, and you don't."

"Implication," Doucet says, scowling, as though he objects to the quantity of syllables.

In Mathers's mind, Sykes is too confident, too much at ease. He almost wants to ram the table against him himself, not that he believes he can pull that off with conviction. Anyway, it's been done. He decides on a different tack to throw him off his feed.

"Tell me about the train tracks," he commands.

"What?"

"The tracks. You know."

"Sorry, I don't. What tracks?" Sykes is staring hard at Mathers now, which he's not done before.

Mathers gently points his forefinger at him. "You know what tracks."

"You got me on that one, Detective," Sykes says, still staring, and wondering what Mathers knows. Doucet repeatedly shoots a glance between them, picking up on the electricity in the air.

"You remember, Douglas, when you lashed a bad guy down to the railway tracks and a train lopped his head off? You stole his feet. Those tracks. Where were they?"

Sykes asks, "Where were the feet, you're asking?"

They stare each other down. "The tracks."

"Nearby. Right behind this station almost. Funny how close. A long time ago."

"Still fresh in your mind, I suppose."

"I almost forgot. Until now."

"This guy's already a killer?" Doucet inquires. The turn in the conversation has pumped up his heart rate, yet he speaks quietly and slowly. "A deep dark past. Nothing about it on his sheet."

"You talked to Cinq-Mars," Douglas Sykes concludes, still looking at Mathers less harshly now. "How's he holding up?"

A knock, then an officer carries in a file folder. He puts it down and leaves. Doucet gives the page inside the folder a perusal.

"This is not nothing," he notes. "Time to stoke the barbecue. Your part, Mr. Sykes, is to be the burnt burger."

Curious, Sykes finally looks at him. Waits. Doucet takes his time.

"What did you do with your socks?" Doucet inquires.

Now Mathers is the one who's surprised.

"What socks?" Sykes asks. "*My* socks?"

"Your socks."

"They're on my feet."

"A nurse says she put them in your shoes. When it came time to get you dressed to come over here, guess what? They weren't there. Where did she find them?"

It's clear that Sykes doesn't appreciate the question. "I believe they were in my pants pockets, yeah."

"How'd they get there?"

"I'm only talking to Cinq-Mars, all right?"

"Those days are gone," Doucet reminds him.

"What's this about?" Mathers wants to know.

"If not Cinq-Mars, it'll be a lawyer. Tell me who to call."

"Don't threaten me with what you don't want to do, Mr. Sykes." He looks over at Mathers. "Sykes got the drop on Officer Matti. Grabbed his gun. Unhooked himself from the bed with Matti's keys. Took the man into the bathroom to mask the sound and shot him. He then went back in bed and pressed the clicker to call the nurse."

"No," Sykes says, not for the first time. He's been whispering *No* all along. "The clicker was on the other side of the bed. I couldn't reach it."

"You killed a cop. Do you know what that means for you?"

"Do your job," he mutters under his breath.

"Excuse me. What did you say?"

"*Do your fucking job!*" Sykes yells as loudly as Doucet had previously. "Where's the gunshot residue on my hands? Come on, where's the GR? If I freed myself, why the hell am I still here and not in Miami by now? Answer me that."

His outburst causes Doucet to grow calm. "Why did we find the key for Officer Matti's handcuffs on your bed?"

"What?"

"You didn't know that? Answer the question."

"I don't know nothing about it. But where's the GR?"

"You did a good job washing it off in the bathroom."

"Who could do that good a job?"

"You, apparently."

"Where's the gun?" Mathers asks.

"Next to the victim," Doucet responds. "Wiped clean, of course."

Mathers and Sykes lock their gaze on each other again. Mathers asks, "Did you shoot him, Douglas? I think it's time to own up, don't you?"

"I want to talk to Cinq-Mars."

"We heard. He got you off once before. He's not getting you off this time."

"Just let me talk to him," Sykes persists. "What are you so afraid of? Either him or I get a lawyer. You choose."

The prisoner can still be pushed on other details, so Mathers is surprised when Doucet taps him on the forearm. He signals to come outside.

Before exiting, Doucet offers the suspect a word of advice. "Long and hard, Mr. Sykes. Think it over. The key was on the bed. How'd it find its way there? Your socks were in your pants. How did they get there from your shoes? Dream up some story while you're waiting. It can be a lie; we're used to those. Anyway, I love a good lie and you're going to need some whoppers."

The prisoner is adamant. "Due respect, why no gunshot residue? Who wins in front of a jury if you're talking socks and I'm talking GR?"

In the hall, Doucet asks, "What don't I know?"

"Nothing I don't know either," Mathers admits. "My best guess? He's a big-league snitch. He may want to cash in his chips. Be handed down a favour for favours in the past."

"Is that what this deal with Cinq-Mars is about? I don't want to lose this guy because he's owed a goddamned favour."

Mathers deflects the question. "Léon, Cinq-Mars will drive us both nuts. Guaranteed. Could be the right move, though. I get the feeling more is going on here than we're aware of. I mean, who shoots a cop then hangs out in the room? Who? Only one answer to that question: Nobody. What's his thinking, doing that? He'll get a lawyer. A good one might get him off on that one point alone."

"Not to mention the GR," Doucet tags on.

"Let's not mention it."

Doucet takes time to consider everything. "You're a smart cop," he says. "I am, too. You're saying we need help on this?"

"It's not about smarts. There's history, like he says. We have to turn over a log, see what bugs live under it."

Doucet takes his time before he consents. "First, let's go after him again. Once more. You be nice. I'll hammer his nuts. And please, don't turn on the fucking recorder. Do you think the damn thing's broken? It's not. We're not recording this."

"You turned it on yourself."

"Remind me to erase. Anyway, I have to damage the machine now in case his future lawyer brings it up. We've been too easy on him, Bill. He killed a cop. Let's break him apart before we interview on the record. I'll tell you one thing. If we don't separate his left testicle from his right, the brass will bust ours."

"Léon, why didn't he lawyer up? Did you make a deal?"

The detective pushes out his big lower lip, then chews on it a little, not wanting to disclose what he knows he should. "Bill, I told him that talking to Cinq-Mars goes from fat chance to less than zero the second he lawyers-up. Something strange, though."

"What's that?" Mathers asks.

"He doesn't want to. It's like he's afraid of lawyers. Strange. Go in?"

Mathers concedes. "I'm on-side. Just tell me you know your limits."

"Sorry if I startled you in there, Bill, but he killed a cop. Fuck limits."

11. Rain and Fire

Nobody on the run makes a beeline for Canada's capital city. A man with a bounty on his head will get noticed in a polite, law-abiding municipality such as Ottawa. A government town, chockfull of groomed civil servants and military personnel. Folks are fined for jaywalking. Or for spitting. They're imprisoned if they forget to say they're sorry for no reason. Loitering can get a man 6-to-10. Months, but still. The jokes go around, but if nobody on the lam runs to Ottawa, Raccoon calculates that he should. Do the unexpected. He's crafty that way.

He chooses Ottawa as the first step in a plan to escape to somewhere else.

A conviction of his: A woman may need love, but a man needs a plan.

He ditches his battered Corolla in the Plateau district of Montreal. That tells nobody anything of significance. It's a hot car anyway with fake plates and ground-down VINs. He'll walk downtown, which will take a half-hour. From there it's public transportation to the West Island. The better part of an hour. Less security out in the 'burbs. More walking after he gets off the bus, but nothing extreme. He's then free to catch the intercity to Ottawa without the eyes of closed-circuit cameras on him or thugs hanging around the depot with his picture in their heads.

Cop or Hells Angel, he'll elude his pursuers. Thanks to the brains in his heels.

Before catching the public bus, he makes a call. Dials the back room at the gym.

"Yeah?"

"Hey, Sharpie, it's me."

Sharpie's response is an extended silence.

"Sharpie, it's me," he tries again.

"Sharpie's not here," Sharpie says.

He figures out what that means. "Syllables? Is that you? Hey, Syllables, how's it hanging?"

"Give me a blow-by-blow, motherfucker, but don't blow me. You coming in?"

"Time and place," Raccoon says. "This ain't neither one of those."

"Come around. We'll console each other."

"Sounds great. Yeah. Like I said, time and place."

"What we heard over here," Sharpie reveals, "the ice-cream man cashed it in. We'll miss him. You gonna miss him, too?"

Raccoon thinks through what that might mean – *ice-cream man*? – and figures out how to respond.

"Yeah, that's right!" Too upbeat. Calm down. "One of his loyal customers, I heard, is springing for the funeral. You know? Paying for the funeral."

"That so?" Sharpie says. "You sure?"

"Yeah, you should tell the guy who owns all the ice cream in the ice-cream factory that the ice-cream man don't need to worry about no funeral. He's got good friends. The expenses? Paid up. The man who owns the factory, he's on the hook for nothing more."

Raccoon listens to the silent delay while Sharpie tries to grasp what he means. Then Sharpie says, "We'll pass it on. I think."

"I gotta go."

"Nothing to say for yourself?"

"Understand it, you know? The ice-cream man? Gone before I got there. Must've been a change in the weather, hard to say. Started out like a sunny day but clouds rolled in. His best customer, gone, too. Never got to see him. We never shared a word. Gone, but you know how it goes, not forgotten."

"Gone before you got there? The ice-cream man?"

"You said it was urgent. Now I know why. You never told me we had a race on. The best customer had his ice cream, then left before me. A change in the weather, I figure. I never saw a thing. Except I saw who was left lying around."

Raccoon's impression is that Sharpie is considering all this.

"Like I said, drop by. We'll have a beer."

"Look forward to it, Syllables. Right now, I gotta run."

"I'll be seeing you then."

"Not if I don't see you first."

Raccoon taps the line. Dead.

And now, he desperately needs to run.

He might as well assume that he has the Hells Angels looking for him. Any dimwit can figure out that the cops want the guy who killed one of their own. That means they'll be after Douglas Sykes, not him. They don't know about him as far as he knows, but he's not going to stick around to find out for sure.

Chances are, though, he's on the Hells' radar. They'll have questions up their butts.

Run to Ottawa. Beat it from there. That's the plan. What can go wrong?

12. Nothingness and Being

The cat's meow.

He's been feeling better. *Ain't that the truth.* His wife has seen the improvement for herself. Doctors and nurses agree that he's on the mend. Anyone who missed seeing him at his worst is alarmed, but that visitor is reading the pallor of his skin, the weight loss, the evident weariness, the strain on his general vitality. His disposition, no great shakes either, has improved. Overall, he's feeling better. *Ain't that the cat's meow*?

Émile Cinq-Mars took a bad turn on his way north from New Hampshire in an ambulance. He'd been ambushed, shot, rescued from being face down in the Connecticut River where he was bleeding out. As his health improved after surgery, his travel insurance company lobbied to get him back across the border, where he would be subject to government care and expense, rather than their own. He can't rightfully blame the ambulance folk – although he does, thinking that he should have been delivered to a hospital along the way as he got sicker. Nor was his illness a direct effect of the trip; the two happened to coincide. Along the highway, he started hallucinating. He had to fight to identify himself by name and fought through a fever that levelled him.

He survived with scant awareness of himself, later describing his state to Sandra, his wife, as alternating between nothingness and being nothing. "Hard to figure out which one I preferred. Either I was in the clutches of misery or feeling discarded on death's door. What be your preference, sir?" How much was due to the insidious drugs? Difficult to decipher. He often felt remote, sometimes hot, sometimes chilled, always nauseous and miserable, his joints aching. Each sway or jolt of the vehicle delivered a precise, needle-like pain comparable to the worst of his back pain attacks. The mere bend of an elbow, necessary from time to time to combat the relentless aching, put him through a meat grinder of assorted afflictions.

"Like crunching razor blades in my joints," he told Sandra.

Mentally, he held on to the *knowledge* of his name, suspecting that he might be enduring his final moments. He held to that thought that if he shed his body, he wanted to retain the ability to identify himself.

A religious man, he prayed less than he'd have predicted. Too dizzy? Too disoriented? Sometimes he perceived himself as jet-propelled, not flying down a highway, rather, veering through tunnels in mountains and emerging into verdant dark valleys. Once, plummeting to the bottom of a lake. "Belly of a whale type thing." He swam to the surface, gulped a great lungful of air. In reality, he had pushed off his rich oxygen tube in his sleep.

He'd cling to his name, *"I'm Émile."* Only in possession of it did he believe that his world was not a dream, that the tremors and terrors presenting themselves were more imagined than real, therefore marginally subservient to his will.

Hospital life in Hawkesbury, Ontario, proved less dramatic in terms of what he endured. His dreams and fevers quieted, the imagery becoming less lucid. He felt a weight on his body at times, and the weakness through his arms and legs felt scary. At his worst, he bullied himself with fears of an imminent stroke. Death vexed him less. Compared to being half-paralysed with a malfunctioning brain yet unable to speak, the Grim Reaper seemed less grim.

Still weak and out of sorts, Émile considers his reprieve to be the cat's meow. He can now imagine returning to full health again.

Even that is troubling.

A name from the distant past has resurfaced, one Douglas Sykes. Despicable crimes are attached to him. Decades ago, Cinq-Mars had helped him slip a murder rap. He believed that Sykes, an adolescent at the time, deserved a chance to reform. Believed the prospect to be at least marginally realistic. Now he was hoping that eluding a conviction in his youth has not led to committing a multiple murder one day and becoming a cop killer the next. The possibility wears on Cinq-Mars, similar to the weight on his chest when his blood was infected. The cat's meow, physically, but in another sense, he's moved from the frying pan of his fever and drug-induced delirium into the fire of a harsh tragedy.

A new thought for him: Some truths are less likely to set you free than others.

The arrangements have been formalized. Émile Cinq-Mars takes a seat in a meditation room down the hospital corridor, one normally reserved for patients to receive Communion or murmur confession, or for a physician to relate heartbreaking news. He's expecting all of that. To commune with Douglas Sykes about the wretched old days, to hear his side of recent events, to exchange confessions as they cover the long gap in their communications, and to reveal, one way or another, wicked news.

Given what they've both been through over the intervening 40 years, being alive is a surprise. They might start there, with the wonder of it. *We're alive. Can you, Douglas, believe it*? Indeed, when a weathered and much older version of Douglas Sykes than he had summoned in his mind's eye appears, and Cinq-Mars, with difficulty, shoves himself to his feet, the two embark on an embrace.

The old criminal and the retired cop: a hug to commence an interrogation. As two old, scarred, sage warriors, who alone know how the battle was fought, who alone know what the war has meant and what it's cost, they slander normal convention.

They hug as though holding one another up.

Then sit.

Officers, who include Émile's old partner, Bill Mathers, are under the impression that they will stay in the room – until

Cinq-Mars dismisses them with a brush of his hand. When they don't budge, he verbally shoos them on their way.

Alone with the prisoner, he says, "Douglas, here we are. You've been lobbying for this. We've got a lot to talk about, you and me. But mostly you. So, yak."

"First things first, Émile," Sykes says.

"Meaning what?"

"What comes first: my thanks. Thank you."

Cinq-Mars utters an audible sigh. "You're welcome. I think. At the end of this, Douglas, will I be thanking you? That's the question I need to ask."

Sykes purses his lips, cocks his chin from side to side. "We'll see," he says. "For now, you have to hear a few things."

"Please, don't tell me you didn't do it. Don't start with that. Time enough later. Confessions first."

Sykes looks down a moment, reflects, then looks back up again. "Not to worry, Émile."

The ageing petty criminal clears a frog from his throat. They begin – first Sykes, then Cinq-Mars chimes in – by discussing their wounds. The former detective grants him that latitude, as the man is just getting started, working himself up to what he needs to relate.

They fall quiet for a spell. Pivot from the everyday, peel away from the pleasantries, turn toward the nitty-gritty.

"Émile," Sykes says. He speaks his name as though it's a plea; yet restrained. An evocation. A last straw of the faint hope that he's been holding on to. "A thing we say is, *'If you can't do the time, don't do the crime.'* We're like a chorus. We say, *'I can do five years standing on my head with my head in a bucket. Touch the ceiling with my toes. Entertain myself that way, walking on the ceiling.'* We say those things horsing around, figuring life out. The ups. The goddamn downs."

PART TWO

FOUND AND LOST

13. Grab and Clutch

Perilous moments – chases, escapes, gunfights – meander through the bloodstream to coalescence, over the long haul, into the vague yet potent notion commonly advanced as being *experience*. "Be glad if you have it," Cinq-Mars has advised rookies. "Be more glad if you don't." For him, across the girth of time, less dramatic episodes reside in the mind with greater emphasis. As though the mind reshuffles what it chooses to retain, and certain idiosyncratic incidents are elevated above the pyrotechnical. Cinq-Mars holds to a suspicion that the mind is not done with these occurrences, that further understanding remains to be gleaned.

A young fellow lugs a flour sack on his back. The lad wears a tie-dyed T-shirt, cut-off jeans, and the buffalo-hide footwear popular in the day. "Jesus" sandals, they were called. Distinguished by the thinnest possible sole, they sport a loop over the big toe and a skinny strap below the ankle. Older boys, the hippies, opt for them, and for this impressionable lad they are his pride and joy. The junior detective takes notice of the teenager yet has no clue why. He does not speculate on the sack's contents and holds no suspicion.

In the sack are two bloody human feet.

Across time, it's difficult for Cinq-Mars to fully reconfigure the moment. To catch sight of a kid who's lugging around body parts on a warm summer's day should be a career highlight, rather than its most perplexing moment.

The boy is hunting for a place to dispose of his cargo. The cop does not know that. Neither now nor then can he explain why he called out to the youth, although he had been on hand earlier in the day when a body was found strewn across railway tracks nearby. He did not connect the two, the boy to the dead guy, not consciously. The feet did not bleed through the sack and no imprint of them was visible. Nor could he honestly call it a hunch. He abruptly shouted to the lad, an impulse, almost an involuntary reflex, like a hiccup, and since then he's put the moment down to chance. It puzzles him still. Instinct, perhaps, or intuition. Little alerted him other than pure, unadorned, ridiculously dumb luck.

A kind of obtuse voodoo or witchcraft.

In a nick, his fellow cops were handed one more excuse to resent him.

He offered a pair of reasons to his superiors and sheltered a third. They wanted something, in their words, "concrete." Whenever he rewinds the film, Émile can't shake the feeling that something else was up. Something beyond his ken. He doesn't want to get spooky or spiritual about it, although every so often he entertains the notion that the boy's better angels had a sit-down conversation with his better angels and together they put together a plan.

Out in the cosmos somewhere, they shook on it.

To his bosses, he pointed out the difference between the boy and other youngsters on the block. A hot sun commandeered the day. A dusty afternoon, a shabby street, the neighbourhood languid and slow. A tough part of town. Through the harsh, dusty summer light a few girls shook out their hair and giggled. They clutched onto one another as if their lives were suddenly at stake. They screeched more often than they spoke in civil tones. Sullen teenaged boys were observing them with feigned indifference and yet oh so keenly. They'd see the sunlight on the girls' cheeks, a line of shadow bend from a nose. One boy did not pretend to not notice the girls: He simply did not notice them. That boy was distinctly unaware of anyone. Off in his own world, he was carrying a sack on his back like a runaway kid in a storybook.

"The boy looked suspicious, you're saying," his sergeant presumed. Cinq-Mars was a green detective at the time, rising to the position only a tad slower than the speed of light. He'd picked up an assist from a powerful senior officer when they worked a big case together, but acrimony over his rapid advancement was prevalent. He was one of a new breed of righteous cops in a corrupt department. Insidious suspicion was often directed his way. Anything he did was microscopically scrutinized. Any fault, magnified.

Cinq-Mars wanted to explain that the boy's suspiciousness intrigued him less than a unique quality to his disposition – not the same thing. As though a humid summer mood suffused the street, and adults were being themselves and kids were being themselves, all sluggardly with a thirst as if they stood as still as folks on a postcard snared by time… except that that one teenager, busily tramping along with a pack on his back, was not being *himself*.

He had places to go. Things to do.

He looked alien to this place. As if hiking through time.

Not much point in attempting to explain that.

"He looked agitated." He explained it that way to mollify senior officers. They could understand a policeman stopping someone out of the blue because he looked stressed, on edge, *agitated*. It made a certain kind of sense. He wasn't going to explain that the teenager appeared to be strolling through another eon.

He did not mention a third impression. The young man kept looking *up*. The rooflines in the area were uneven and low. Most buildings a squat two storeys, maximum. Single-storey dwellings were stunted. They'd been erected during the Second World War or in the boom afterwards when materials were at a premium. One way to cut costs: keep ceilings low. The boy kept looking at the rooflines. Who walked down a street like that? Émile Cinq-Mars, for that obscure reason, without understanding it himself, called out to him. Hard to say who was more surprised by his shout, the boy or the policeman. The boy turned, and the detective displayed his badge.

Immediately, the kid ran.

The cop knew then that somehow, some way, by some fluke, he was onto something.

He did not speak about low rooftops or upward glances during his debriefing. He was receiving a ton of credit for finding a boy with two human feet in a sack, and if certain bosses could deflect any of that credit and take him down a peg, they would. To say that the boy kept glancing up was too fine a point to attach to the arrest; fellow officers would interpret the acuity of his observation as bragging. He had responded to nerve endings alerting him and had called out, "Hey, there!" He didn't know why.

The chase proved comical. Not only did Cinq-Mars have the advantage of his height and long stride, but the boy was impeded by his Jesus sandals. A girl experimenting with a first pair of high heels could run faster, and as the sandals repeatedly slapped the boy's heels, the policeman's biggest issue was not breaking into laughter.

When he did get close, the boy stopped and swung his sack at him. With an anvil in it and momentum behind the blow, the cop might have been in trouble. Instead, he easily blunted the assault on one shoulder, slipped inside the arc of the swing, and bound the boy in a hold jarring for its immediate vice-like imprisonment.

Growing up in the Quebec hinterland, Cinq-Mars had on occasion subdued injured horses. Wrestling this skinny kid to the ground proved a lesser challenge.

And yet, another moment astonished him, never to be explained. Further struggle on the lad's part proved futile, although he continued to kick and squirm. His eyes conveyed a look of "forlorn abandonment"— a phrase Cinq-Mars used to describe his impression to a friend. Another aspect that he left out of his report: his sympathies were inexplicably aroused. Even as he bent the boy to his knees and handcuffed him behind his back, he discovered that he was on this boy's side.

Not something he wanted to explain to his superiors.

Especially after he checked out the sack.

An opaque plastic bag was inside. Without extracting it from the outer sack, he opened that bag, too. Cinq-Mars discovered the bloodied feet, cut off at the ankles.

He looked back at the boy who was looking dolefully up at him from the sidewalk, and, in a kind of shock, asked, "Tell me this much, kid. What did you do with the poor guy's head?"

The boy nearly burst out bawling. He fought to maintain composure but sputtered. "That wasn't my job. I didn't get the head."

Cinq-Mars tied up the sack again. "There was what, a lottery? You chose straws? What job was yours?" The sympathy in his voice was palatable. It affected the boy.

His answer sounded more like a question. "Get rid of the feet?"

The people who were gathering around them did not grasp the magnitude of the crime involved as they had no idea what the sack contained. They knew only that a man, presumably a cop, had handcuffed a local teenager. Folks didn't act up against cops back then, but the onlookers expected to hear what the fuss was about, to ascertain that the detective had good reason.

His unmarked car was across the street. Cinq-Mars waited for a break in traffic, then escorted the lad across, the bag of feet looped over his forearm. He guided him onto the rear seat. Slammed the door. The severed feet were deposited in the trunk. Then he drove the boy away from the crowd and from that community, dipping under a railway overpass on Jarry Avenue and stopping by a large park.

He shut the engine off and turned to face his prisoner.

"What gives?" the boy asked. His voice trembled. He wasn't speaking with any fake bravado. Fair to say that he was scared witless.

"I'm bringing you in. First, I want to know a few things."

"Like what?"

"Like what. For starters, I want to know the full extent of your involvement. Did you kill that man on the tracks? Was that you?"

"No. No. No way. That wasn't me."

"You know about it. That's obvious."

"I was there."

"Where?"

"On the tracks."

"When?"

"When he got run over."

"When was that? Give me a time."

"Ten o'clock around."

"This morning?"

"Yeah."

He had that part right.

"Were you there when he got tied down to the rails?"

He didn't say yes; but nodded. Good; he was not prone to lying.

"But you didn't do it."

He wagged his head no.

"You know who did it."

The boy nodded yes. He was set to cry again.

"Tell me who," Cinq-Mars instructed him.

The boy stayed mute.

"Just tell me."

The boy didn't and shook his head.

"What's your name?"

"Douglas."

"How about your full name, Douglas?"

"Douglas Michael Sykes," he whispered.

"Do you live around here, Doug?"

"Douglas."

"Excuse me."

"Douglas. Not Doug."

"Okay. Douglas. Do you live around here?"

"A few blocks away, yeah."

"Douglas, I found you with a dead man's feet in a sack that you were carrying. Do you understand how much trouble you're in?"

The detective had an inkling, then, why his attention was first drawn to this lad, and why he was interrogating him in private. The whole situation was different than anything he might have expected because the boy was different.

"I do know," he said. "Heaps."

The way he said that. His tone. That choice of word. Cinq-Mars believed, without knowledge to back him up, that this boy, in *heaps* of trouble, welcomed being picked up and placed in police custody. He had no opinion as to his specific guilt or innocence, and yet the boy preferred police custody over whatever else he'd been through and over whatever else might lie ahead of him. A murder suspect was glad to have been picked up by the cops. This was novel.

"Do you live with your family?"

"With my mom, yeah."

"Just your mom?"

"Yeah."

"She's going to be upset."

"She'll be devastated."

The boy didn't use words he expected. Émile, university educated at a time when few cops were, had a similar problem within the police department. Fellow officers not only resented his education, his success, and his advancement – not to mention his moral deportment – they also objected to the words he emitted. This kid had the same problem among his peers. Especially in this neighbourhood.

Sympathy aside, a man had been lashed to railway tracks and run over by a train. This boy carried the victim's feet in a sack. The head and hands were missing. The future for Douglas Michael Sykes was looking grim. The kid knew it, too, and he and Cinq-Mars shared a glance that seemed to confirm exactly that.

"I'll take you in now, Douglas. Prepare yourself. This won't be a good day for you."

The boy nodded, as if giving him permission to book him. Then his lips trembled, tears needed to be wiped away on a bicep sleeve, and suddenly he was overcome. He began to cry like a five-year-old, and Cinq-Mars believed the lad's torment to be genuine.

The boy was overwhelmed. He may have spared a thought for his mother. That gave Cinq-Mars an idea. When the investigating detectives on the case took over and eased him, their junior, off the case, the younger cop could dangle a carrot before them. Why not offer to be the one to inform the mother? Someone had to do it. He'd even bring her in to visit her son. Cinq-Mars kept to himself that he'd share a few words with her on the drive to the station to advance his knowledge of their situation. He'd do it all because he was intrigued by this kid.

The detectives preferred that he just got lost. They knew he was only itching to stay involved. On the other hand, the job of informing the mother was a hard one, and no other officer was hoping to be assigned.

They let him take care of that part.

14. Bows and Buttons

"What I did for you, was unusual. I still don't fully understand it."

In the hospital's quiet room, Émile Cinq-Mars has not gone listless, although a physician passing by might presume that medications have compromised his focus. In the moment, an excursion into the past has dredged up old memories. A wistfulness has nabbed him by surprise. For all the trouble and travail of the old days, he misses those days.

"I understand it less," Douglas Sykes admits. "Mostly I remember our talks. They were wild. Thinking about the universe. Stars. Philosophy, even. Religion. How crazy it is to be human. Are we monkeys in shoes and shorts? Remember those chats, Émile? You had them with other people, I'm sure, but for me it was special. Rich. Something new."

"We got off on our tangents. You were 15, 16 years old. Reading *Being and Nothingness.* I admit, I found that curious."

"Do you still treat criminals like that? Do you check out their reading habits?"

"Virtually never. In your case, I wasn't convinced of your criminality. Not back then."

"Now you are? Sometimes ...." His voice trails off, as though he's become interested in a different tack than the one he started out on.

"What do you mean to say?" Cinq-Mars prompts him.

Sykes breaks off eye contact, tries again. "Sometimes I tell people... you know, when I'm shooting the breeze... I tell them, that you must've seen something in me."

"Could be true."

"I recited the story to a few ladies, hoping they'd see something in me, too."

"Glad to be of help." He smiles.

"Except that I don't believe it, Émile. Not anymore. I repeat it in the company of the ladies, to make myself look good. But face it, it holds no water. I'm not anything I'm not. Tell me, why *did* you save my sorry ass?"

Cinq-Mars honestly isn't sure. "My colleagues rushed to judgement. Right off the bat, they wanted your sorry ass in a sling. Something about the speed of their condemnation, its swiftness, the potential finality of it – no way was it professional. As a cop, I was offended. Also, I had this sense that there might be some recourse for you other than eternal prison. A kid like you, if you worked your way up to an adult penitentiary, you wouldn't come out alive."

"Proved you wrong there. I've been inside. Scarred, but here I am, still upright."

"My point. We kept you out of jail long enough to give you a chance to survive."

One small table lamp shines in a corner. Despite a noble effort to be a comforting space, the windowless room comes across gloomy.

"Thing is, Émile, you were on my side before that. You told me so."

He knows what Sykes means. "Sure. Okay. But there's a difference between being on your side and letting you slip a murder rap. One doesn't necessarily follow the other. As my career went on, I was on the side of a few guys I put away for decades. I wished them well, then tossed away the key. In your case, being a kid had a lot to do with it. I think my youth did, too. You can't count on either anymore – neither your youth nor mine."

Sykes deflects the negative comment by dipping his chin. He points out, "Looking back, I'm not sure you could've proved murder on me. Not to mention I was a minor."

"Damn, Douglas, you could be right! Still, we didn't put disrespecting a corpse or tampering with evidence on your sheet either. Charges like that were a slam dunk. Accessory to murder would likely be a snap."

"Juvie home," Sykes says, as though to dismiss the rap, although his shrug is a concession. Time passes before he asks quietly, "Why, then? Is it because you wanted to set me up? You had your intentions for somebody like me."

"We weren't setting you up back then, Douglas. That came later."

"If you say so, Émile."

Hands on his inner thighs, elbows jutting outward, trance-like Cinq-Mars stares at a patch on the floor under a small side table. No nuance to the patch is evident, only the shadow of the table creating a dark line precisely parallel to a whitish grain in the tile flooring. A bitterness in the other man's tone caused a thought to ricochet. Mentally, he's wandered off.

Finally looking up again, he says, "I never quite tied it up like this, Douglas, with a ribbon and a bow. Partly, it had to do with your mother. The way she fought for you; I was moved by that. I should not have been swayed, professionally speaking. Her love for you clouded my judgement, made me want to believe – if not in your innocence – in your possibilities."

Douglas Sykes appears saddened by the mention of her, or by the allusion to his long-lost potential. He nods in guarded agreement and quells an emotional slurry.

"Yeah," he concurs. And let it go at that, for now.

15. Son and Mother

Émile Cinq-Mars climbed the interior switchback stairs to the second storey of a duplex, knocked, to be greeted by a petite woman excited to see him. Her hair was a sallow grey, partially held in place by a kerchief looped behind her neck and knotted on top by an off-centre bow.

"Mrs. Sykes? Montreal Police Service." Detective Émile Cinq-Mars displayed his badge. "May I come in?"

She admitted him, closed the door, and guided him into a narrow living room. Her last few steps before she sat resembled a pony's prance. A peculiar spasm, then she chose the sofa. Cinq-Mars sat across from her, his elbows at rest on a chair's broad arms.

On the coffee table between them sat a glass of ice water or lemonade, with cubes. A Hollywood gossip magazine lay open to the shocking news of a star's secret infidelity. *What Jan Said When She Found Out!*

"My errand is not a happy one, Mrs. Sykes. Douglas has been detained by the police as a material witness. A terrible crime took place this morning. He has knowledge of it. As we speak, detectives are questioning him regarding his involvement."

Her visage was creased by a slight smile that never relaxed nor expanded. He couldn't be certain that he was making contact. Furtive glances, with an element of the coy.

"Mrs. Sykes?"

Her expression did not change as she dipped her fingers into the glass, pulled them out wet with what proved to be lemonade, then flicked them at her visitor three times in an attempt to spray him. Sitting slightly beyond her range, Cinq-Mars, flexed backwards, and for the most part, stayed dry. His knees were slightly spotted, and he detected the taste on his lower lip.

"Mrs. Sykes." He felt spat upon.

She held that half-smile, which no longer struck him as benign.

Just then, the front door sprang open.

A woman stumbled in. In her 40s, she carried a large grocery bag that threatened to slide from her grasp to the floor. A purse dangled off a wrist. She kicked the door closed behind her, turned, and spied the visitor.

"Who be you?" she demanded. "Mo? Who've you let in here?"

"Detective Émile Cinq-Mars, ma'am. Montreal Police Service." He stood.

"Police? Maureen, what have you done?"

Rather than answer, the woman pulled an ice cube out of her glass and hurled it at Cinq-Mars. He failed to duck as it careened off his forehead.

"Maureen!" The woman dropped her grocery bag on a chair and rushed into the room. "Stop that!"

She stopped.

Struck hard and startled, Cinq-Mars moved closer to the woman who had just arrived, as though for her protection. "Who are you, may I ask?" A hand on his forehead. More stunned than hurt, although being hit by the cube did smart.

"I'm Martha Sykes," the arrival told him. "I live here. Why are you here? Police? Has something happened?"

"You're Douglas's mother?"

Her face changed in an instant. "What's gone on?" Her tone implied the worst.

"Are you the mother? Not this lady?"

"For God's sakes! *Yes!*"

"Your boy is safe, Mrs. Sykes. He's unhurt. He's in some trouble. I'm here to inform you about that and take you to him. I'm sorry, I thought this woman was Douglas's mother. She didn't tell me otherwise."

"She doesn't talk much," Mrs. Sykes said. "People think she's mute. She's not. Mo? Excuse us, please. Be a good girl now. Wait in the kitchen."

The woman known as Maureen arose, and was guided out to the hall, then proceeded on her own from there. Mrs. Sykes turned fearfully back to the officer.

"What's happened?" Her tone aggressive, distrustful.

How to explain to a woman that a man was dismembered on a railway track and that her son was subsequently found carrying his feet in a sack?

"We believe, Mrs. Sykes, that your son witnessed a most serious crime."

"How serious?"

"A murder, ma'am. In any case, a man is dead."

"Oh my God."

The shock of his words sat her right down on the sofa. She held a hand to her mouth.

He had to finish his core message. "For some reason, ma'am, unexplained so far, your son participated in concealing evidence."

The woman's eyes were darting around, frantic with concern for her boy, and puzzled by this slow drip of incomprehensible information.

"What're you talking about? What evidence? Conceal what?"

"Douglas took away the victim's severed feet, ma'am. It appears that he was attempting to get rid of them somehow."

Another jolt went through the woman, she was abruptly displaced, thrown out of herself. Cinq-Mars saw her battle through that narrative to arrive, within a few seconds, at a singular and fierce conclusion, speaking with her teeth clenched, "Where is he? Take me to my boy!"

He had no opportunity to issue any word of calm, for at that moment the other woman returned with a kitchen knife – nothing too lethal, it looked flimsy, although it had a jagged edge. The weapon didn't pass muster, but it could nick the skin, scratch a vein, take out an eye, and he reacted to thwart her attack. She was all over him as he clutched her wrist, then bent back her fingers, the mother joining the fray – on his side, although in the melee that took a second to discern.

"Mo!" the mother was screaming.

Cinq-Mars methodically removed the knife from the woman's hand. He did his best not to break her fingers in doing so and, in that, succeeded.

Pulled off him by the other woman, the attacker settled quickly, as though nothing had happened. The woman whom he now viewed as the sane one treated the other as a child. "Mo! That was bad! *Bad!* Go to your room! Now!"

Miraculously, with reluctance, the woman bent her head and did just that.

"She'll be my death, that one."

"Who is she?"

"My tenant. Social Services pays her rent and then some."

Mrs. Sykes turned to challenge Cinq-Mars.

"I'll apologize for her behaviour another day," she announced, not calmly, yet under heroic control. "First, take me to my boy. Immediately."

"Certainly. Ma'am? Douglas was wearing a T-shirt, shorts, skinny sandals. He might appreciate a better shirt, proper pants, shoes, and socks. If the shirt is less casual, with a collar, it can give one a sense of self-worth that might be necessary, under the circumstances. Proper clothing will help him to look presentable when detectives are questioning him. That can help. Not only him. It might help the detectives see him in a better light."

The look she gave him caused him to feel like an alien. He supposed he earned the part, with his gargantuan nose, his height, his suit and tie, and his remarks which sounded so foreign to her.

"Fine." She left him in the living room while she went to hunt a few items.

Cinq-Mars didn't care what the boy wore; he appreciated being alone in the apartment to have a quick glance around. Someone who lived there was a reader. He browsed through second-hand paperbacks, marked down to a nickel or a dime, that topped the side tables and the TV. Hemingway. Camus. Sartre. Dos Passos. He was getting an inkling of where the boy derived his vocabulary. A pile of magazines next to the TV revealed varied interests: hot rods, locomotives, jet fighters, and firearms.

Mrs. Sykes returned with a small shopping bag filled with clothes and toiletries for her son as if he was off to summer camp. Émile Cinq-Mars then escorted her to the downtown *poste*.

16. Arrows and Slings

He'd never been inside a museum. And like holy wow, man, how weird is this?

Raccoon got off the bus in Ottawa, then caught a cab across the river into the city once called Hull, now called Gatineau for some crank reason – why don't people make up their fucking minds? – where he found a rooming house that suited him. Rundown, real cheap, familiar that way. If dipsomaniacs aroused themselves at night to curse and lament, he'd heard their mournful tune before. Music to his ears.

Ottawa was his plan, but a man must always be willing to adapt. A tattoo above his left eye and a con look to him: better to blend in with derelicts and the older poor than among civil servants and students. He went out to eat, grabbed a bite at a greasy spoon and that was comforting. But the day was hot. He wanted to beat the heat. The huge museum down by the waterfront looked impressive. Had to be air-conditioned, right? He'd cool off there.

Somebody in the line to buy tickets commented, not to him, that there was more copper on the roof than on any building in the world. He hadn't looked up. He did then. Wow. Wow. That was a lot of copper. That would be a heist, stealing a roof. He could carve off a piece every day and nobody would notice while he got rich. Inside, he was amazed. Never mind that the entry fee for one cost more than a movie for two, and what nut bar came up with that idea? Once inside, he felt that he was still outside, and in another world. A native world, like it used to be in the olden days, and that was chill. Totem poles. He could walk around inside and breathe cool air and be in another place, another time, and feel the stress, the fear, the gnawing darkness leave him. Lift away.

Still, seriously, five million artifacts? Way too many. Whose idea was that? Did nobody ask nobody else, *who has time to look at five million useless things*? Most of it nothing more than old stuff anyway. Like an old spoon. An old bed. A spinning wheel. A few beads and bows and arrows. Somebody cares? They should slash that number down, make it an even thousand. That should do it. A person has a half a chance to see junk if there's less of it. Five *million*? He should help them out, snitch a few items.

Like Samuel de Champlain's astrolabe. This museum bought it from a New York museum for a quarter of a million bucks 25 years ago. That's what it says. He's beginning to see why they charged him what they charged to come in and look around while he cooled off. A museum has expenses. Especially if they're getting ripped off that way. Now, if he could relieve them of Champlain's astrolabe, which he could fence for a grand, minimum, they'd still have five million other things to show.

That would be something.

Except, the astrolabe is secure.

Under unbreakable glass.

Guards everywhere. Even though they look like they haven't had a dose of excitement in their veins since landing the job, they're still guards, they're still looking for *something* to do. He can't let himself become that something.

Anyway, he's not there to make trouble.

The wrong time for that.

He's on the run. He's here to breathe air-conditioned air and that's it.

It might've been fun though. Stealing Champlain's astrolabe, whatever the fuck an astrolabe is supposed to be.

In wandering around he entered a temporary exhibit. "Gold Rush! – El Dorado in British Columbia." Gold sounded up his alley. A lot of pots and pans and pictures of donkeys and guys with beards down to their dicks. They looked like the bikers of their time. With mules, instead of Harleys. He sat in there and took a load off and that was cool, too. The lighting was subdued, as if nobody wanted to wake up the dead, and the hall had that cavernous feel, tomb-like. A good place to relax. He relaxed. He'd prefer to smoke but that was outlawed. Banned. A worse crime than theft if you go by the signs up everywhere. He'd put up a sign like this: *Steal something, take your chances, but don't you dare smoke.*

He gets it. Anyway, he's only in here so that he doesn't have to sweat. He can obey.

Raccoon keeps hearing indistinct sounds coming from a room across the way, then people walk out and there's silence again. Then people go in, and the sounds start up. The room looked dark. He could shut his eyes in there, catch a few winks sitting up. He went in and the small room was empty with nothing going on. He figured the lights were dimmed on purpose. Benches. He sat down on one. He thought that he could try lying down. Other people came in and a little girl, no bigger than a hydrant, with pigtails, said, "Press the button," and this kid's dad did that and a movie started. Just like that. You could run the projector yourself in here. After he watched the movie about old geezer prospectors freezing their nuts off then panning for gold then losing all their money in the brothels and starting over again and getting their nuts frozen off again, he punched the button himself and watched the movie on his own, which was a bit of a dud really, with just one quick still of dancing girls doing the cancan, kicking up their heels, and then he goes to leave the little room the way he'd come in but stops cold. He freezes like the guys with the frozen nuts.

Why are three biker dudes loitering around the Gold Rush! section of the Canadian Museum of History? Apart from their physical and stylistic resemblance to prospectors, he can't think why they should be there.

His heart is palpitating now. He feels the sweat on his skin pop and wipes his neck dry on a sleeve. His nuts have shrivelled to the size of peas, they might as well be frozen. He stops himself from manually checking.

He risks another peek out the door.

He didn't imagine them. Bikers can mean anything. Just because they rode in on Harleys doesn't mean they're gang-connected. Far from it. Geriatric bikers outnumber the bad guys about a million to one. For all he knows these guys ride Hondas. He doesn't want to go closer to find out. They're strolling through the exhibit, and they don't look interested in the gold rush.

Another two families come into the room and just sit so he tells the dad, "You gotta push the button." The dad does that. One kid is pissed that he didn't get the chance first. The kids squirm around and complain through the whole reel. Raccoon wants to spank them. Or spank the mothers. He snorts out loud, involuntarily, when he has that thought. Then they leave, and he takes another glimpse out and can't see the bikers through the entryway. He looks for them out the opposite door, the exit to the little room, and there they are, three bikers who at that moment are leaving the Gold Rush! exhibit.

Raccoon waits alone in the dark. Stone still.

Once they're long gone, he turns back the other way. He knows he's being paranoid, but paranoia can keep a man alive.

He quick-walks back through the museum the way he came in, hurrying against the flow of human traffic, of families and upstanding fucking citizens until he reaches the entrance where the turnstiles click in one direction only. In, not out. He departs by ducking under one. He figures no one will arrest him for breaking *out* of a museum into the open air, especially when he never got his money's worth for his ticket and never stole nothing.

He comes up with a simple plan in a hurry. Those quick-thinking heels of his again. He'll grab a couple of hot dogs. Take them with him. Add a six-pack. Extra smokes. Take it back to his place. Stay in for the night. Lie low. That should do it.

He can't help himself, though. On the return walk to his new digs, he catches sight of three Harley-Davidsons stacked against the curb. He saunters by. Pretends not to look. But he looks. His blood freezes solid as if he's a Yukon prospector. A patch on a saddlebag gives it away. They're Hells. Wanderers. From Mittens' club. The goddamn Hells Angels are in the Canadian Museum of History and what other reason can they have to be there? To learn how to pan for gold?

He wishes he was panning for gold in the goddamn Yukon right now.

Someday, he'll head up there. When he gets away from here. Find his way back into time, into history. Pan for effing gold. Now that's a plan.

For now, he wants to get off the streets.

Raccoon buys his hot dogs. He'll eat them later, cold.

Heading back to his room, he feels more dead than alive.

17. Death and Life

Sandra Cinq-Mars returns to the hospital to find Montreal police officers loitering there and her husband absent from his bed. Sergeant-Detective Bill Mathers, her husband's old partner, is reading the morning paper in Émile's room.

"Bill, where is he? Why are so many cops here?"

"Not to mention me."

"Not to mention. Yes. Why are you here?"

"We brought in a suspect to talk to him."

"Excuse me? What suspect?"

"Our cop killer."

She folds her arms across her chest. A confrontational pose. "You brought a cop killer to talk to Émile. Are you mad?"

"Sandra, it's okay. He said that they're old friends. Or something."

"He said," Sandra notes. Her tone underscores that Émile should not be depended on to take his own well-being into account. "Where is he and this old pal at the moment?"

"There's a meditation room down the hall."

Sandra spins on her heels.

Despite her choler, she's intercepted by a nurse who parks her under a clock in the corridor. The nurse spritely marches off to find Émile's physician who has been waiting to have a word. Reluctantly, Sandra accepts that the opportunity to learn about her husband's progress trumps wringing his neck, for now.

The doctor had put *speak to the spouse* on a checklist. No great urgency. Yet what he enunciates alters her mood entirely.

"In layman's terms—" he starts in. Thinning white hair. Considerable girth. A warm smile. Ear tufts snag her attention. Some child's jolly uncle, she presumes.

"I raise horses, Doctor. I speak to vets every week. I don't require layman's terms."

He looks at her without comprehending. As though he considers pointing out that her husband, who might be a stallion in her mind, is no horse.

"In medical terms," she adds.

He studies her again, noting that she seems unsettled.

Then says, "Asystole ischemia."

She stares back at him.

"Mrs. Cinq-Mars?"

Her look grows sheepish.

"Run that by me again. This time in layman's terms."

They both smile. "Essentially, his body was quitting on him."

"Quitting?"

"Aggressively. His immune system chose to work against him."

"Chose."

"In a way, as if it had a mind of its own. His body said, 'Okay, enough of this,' and began to stop, as if intending that he die. His mind, and I suppose our intervention, a few shots of adrenaline, saved him. His mind fought back and kept him alive. That he's alive is a credit to his will."

"His body," Sandra interprets, "tried to kill him."

"In a sense. The shock. After all, a bullet hit next to his heart. Few survive that."

"But he recovered! He was doing fine!"

"He recovered, then suffered a delayed reaction. The blood poisoning was separate from that, most likely, but contributed. In layman's terms: Shock. Although more serious than garden-variety shock, which is serious enough."

Sandra is rattled, knowing it had been touch-and-go with Émile; what the doctor was impressing upon her was how delicate had been the touch, how feeble the go. "And now? He's fully recovered?"

"Mrs. Cinq-Mars, his mind fought back. Sheer will. Rest is required now. Rest is everything. We'll keep him another two days, then we might consider a discharge. He's doing that well."

She could kiss him. "Thank you, Doctor."

She takes a minute to quell her anxiety, then departs to go strangle her husband.

"Out of my way," she directs the officer at the door to the quiet room. The young woman is befuddled. She either forgets her own authority in this situation, or she acknowledges having none, given that she's trespassing from another province and jurisdiction. She stands down.

The door's locked. Sandra knocks. Under the circumstances, remarkably gently.

"Not to be disturbed, thank you," her husband's voice calls from inside.

"Émile," Sandra instructs – again, restrained – "open up."

He opens the door partway, takes a look at his warrior wife, and permits her entry. He locks the door behind them. In turning to face her, he anticipates her umbrage, only to find that she's directing her attention to the prisoner in the room.

"Hello," Sandra says. The man seated before her has long scraggily hair, a description that might serve for his overall frame. He's scrawny and weathered, his visage seems hollowed out, the cheeks and eye sockets sunken, the nose and chin pointy. She does not know that the reason he's so pale is due to a pair of operations after being shot in the thigh, but the news would not surprise her.

"How's it going?" the prisoner replies. He rustles up a smile. He's dressed in a baggy blue sweatshirt and jeans and wearing summer sandals. He's not cuffed, she notes. A cop killer, sitting alone with her wounded husband, has not been cuffed.

"Not too well. I just found out that my husband tried to kill himself."

"Sandra, what—?" Émile balks.

She turns to confront him. In light of the situation, his appearance strikes her as comedic. Dressed in a plaid bathrobe brought from home and worn over his hospital gown, his feet nestled in slippers lined with lamb's wool, he resembles a super-sized, ageing aristocrat, lacking only the requisite young stick of candy floss attached to a hip. He hasn't smoked in a dog's age, yet she pictures him in this get-up cradling a pipe. "Your body tried to kill you, Émile. And now, when you should be resting that body, giving yourself half a chance at survival, you're interrogating a cop killer." She turns back to Sykes. "No offence."

"None taken. But I didn't do it."

"They all say that, I hear. Émile?" She's not demanding an explanation; she wants an abrupt change to his behaviour.

"Sandra, may I introduce you? This is an old friend, Douglas Sykes. I've told you about him in the past."

The name sounds familiar. He's standing to acknowledge the woman in the room.

"Friend," she notes.

"Friend. When he was still quite young—"

"The feet," she says, putting his name to the story now.

"The feet," Émile confirms.

"Those feet," Sykes adds, and shakes his head. The sorry tale will forever be ascribed to him. He sits again, the mention of the unattached feet sapping his energy.

"What's going on?" She addresses the prisoner. "He got you off once, you expect he'll do it again?"

"Twice," Sykes says.

Émile grimaces. He'd prefer that that matter not come up.

"Right," Sandra recalls. "The worms."

"Ah. You heard that story, too." His head slumps further down. Forlorn.

"Yeah. That story. Émile—"

Unexpectedly, she stops talking. It's as if a page in her head turned and the script for her argument diverts through a surprising twist. That Émile's body plotted against him, and attempted to annihilate him, jolted her, and she's dismayed. Yet a fleeting, alternative viewpoint arises on its own wing. *His body tried to kill him, but his mind saved him.* That mind, *that mind* that spent a lifetime shaking down thieves and obstructing killers, *that mind* that in its day assailed the ramparts of criminal organizations, *that mind* then rescued him from a likely death. At it again, talking to a miscreant, a waif of an individual, who is accused of multiple murders including a police officer, Émile is conducting the *interrogation* – her word – as a quiet, intimate chat between old friends. *That mind,* then, is not his enemy, and never has been, having fought against the subversive dictates of his own body and won. The doctor recommended rest, a standard prescription. And yet, does she not possess a better understanding of her husband? For if his body is under no special duress at the moment, keeping his mind exercised and engaged is as good an anecdote to failing health, for him, as she can imagine.

In that twinkling, she changes her approach.

"Sandra?" Émile asks, concerned.

"Okay. Talk. Interrogate. Whatever. Mr. Sykes, good luck with that."

"Douglas," he says.

"Hmm," she demurs, unwilling to go that far. She opens the door, then pauses. "Don't lock yourself in," she demands of her husband. Her one compromise. "You're in here with a suspected killer. No offence, Mr. Sykes."

"None taken. But hey, if I got physical, he can take me."

"He's been shot, Mr. Sykes. He's been ill. He's weaker than normal by half. You might stand a chance. By the way, I always wanted to know this. Why were there only bare feet in that bag? What happened to the man's shoes? Did you remove them before or after he was killed? Émile, don't lock this door. Or else."

The former detective, now hospital patient, consents to her edict. He has no clue what's gotten into her. Only after she's gone does he grasp a notion that she left behind.

"Good going," Douglas Sykes says. "You did well with that one, Émile."

"What about you? Never marry?"

"I had a few loves. Nothing long-term."

Always, with him, a sadness underscores the moment. Émile wonders if he's being played.

"Douglas, Sandra inquired about the shoes. Years ago, when I told her the story, she asked the same question, and I couldn't believe that I'd neglected to ask it of you."

"Shoddy detective work, Émile. Don't sweat it. You were a beginner."

"That's true." He won't be pushed off his stump. "What about the shoes? Would it have mattered if I learned about the shoes back then? Would it affect the investigation?"

"Might've. Could've, yeah. Sorry. I'm teasing you. Doubtful."

Humbling, to have one's lapses brought to the fore. "And now, the worms, Douglas, that murder. Since Sandra brought it up. What can you tell me today that you couldn't tell me back then? Such as about the feet. Time's gone by. Surely the shoes no longer matter. Hell, the feet don't matter. Do the worms?"

His suspect seems to dwell upon the questions at a deep level. He takes his time responding. "There is a necessity, Émile."

He waits.

"A necessity prevails upon me not to reply."

He always spoke in an unusual manner. That may have suckered Émile into siding with him. They had that in common, although Sykes has kept it up and expanded upon his elocution, whereas Cinq-Mars's speech has grown more commonplace as he grew adept with English. He always resisted the vernacular, what he refers to as "cop talk," a resistance that has not been wholly successful. He must be careful to not be lulled by his appreciation for the man's diction and vocabulary, nor by his own venerable fondness for the old days, that his judgement be impaired. Back in the day, his thinking may have been compromised, when he assumed the boy's innocence from the get-go. This time around, it's possible that Douglas Sykes is guilty of heinous crimes.

Another thought – as Sykes might put it – *prevails* upon him.

"You still read?" Cinq-Mars asks. Always, keep your suspect or witness off guard.

"Yeah. You?"

"Cosmology, mostly. You?"

"History. Biography. A little philosophy. You remember our talks. True crime."

"*True* crime?"

"Honestly, I've never found it all that true."

"Here's the thing, Douglas. If you still don't want to talk about murders that occurred decades ago, even with your life on the line, that gives me a certain indication. A signal."

They stare at one another a moment. Sykes bites, "What signal?"

"I'm inclined to wonder if the past does not pertain to the present."

The man's eyes wobble in their sockets.

"Let's go through it again," Émile dictates. "I'd like to hear that tale."

"What tale? Go through what again? Which?"

"The worms," Cinq-Mars guides him. "Let's do the worms."

"Really? That again?"

"It's what cops do, Douglas. We ask people to repeat themselves, to see if they slip up."

"You can remember what I said way back then, to compare?"

Cinq-Mars issues fair warning: "I've got a mind like a steel trap. My best advice? Be truthful. You can't go wrong. Whereas a lie, today, with a police officer dead, not to mention a trio of hooligans coming to a bad end, a lie today can sink you for yesterday, and for 40 years ago, too."

"It wasn't that long ago. Was it?"

"Seems like last week. Douglas, tell me about the worms."

Cinq-Mars resumes his seat for their talk about old times.

18. Girls and Boys

He'd travelled across a wide country.

Learned a few lessons. Saw stuff. "Made my mistakes," he'd say.

His early childhood had been harsh but not unsatisfactory.

Adolescence took a detour and left him mangled.

Adulthood found him lost, wary. He trusted no one.

His hometown presented itself as different when he returned from a prolonged absence. New buildings and altered streets. A spirit of activity snagged him by surprise. He considered that, as an adult now, he was viewing his former haunts with an altered perspective. Favourite playgrounds from the old days appeared shrunken. He'd swear the trees were shorter, buildings half their former size.

In his old neighbourhood, he found strangers in places his pals used to inhabit. Park Extension, long a drop-off point for immigrants, had been welcoming different nationalities than the ones he'd known. He was the foreigner now. He'd been away, had endured troubles and done a little time. At intervals, he had also worked hard and made a few honest bucks. He travelled on the extra cash and now, home again, broke again, he was rooting about, bewildered.

His mom had died young.

In prison, he had missed her funeral. He wanted to put flowers on her grave, at least do that, and so had returned.

Douglas wasted no time chasing down a couple of jobs and was deflated to be bypassed. He did not speak French; during his absence that had become a requirement for low-level employment. A dishwasher, a car washer, a window washer or a parking attendant had to speak the language of the majority to work, and he could not do so. He understood why, he cosseted no grievance. He had simply returned to the wrong city. Or the right city was now the wrong time for him.

The absence of any form of welcome felt palatable.

He was sitting on a park bench one afternoon feeling blue when an old connection popped up. The former acquaintance bought him a draught beer, then offered a sofa to sleep on. He moved a newspaper off the sofa, but first he read through the classifieds. He spotted a request for worm pickers.

Hey! Can I do that?

Worms spoke neither English nor French. Everyone who showed up was hired, the ad claimed, and it was written in English. All he had to do was arrive on time in the evening, work all night, get paid in cash the next morning. A penny per worm picked. By the time the sun came up above the rooftops he could be eating properly.

Douglas Sykes walked miles on an empty stomach to go pick worms.

Prospective worm pickers, waiting for the boss, hung together in the underclass district of St Henri, a little southwest from Montreal's downtown. Sykes felt leery, being cautious in neighbourhoods that had reputations for being as tough as his, especially as he was arriving on his own. He was hoping his trepidation didn't show.

The workers were divided between those who had done the job previously, and first-timers. The experienced crew gathered up equipment; new arrivals received a lesson. Each person strapped on a headlamp provided by their instructor and were offered a singular tip. "Shine your fuckin' light right on a worm. It'll vanish before you can touch it, even if you're on your belly in the grass." Instead, they were to search for worms along the outer rim of the lamp's beam, keeping their heads turned to never worry the worm with bright light. "Graze the grass with your fingers. Worms are slippery devils and super smart."

He was sceptical about the aptitude of worms.

Forewarned, he stayed away from areas where sprinklers were in service. Such territories were reserved for regulars who had seniority.

Each worm picker was supplied with a can of sawdust, strapped to his or her left shin, in which to dip their fingers, and an empty can strapped to the right shin to collect the worms they caught. Sawdust on their fingertips gave them a fighting chance against slippery, slimy, super-intelligent worms. They were also issued shallow, wooden boxes in which to deposit their bounty once their leg-cans filled up.

A full box equalled a hundred worms. A buck's worth.

Fill five boxes, then get more from the field truck.

Sounds easy enough.

Suited up and, with his headlamp on, Douglas Sykes felt somewhat like a miner. No descent into a coal mine, although the pending black night might feel akin to that experience.

Ready, the newbies proceeded onto a school bus and joined the regulars. They were driven to a golf course on the edge of town. A different location every night, a veteran mentioned. He was thinking that he'd take note of the traffic signs to judge his destination, merely out of curiosity, a plan that was dashed once they were underway. Jostling along in Uncle Harry's yellow school bus, his concentration went out the window because Douglas Sykes discovered that he had fallen in love.

The young woman, under 20, had such pale skin that he wondered if she ever saw the light of day, picking worms by night then sleeping while the sun shone. She looked shockingly fragile; her poverty imprinted on her skin. Sickly, as if a critical illness lurked.

Sykes was borne into a cloud of empathy, wanting to help her, protect her, nurture her back to good health and, of course, offer her a life of happiness and love. She seemed emblematic of tragedy, an aspect that attracted him. Rather than being especially pretty, she possessed an allure that, he guessed, others might miss. Through furtive glances and by sneaking in the occasional long gaze while her own was focused outside the window, the delicacy of her features and a plaintiveness to her disposition arrested his sensibilities. In love at first whimsy.

An exchange she had with another young woman informed him that she was French, a knowledge that handcuffed his courage. To approach her in his halting French, or in English which she might find incomprehensible, thwarted his initiative. He resorted to silence instead, which did no good. The pair disembarked, and as worm pickers spread out across the golf course, he followed her at a distance into the deepening dusk.

Night fell, and Douglas struggled to pick worms. He also struggled to keep an eye on the woman he desired to know. She was little more than a headlamp to him most of the time and could easily be mistaken for any number of headlamps. He did just that. Screwing up his courage, he approached, only to find that she had morphed into a 50-year-old man down on his knees whispering a hymn as he wrestled worms from the ground and, when he was victorious, naming his captive after a movie star.

"Marilyn Monroe."

"Clark Gable."

"Jayne Mansfield," he'd say, then get back to murmuring *Rock of Ages*.

Sykes stayed on a minute to observe the fellow's technique. In 10 minutes of observation the old guy plucked five or six worms, much better than the two he extracted in well over an hour.

He had lost sight of his soulmate.

Then found her again.

She was infinitely more adept than the hymn singer.

He couldn't believe her success in picking worms. As far as he could tell, they leapt unbidden onto her saw-dusted fingertips.

The night went poorly. He slept in the woods for a half-hour at a time, here and there. His bones ached from the chill of the damp earth. Weariness took a toll and while he didn't hallucinate, he did engage in a conversation where he was not only speaking aloud but speaking for someone other than himself. Two-way banter became three-way, and he was the only one around. He dropped his can of worms into his shallow box and counted them out. Eleven worms. Eleven cents. Not a lucrative night. He would not be buying breakfast or a morning coffee. If he knuckled down, he might manage bus fare back to his old neighbourhood and an awaiting sofa.

Otherwise, he'd have to stagger home on foot, miles without sleep or nourishment.

Eleven worms. Eleven cents. By the time he was done, with travel, he'd have logged 12 hours. This gave starvation wages a whole new threshold.

The night temperature grew chillier. He was wearing light summer clothes. He tried to stay warm by moving and wandered around aimlessly. Sometimes he hunted for worms but what was the point when he might miss three and then grab one only to have it wiggle free into the grass.

Smart-assed worms. Sometimes he talked to them, plaintively pleading.

He felt rain. Oh, great. In checking the sky, he saw stars. The rain vanished, then returned. He was being hit by a sprinkler. No one was around. He had a sprinkler all to himself! He searched for worms. And worms were there! Everywhere! Worms! And more worms! He got down on his knees. He lost a few, he plucked a few. He accidentally ripped a few in half and tossed away the pathetic portion left in his hand. Yet, suddenly he was making money! Suddenly he could imagine breakfast. Then the light from his headlamp seemed too bright and too broad. He turned around. More lights. Hands were on him. He was knocked down. Hauled up. Pummelled by fists. His attackers, invisible in the dark save for their headlamps, were remarkably silent as they went about the task. They hit his face, aiming just below his forehead lamp. His nose, his eyes, his teeth smashed, and when he fell his body was kicked indiscriminately. Blows to the belly, face, thighs, and back.

Boot kicks. Then, finally, at last, his attackers spoke.

He didn't wholly understand the language, it being French. He grasped that he had trespassed. They were saying something to that effect. He was being advised to avoid sprinklers. Then they dragged him beyond the range of their turf and rolled him into a sand trap.

Their final parting gesture was to expel his own worms over his head, then throw down his empty box. At least, they didn't steal them. Douglas Sykes scrambled quickly to retrieve as many as he could before the buggers escaped underground.

In the grey light of dawn, he saw his one true love again, and she him. She noticed, he could tell, the damage done to him. Welts were still forming. She gazed at him, then moved along to have her worms counted. She cashed in 18 boxes. Eighteen hundred worms.

Eighteen hundred!

Eighteen bucks.

By comparison, he was left with 19 cents earned.

The tallyman gave him a full dollar.

A charity he accepted.

Grateful. In those days: bus fare and a cup of coffee.

Douglas Sykes stayed resolute. He'd been pummelled. Yet his life was not over. Due to his humiliation, the girl had noticed him!

He still did not know her name, or if she spoke English, but Douglas Sykes experienced a wellspring of hope, unexpected and keen, that was rare in his life.

He'd be back.

19. Glitter and Glitz

Facing the murky bathroom mirror in his squalid room, Raccoon studies the infinity tattoo above his left eye as though gazing into an abyss. What comes to him as a revelation is something he's known all along. This is why he fled to Ottawa, the real reason, and had crossed the bridge into Gatineau. Stuffed to the gills with routine lies, sorting through those, as he's told himself, takes time.

He quaffs a beer and heads out into the night.

Whenever he's stressed, there's only one place to go.

He hails a cab on *rue Principale*.

The driver pokes out into light traffic, waiting to be advised on a destination.

Finally, he asks, "*Où t'va?*"

"*Le Casino*," Raccoon tells him, as though that should be obvious to anyone.

It's obvious to him now. He was always headed there.

The big one on the edge of town is as bright as an intergalactic hotspot. Cars pour in. He won't feel so lonesome now. He has enough cash on hand to pay the fare and heads inside to an ATM. Extracts his maximum allowable. Six hundred bucks. Raccoon heads into the cacophonous buzz of honking, ringing, blaring machines, a bedlam that is a comfort to him, a peace. He needs to settle in, relax his nerves, take a deep breath, and exhale slowly. He seats himself before the wild wolves on a dollar slot machine. Over the years, the wolves have been kind.

On his fourth spin, they pay out 20 bucks. He's home free.

After that they horde his money for themselves.

Howling bastards should be shot for their pelts.

He prefers playing the slots down in the United States where they let you drink hard liquor while you bet. In Canada, the thinking is, you might run somebody over if you press a button while under the influence. Crazy country. He accepts a couple of free Cokes, then raises his glass for more. Anytime you're offered a freebie, take it, then take another until the well runs dry.

A three-buck payout costs him 17.

Damn wolves. They should be extinct by now.

Raccoon stays put. Doesn't want anyone to score big off his contribution.

Then he gets nervous.

A big-bellied dude on the periphery of his vision steps away from his line of sight into the next row over. Could be nothing. Could be something. He plays on, tense now. Peering between machines, he fails to pick anyone out. He fakes a stretch, stands tall, gazes over machines to the next row. No one's there except old folks hooked into their units with their telescopic counters, umbilical cords to Mother Lode. Two young Asians, also. But no bikers.

Then two appear, one at each end of his row, and he has no fucking chance of escape.

They close in on him. A studied casualness to their attitude.

He cashes out. Extracts the printout.

They're on either side of him 10 yards away. The one on his left seems in charge. A sports jacket might well conceal a hip holster. Khaki chinos. A blue shirt with an embroidered cowboy motif. No tip-off that he's a biker thug, yet anyone who knows, knows. When Raccoon hazards a glance up, he recognizes him. The bulge of bone at the crest of his forehead. One battered ear. Pudgy. He can outrun him. Never out-brawl him. He's a full-patch and he's seen him in his gang colours with his bicep tattoo: *Filthy Few*. Meaning, he's killed on gang business.

His helper is tall and thin. He's cognisant that this is a public venue, as though he's sizing up the opposition should things get nasty. Cameras everywhere and security guards abound. This is not the most straightforward extraction. It's both public and secure, and they all know Raccoon will try to work with that.

"What's the story?" he asks the guy who's a *Filthy Few*. He looks past him where the big-bellied biker he first noticed is lounging at the end of the bank of slots, close to the nearest guard. If the situation goes south, that guy will neutralize the guard.

Rather than answer, the man has a question of his own. "How's it hanging, Rac?"

"No complaints. You? How'd you find me anyhow?"

"Who says we're looking? Dropped by to say hello, maybe."

"Okay. Why not? Hello and goodbye. I appreciate the visit."

"You really want to know how?"

"I'm interested, yeah."

"It's in your file, Rac."

At first, he's about to ask, "What file?" This is no time for stupid questions, so he inquires instead, "What is?"

"When you take off, it's never far from a casino. You didn't know that? You didn't know you were that dumb a shit or is this like a front-page headline to you?"

He looks away to think about it, feeling a nudge of regret.

Raccoon pulls himself together. He's in a public space. "What's the outcome of this supposed to be in the long run? Nothing too shabby, I hope."

"You're not under house arrest."

Raccoon knows the parlance. The man is advising him that he has no instruction to kill him. That makes sense, given that he's been contacted in public like this.

"Good to hear. Then what?"

"I don't know if you're in for a drink or a talk," the man explains. A drink means conversation, where he will be obliged to explain himself. A talk means torture, where it won't matter what he says. "Won't be with me. I only provide the limo."

"I appreciate that. Do we have time? Can I play a little blackjack first?" He knows what the answer will be. The answer is so obvious that the man accosting him does not bother to reply.

"How about I cash my earnings?" Rac holds up his tally chit.

The tall man steps up, reaches from behind and takes it from him. "I'll keep that," he says. His deep voice sounds incongruous for a man so thin. "For expenses."

Rac knows not to argue.

The man who has come for him says, "Don't make trouble, Rac. I have permission."

The code means that he's to be taken alive, that's preferred, but if there's a snag, then the man is permitted to execute him on the spot. More likely, he'd wait for him to leave the building, travel a respectable distance away from the general public, then waste him.

"In plain sight?" Rac comments, "I never done one of those for you guys."

"Don't let it go that far." The man nods. "Couple of guys coming down from Montreal. Like I said, a drink or a talk, I don't know. One out of two, better than blackjack, the odds. How about it? Nice and easy or are ya going to be a pussy about it?"

Raccoon faces the wolves again and presses a few buttons as though he has money in the machine, which he does not. Both men follow his eyes to the machine, which gives Rac a millisecond to stage his revolt. The man at the end of the row has his attention on a security guard. The other way he doesn't know for sure, it could be clear, but in that direction he'll need to get past the tall man, who looks limber and capable of a winning stride. He sees only the one option and launches himself back across the aisle. He leaps up on a stool with one foot, the other is already ascending to the top of the slot machine, and he goes over its roof. He loses his balance and tumbles into the next aisle. Then he's on his feet again and leaps to another stool. Up and over a second line of machines. This time he lands well, and runs to his right, which means he might encounter the big-bellied guy who'd been at the end of his row. That one might have had a slow start due to the guard in his vicinity, and anyway, he can outrun that guy. He's off. Through a row at full speed, he dodges and turns and tries to create a trail that's a maze, then frees himself from the slots and races through a plateau of roulette tables, then upstairs, more slots, with automobiles parked above the rows of machines offered as ultimate prizes, all glitz and glitter, great wax jobs, and he's heading for the doorway. Casino guards, a pair, look to stall his progress. They know nothing of the situation except that a man is running at breakneck speed, and he pulls a neat feint to the left and is by them. Raccoon is suddenly, wildly, out the door. A quick stop to gain a breath, then he dashes to the parking lot to lose himself amid the cars and hide like a slug on a leaf.

He crouches down when his adrenaline and oxygen intake can't keep up. Breathes heavily. He waits. If anyone approaches, he'll slide under the van that's next to him, then do what others do in church. And yet, when he hears footsteps, they are not approaching from any logical direction. They are coming from the far end of the lot and heading toward the casino. Just a new player. As the steps come closer, he can picture the sound: a woman in high heels. He waits to see what she looks like. Rather than walk right by him, she stops, and rather than ignore this man sitting on the pavement jammed up against a van's front tire, she turns to face him, and steps his way. He's too startled to budge. "Lady," he intends to say, "Beat it." She's opening her purse, and he's going to tell her that he doesn't want her charity unless she plans to give him her car keys. He's shocked, then, when she pulls out a pistol and aims it at his face.

"Bitch," she says. "Stay down. Stay put."

He hates it when a woman calls him that.

She frees a hand, gives a quick wave over her head.

He knows he's doomed now.

The bikers soon are on him.

He's hoping for a limo – a guy needs hope – or, second choice, a van, but gets to ride in a nondescript Camry, down in the dark of the trunk, knotted and gagged.

He can tell when he's left casino property. The road runs bumpy. A construction zone. Then the speed picks up and other cars surge past him. Regular people in their decent lives, free to come and go. But not him. Maybe never again.

20. Taradiddle, Then and Now

Cinq-Mars seeks to drill deeper into the yarn that Douglas Sykes has spun. The details line up precisely as they did years ago, a level of accuracy he finds disconcerting. Surely, after a prolonged passage of time, an occasional discrepancy might emerge. Elaboration and forgetfulness being human tics.

"That second night, did you go out to seek revenge?"

"I did not."

"You got beat up," Cinq-Mars points out. "You're a young stud. Hormones are popping; adrenaline is snapping through your veins. What's a poor boy to do if not fight back?"

"I went back there to pick worms, Émile."

"Oh, for the money? Come on. I wasn't born on another planet yesterday."

"Fine. I'm kidding. I went back to see the girl."

"That I can believe. To impress her, you brought along a gang?"

"What gang? No."

"You weren't alone on the battlefield. If you were, you're the killer."

"Stop trying to mess with me, Émile."

"Stop trying to string me along, Douglas."

"What's with the attitude?"

"*I* have the attitude? *Me*? Three dead in a biker's bank where you were hanging out, where you took a bullet, and now, as of yesterday, a cop is dead in a hospital room. Oh, wait. It was your room. Coincidence?"

"I thought we were talking about yester*year.*"

"That's right. The good old days. Note the similarity."

Sykes doesn't catch the reference. He's losing his footing, his confidence. "What similarity?"

"A man had his head and extremities sliced off by a freight train. You were there. You absconded with his feet. Another man had a knife plunged into his heart on a golf course where he's picking worms. On the 14th green, as I recall. Oh, look, you were there again. You're always in the vicinity when people are murdered, Douglas. If you were me – hell, if you were anybody else for a hundred miles around – wouldn't you find that a tad suspicious? A tad incriminating? Guess what. The police, the ones who aren't retired yet, they sure do."

Cinq-Mars and Sykes had returned to the small antechamber in the hospital after a chaplain had displaced them. Douglas Sykes revisited the story of the worms while wheeling Cinq-Mars around the corridors in a wheelchair as he hobbled along behind. They found an alcove by a window to talk in private, with plenty of potted plants at hand, then did another tour of the ward. Noticing the chaplain depart with a grieving family, they reclaimed the small room to continue their talk, and this time Cinq-Mars alters his tone, becoming confrontational.

"All I can do is tell you what happened," Sykes complains. "Proving my innocence is up to you."

"Your guilt, as I see it."

"Whatever."

"You don't care which?"

"Come on, Émile. I care. My life is on the line here."

"As it should be. That's one helluva body count piling up around you."

Sykes is discombobulated by this shift in the conversation. Being in the company of the man who rescued him in the past has been a salve on his anxiety. To have him suddenly adversarial creates distress that's difficult to manage. For his part, Émile sees that the long-time, small-time hood is agitated. Typically, suspects who are mentally upended seek stable ground, which can take the form of the truth, whatever that might reveal, or the form of a deeply ensconced lie, an embattlement that can then be assailed. Either way, he needs Douglas Sykes to retreat from what comes easily to him – his security in old tales – and force him to defend what's difficult.

The man is mentally agile. His vocabulary, a sly mix of the vernacular and the sophisticated, is limber. He knows how to parry in a joust. He's a challenge.

"This is what you want me to believe: You returned to pick worms a second night because the love of your life, your soulmate, would be there."

"Soulmate. Don't make fun. I never found out her name, even."

"You've never stopped thinking about her, is that the gist of what I'm hearing?"

"She's never left my mind. Hasn't that happened to you? If not, I feel sorry for you. If it did, I feel even sorrier."

"Did you talk to her that second night?"

"She was French. I was English. Hard to communicate."

"You must've had some French in you."

"A little. Hadn't used it for a while. Never with romance in the air."

"You had to know some French to get involved in a brawl."

"My lack of French helped generate a misunderstanding that led up to it."

Cinq-Mars lets that stand a moment, staring down his imperious nose at him.

"What?" Sykes demands back, unhappy with the interrogation.

"Do you still like guns?" Cinq-Mars asks quietly.

"Since when do I like guns? Is that some kind of trick question because you think I shot people the other day?"

"And the cop."

"I didn't shoot nobody. Why ask me that, about guns?"

He won't reveal the finer details of his strategy. "Never mind why. So, the brawl."

"On the 14th green. Good memory," Sykes states.

"You remember that, too."

"I read it in the papers the next day. I remember they wrote it was the 14th."

"That's not true."

"What's not true? I read it in the papers. The 14th green."

"You knew it was the 14th. You didn't have to read it in the papers."

"How the hell do you know that?"

"You called me out there, remember?"

Sykes takes a breath, sits back in his chair, and reflects on the time. "Something I ate. Bad stomach. Comes from being punched in the gut over two nights, multiple times. Could be I had internal bleeding. I had to shit. I was willing to go squat in the woods, except they took me to the clubhouse. A cop ordered the night guard to open up for me. Whoa, lordy, the best place I ever took a crap in. Beautiful floors. Coming out, down this curved, corridor-type ramp, I spotted a row of payphones. I gave you a jingle, for old times' sake."

"You carried my card across the country and back?" He had said so at the time.

"Getting out of jail, they handed me my wallet. Your card stayed stuck in there through the years."

"You called. You directed me to the 14th green. Long before it made the papers."

Sykes nods. He's impressed. "Right you are. You got me on that one. I forgot. I must have known it was the 14th. Seen a sign, something like that."

"I didn't do homicide normally."

"I didn't consider it a homicide. More like an accident."

"Knives don't land in a man's chest by accident. You say it wasn't your knife?"

"Not mine and my fingerprints weren't on it."

"Nobody's were. Wiped clean. Let's say the killer wore gloves."

"I didn't own a pair. Or a knife. I didn't slay the man, Émile."

"You know what I don't like here the most?"

"What?"

Cinq-Mars doesn't let him in on that just yet. Instead, he asks, "First, tell me, are you still into hot rods?"

Douglas squints, not knowing where the question is coming from.

"I don't give a shit about hot rods. Why?"

"Really? Honestly?"

"Yeah." Sykes shrugs, befuddled. "Honestly."

"And trains. You loved trains."

"I never did. Especially not after the feet. Your memory's slipping away there, Émile. I've seriously worried about you."

Douglas Sykes ducks his head just then as if a corollary thought suddenly occurs.

Cinq-Mars doesn't let on that he detected the other man's brainwave, although he has no handle on what it portends. "I got shot recently," he remarks, as though to concede that he might be off his game. He's willing to let Sykes think so.

"Yeah. Sorry about that. It sucks to get shot."

"The drugs lay me low." He returns to his previous question. "Anyway, what do you think I don't like here the most?"

"No idea, Émile. The food, I guess."

"I can digest the food." He takes a moment to run his right hand through his hair, first on one side, then the other, and offers the back of his scalp a scratch. Ever since he's been in the hospital, he feels his skin crawling as though infested.

"Douglas, years ago, you were caught with body parts. We never got to the bottom of that, only that a man was dead, and you swiped his feet. Back then you admitted to seeing him die. Awfully gruesome. Hard on you, especially being a kid. A few years later, you pop up again. Lo and behold, a young man lies dead on a golf course with a knife in his chest and who, pray tell, is held for questioning? None other than Douglas Sykes. Fancy that."

"I called you out to the 14th green because I was innocent."

"I went out there because I was curious. What don't I like about it now?"

"*That* I don't know, Émile. Waiting on your reply."

The former cop doesn't mind that the prisoner's patience is draining.

"Douglas, I won't dredge it all up. But here's a question that intrigues me: what happened back then that was so off-kilter that you don't want to talk about it now? What happened a billion years ago that we cannot revisit? If you're embarrassed, or implicated, it doesn't matter a whole hill of beans because you're in the clear by now. It's ancient history." Cinq-Mars wags an emphatic finger in the air. "Yet you still don't want to tell the whole truth about way back then. Not even to the man who helped you escape the muck. I'm sitting here thinking there can only be one reason why."

"What's that?"

"Back then has something to do with right now."

Rather too quickly, Sykes contends, "I don't think so. They're not connected."

He lacks conviction to Émile's mind.

"It's unravelling, isn't it?" he asks him, somewhat kindly.

"What is?"

"Whatever shit you're in."

"Émile," Sykes says, then he's stymied.

The retired cop presses his advantage. "What did I miss back then that I better not miss now?"

Sykes shrugs, an indication that nothing will come easily, that Émile will have to work for anything he gets. Even then, he'll fall short.

"Did you go back to the worm picking job—"

"To see the girl again, like I said."

"Did you go back with a gang?" Cinq-Mars asks. "If I'm overstating it, did you go back with a pal or two, intent on revenge? Did you exact your revenge? Before you answer, allow me to remind you of your own words. Your life is on the line here."

Inclined to blurt out a reply, the reminder turns Sykes mute. It's not that he doesn't know how or what to say, in Émile's assessment, he doesn't know *if* he should say it. Will it be to his advantage? Life gets complicated when people die around you, and you're the one bearing the brunt of the blame.

"Cat got your tongue? You? Of all people."

He shakes his head, distressed, and tries to alter the current coursing through him by shaking his shoulders and clenching and unclenching his fists.

Finally, he imparts, "No gang, Émile. Okay? No gang. People asked me, other worm pickers, what happened to me, how I got banged up the night before. I told them. Some guys got mad about that. Some guys – the women, too – were pissed off that we can't pick worms around the sprinklers. That never seemed fair. Bad blood was building before I ever showed up. A union type thing. Some said they weren't taking this shit no more."

"And you were the boss. The union agitator."

"Don't make fun. I was just sitting there with my bruises, wishing everybody would go away so I could chat up my girl. Who cares in what language."

Cinq-Mars mulls it over. Then says, "The cops talked to everybody left behind on the 14th green. To every person involved in the melee who stayed on. In our considered opinion, the people proved to be honest with us. You, less so. None of us felt that the man, or woman, who killed the boy on the 14th green was among those who were brought in, unless it was you. Because it happened in the dark, nobody knew who did it. If it wasn't you, then he or she got away. Whoever did the killing, if it wasn't you, was smart enough to run. That's the main reason I could get you off – you didn't run – because you must admit, circumstantial evidence was butting up against your hide. Motive, too, given what transpired the night before, you getting your ass kicked."

Sykes shakes his head, as though to express an honest lament. "Dark out, Émile. We had a tussle. You call it a battle; I call it a minor scuffle. You never knew who you were hitting or who was grabbing hold of you. Scary that way. Then in a few beams of light – you know, from our foreheads – we see this guy on the ground, a knife in his chest. I don't think I was the first to shine my light on him. When I did, Émile, the fight went out of me. True for everyone else, too. We sent a girl away – yeah, my mystery girl, as it turned out – to make the phone call. To tell our worms' boss to call the cops. When they showed up, I don't know why, I happened to get sick. Needed to take a crap in the worst way. Like I said, I'd been punched in the gut a few times. I ended up calling you. Seemed like the right move."

"You knew you'd be a suspect."

"Been down that road before, that's true. Some people, no pun intended, shone a light on me, because I'd been whipped the previous night. The cops seemed more interested in me than anyone else. I looked the part; all beat up from the previous fight. Soon as they found out I had a record, I needed help in my corner. Gave you a jingle."

"Figured you'd suckered me one time, you'd try it again."

"Come on, Émile. I never suckered you. Not ever."

"This'll be the first time then?"

"Don't be that way."

"Then tell me about your love of cars, trains, pistols."

"Émile." Exasperation now. "What the fuck are you talking about?" He turns to confront his former helper, only to be struck by the look that has dawned across the patient's face. Émile's mouth is open, his jaw gone slack. Sykes might think that the man is having a stroke if not for the glint in his eyes. Cinq-Mars is onto something, and the derelict-looking vagabond can tell that's true. "What?"

"I made mistakes back then, didn't I? Don't lie to me now! I screwed up royally."

Sykes protests, "I don't know what—"

"Yes you do! You were covering it up. Not once. But twice. Twice! Is that what you're concealing today? Oh my God! I'm a religious man, Douglas, I don't invoke His name in vain. Oh my *God*. What kids today write in their text messages: OMG."

"I don't get you," Sykes says.

"OMG, I screwed up." Cinq-Mars clamours out of his chair, then discovers that the effort isn't worth the trouble. He sits back again as awe swipes through him. "I was a young cop. I was prone to screwing up. How else does anybody learn? Except, Douglas, we learn from our mistakes when we recognize them as being mistakes. Is this what's happened here, Douglas? Has history repeated itself? OMG."

"Will you fuck off with the OMG?"

Cinq-Mars may be flabbergasted, although he's playing it up beyond his actual reaction. Pieces are falling into place, and that process fascinates him even as he's in the middle of the experience. Arms folded across his chest, slumped back into his wheelchair, he's no longer glaring at Sykes. Instead, he's virtually beaming.

"You're right," he agrees. "It's no better than taking His name in vain. I'll let it go. How stupid could I have been, Douglas?"

"What are you going on about, Émile?"

"You know what. I spoke with your mother several times. You have no siblings. Someone in your household had a thing for trains and hot-rods and, yes, guns. If it wasn't you, or your mother, who was it, Douglas?"

"I don't know what you're talking about." He can't say that without staring the ex-cop down, as though trying to embed his lie as being true.

"If you don't want to say, is it because it connects to current events? Douglas, I was in your house back then. I met your mom, *and* I met your rather strange boarder." The man's head goes right, then up, then back down again. "I'm pretty sure she wasn't responsible for the magazines on cars and trains and guns. She was not the only tenant in the house, was she? She had a son of her own! I was not told of his identity for one specific reason. Neither by you nor by your mother. If you were not alone on the railway tracks that dreadful day, the other boy who lived in your house was with you. Was he the one who took away the head and hands?"

Despite his evident excitement, Émile is monitoring the other man's reactions to his line of inquiry. Sykes is not being defensive. Rather, he appears to have gone sad, as though the revelation depresses him, or takes away his hope. When he tries to speak, it's almost as though Sykes no longer can.

"People do this sort of thing," Cinq-Mars goes on. "I can understand why you might want to protect a friend back then, but now? Today? That makes no sense."

In the gloom of the room, Sykes still does not want to say. He's struggling to respond.

"What's his name?" Cinq-Mars asks him.

He offers back a quick shake of his head.

"I have ways of finding out."

The man still does not respond.

"Open the door," Cinq-Mars commands.

"What?"

"You heard me."

Sykes opens the door and Cinq-Mars yells to the cop outside. "Get Mathers in here! On the double!" The policewoman tears off down the corridor as though Cinq-Mars holds rank over her. He won't remind her that he's a civilian.

Sykes dolefully hangs his head while they wait.

"What's up?" Mathers asks from the doorway. Cinq-Mars waves him in. The detective closes the door behind himself, to stand with his hands on his hips.

"When this man was 15 years old he lived in Park Extension with his mom. Back then, I brought him in for questioning. You can get the exact dates from the records into the murder of a man—. What was his name, Douglas? The victim?"

"Who? The dead guy?"

"Yes, the dead guy!"

"I forget. Did I ever know it? I can't recall."

"You can't recall. Something *chuck*. Starts with an R, I think. Rubba? Rubbachuck? English names. They never stick with me."

"Sounds Ukrainian. Not English."

"Same difference."

"Hardly."

"Rybachuk," Sykes says, as if he can't stand the error. "Don't ask me to spell it."

"So, you do know the name," Cinq-Mars notes.

"Now that you reminded me, yeah. Only it's *Ryba*, like rye bread, not *Rubba*."

"Rybachuk?" Mathers asks. "That's what you said?"

"If that's what you heard."

"At that time," Cinq-Mars points out to his former partner, "Douglas's mom had a deal with Social Services where she took indigent women into her house – and their offspring, I bet. I need to know the name of the woman who was living with her back then and the name of that woman's son. Social Services can find it."

Mathers doesn't respond, his gaze fixed on Sykes. "Rybachuk," he says once more.

"Come on, Bill, you're supposed to be the one who's good with names," Cinq-Mars admonishes him. "It's Rybachuk, yes."

"That's why I'm repeating it. Look at him, Émile, he's squirming."

Cinq-Mars does look. Not a sight to which he's been privy previously. Douglas Sykes is clearly agitated and unnerved.

"What's going on?"

"I know a Rybachuk," Mather states. "Could be all the same."

Cinq-Mars looks back and forth between the two men, who are now riveted on each other. He asks, "Okay, Bill, what does 'all the same' mean?"

"The mother, the son, the dead guy. Could be they were all Rybachuks."

Sykes barely protests the theory. He says, "Quit clowning around." He looks steamed.

Mathers moves a few steps closer to him. He repeats, "Rybachuk." He pronounces the last syllable as *chook*. The name appears to cause the other man a degree of unease.

Sykes looks as though he's recovering from being shot in both legs, not just one.

"Stop that," he says.

"Stop what?" Cinq-Mars asks him.

"Stop clowning around!"

"You think I'm wearing a costume?" Then he glances down at himself, in a plaid bathrobe and slippers, and smiles at the contradiction. "Okay. Don't answer that part."

"You're pissing me off."

"I can see that. Why? And how? Bill? Can you answer?"

"I know of a Fedir Rybachuk. That's not the name he usually goes by."

"What's the name he goes by?" Cinq-Mars inquires, his eyes on Sykes.

"Raccoon," Mathers says.

Sykes flinches as though stung by a whip. Cinq-Mars takes note of that, then looks back at Mathers for further explanation.

"He's a killer. A Hells hire."

"Full patch?" Cinq-Mars asks. "Filthy Few?"

"No chance. He's not *bona fide*. Too many issues for the gang. He's messed up but the Hells like him as a hire. Special details. You can imagine what."

"What kind of issues?"

"He's not French. That's one strike against him. He uses. That's two. Addicted to gambling. That's three strikes. You know how it goes. They prefer their bad guys to be choir boys even when they look like sin's shit."

"They have standards." Cinq-Mars crosses his arms and confronts Sykes. "Who's he to you, this Raccoon?"

"Nobody I know," Sykes maintains.

The former cop, sitting in his wheelchair, and the current cop, let him stew in silence. They know he's lying, and Sykes knows they do. They won't give him the satisfaction of challenging him. His fabrication won't hold, they're saying, without speaking a word. Finally, Cinq-Mars asks, "Why is he called Raccoon?"

Cinq-Mars has asked the question of Mathers and expects him to answer, yet they both notice that Sykes is considering the question on his own. Mathers remarks, "I'll find out the name of the tenant, the boarder, when he was a kid to confirm. That can be done."

That can't be done, the lie a mild one. Failing, as usual, at a crossword one time, Émile received instruction from his wife and added a new word to his English vocabulary. Taradiddle. Defined as a petty lie or pretentious nonsense. Finding the word comical he taught it to Mathers. Nearing the end of their time together, they used it on occasion while interrogating a witness or a suspect for the sake of expediency. Sometimes they needed to communicate that they were fibbing, whereas on other occasions one or the other grasped the assumption on his own. Cinq-Mars is aware that on this occasion Mathers has brokered a *taradiddle* to provoke the truth, an understanding that passes naturally between them. The moment is welcome, a throwback to the good old days.

Sykes draws out a long sigh. In computing his choices, he replies to the original question. "Dark circles around his eyes. Even when he was little he had them."

"Last name?" Cinq-Mars asks. "For the record. Confirm it."

Reluctantly, Sykes tells him, "Rybachuk."

Cinq-Mars and Sykes stare at one another until the prisoner breaks the contact off.

"Your friend killed his own father, then took his head away?"

Tears well up. Under his breath, Sykes maintains, "He didn't have much choice."

With a nod, Cinq-Mars directs Mathers to depart to let them talk in private again. Mathers acquiesces, somewhat unhappily. The two left behind are seated and silent. The retired cop gives his chin a scratch. The prisoner knots and unwinds his fingers.

"Why?" Cinq-Mars asks.

"You don't understand," the man whispers.

"That's why I'm asking. Explain it to me."

“We’re all we have.” His voice sounds broken, emotional.

Another deepening silence.

“Elaborate, please.” He can use a word such as *elaborate* with Douglas Sykes, guessing that it might be an effective choice in terms of evoking his cooperation. He knows that this talk will go deep or go nowhere. If they are to find light, they cannot avoid entering the dark.

21. Release and Catch

Rac lined up the ball of his life with a stick, then fate stuffed a fist in the corner pocket.

Now this. Life behind the eight ball.

He's stuck in a skylight shaft. Any quick slip, he breaks his neck.

The Hells pulled him out of the trunk. Bound. Gagged. Blindfolded. With the car motor off, he heard a gate squeak shut. They packed him between two big guys, which meant they did not desire attention. They weren't on a street. Gravel underfoot then grass, probably a backyard parking spot. If anyone on the lane glanced out a window, he might be seen. Less likely if he was under shade trees; he heard leaves rustle overhead. If people knew the sort of people who sheltered here, what neighbour would dare raise an alarm?

A handler to each side of him, he was guided up steps. Steeper than the norm. A back porch? They shuffled him through a door where they got rougher.

He quelled a fart. A choice that struck him as relevant.

As though he'd be okay if only he squeezed extra hard and kept his dignity.

Stairs to climb again. Two flights. He was on a third floor. Any breakout through a window, if a window existed, was not on. They strapped him to a chair. French voices. One or two wise guys stayed behind to guard him. Now he was up that famous creek.

They removed the gag. Which told him that screaming was a useless crusade.

"Guys, guys—" In French, he was saying, "*Les gars, les gars,*" trying to remind them that he was one of them, if not deserving of mercy, then at least an explanation or a chance to converse. "*Les boys,*" an even more familiar French salutation, "what's going on, hey? The blindfold – we know each other, hey. Not necessary."

"You don't know me," the guy who stood behind him said.

His chest stitched with dread and fright; Raccoon felt another chain of desperation cinch him tighter. Then the talk turned.

"You know me," a guy in front of him said.

He didn't recognize the second voice. The man moved to unwrap his blindfold, and the other man in the room took his cue to leave. He was down to one guard, and he could talk now, and he could see. This was going well.

The biker left behind was someone he'd hung out with years ago until the man had been elevated within the gang, leaving Raccoon still knocking on the Hells' door, still doing what he was told to do when he was told to do it. His guard was not an especially menacing man from his appearance. A grey beard fell from his lower jaw to below his heart. A black leather vest over a maroon shirt and loose frayed jeans. A shiny Harley belt buckle. The flesh under his eyes was swollen and saggy. Silver rings rimmed his ears. His forehead jutted forward, a button nose had a punched-in look, a combination that made him look goofy.

"Cutter," Raccoon said, to show that he recognized him.

"How's your shit cooking, Rac?" Although French, he chose to speak to him in English. A friendly gesture. Another good sign.

"What's coming my way? Any idea?"

Cutter shrugged, a gesture to say he didn't know.

"You don't get told, huh?" Make him feel insignificant, badger him into revealing what he did know, if anything.

"Car up from Montreal."

"Who's in it?"

This time the man didn't shrug, which indicated that he knew the answer and was weighing whether he should speak it. "Find out soon enough," Cutter said.

"I'm not feeling that patient. Tell me now, hey. Do you know?" Challenging him.

Cutter chose to pick his nose for a moment and examine what got dredged out. He flicked the debris onto the floor, and revealed, "Sharpie's coming in. Chiclets' driving, I hear."

The room, Raccoon observed, was predictably nondescript. It hadn't been painted in his lifetime and the lone window, oddly modern, was less than opaque from city dust, weathered grunge. The overhead was a dim 40 watts, bare and harsh. At his back, an old sofa. An end table balanced a radio. An upright wooden crate looked stitched together by cobwebs.

"You know why I got brought in, why you got left out, way back?" Cutter asked.

Raccoon had been demoralized at the time. He'd put it behind him.

"You're French. I'm English," Raccoon pointed out.

"If you wanna believe that."

Cutter's expertise included torture. That's what earned him a patch. Rac wasn't going to say so. Not out loud. He hated that the man brought it up.

The first man returned and passed Cutter an instrument. In the way that a dentist hides his needle, Cutter kept his choice of tool a secret. Though he twirled it once. A slim, handy gizmo. Rac caught a glimpse. A barbecue lighter.

Not much is worse.

"Cutter," he said. "Cutter." Appealing to a lost connection from the old days.

"I never liked you that much," Cutter pointed out. "Makes no difference anyway, right? Rac, meet Ziggy. Here to learn a trade."

"Hey, Raccoon," Ziggy said.

"Hey, Ziggy," Raccoon said, his voice barely audible.

"You better speak up once we get started," Cutter instructed him. "Ha! What am I saying? It won't be no problem."

"Cutter."

"Ever heard a rabbit scream?"

"I'll try to keep it down."

"Let me explain it. Ziggy unties you from that chair. We keep your hands knotted behind your back, see. He pulls your pants down to your shoes, stands you up against that wall there." He uses the barbecue lighter as a pointer. "I'm telling you this for your sake, Rac. You will let him do that. You will not make that part difficult. Don't squirm."

He had no voice. He nodded.

"Good man."

They unwrapped him and bared his genitals and shoved him against the wall.

"I gotta keep you alive, Rac, on account of the guys coming in from Montreal. They want a piece. But I got permission to burn your balls off. I don't have to. Up to you."

"Cutter." Finding his voice again. He knew better than to plead. That would be the worst thing. He had to stay in contact and you're not in contact when you beg.

"Just answer the question, Rac. I don't mind, either way. No skin off mine, right?"

He heard the click of the lighter and the man commenced down low, slowly raising it up between his legs so that he felt the heat on his inner thighs first and immediately he capitulated. "Cutter! Cutter! Just ask the question! Ask the question! Cutter! I'll answer! Okay? Come on. I got no problem, Cutter. I got no problem."

"You want the question?" He raised the flame higher. Raccoon *thinks* he feels the heat on his testicles. On his thighs, he does for sure.

"*Cutter!* Yes! I want the question! Give me the question! Fuck!"

"You want the question, Rac. I want the answer."

He scorched him a second and Raccoon hollered.

Then heard the lighter flick off.

"Since you're cooperating, I'll let you know the question. Make real sure you give me back the answer, Rac. Do not offend me. No bullshit fuck."

"Yeah. Yeah. Okay. I got no problem. I got nothing to hide, me."

"We all got a shitload to hide, Rac. Just don't hide nothing from me," Cutter warned, and pressed his weight against him as a rapist might to whisper in his ear.

Raccoon consented to the terms.

Cutter physically backed away from him.

"Big question, Rac. Answer back. Why the hell did you go into that hospital room, whack a cop, then leave your target in there sleeping like a sick kid with a thermometer up his ass?"

Raccoon coughed, then gasped, up against the wall.

"No BS, Rac, or I'll roast them, one at a time, real slow."

"No BS! It's just weird what happened. I go in the room, and the target, he's not there." He coughed again, then hurried on as though to make up for that lost time. Cutter ignited the flame again, several feet away. "I check the can in case he's there. What do I find? A cop. Dead on the floor. Bullet in his head. Blood the fuck everywhere. I didn't fucking shoot him, man! The target is not in the room!"

He waited then, pressed against the wall, to learn how his news goes down.

"Rac," Cutter said, "I bought this thing new. The lighter. Gas full to the brim, man. I can burn you for more hours than you got on your watch. You'll see the hour hand go around and around. I'll stick it in sensitive places. More effective that way. After I burn your balls off, think about the soles of your feet, your nips, the *tip* of your cock—"

"I swear," Raccoon proclaimed, "it's the only goddamn truth I got."

"Under the chin. Burn a hole right up into your mouth."

"I swear, Cutter. I swear. I so swear. No bullshit out of me."

"Your tongue. Burn the roof of your mouth. Guys lose their minds when that happens."

"Cutter." A mere whisper. Despair.

"You'd think – seriously, wouldn't you think? After a guy gets his balls burned off, he don't care about nothing else. Seen it for myself, Rac. Balls on toast, but he still don't want me nowhere near the soles of his feet. It's amazing to me."

"I swear. I swear. Cutter!"

"Then how come," Cutter wanted to know, and he moved right against him, dry-humping his bared bum and whispering in his right ear, "the dude was handcuffed to the bed when the cavalry showed up? How come, huh?"

"What? Yes! I heard that! That's the fucking question! Look. Cutter. He shot up your bank the day before. That's why! He doesn't want to be on the street! You'd burn *his* balls off if you found him! Am I right? He wants cop protection now. That's my theory. I don't know why he did that cop. He didn't want to take the blame, didn't want to be out on the street with you guys, so he ran. Had second thoughts. I came in. I left. He ran back to his bed after I left. The only explanation, right? He climbed into his bed again, handcuffed himself back in. Waited for the heat to show up. Now he's innocent, see? How'd he shoot a cop in another room if he's chained in? He says some crazy guy came in and shot their man. Cutter! When I was there, he wasn't in the room. Why the hell, *why the hell* would I shoot a cop for no goddamn reason then let the target, if he was lying in his bed, why the hell would I let him go free? Answer me that!"

Cutter never said another word. He backed away from his prisoner. A silent gesture might have passed between him and his apprentice because the other man in the room pulled Raccoon's pants back up then manhandled him back onto the wooden chair. He bound him again. Cutter had nothing further to say and strolled around aimlessly. He was relaxed. Ziggy left, then returned with a chainsaw, which he put down on the floor. Raccoon looked at it and noticed that the man no longer cared if he saw him or not. He could make him out now and identify him if he had a reason to do so but that was no longer a concern. Not a good sign. The chainsaw was not a good sign, either. Usually, it meant that somebody was losing his legs before he was allowed to die.

Cutter gazed at the chainsaw as well, then back at Raccoon. "That's not too promising," he pointed out.

"Shit, no. Jesus Christ, no. That's not promising."

Still, they were showing it to him ahead of time. Mere intimidation. Which meant they wanted him to talk. Get it all out. Every lie, every stitch of the truth, whatever was swimming around inside him, they wanted out. That's what they cared about. Not that he had anything to add to benefit his own cause or keep himself alive.

Ziggy had stayed in the room, checking on his reaction. When he got what he came for, apparently, he departed.

"Cutter," Raccoon entreated his old pal, who had never been much of a pal as neither had enjoyed the other's company. They had hung out only because no one else was around at the time. The shakiness and plaintiveness in his voice was obvious to both men.

"Don't go squirrelly on me," Cutter warned him.

"Shit happens. Speaking about that. Hey, Cutter."

"What?"

"I need to take a crap, man. Real bad."

"Come on."

"Serious. Get permission if you have to. You got to let a man take a crap. Better now than later when I got no control. You want to clean up that stink?"

The man considered the request. He could imagine that a man might need to evacuate his bowels when confronted with having his legs sawn off. He also wasn't going to let himself be conned. He went to the door and opened it to the hall, where he called out, "Ziggy!" The guy didn't answer. His big boots, though, soon were heard clomping loudly on the wood steps. He came back up. Cutter explained that he was taking their prisoner to his final crap.

"Yeah, so?"

"So hang around, asshole. Make sure he don't try nothing."

Raccoon was untied from the chair. He massaged each wrist. He rolled up his shirtsleeves. Cutter pulled him up by the collar, then walked him down the hall gripping the back of his shirt. Ziggy followed dutifully behind.

When they reached the washroom, Cutter instructed Ziggy to check it out. The man went in, then shrugged, then Cutter told him to check the medicine cabinet. Old junk was abandoned in the cabinet behind a mirror that swung out. A rolled-up toothpaste tube. A brush self-respecting folks would not permit near their hair. No razor blades. No scissors. Nothing useful to someone carrying around a stupid ambition inside his head.

"Go shit," Cutter told Raccoon.

He went inside. His heart leapt. He saw hope. A skylight.

Still. They were keeping the door open. Taking no chances.

"Fuck me, give a man his privacy."

Cutter gave him a hard look instead.

"This won't be pretty. It's embarrassing. My shit's gonna explode."

Cutter warned him. "Lock it, one second later I bust it down. Then I start up the chainsaw. No waiting. Hang on, I'm going to help you out." His guard unbuckled his belt and removed it. "In case you feel reckless or stupid."

Definitely, they wanted to talk to him. They wanted him alive. For now.

The door closed but not tightly.

Given the opportunity, Raccoon suddenly needed to piss. He pulled down his pants and squatted and urinated, desperately looking around for anything. He finished and pulled his pants back up and hunted through the medicine cabinet himself. Nothing. The toilet then. He could remove the porcelain lid over the tank, try to smash his way through two guards. Die trying. Or they'd lead him back to the chainsaw, and he'd find out then how much they wanted him alive. Probably not that much. He'd lose his fucking legs. Bleed out. He lifted the porcelain lid anyway. Felt the weight of it in his hands. One solid blow. Then another. A chance. He'd need to flatten them both with perfect swings in quick succession. Trouble was, he had no confidence in his superman credentials.

"Get on with it, Rac!" came the call from outside the door.

Think. The wings on his heels. Rapidly, Rac removed the chain from the toilet tank that operated the plunger to release water, detaching the small hooks at each end. He then manually lifted the plunger to create the flush, extra loud with the top cover off, then wrapped the chain in his fist and yelled, "Ready in a second!" at full volume. He intended to smack the mirror with the chain but then had a better idea. He yelled again and gave the mirror a moderate tap with the heavy porcelain, cracking the glass, and a few pieces fell into the sink. He palmed a shard the way a magician might do. The chain he ditched in a pants pocket which his captors had emptied, adjusted the plunger to stop the water flow, dried his hands and flung open the door before suspicions were aroused. He did them the courtesy of flicking off the light behind him.

The men led him back to his chair and tied his wrists behind his back as they had before, and lashed his chest, thighs, and ankles to the chair itself.

Raccoon waited. When nothing happened, he let his head droop forward as though the experience had exhausted him, and he feigned the sleep of the damned.

A ploy that worked.

When his captor grew restive with silent company, Raccoon was left on his own, tethered and immobile. Rac continued with the effort he'd begun even while the man was still in the room, sawing through the rope that bound him.

Difficult to find adequate purchase. Yet he progressed, working the glass shard against the braid. Before the rope was cut through it loosened, and he was able to free his wrists completely. He unknotted himself.

Now what?

He had to think on his flying feet, depend on his ankle wings.

They'd locked him in. A complication. Raccoon went to the window only to confirm it was modern. A security measure. A bar jutted out from the face of the building, preventing the casement window from opening any further than ajar. Smash the glass? No inducement to take that option – what could he do outside except hang there? Pray for rescue by the fire department, like they do with treed cats. If the bikers saw him first, they'd hammer his fingers, then crack his head open after he hit the ground.

He returned to the door. Locked, but the hinges were exposed on this side. They were tight in place, yet no match for his desperation. For the higher one, he pulled over the chair he'd been lashed to, stood on it, and got high enough to gain purchase on the hinge, making it yield. Prying open the door from its wrong side, he managed to squeeze himself through. An added benefit, it sprang back into place and still seemed both closed and locked. Like magic, then, *presto!* He was a missing captive.

Raccoon crept down the hall and tried the stairs. A few steps down. Below, him, on the next level, gang members were hanging out. No way through. He retraced his steps.

He checked two other rooms, with no luck, then returned to the washroom. He locked the door behind him and stood on the tub to open the window to the skylight. He looked up. By the light of the moon and the city, he could tell that the exit had been secured: a metal grate barred entry by police from above.

No way in, so now there was no way out to the roof, either.

He looked down.

Each floor below had a window to the skylight identical to this one. He had no other choice. And no way to soften the damage should he fall. If he pinioned himself between the walls, he might be able to creep down to a lower level and bypass all guards.

First, he unlocked the washroom door. Turned off the light.

Then he pulled himself out into the vacant space of the shaft, holding onto the ledge of the window while he managed his positioning. The time came to let go of the ledge, reach up, and close the window to conceal his escape route. They'd figure it out, yet any delay helped. He took his time, didn't fall, and the window looked closed.

Then he nearly fell. He grabbed the sill in a nick and saved his life.

Lower down, there was no sill to grab.

He glued his feet to the opposing wall and forced his shoulders and head hard against the surface behind him. Propped in that bent, cramped position, Raccoon scraped plaster with his fingernails to control his descent. Anytime he looked down or slipped an inch, a silent scream erupted through his torso. He thought about diving down, head first. Had to be a better end than the barbecue lighter or that bloody chainsaw. Still, he held on, and in scant increments battled his way lower.

He stalled once. He felt a revulsion come on, his body distressed, his emotions out of whack. He could weep. He could drop down to oblivion. Everything before him and his life behind him kept jolting him with a series of spiteful laments and grievances, as if the very unfairness of life itself kept him alive, kept him battling out of rage. That sorrow had the double effect of awakening adrenaline, which brought him strength and fortitude as deep-seated gripes and fallacies vied for attention.

He wanted his father alive again, so he could strangle him. He'd taught him how to kill, that man did. He'd love to show the old man what he could do now. Except that he was trapped inside a skylight shaft. He didn't kill the man himself; his father had died as part of an elaborate suicide scheme. Raccoon, constrained in place, feeling out of his body and half out of his mind, fit various pieces from that time into a vile and repellant whole.

"Okay, so they're ghosts. Dad, I still don't get it. What're they for, these ghosts?"

"A diversion. Always, you gotta have a diversion when you kill somebody."

"A diversion."

"Yeah."

"For what?"

"You'll find out."

He did.

They made the ghosts out of bedsheets and sticks of balsa to give them form and stability. Tied strings. With the strings, they could hide the ghosts amid the trees overnight, then raise them to be visible the next morning when it counted.

His father had two reasons to die. A malevolent cancer was moving through him quickly and causing him great misery, yet even that early end to his life would not spare him the venom of two criminal gangs, both eager to strip his skin from his bones. He had no hope, although he had one last card to play, one final sting to run. An insurance policy for 10 grand would set up his family, he told Raccoon, as if looking after his family had always been his primary interest, rather than an afterthought.

"It won't pay on suicide," he explained to his boy.

"So hide," the boy counselled his dad. "Let the cancer kill you. It'll pay on cancer."

The man looked at him as if he had just emerged from primal muck and not yet grown limbs or a set of lungs. "Where'd you come from?" he asked him.

The boy found the question difficult.

His father wasn't going to wait for the cancer to rip him apart, or for angry thugs to invent a more terrible way for him to die than the last time they committed butchery. He chose to do himself in.

"What about the insurance?" Raccoon was interested in that. His mom was broke and crazy, and he had only the paltry sums he stole snatching purses. Sometimes he had a decent payday but either he blew the money quickly or his dad got wind of his good fortune and dropped by to confiscate his earnings.

"Create a diversion. The engineer, the brakemen, they'll see the ghosts dancing in the breeze. But they won't see me, tied to the rails, until it's too late. *Tied* to the rails," he repeated. "A suicide *lies* down on the tracks. A man who is murdered is *tied* down. See the difference? Plus. To make it work. To convince everybody that I didn't do myself in, you will take away my extremities."

"Your what?"

"My head, see. My feet. My hands."

"Take them away? What do you mean, take them away?"

"You want the insurance for you and your mom or not?"

He couldn't deny that he did.

"Create confusion, Rac. Remember that. Then nobody knows what's going on. I'll be headless, handless, footless. No cop and no insurance suit can say I did myself in and then somehow walked away with my own body parts. This'll make it look for sure like somebody took a personal interest in my slaughter. The shitheads out to get me will sweat. They'll be questioned because I'll leave the right trail markers. Meantime, insurance pays out, Rac. They gotta."

Raccoon solicited help from his good buddy, Douglas Sykes, and the die was cast in blood. Then everything worked as planned, until Douglas got caught with the feet. The insurance policy paid out, but every last penny of the 10 grand went to his dad's girlfriend. Nothing for his kid or his ex who was now officially his widow.

Raccoon revenged his dead father for that. Raccoon snuck into his father's mistress's apartment after her current lover had left for work and stabbed her to death while she slept. The only prints left on the knife were the lover's. He wetted the man's running shoes with the victim's blood, dropping them into the bottom of a garbage can, partially concealed under trash in the backyard. Somehow, not enough evidence could be uncovered to convict the lover, or he bribed his way out of that one, and yet for a year and a half the cops pursued him without bothering to consider another killer. By then, his own trail had gone stone cold. Raccoon had found a diversion – the spectre of a married man with his prints everywhere in the dead woman's apartment – and created chaos with the murder itself, making it bloody and horrific, "2 Timer" scrawled in blood over the victim's bed. Investigators fixated on the crime as one of carnal passion. Nobody searched for an 18-year-old aggrieved by an insurance policy and a dad's betrayal.

In committing a well-planned suicide right before his eyes, the head lopped off and rolling down the railway grade to land in his lap, his dad had taught him how to kill. In betraying him and his mom he'd taught him to *want* to kill. Raccoon was learning a profession. The next step had been to make it pay.

After that start in the life, the only thing that counted with Raccoon was loyalty.

Douglas Sykes proved his loyalty. He was the only person on the planet he could trust. And vice versa. They were more like brothers, he told him, than most brothers.

They made a pact to be invisible to one another. That was important with respect to the father's suicide, and it could work to their advantage in the future. Raccoon argued that they could better look out for each other in tough company if no one knew they were brothers in secret.

Douglas had no problem with that.

They'd made a pact. That Douglas had returned to his hospital bed – *after* Raccoon had rescued him, and *after* he warned him to beat it out of town – was more peculiar than he could figure out. What the hell went wrong? It had been the perfect plan. Did Douglas betray him? Why the hell did he go back to bed when he was supposed to run for his life?

At the next window, Raccoon takes a break, leaning an elbow on the sill. He clamps the fingers of his opposite hand on the sill as well, alleviating the stress on his thighs and stomach muscles. Relaxing too much, he nearly catapults down again. This time he recovers his leverage and feels heartened that the depth of any potential tumble has been reduced. Only two floors to the basement level; only one floor to his escape route. If he lands on his feet after a fall from this point, he might survive with broken ankles. They'd be repaired with a chainsaw. Still, achieving the first window shows that his gambit is succeeding.

Encouraged, more confident, he increases the speed of his descent. He's surprised by how little time it takes to reach the lower window. Opening it is the next obstacle. Raccoon puts his ear to the glass, listening. Off somewhere, rock music. With luck, loud enough that no one will hear a little racket.

He jiggles the latch. The window is meant to open like a cupboard, inward to the bathroom. Gentle persuasion fails to trip the mechanism. Raccoon edges further down and presses his hips in under the ledge. He raises his elbow to the glass but nearly slips. He reconfigures how he adjusts his legs to keep himself pinned in place. Tries again. His elbow cracks the pane. Another nudge and he breaks a jagged hole in the glass. Shards tinkle into the tub. Not wanting to make any unnecessary sound, he slides the chain he lifted from the toilet upstairs from his pocket – then suddenly winces from a leg cramp. He needs to stretch the muscle out. Not easy. Carrying on, he finagles a small loop in the chain and eases it upward, over the latch handle and tugs it downward. The chain slips off. He tries again with the same result. The third time, he presses outward on one side of the window frame which effectively reduces the pressure on the latch, and when he pulls down, it springs open.

Rac dangles from the windowsill, then pulls himself up and in. The only light in the room funnels down the skylight, and at this depth not much is received. His eyes have adjusted to the dark. Raccoon spies a gleam off his bald scalp reflected in the bathroom mirror. He steps out of the tub and opens the door to the hall.

Someone speaks and turns into the hallway and Raccoon darts back the way he's come. He thinks to lock the door but realizes the stupidity. The steps are approaching and he's willing to place a bet on why. In returning to the tub, he whacks his head on a corner of the open window. A murderous pain. He holds in his outcry, closes the window, ducks behind the shower curtain and gives his scalp a rub.

To be on the safe side, he keeps the toilet chain handy, holds it in both hands.

Stretches it taut.

In another moment, a biker enters the room.

He takes a long, impressive piss. Raccoon figures him to be part horse.

The cramp in his leg seizes on him again. He tries not to gasp. Or breathe.

The stream stops, and the man zips up. Raccoon measures his breath. Keeps still. What goes wrong happens fast. He doesn't know how he's given himself away, only that the biker checks behind the curtain, poking his head around the edge.

Then throws the curtain back and hurls himself on him.

He's shocked but reacts on impulse.

Raccoon gets the chain around the man's neck in a twinkling and is turning it, squeezing, cutting off his air as the brute stumbles into the tub. The biker is prototypical of his species, all beard and wild hair, with a neck the width of a mature oak and biceps the size of pumpkins. The man awkwardly punches him in the gullet once, grabs a breath, tries to smother him against the tub wall, then reaches for his throat. In that moment, Raccoon, still twisting the chain, steps onto the rim of the tub with one foot and gains position on him and as he falls forward the biker stumbles back. The big man strikes his skull against the sink. Seizing that advantage – his brain firing wildly, calculating his chances – Raccoon drives the man's head down hard against the rim of the toilet, then drives his head back down against the porcelain rim again, and again, and cracks his skull.

The man's just lying there after that. Bleeding. Completely still.

He removes his hands from the biker's throat, his fingers pinched under the chin and detects that the guy still breathes. Let him. He won't be coming after him anytime soon.

Raccoon is out the bathroom door in a split second. Moments later he's worked his way to the street, walking fast, beating it out of there and down the block. As soon as he turns the corner, he's already looking for a car to swipe.

PART THREE

RUN AND HIT

22. Hell and Heaven

Fatigue overtook Émile Cinq-Mars, ending his initial talk with Douglas Sykes. The prime suspect in the policeman's murder was hauled back to the city, only to be returned to Hawkesbury Hospital the following day. Advised that Douglas Sykes was expected soon, the retired detective waited for him in the ambient dark of the alcove where they spoke previously, exiled from the realities of his world by pernickety thought. He's surprised, then, when Sergeant-Detective Léon Doucet arrives first, unannounced and on his own.

"He's in a van outside," Doucet tells him. "The little shit."

"Ah, you're expecting me to go out to the van? I'm to force-march him in here? Will you be pushing my wheelchair while I wrestle him to the ground?"

"That won't be necessary," Doucet affirms. He sits.

Muscular, well-coiffed, the officer sports a style of haberdashery above the norm. The policeman's protuberant lower lip is disconcerting, which rouses in Cinq-Mars an unexpected curiosity. Inclined to stare at the lip, he checks himself, and wonders if this is how it goes when people first encounter his own prominent proboscis. The man opposite him is handsome enough otherwise, which, Cinq-Mars reflects, might be how others sum him up. *Otherwise*.

The visiting officer is sluggardly in getting underway.

"Sergeant-Detective Doucet, do you expect me to yell out the window and across the parking lot? I'm not feeling that rambunctious. I'm not convinced these windows open."

The officer declines to dignify the sarcasm.

Having gotten nowhere with the outburst, Cinq-Mars chooses a conciliatory approach. "What's the trouble, Sarge?"

"Feel free to call me Léon if you like. Bill does."

"You two are getting along."

"Mostly. Yeah. I think so."

"He's a good man. I trust him."

"Yeah. A good man." He pats his inner thighs.

"Detective," Cinq-Mars nudges him, his patience limited.

"Look, I can't keep bringing Douglas Sykes out here."

Why was that so hard to say? Unless there's more to come. "I'm not going into town."

"Due to your health," Doucet assumes.

"Sykes will need to suffer the commute, not me."

"I have a boss," Doucet explains. "I'm being forced to put Sykes into the system."

"He's not in the system?"

"How can he be when he's out here half the time? *More* than half the time."

"You exaggerate."

"Not if you include road construction and the goddamn detours. It takes time to dodge falling cement slabs."

"Ah, yes. Montreal roadwork. Still, he's in the system."

"We've kept him in our station lockup overnight. We figured – I did anyway – that he might be safer there."

Safer is an odd choice of word. It's more convenient to hold him in the lockup. Paperwork is not without material force; when avoided, legal repercussions may ensue.

"You're worried that he'll bust out of Parthenais, try that trick with bed sheets from 30 storeys high. A valid concern."

"One guy made it. Another came up short."

The memory evokes a chuckle between the two. A criminal had scaled down more than 20 storeys from his cell at the top of a police high-rise, only to be left dangling several stories above the street because he failed to account for the effect of knots on the overall length of rope created by tying prison bed sheets together. Firemen had to rescue him with a ladder truck.

The ice between them has cracked. Doucet endeavors to elaborate. "Escape is not my concern. On the other hand, if we isolate him, he can still slip in the shower. Or take a heroin overdose after a visit to the chaplain. Or his lawyer gets him off on a technicality 10 minutes after he mysteriously has his throat slit, although the shiv went missing."

"Right. He might be safer in your house."

"Except, I can't keep him there. Boss's orders. Which are his boss's orders and the boss of that boss's orders. Have you heard of it? It's called the chain of command."

"My tendency was to ignore it."

"How you did that I do not know. You should teach a course."

"Sorry. A few state secrets will go down with the ship."

"Mr. Cinq-Mars, I have to stick him back in the system. To sink or swim. Officially, he *is* a cop killer."

"Not until proven guilty."

"You know how it works. Animosity builds against him with only a speck of evidence. One is not equivalent to the other. As far as anybody up the chain is concerned, no matter what they say in public, he's being measured for the rack."

Cinq-Mars takes a moment to consider their options. Unconsciously, he rolls his wheelchair back and forth slightly, as if he's at a starting gate revving his engine. "Your use of the phrase, Léon – sink or swim – is interesting."

"How so?"

"Reminds me of – how shall I say this? The darker recesses of human history. Witches were publicly thrown into icy rivers in winter to sink or swim. If one survived, she was a witch. Proof positive. She could then be burned at the stake or some similar ritual without a stain on anyone's conscience. If she drowned, that didn't necessarily prove her innocence, only that her powers were feeble on the day. Or that God chose to carry her home. I do lament the excesses and the trespasses of my so-called Christian forebears. At any rate, if a woman accused of being a witch was going to clear her good name, her best chance to do so was to drown."

His housecoat opened slightly; Cinq-Mars wraps it more comfortably around his chest. He'd had a good walk after breakfast and overheard serious, if conditional, talk of him going home soon. He can hardly await the hour.

Across from him, Léon is rubbing each of his knees in opposing circular motions. "You're saying, if Sykes survives in the system, it shows he has more pull than we know. If he's jacked on the inside, if this or that biker gang garrottes him, we can take a fresh look at his possible innocence."

"If he's on a slab in the morgue, we can do that. Except, no one will bother with a fresh look. What's done will be considered done. Justice for one, if not all."

"About the size of it," Sergeant-Detective Léon Doucet concurs. "Look, Mr. Cinq-Mars, I've let him come out here because he makes a valid point. My superiors expect me to ignore it, and Lord knows I've tried.."

"What point?"

"The GR. Not a trace of gunshot residue on him. He could have washed, but not that thoroughly and not his clothes, too. I haven't admitted it to him, of course, but it's compelling. If he's guilty, you can help me figure that out."

Crossing his wrists over his lap, Cinq-Mars engages the other man with a look that's squared-off. "Are you going to let me have at him today? You drove him out here, Léon. He's in the van. I presume you want me to take another crack."

"That's what I'm here to tell you, Mr. Cinq-Mars," Doucet forewarns. "One last shot. That's it. The clock, she ticks. We need results."

The retired cop declines to give the one who is still on the job permission to call him by his given name. Aware of that, the detective excuses himself to fetch the prisoner. He's no sooner out the door than Bill Mathers, who's been waiting on the opportunity, slouches into the room.

"Did you know that, Bill?" Cinq-Mars inquires.

"Know what?"

"The clock, she ticks."

Mathers looks at him as though he's sprung a leak.

"I have it on good authority," the older man defends.

Detecting his mood, Mathers doesn't press his old friend for further explanation. He plops himself down on the sofa and exhales as if he's the one who's feeling weary. All this driving out to the countryside is wearing him out. "How're you doing, Émile?" he inquires. "Scale of 1 to 10."

The question carries no interest for the retired detective. "Who knows? I'm in a drug-induced fog. When I'm in a coma, you're nothing but a figment of my dream. Anything I say should be held against me. How are you, Bill? How's the family?" Willing to answer, Mathers is promptly interrupted. "What do you make of him?" Cinq-Mars asks.

"Sykes?"

"Doucet. *'Feel free to call me Léon.'* That guy."

Instinct, and experience in his former boss's company, alerts Mathers to the question as being of special interest, rather than flip or idle.

"We get along."

"He mentioned it. That's suspicious, but my question is, what do you make of him?"

"Not sure. He has an edge. I think he has boundary issues."

"That's how people talk, isn't it? We speak of *issues*. I think it's a way of talking in generalities while pretending that vague words are meaningful."

"Okay. Specifics. He'll stomp on a wounded man's bullet hole to get him to speak. When working a suspect, he can be gung-ho rough, borderline temper tantrum. Dip over the line. Those are his *issues*. I think he knows when he's pushed himself far enough, when it's time to ease off. I'm speculating, of course. Everything needs to be checked out over time."

"Mmm." The murmur is neither judgement nor conclusion. "I've heard worse. Did Douglas tell you about the stomping? He could've been lying."

"Not him, no."

"Trusted source?" Cinq-Mars waits for him to explain himself.

"It's a guess," Mathers admits. "Partly, Doucet said so on his own, and I've seen him inside an interrogation room for myself. I nearly pissed myself. If he does have issues – sorry, I like the word – he's also a smart guy. His head is screwed on okay. I think. Proof of that, he brought me into this to see if I could bring you into this. That puts a few brownie points on the right side of his ledger."

Cinq-Mars appears to agree, as shown by a fleeting facial notation. Nothing more is said on the subject as Douglas Sykes, in the grip of the man they've been discussing, is shuffled into the room.

The two exchange a non-verbal greeting. The former cop then repositions his right elbow on the armrest of his wheelchair as his forehead droops into his right hand. Perhaps he's taking a catnap, no one's sure. Looking up again, Cinq-Mars is surprised that two policemen are still in the room.

"What's up?" he asks them.

"We're staying," Sergeant-Detective Léon Doucet informs him. Then he qualifies that remark. "I am, anyway."

"I'll stay," Mathers tacks on, as if declaring himself a counterweight to the other badge in the room. Rather than argue, Cinq-Mars gives a slight flick of his hand, as he might dismiss a fly. While it's not his purview to grant them permission to stay, he's adopted that privilege.

"The clock, she ticks," he mentions to Sykes.

"That's supposed to mean something?"

"Time's a-wasting. Your ass has not yet been cooked. These two detectives are being leaned on. The weight above them expects you to emerge from this meeting adequately tenderized. No more raw meat on their plate. They want you browned off, Douglas. Sizzled. What do you think? Are you game?"

"You're bright and cheerful today, Émile. Rough night?"

"The contrary." He smiles. "A source of my dismay is the news that you're to be tossed into the system. No more perks. No further travels out to the bucolic countryside to meet your favourite cop-buddy. We need to make strides. I hope you're feeling—" He stops himself, and the men behind Douglas Sykes, who are settling onto the sofa, detect the twinkle in his eye when he glances back at them to secure their attention. "Give me a word, Douglas. Complete my sentence for me."

The prisoner requires a moment, then says, "Loquacious." A twinkle in his eye, too.

"Hear that, gentlemen?" Cinq-Mars addresses the pair of detectives. "Now what low-life, bottom-feeding, thieving, pimping rascal that you have ever had the pleasure of interviewing can feed you back a word like that? Loquacious." He continues in a whisper to Sykes in a voice loud enough for the others to hear, although his words are intimate: "You've always been one unique loser, Douglas."

"Carve it on my gravestone, Émile."

"What will you write on mine if I precede you? *Here lies a sucker. A man I duped.*"

Sykes shrugs. "I don't believe you think that way."

"Let's find out. The clock is ticking. That cloud of shadow over you, residing inside you even, let's blow that darkness off."

"Poetic today, Émile." He intends his comment to make light of the older man's purpose, failing at that. Head-on, he meets the eagle-eyed stare he has rued previously. That penetrating glare brooks no substitute for the truth. They take each other's measure. The two cops at the prisoner's back notice the exchange, and Mathers for one thinks of it as a forcefield being bent out of shape. This is not going to be a rudimentary conversation between adversaries or friends. Doucet is less able to ascribe a description to what he observes. The retired cop has a reputation, and Doucet feels the tug of opportunity to learn what the fuss is about regarding this legendary figure.

All this, with no other word spoken. Only a mutual circling around while standing still. Two fighters affirming their ground, parrying in a ring.

"Sopwith Camels," Cinq-Mars declares finally, inexplicably. He passes a hand in front of himself as a priest might do for a blessing. "Something occurred to me with my morning coffee. Colourblind people have certain advantages, Douglas, I don't know if you're aware."

"I never took an interest in Sopwith Camels – the airplane, first World War? The colour-blind? Also, no interest."

"Biplane, yes. The colour-blind, Douglas, discern patterns in a range of hues others do not. In World War One, colour-blind pilots could spot artillery installations beneath the German camouflage. Pilots with normal vision could not differentiate camouflage from the trees. The Brits conscripted colour-blind pilots since they were effective at bombing those targets."

Sykes offers up a small toss of his hands, asks, "Your point?"

"I'm sharing, Douglas. It's something people do. They share. Practically my entire adult life I have wondered how on earth I stopped you as you walked down the block with your sack full of feet."

"Ah, Émile, only two feet. In the sack. It wasn't full."

"I stopped you anyway. This morning, coming out of my druggie befuddlement, I was enlightened. Like a colour-blind Sopwith Camel pilot, I saw though the camouflage. You walk down the street as a kid with a sack on your back, and I see through it. Or, at least, I respond. Yesterday, you established your camouflage of deceit and lies, using truths and storytelling, which doesn't yield much substance to us investigators. With me, though, because I suffer an equivalence of colour blindness in some other regard, I see through it. Can't say how or why, except it's what I do. It's why I am what I am. Ultimately, it's who I am. I'm *sharing*, with you, Douglas, this wonderful breakthrough of mine. It's a promise, in a way, from me to you. Please, be confident that I will see through your fabrications the way those impaired pilots saw through the camouflage. You should be glad, though, as your life might depend on it."

Sykes considers the analysis, dismissing a portion and retaining the rest. "From now on, I'll think of you as you're an impaired pilot," is his final assessment.

"I'll accept that as fair," Cinq-Mars plays along. "Wise, even."

"Where did we leave off, Émile?"

Mathers and Doucet react to what they've heard. Mathers, who knows Cinq-Mars well, is surprised by the inherent braggadocio in the man's introduction. Out-of-character for him, yet in trusting him he assumes that a reason for the commentary will surface. Doucet, on the other hand, without prior experience with the man, assumes that his ego has run amok and is already counting the entire exercise as wasted effort.

"Why," Cinq-Mars ponders aloud, enfolding his arms along with his concentration, "are you loyal to someone who has not been loyal to you? Start there. Your bosom buddy, this Raccoon friend, in the money-counting room, shot you. He left you to the mercy of the cops with a triple murder hanging around your neck. Next day, he shoots a cop in the head and leaves you to take the blame for a cop-killing. You've been clever in trying to avoid blame – and please, don't bring up the matter of the GR with me. We're going under the surface here, Douglas, we don't need to discuss gunshot residue. That's on the surface. Today, we want what's underneath. He's pointing the finger of guilt at you, Douglas, at *you*, and still you respond by staying loyal to him. How come?"

The question slices below the skin, beneath his defences. The man's body language and reactions confirm a direct hit. He squirms in his chair as though he'd like to pick it up and fling it at him.

"Understand what I'm asking, Douglas."

"I do."

Cinq-Mars expresses doubt by shaking his head. "I'm not asking that you say anything about Raccoon. Protect him all you want. I'm asking you instead to *explain*, okay, explain to me why you're loyal even when the other guy in the pact shoots you, then leaves you on the hook for three homicides of deadbeats and one homicide of a police officer. Everybody's life is important, but the cop-killing, that's a capital offence. You don't get to walk on that one. Explain why you let the other guy treat you this way."

The question works through Sykes. His torso involuntarily flexes.

Cinq-Mars presses on.

"You stayed in bed. At the hospital. That's not what he wanted, was it? Not what he expected you to do. You were already *out* of bed, already dressed. Socks in your pants, shoes on your feet. Am I right? You were on your way out of there when he left you. On the run. But you turned back. Got undressed again. You climbed back into bed and handcuffed yourself in place. You defied him, Douglas. I guess you're not *that* loyal, are you? Yet, with us, you defend. You deflect. You squirm around trying to keep your shit in place. As if that'll do you any good. Thrown into the system – I'm not threatening, I'm only stating the obvious – thrown into the system you can't be protected, Douglas. Not with biker gang thugs living in the wall cracks."

"You're not threatening me. Like hell." He seems morose.

"Why protect him? Just answer that part. You don't have to betray him or say a word against him. Explain to the people in the room why you insist on being loyal when it's not in your own best interest. I'm not asking for a bone, Douglas. Throw me a crumb."

Sykes takes his time getting started, although it seems obvious that he will reply.

Ready, he says, "Raccoon always counted on me to make my own way. I'm smarter than him, that's how he thinks, although he's smart enough. A street-smart guy. Old school that way. Also, he figures I'm connected. To you, among others. That I can wiggle my way through anything. Shooting me, sticking me in a bad situation, he counts on me to slip free. He's playing the odds. He doesn't slip free himself. He goes his own way and that never turns out good."

Cinq-Mars offers a particularly pensive nod. Even as he turns his head and looks around the room, he continues to emphasise his nodding. He says, "Douglas, I understand. Know why? In a sense, Raccoon has been counting on you the same way I do."

"Counting on me?"

"To be your same old self. You'll keep a secret. You'll protect a friend, even when it's not in your own best interest. Raccoon doesn't do that – he'll shoot a friend, implicate him in multiple homicides, then count on him to be loyal."

Sykes considers that perspective, then asks, "You're counting on me the same way, you said. I don't get that part."

"Think about it for a minute on your own. First, let me tell you what's on my mind. I had a long night. These damn drugs. Half the time I don't know if I'm awake or asleep or on what planet. I can't believe people take these pills for recreation."

"Don't look at me. I'm whistle-clean. The occasion spliff to take the edge off."

"I prefer to keep my edges on. I was thinking in my delirium overnight why you were wounded but not killed. Initially, you wanted the good men who are sitting behind you to believe that things worked out a certain way. Bullets were flying. You caught one in the thigh when every other bullet landed in somebody's brain or chest. One bullet, one only, goes awry, and nips you in the leg."

"Some nip."

"Some leg, to more or less quote Churchill. I don't buy it, though. I certainly won't pay top dollar. The men behind you don't buy it, either. None of the patients in this ward buy it. I was yammering to them at 3 a.m. Since you've been stingy with the facts of the case, we're left to our imaginations. Mine goes wild sometimes, especially when I'm doped up. Imagine, then, that your name was supposed to land in the obituary columns. Only it doesn't. Instead, you're a survivor. The people who survived the loss of three of their employees hear that you did it and find out that you're holed up in a hospital. They send in a killer to exact revenge. Understandable. Trouble is, they don't know that you didn't do it – for now, let's go along with you on that – and send in the same killer who botched the job the day before. A guy named Raccoon."

"I never said Raccoon was at the hospital, Émile."

"As far as that goes, no one's told me anything. The two gentlemen behind you haven't told me about the video from the hospital or from around the neighbourhood. It's called Little Italy, Douglas. The emphasis is not on the word 'little.' Trust me, there's cameras. Know why?"

"Won't matter. He was wearing a hat."

Cinq-Mars raises his right hand. He then draws an imaginary vertical line in the air from the height of his reach down to the level of his chin.

"What's that supposed to mean?" Sykes asks. His eyes had carefully followed the finger's stroke.

"I drew the number one in the air. A point for my side. You just identified the killer as wearing a hat. Sergeant-Detective Doucet, did the killer in the hospital wear a hat?"

"He did."

"There you go. So far, Douglas, I'm winning, in case you also want to keep score."

"Lots of men wear hats."

"On warm summer days, fewer than you think."

Cinq-Mars requests a cup of water. A large upside-down bottle with a tap is available in a corner and Mathers does the honours, bringing over a cup for Sykes as well. The two policemen go without.

"Here's the lay of the land. Two crime scenes. People dead at both. You escape each time. Could be you know the killer and the killer knows you. He spared your life, accordingly. That indicates Raccoon to me. If that's true, let's give him full marks for that. Although he's also putting the noose around your neck as the perpetrator and relying on you to keep your mouth wired shut to let him get away with murder. Meantime, you get life. Tell me again why you're so damn loyal? You haven't convinced me yet."

Sykes is not interested in travelling down that road again. He knows that if he explains why he's loyal he is effectively agreeing to defend the man, who is not defensible, giving him nowhere to turn.

"Thought so," Cinq-Mars concludes.

"A fly in your ointment," Sykes points out.

Cinq-Mars leans to one side to get a better view of his old partner, Bill Mathers, and asks him, "Don't you love the way this guy talks?" To Sykes, he says, "What fly?"

"If Raccoon – let's say it's him for now—"

"I'm happy saying that."

"If Raccoon was sent to kill people and botched the job, what gang would send him back to fix his mess? Since when do the Hells – let's say it's them – when do the Hells send somebody back for a do-over? He gets a screw-over before he ever gets a do-over."

Taking that in, Cinq-Mars is inscrutable for a minute or so. Possibly, it's an effect of the drugs he's been complaining about. When he emerges from his trance, he raises his left arm this time and again draws a vertical line. "One point for you," he remarks. "We're tied." He sips water and thinks the matter through.

Eager once more, he says, "This is what we have. Day One, you kill three gang acolytes. Day Two, the gang seeks revenge. A cop is killed instead by an unknown party. In that scenario, you're a killer and should go to jail. Next possibility, Day One, you're supposed to die in a hail of bullets. You get away with a flesh wound. Day Two, a killer arrives to finish the job while you're lying in bed. You conceal the killer's identity and should go to jail for that. Or, door number three, on Day One you get shot then on Day Two you shoot a cop for no good reason. As if there could be one. Go to jail for that. Or, and this is where you get to claim your innocence, behind door number four you're in the wrong place at the wrong time and three people die. The next day, same thing, wrong place, wrong time, and a cop dies. You're innocent. Mind you, since that's ridiculously far-fetched, you will, in all likelihood, go to jail for that. Meantime, you're tossed into the system to sink or swim, and you know what happens. You sink like a stone. Does that about cover it?"

Douglas Sykes, if hopeful upon his arrival, is now subdued.

Slowly, Cinq-Mars wheels in closer to him, so tightly that the suspect shifts his legs to make room. The retired cop sets the brakes on his chair.

He speaks quietly. The cops in the room lean forward to hear him better.

"My friend, we've seen you through troubled times before, haven't we? This one's a pickle. We have different scenarios. I think the one that you want me to work on is whichever one is true. Otherwise, what's the point? A lie won't benefit you. I can't get you off with an invented wild tale. If the truth comes out that you were shot to preserve your life, which puts you on the run, let's work from there. And if the truth comes out that the same shooter came back to finish the job, shooting that poor policeman instead to get you off, putting you on the run, let's work from there. You didn't run. You knew better. That would have confirmed your guilt, and we wouldn't be talking today if you'd been caught."

Cinq-Mars draws a deep breath, then continues.

"You made a good point. I drew it in the air. Why would they send the same man twice? Unless, unless they didn't know they were sending the same man twice. The Hells, or whoever, thought that you did it on Day One, and sent in a trusted man on Day Two, not knowing that he was the same guy who let you escape. Which means, and I need you to think about this, Douglas, whoever gave the order on Day One was not the same person or entity who gave the order on Day Two. Or, if he was, he knew what he was doing. So, let's ask, who gave the order to kill you in the first place? Are there two gangs involved? Or is the head of one gang not letting his people know what his right and left hands are doing? Either way, your life expectancy in prison, even awaiting trial, is negligible. I can use a word like that with you. Negligible. It also means I won't be betting on Raccoon's life expectancy, either. What do you think the Vegas odds are on that?"

Cinq-Mars leans back in his chair, giving the captive a touch of personal space.

"Are you being loyal to a dead man, Douglas?" Cinq-Mars inquires.

As Sykes speaks, his voice feels far away to him. Out of the depths of himself, he contends, "Him and me, we're like brothers. In this world, it's what we have."

Not *he is all I have*, Cinq-Mars notes privately, but *it's what we have*. The loyalty. More important to him than the person to whom it's attached. The concept, of two people bound to each through circumstance and shared experience, is the only true bond this man has known, the only true bond he's held onto. Cinq-Mars understands now what he's up against in terms of penetrating his defences.

He takes the brakes off his hand-powered vehicle, spins the wheels that move him backwards.

"I said, earlier, that I was counting on you the same way Raccoon is. He's counting on you to keep your mouth shut. I'm counting on you to be loyal to your friend. This way, you'll be imprisoned for murder. A capital offence, killing a cop. If you've been guilty in the past, Douglas, and I got you off, that won't be on my conscience. Guilty or innocent, it looks like you'll go down for this one. I'm counting on you for that."

"Émile—"

"Don't bother, Douglas. I'm sorry that I can't help you. In all sincerity, take care."

Notably, the two policemen rise with a sense of regret, even lassitude. As though they don't want to do this. Sykes is cuffed, and Doucet leads him away to uniformed officers in the corridor. The detective pokes his head back in to find out if Mathers is coming, too, and notices that his colleague has scarcely moved. He seems aware of something that leaves Doucet mystified. Both men stand in the room, virtually motionless.

Cinq-Mars suddenly becomes conscious of them.

"What did you see, Mr. Cinq-Mars, peering through his camouflage?" Doucet asks, his voice lanced by a strain of doubt.

The patient in his wheelchair smiles briefly. "No need to get your back up, Léon. I don't consider myself to be a Sopwith Camel pilot. I don't share their abilities. What I said about them is true; I only told Sykes that I could see through his BS for his benefit. To help him think twice about lying."

"Is he? Lying?"

"His comments strike me as truthful. I'm also quite certain that he's holding stuff back. What he's telling us is not the lie. In what he refuses to say, he's less than truthful."

"Is he guilty?" Doucet inquires. "I mean, you're sending him up."

"Only the courts can send him up. As far as Parthenais goes, I'll make a call. That should keep him safe in there."

"A call."

"A call. One of those. Do me a favour, Léon. Don't tell him I said so."

"You want him to live in fear."

The older man rocks his head from side to side, not agreeing. "I want him to believe that we're done here. Even though we're not done. I need to break apart this bond with a so-called brother that he carries around with him like a sack on his back. Brother-at-arms, more like. Knock that wall down, we go inside. Once inside, we figure this out."

Doucet's eyes travel from Cinq-Mars to Mathers and back again. "I'll be seeing you, then," he says, and takes his leave. Bill Mathers still has nothing to say, yet before departing he places a hand on his mentor's shoulder; holds it there a moment. A connection between two old pals.

Before exiting the room, Mathers turns, and offers his assessment of his mentor's performance. "Nice taradiddle, the Sopwith Camel."

A petty lie, to trick truth into the light. "All I had," Cinq-Mars admits. "Sometimes, when you got nothing, you go with what you got."

23. Out and Down

Raccoon located a high-traffic convenience store in a strip mall. Only a matter of time before a driver chose to not turn his engine off, to keep cool air flowing while he popped in for smokes or a six-pack. A flashy red Mazda3 fit the bill. Climbing in, Raccoon appreciated the cooled interior. Less happy that it used a keyless start, and that the fob was in the owner's pocket. He could drive only until he turned the engine off or ran out of gas.

The meter displayed a trickle less than half a tank.

He could get out of town on that.

Toronto was out of range. Ditto North Bay. He could make Kingston easily or Smith Falls with miles to spare, but those towns had surrogate chapters of the Hells. With his shiny pate and forehead tattoo, he'd stick out in those small towns. Raccoon merged onto an expressway and headed home again to Montreal.

His hopes up, his speed down, he relaxed behind the wheel. The bland scenery of woodlots and fields encouraged him to deny the circumstances of his existence. Passing a parked cop car altered his focus. By now, the sporty number would be reported stolen, and the red colour was easily picked out on a highway. Some keen-bean copper might take a closer look. The one he passed suffered no such fervency, interested only in the numbers flashing on his radar detector, yet at the first opportunity Raccoon pulled into a service station. Obliged to leave the engine running, with the doors unlocked, he parked as far from the pumps as possible. In the convenience store, he pilfered a cheap pen that had the advantage of a sturdy pocket clip, then returned to the busy section of the parking lot, knelt, and used the clip to unscrew the rear license plate from a Dodge Ram truck. Quebec plate. Back on his far side of the lot, he removed the front and rear Ontario plates from the

Mazda3, mounted the one freshly minted by the Dodge – only the rear one for Quebec – and anointed himself as immune from prosecution.

He settled into the drive again, yet he had to evaluate. No money. No credit card. No wallet, no ID, no chance of escape, nowhere to run and nowhere to hide. He didn't even possess a proper screwdriver. Police were one enemy: the bikers vastly more frightening. Yet if he turned himself in, *as a cop-killer*, how would he catch a break? Bikers ruled the prisons. They'd waste him. Worse, they'd devise some incredibly gruesome method.

In the store, poker machines lined the far wall. They elicited such a yearning in him he could scarcely calm his heartbeat. He'd seen the row of tall fridges with glass doors and desperately wanted a beer. Or six beers. Or uppers or even downers. He wanted to get high then sick to his bones. He wanted to be totally trashed, barely breathing, incapable of discerning when one day flipped to the next.

He had to get back to thinking with the wings on his heels, because this fuck-up was unlike any he'd known. The worst people on earth and their sickoid cousins were out looking for him, with switchblades and knuckledusters, Uzis, dynamite, and all he could do was drive until he ran out of gas.

He'd need to steal another car. What he did then, where he went, how he survived, all that was so far up the air he felt absent from his bones. His nerve endings felt lit by matches. He failed to detect that his speed had crept up to 150 clicks an hour, and when he did notice, his control slipped, sending the car swerving on the asphalt.

Raccoon slowed down. He set the cruise control at 105. Slightly breaking the law made him look normal, he thought, less suspicious. He tried to get a grip. An inner panic thrummed in his bloodstream. His brains felt roasted to a golden crisp.

Driving on, he was desperate to figure this out, and by the time he reached Montreal two hours later, he perceived an inkling of what to do.

Was he not a killer? Then that's what he should do. Kill.

For that, he needed food, first, then weapons, then a little support.

Who to kill? For sure, some people deserved to go down. He could shoot up the biker's gym, killing Hells Angels and innocent fitness fanatics alike. He could shoot up a cop house. Pick a *poste de quartier*, taking down uniforms and detectives both. He could arrive outside a major prison and pick off the guards emerging from a shift. He could drive to a beach and eliminate sunbathers. In any scenario, he'd die, too. He'd make a point of it. That was not a negative. He had lost hope of surviving.

He desired a dramatic move to go out in a blaze of glory. Not unlike what his dad had tried, a man who thought he was going out in style but screwed everything up. His dad's former wife was left penniless, his girlfriend got sliced and diced by his angry offspring, his son embarked upon a life of murder, and he was too dead to know what happened. *Way to go, Dad*. His father's dramatic demise was useless. Raccoon would not follow in those footsteps. That man, after all, had been left without hands and feet. Not to mention, no head. His cranium had rolled down the railway embankment right into Raccoon's lap. No, he would keep his hands and feet and his head, too. Be proud of the bullet holes emblazoned on his chest. He could see the photograph now, page three of some rag, showing him spread out on the pavement, oozing blood.

People had to pay for his situation. The only question was to choose what group most deserved to be annihilated. He could shoot up a mall pretty easily, slaughter the innocent but fewer kids than at the beach. He gave the thought only brief consideration. Those killers were nutbars, unworthy of a second's admiration and he did not want to be numbered among them. That was no legacy. He wanted his action to count for something, to show that his grievances with the world were wholly justified. He wanted to pay people back.

A man needs a plan.

He's lived by the dictum.

Driving, one begins to formulate.

A whore who lived on Ontario Street East would be his trusty cohort, providing food, support, and even a measure of comfort. He referred to her in a derogatory manner because she had done him the dirty, ditching him years ago for one or two other men – or three, he wasn't sure – although she tried to explain back then that one or both or all three *preceded* him, that she was cheating on *them* and not on *him*. He could never get his head around that to see it her way.

Her neighbourhood posed a risk, the apartment within a block of the old Rock Machine bunker, abandoned now. The Rock Machine had gone to war with the Hells Angels, an epic turf battle with more than a hundred and fifty bombs igniting on the streets of Montreal. The Hells prevailed, the Rock Machine retreated; the Hells went to prison *en masse*, the Rock Machine quietly folded into an American gang, the Bandidos. Then eight former Rock Machine members were slaughtered by their new friends, those same Bandidos, and after that the old gang went low, remerging only slowly, cautiously. Scared of their own shadows. Lately, the Machine's patch has reappeared, the gang cobbling together its resources to coincide with a large contingent of Hells Angels on tap for release from prison. A return to open warfare was a growing possibility.

An entirely new option when he thought about it. The Hells were threatening him. Why not see if the Rock Machine would take him in? He could offer them a hit. Name a Hells Angel you want dead and consider it done. After that, they could be his protectors and new brothers from a different mother.

Hope, then, keeps staggering to its feet. Raccoon felt himself tilting back toward upright.

His good friend Clara had walked the streets in her teen years before she reformed and became a barmaid in a strip club, then graduated to being a stripper herself although she lacked basic rhythm. She spent time out in Vancouver taking her clothes off slowly. An addict. Living the high life, she garnered a biker boyfriend who brought her back east. She saddled up for the romp which suited her to a tee until he washed up downstream in the St. Lawrence River, seven bullets in his chest, four more clogging his brain cells. Not that the wounds mattered much, given what the river did to his corpse. Later, as she got older and less attractive to former clients, due in large measure to various addictions, Clara managed to get by through a clever combination of welfare payments, panhandling, and discrete hand and blow jobs, usually in cars or alleys around the neighbourhood. She preferred to not go to bed or even indoors with johns, as she had figured out that anyone who took her to a room at this stage in her life usually wanted to beat the crap out of her, not an interest she shared. Those men were vermin. On the other hand, she was fond of poor wretched fellows, mostly aged working stiffs who were also drunks, who took pleasure in what her fist could do up against a brick wall. She never mocked them when their pleasure remained soft. Boyfriends – real boyfriends, men with whom she might watch a TV show or share a meal – were few and far between, as she liked to put it. She confided to Raccoon that she meant she kept the few she liked far between each other. He got the joke without really appreciating it.

"I can afford better," he told her.

"You cheap bastard. You prefer free."

He did. They hit it off, even post break-up. He couldn't deny that, and as time went by and they became increasingly forlorn they'd sign up for an occasional binge and get sincerely wasted together. They started doing Christmas and birthdays at her place. They called it a lasting friendship.

Now that he was desperate, running down a very short list of possibilities, he chose to call upon Clara. She was awake in the middle of the afternoon and came downstairs from her apartment when he rang her bell. She seemed happy to find him at her door even after he told her he needed a favour.

"Why is that car running?" she wanted to know first.

"Never mind. You didn't hock your computer yet, right?"

"God, it's a piece a shit. Fucking out of date. Nobody will take it off my hands."

"So, you still got it?"

"Kitchen table, hon. Where it's always been."

"I need to wire you some money."

"Yeah, I thought you looked different today. Must be the light reflecting off your shining armour."

"Shut up. Look. I got no money."

"Oh, hon, you know I can't help you out. That's the deal. It's called tough love."

"Tough tit to you, too. I got money *in the bank*, Clara, that I can't get out. No ID."

"How come?" They were already walking upstairs to her dingy apartment.

"Never mind. I can send money over the internet."

"You can do that?"

"Piece of cake. I'll send it to you. Then you go to the bank and get it out."

"If you say so, hon. This high financial transaction is worth what to me?"

"I'll give you my car."

"The one that's running outside?"

"That one, yeah."

"I'm serious," Clara emphasised. "The shine, on your armour, it's like blinding."

"You can't turn it off, though. No keys."

"Always a catch. Disappointed but not surprised. Rac, you're a prince among motherfuckers, know that?"

"Take the car to a chop shop. I can show you where."

"I know where."

"Good. They won't have to restart it, see? They'll turn it off and take it apart. Nobody's the wiser. You're the richer."

"I tell them I'm in the business of jacking cars since when?"

"Make up a story."

"Like?"

"You're helping a friend. Tell them, your friend has a 14-year-old kid who stole a car. You want to keep him out of juvie. Junk the car, everybody forgets about it. Tell them that. They'll like the story. They'll believe it. They might pay extra for the entertainment."

"I like that story. You think fast, Rac."

"Flying wings on my heels, Clara."

"I won't go that far."

"Guess what?"

"What?"

He looks up from her computer. "The money's been sent. It's in your account."

"You know my account?"

"Of course.

"All you got to do is type your acceptance and answer a trick question. The answer is *sunlight*."

"Sunlight?"

"Came to me on the spot."

"Now what?"

"Type that shit in. Then we go to the bank. You get my money."

"While you leave the car running outside."

"You got it, Pontiac."

"I hope no cops're around. That's illegal, letting your car run. Okay. I'll type it in. Oh. My. Look at that. There's money in my account. God! Fuck! I'm flush. Let me find my purse. You have plans for the cash, Rac?"

"Trust me, Clara. You got no interest in being involved. And by the way—"

"Yeah?"

"Not only for my sake, for yours, too, you're not looking at me right now. You haven't seen me in two months."

"I'm blind to you, Rac."

"No matter who asks."

"Can't see you. Can't hear you."

"Thanks, Clara. I appreciate that."

"Anytime, more or less. Oh, sorry. I'm just talking out loud to myself here. You don't exist. You're a figment of my goddamned imagination. Jesus Christ, I'm rich."

"Not very."

"Still."

Waiting down the block from the bank in a No Parking zone, Raccoon figures a few things out. Part-way, anyway. The key to his thinking turns on who hired him and why. The old left-hand/right-hand thing. How come one hand didn't know what the other one was doing? He once diddled a woman with one hand while counting his take from a heist with the other. That might have been Clara, he'll have to ask her, but this is different. This is serious business. How come he gets hired by the Hells' boss, who's on the inside, to shoot four guys in a Hells Angels' bank while the top guys in the organization, who live on the outside, know nothing about it? Then those know-nothing guys assign him to kill the one guy he missed killing in the first place. Left-hand/right-hand. More importantly, who in the universe would like to know that information now? More importantly, who wants to get that information through torture or death, if necessary? Could he not hold a friendly fire sale instead? He could say to the right person if he knew the right person: "I know what you want to know. It'll shock you. Fair trade: we'll shake on a deal. I'll give you information that's such a mind-fuck you'll think you're on acid, and all you got to do for this silver and gold is to lay off killing me. Fair deal, right?"

Somebody might want to take him up on that. The question is who? Who needs to know what he doesn't yet know he doesn't know? Who needs to know what he doesn't yet know more than anyone else?

He thinks of Sharpie, who was willing to make the boring drive to Ottawa to talk, then run a chainsaw above or below his kneecaps.

Clara is emerging from the bank. She was a biker's moll once, had her shit together. Now she's hanging tough. He admires her, and her beauty, in a way. She still comes in at several notches above bag-lady status. They should talk. They're on a downhill run together. They could partner up. If she's lucky, she'll make it to the chop shop before running out of gas. In the meantime, he has more figuring to do. His life has improved over the last 20 minutes. Among other things, she's looking good to him. Raccoon feels a shimmering glimmer of hope.

She gets in the car and hands over the money he transferred to her account. All of it, to the dime. She's taken no cut, satisfied with their deal to take the Mazda3. She wants to breeze down St. Catherine Street in a car like a regular human – that's as important to her as collecting on the sale.

Her moment in the sun.

Raccoon now has money.

Next, he needs guns.

You can't strike a bargain, not even with the devil, without guns.

Once he chooses a target, he'll need to devise a diversion. His dad taught him that. Down on the railway tracks, slicing his own head off, he first had to have a diversion. Raccoon has learned his father's trade well: How to commit suicide and make it look like murder.

24. Day and Night

His hospital window frames a ruddy western sky. Cinq-Mars switches off the fluorescent overhead, which he blames for a low-grade headache, and sits with a reading lamp on. His disposition, Sandra notes upon her arrival, is compatible with the room's gloominess.

"Sweetheart, you look terrible. What's wrong?"

She almost never calls him that; he must be looking poorly.

"Hey, San. I'm fine. My head's off a touch. Why are you here so late?"

"Do you want me to leave?"

"Sandra. No fights. I'm happy you're here."

"Be still my heart."

This time he laughs, and she picks up on it.

"Restart. What's wrong, Émile? Don't say nothing. And – I'm turning on another lamp. The dark does nothing for your appearance. Not much for your mood either, apparently." The extra light is no help. The room feels designed for melancholy. "Please, cough it up. What's wrong?"

He relents. "Being here. I'm not suffering, but it's depressing. They tell me I'm going home, then I'm not going home. It's getting to me."

"Perfectly understandable." Intuitively, she knows that that's not the heart of the matter. Sandra can usually intuit when to leave her man alone, and this is not that moment. "What else?"

Tonight, a sadness feels embedded in his expression. When she's onto him like this, it's face-the-music time. "Rapping my knuckles on death's door – I don't mean when I was bleeding out, when I was both conscious and sick – I experienced... *something*. I've thought of it as the opposite of an epiphany. I have no tales of a bright white light when my heart stopped for a spell. I'm okay with that, although, honestly, I feel a little cheated. I could have used a white light. Too much to ask, I guess."

Laughter bursts from her, and this time he's the one who joins in.

"I'm referring to when I was conscious, not overly drugged, struggling to keep my organs functioning. You know, when my body quit on me, like that doctor said."

"I'm still pissed at you for that. Émile, what's the opposite of an epiphany?"

"A sudden surge of dullness," he blurts out. Then shrugs. "I wasn't… I wasn't as *spiritually* vigorous as I expected myself to be. I wasn't strong. I've always believed that no matter what, I could count on myself. At the hour of my death, I assumed I'd be strong, even *expectant*. I feel that I let myself down."

He can usually articulate an experience, even an emotional one. What he's broaching is unfamiliar, unexpected, and certainly unwelcome. She assumes that that's why he's struggling.

"I'm a half-assed decent Catholic. A heretic to some, but not first in-line for the next Inquisition. The new pope is coming around to my way of thinking. And yet, when I required my prayer life to be at its peak, it was insipid. Barely half-hearted. My conviction was flimsy. I'm not saying my faith was being challenged – had I thought so, I might have had more spark. Instead, I was unprepared to be so lackadaisical right when I was on the precipice of death. I certainly thought I might die but I had so little fight left in me. That reaction bothers me. When it counted, I just didn't care. I'm out of sorts, San, as disappointed with myself as I've ever been. Mentally, spiritually, I wimped out. I'm upset *now*, when it's too late, when I'm halfway healthy. Back then, nothing. Sorry. I'm being muddy."

"The doctor thought your mind kept you alive."

"If it did, that was purely out of habit."

He gives the top of his forehead a massage with the fingers of both hands.

His lament surprises her. She can grasp why he finds the experience troubling, for his reactions contradict what he has always taken to be his nature. "What else?" she asks once more, gently. Her tone does not imply that what he's presented is trivial, only that she feels there's more to come.

"On top of everything," he confides, "there is the case."

Right. The case.

"Émile, why are you dealing with any so-called case? I know! I wanted you to take it on. My thinking, it would perk you up. Did it? Except now you're borderline morose. You're retired. You're in a hospital bed recovering from a bullet wound. Why, for the love of the God you ponder all the time, are you on any case?"

"Because it's there?" Flip for the moment, he turns dour again. "Like Everest, it's a tough one. People are dead. A policeman included. That's part of it. Then Douglas Sykes returns from the past. That's part of it, too."

"The bigger part," Sandra infers.

"How so?"

She gives it another moment's reflection. "Friends come over to the house, relatives, strangers. At some point, you regale them with police stories. Less because you want to tell the stories than you know that it's expected of you. You're being a good host. Over the years, one story that repeatedly comes up is the one about the feet."

"Little kids, especially, love the one about the feet."

"So do you."

Cinq-Mars shrugs. She's right.

"You keep coming back to it, I'm thinking now, not only because the story makes the kids squirm. It's a living thing. The tale squirms inside you. It's one that has neither settled nor gone to an inglorious demise. Émile, you have a stack of unsolved cases on your docket. None, I suspect, have so consistently agitated you as the feet."

He's reluctant to concede ground, unable to determine a reason to do so.

"You haven't told me about every police chase you were involved in, or every misadventure. I know because I've heard a few from others. This one, the Douglas Sykes case, has weighed on you. You've brought it up often, and usually when you're feeling vulnerable. It's like a reverse security blanket for you."

"Ah," he asks, brightening a little, "what the hell is a *reverse* security blanket?"

"Something akin to being the opposite of an epiphany?"

"*Touché*." They share a fleeting chuckle.

"It surfaces," Sandra asserts, "when you're feeling vulnerable, worried about a mistake, or when an evaluation weighs on your mind. If you're up against a foe who manages to keep ahead of you, what do you do?"

He looks at her to provide the answer.

"You mention the feet in a sack, the boy with no dad who may have gotten away with murder. Why? If you made a cut-and-dried error in judgement, you'd own it, you'd learn from it, you'd avoid making the same mistake twice. But you could never determine if you were right or wrong. That's what gets your goat, I think. When you're vulnerable, you revisit the time: a reverse security blanket. It doesn't give you comfort, the opposite, it keeps you on edge. Agitated. Unsure. At key points in your career, you have preferred to be unsure. Buffeted about by the four winds, or however many there are. You were hoping, perhaps unconsciously, that it might help you."

Her points are being taken in by her husband. His smile offers a glimpse of thanks.

Sandra's not done.

"For me," she says, "the basis of the enigma is different than what you've put out there."

"Ah, the basis of the enigma?"

"Oh hush. A little hyperbole isn't a crime."

"Okay. What basis, then? What enigma?"

"You won't like this. Ask yourself, Émile, who do you feel you failed, way back when? Douglas Sykes? Or Émile Cinq-Mars?"

She may be hitting the proverbial nail on the head, although Cinq-Mars feels that she's using a battering ram rather than a hammer. She needs one, too; as predicted, he resists the discussion. Rather than answer, in a roundabout way he fills her in on progress with the current case, on how it connects back to the incident with the feet years ago, and the worms. He tells her about the emergence of a second person, one he missed identifying in decades past. "He calls himself Raccoon. Last name, Rubbahchuk? No, Rybachuk. You know me and English names."

"Hardly English. Ukrainian, more like. Or Polish?"

"Same difference."

"Hardly!"

"Anyway, his father was the man who lost his extremities. He and Douglas are close buds, even though they pretended not to know each other."

He explains that the bond between the two men runs deep and that his task must be to disrupt that bond, tear it apart. He believes that Douglas will only guard his own skin if he cuts Raccoon loose. Only then can they delve deeper into what happened, both recently and in the past.

"At that point, I won't worry about who I let down in the distant past."

Sandra interprets his thesis differently. "That's why you're in such a sombre mood."

He's brought up short. "Meaning?"

She needs the better part of a minute.

Then speculates: "That might be what's eating you. You're making a mistake. Yes, you, the great Émile Cinq-Mars. You're doing something that's wrong. That's why you're depressed, why you're such a gloomy Gus."

He's wholly confused. "What am I doing wrong? I'm not aware of any—" Émile searches for the right word; finding none he makes one up. "Wrongedness."

"No such word."

"I'm French. I'm permitted a wrong word in English."

"Not *wrongedness* you're not. You're avoiding the issue."

"Now there's a word to remove from the dictionary. *Issue*."

"You're blatantly trying to avoid *this*! It's why you're so down in the dumps."

"What am I doing wrong?" Émile fires back. "Sandra, I do not understand you."

"You're saying that the way to solve your case is to take two friends and tear their friendship apart, strand by strand. Cause one to betray the other. Right?"

"I wouldn't put it quite that way, but—"

"And that's wrong. It's plain wrong, Émile, and you know it."

"Come on, Sandra. My job – okay, my *former* job – does not allow for sentimentality to creep in. I deal with dark criminals. I can't hum and haw about their *sensitivities* or their *feelings*."

"Sure you can. And you do. Although that's beside the point. All those two men have is their bond to each other. Take it away, they have nothing left. That's what they hold onto in life, why they protect it. They have one connection in their world to another person and that is the sum-total of their existence. Correct? Take it away, what's left?"

Seeing at least part of her point, he says so. "I still have to tear the bond apart."

"What if you don't?" she fires back, even before she's thought her notion through. "I have no clue how to implement this, but on a philosophical basis, instead of breaking the two of them apart, why not work with their friendship. Honour it. Invite yourself in. Just don't tear down the one thing in life that holds each man up. They're accustomed to people who demystify or destroy their childhood pact. They keep it a secret, right? Neither one of them, I bet, has any experience with someone who supports them. Support their pact, Émile. See what that does for them. And for you."

"Mmm," he says. At this point in their talk, that's more than Sandra has expected to draw from him. Satisfied with the victory, she tucks in for an evening of TV. It's high on the wall opposite the bed, where it abuts the ceiling. Together they snuggle down on top of the covers, tuning-in a summer rerun of *Downton Abbey*.

25. Country and Town

After Clara drives to the chop shop, Raccoon waits out of sight down the block while she negotiates a deal. She comes away with $400 for the Mazda3 and is happy with that. He's not amused.

"It's worth twenty thousand."

She tells him, "I take what the market will bear."

"You take what?"

"Hey, not your car, not your money. No big booger out of your nose."

Grumpily, he hails a cab. At her place, she propositions him and gives him what she wants to call a roll in the hay. He maintains that his effort was more for her than for him; she tells him his monkey is up a tree. He doesn't know what that means. He tells her that they both got what they came for and that they were both ripped off, so they're square. She has no clue what he's talking about, either.

Making small talk, she mentions, "Crazy about those murders, huh?"

"What murders?"

"Pulling Sykes in for that. I can't figure that. For the cop, too. You know him, right?"

"The cop?"

"Sykes. Douglas."

"You do him, too?"

"Back in the day, yeah. Out west. Those sweet old days. He was a broom at a bar I worked in. Nice guy. Complicated though. Jesus H. Oh, don't sweat it, hon. I felt sorry for him, nothing more. Kind of like you today. Hey, are you bugged?"

She means emotionally. He thought she was asking if he was wearing a wire and they had to sort through an auxiliary universe of misunderstandings. In the end, Raccoon was fuming without a floor to stand on. The whole time she was talking she was separating her laundry in the kitchen, colours from the whites.

"You're supposed to be the killer-boy, Rac. Not Douglas. Never figured him for the hired-gun type. I guess anybody can get that desperate, hey."

"I gotta run."

"Not on my account, hon. Stay over."

He might. He figures that Clara's place isn't like a casino, where bikers expect him to show up. He's safe with her. During sex, he felt he was in his death throes and that she was, too. In part, that's why he wants to leave.

"They say he's got that cop involved," Clara says.

"What cop?"

"You know. The real famous one."

"What cop?" He can only think of one. He heard he retired.

"The old fart. The retired guy. Cinq-Mars. He send you up ever?"

A man needs a plan. A killer needs guns. He also needs a target.

"What do you mean, involved? What's that supposed to mean exactly?"

"Radio never said. Just that they brought Sykes to talk to the old guy. On the news. Everybody's been talking about it. Where've you been?"

"I gotta go. I might be back."

"You into something, hon?"

"You don't wanna know. You absolutely don't wanna ask."

"Oh, shit, you can trust me. But don't bother! See where that gets you. Not into my pants again, that's for sure."

"I didn't want to go there anyway."

"Now you tell me. When your monkey was riding high you sang a different tune, didn't you? Didn't you, Rac? Wait 'til later, hon. You'll sing that song again. Anyway, who cares? I think that was the worst sex a poor girl has ever had to put up with."

He doesn't answer, and she sets her laundry down to look at him.

"Oh, hon, I'm only kidding. You can rock my bones any day of the week except Mondays. Strictly on the house. It'll be my pleasure. Seriously."

He stands and is leaving. "What's wrong with Mondays?"

"A girl needs her day of rest. Especially after a hard weekend."

"Remember," Rac warns her, "I was never here. You got to take that serious."

"I do, hon. I do. Trust me. I never laid eyes on you for such a long time, I can't even count the months. Back when I did, you were forgettable then, too. Ha! Teasing. Teasing! Give a girl a kiss before you go."

Raccoon slips an arm around Clara's waist and enfolds his lips upon hers with an abandon that takes him by surprise even more than it does her.

On the street, Rac takes a breath. Money in his pockets. He knows where to pick up a gun. As for the rest of his plan, it's coming together in his head, he just needs to work out the details.

Sandra returned to the farmhouse after the hospital. All seemed quiet across the broad expanse of fields that spread into the distance beyond her property lines. Starlight and moonlight above. The horses in their stalls were still, barn cats stalked mice, and the loneliness of her home was accentuated both by her husband's absence and by the ghost of the family mutt, now deceased. Another dog hasn't been decided on as they have not chosen where to live next, or if they'll bother to sell. Way out on her own, without Émile, she is suddenly convinced that sell they must. With Émile 19 years older than her, to be left alone is an inevitable outcome. Sooner rather than later she won't want the farm and she's already declared that she's done with the burden of caring for so many animals.

For now, she's hired a man to help out. A stopgap solution, if that.

So. The sign goes up tomorrow. She means metaphorically, yet her resolve has finally coalesced. No more farm. She'll let Émile know in the morning.

The phone rings. At this late hour, it's either someone checking up on her who's been calling for hours, or someone checking up on Émile. She doesn't want to endure either conversation. She answers to get it over with and hears a voice she doesn't recognize.

"My husband's not here," she says when his name comes up. She immediately regrets saying that. Émile coached her to never admit to being alone on the farm, given his job.

"Yeah, yeah, I know," the male voice says. "He took a bullet. It's in the papers. He okay? Must be if he's giving the gears to Douglas."

"Who's calling, please?" He's not identified himself as being the police and he's not an acquaintance. The most credible option: *trouble*.

"I'm Raccoon. They call me that."

"Can you repeat that, please, sir?" She thought she heard him correctly. Anybody who uses an animal for his nomenclature is a bigger problem than she needs right now. Sandra fishes out a pen and paper from the desk drawer.

"Raccoon. The critter, the one looks like a bandit."

"I'll let him know you called, Mr. Raccoon."

"I got a message for him."

"Fine. I'll write it down."

"Tell him I'm glad he's talking to Douglas. That's important to me. Custody's the best place for Douglas right now. All good. Tell your husband I said so. Tell him, whatever he does, don't let him loose."

"Don't let him loose," she repeats, to let him know she's writing everything down.

"That's the first thing."

"I got it."

"It's not the last. We'll wait on the rest."

"Okay. I'll give him the message. Can he reach you?"

"Naw, we'll do it this way. I'll call you. You talk to him."

"I see."

From time to time, rough-talking men gathered in her husband's orbit. Sometimes their appearance was a fright, too; yet the ones she encountered had been benign and on rare occasion gracious. She was guessing that this man did not fit that bill. She was talking to the kind of man Émile would never admit into their vicinity. One of the good reasons for living out on a farm: Keep the bad guys at a distance.

"Tell your man, if he wants to save his fink—"

"His fink. I'm writing this down, Mr. Raccoon. I guess you're not done."

"Sykes. That's who his fink is. If he wants to save him, he's got to save himself."

"Excuse me?" She's growing increasingly leery.

"Saving himself means saving me. You got that so far?"

"How does he save himself?"

"By saving me."

A tremor jumps through her with the notion of a threat.

"How did you get this number, may I ask?"

"Internet."

"My phone number is not on the Internet."

"Sure it is. On the internet, like I said, I was reading about Sergeant-Detective Cinq-Mars. Found out he had a wife. Found out she had a name. Found out she had a company for her horse business. Found out the company had a name. And that company has a phone number and that's how come I got through to you."

"You went to a lot of trouble."

"Not so much."

"How does saving you save my husband? Or do I have that backwards?"

She wants to ask what he'd be saving her husband from, except that she doesn't want to hear the reply.

"He'll know what I mean. He can figure it out, anyway. I'm a dangerous man."

Not an admission she anticipated. She's momentarily stunned before getting her wits about her. "Let me get this straight. You *are* threatening us. You're threatening my husband. And me."

"No, ma'am. Don't think that way. Not for a split second. I'm leaving you clear out of it, see. But you know how it goes sometimes."

"I don't. Not really. Explain it to me."

Her husband would want her to keep the other man talking. For the life of her, she can't remember why that would be right now.

"Sergeant-Detective Cinq-Mars will understand. It's a crossfire type thing."

"You're threatening us. Me, included. No, you are. I hear it in your voice. Are you proud of yourself, threatening a woman?"

"Don't get all – Look, just tell him what I said. That's all you need to do."

"Give me your exact message again. To make sure I have it right."

"Save me, too," the caller instructs. "Put it that way to him. Save me or else. He'll get it. To show I'm serious, I'm going to take down a leader. Tell him that. He'll believe me then. He'll know he's got to help us both. Me and Douglas. The two. Not just one. This time, tell him, make it him and me both."

"This time," Sandra repeats.

"Tell him. That way, you won't be sorry about nothing."

"I'll pass it on. Nice talking to you Mr. Raccoon."

"Just Raccoon will do. Thank you, ma'am."

"You're welcome, I'm sure. Please don't call again."

26. Loathing and Fear

Taking a shower at Clara's place is an undertaking. Raccoon ducks under Clara's underwear and sweaters, a blouse, nighties and a dress, everything hung over the stall and on the back of the door and from a line criss-crossing the room. A jungle in there. The shower stall is a bazaar of creams, shampoos, ointments, hair dyes, and products he cannot identify. He can't relax under the shower-head, afraid of knocking jars off the tiny shelves. Getting out again, he's nearly strangled by a bra. He can't stand it and thrashes his way through to towel off.

He's hoping tattoo parlours open before noon – or that a special one does.

He's out the door at long last and on the street and soon in luck.

"Morning, Jacques." The bell jingling overhead tells him an angel just got its wings.

A man in his mid-30s, stocky, of average height, balding prematurely as Raccoon once did, a scruff of facial hair, ornate ink visible on the right side of his neck and on his left forearm, looks up from a drawing. The art is intended for a woman's shoulder blade. He slumps back in his chair and adjusts his wire-rim glasses. A distinctive sharpness is inherent in the man's gaze; a squint that conveys intelligent oversight.

Jacques looks past Raccoon, out the store windows to the street. Satisfied that they're alone, he keeps it that way, standing and going around his visitor to lock the front door. He flips the sign that faces outward to show an animated frown. A smiley face grins into the store now. Raccoon steps further down into the partially subterranean tattoo parlour and leans up against a counter. Suggestions for heart shapes lanced by arrows are spread out before him. Those in love presume it will ever be so.

The tattoo artist known as Jacques comes past him and resumes his seat.

"What're you working on?" Raccoon asks, feigning interest.

"Snakes and ladders. I can do something similar for you, Rac. Darkness and dread. Roulette colours, red and black. The ladies will want to mount you from behind just to stare at the evil painting on your back. You'll need to beat them off with a stick, Raccoon. I can promise you this."

"I believe you."

"What are you looking for?"

"A Glock'll do."

"I shipped an M&P Shield your way not so long ago."

"Time flies when life's a party. I sold it."

"Right. Sold. You should tell me what trash cans you bank at. We recycle in the modern world now. We consider the environment."

Rac checks around the room, to assure himself that they're alone as the other man had done. "Not into recycling," he points out.

"I heard about a G42," Jacques says. "Real nice piece, a .380 cal. Light. Subcompact. Spanking new. No record of it in this country. I also got a G36 to show. Used, but not in the trade. A heavier .45. Both are autos, natch. A single stack and a double. I can get you lots else but those are ready to go out the door. Gotta tell you something, Rac. You won't like this next part."

Raccoon steps away from the counter, peruses the room. "I never like it when you start jacking up the price."

"Not jacking. It's the high cost of doing business. I got expenses."

"Tattoos take care of the overhead."

"I got inventory! You freelance guys don't know what it is to put up a shingle, go legit."

"Put the price up 20 percent, knock off 10 as my discount, we call it even. I'll take the G42. It's a new gun, right? You're positive?"

"Mine's crystal. Comes with its own birth certificate. People hold their breath to get their hands on a piece like this. Very high demand."

"Don't give me the pitch, Jacques. I'm not looking to fall in love with a fucking gun. When's delivery?"

"On-hand, like I said. Come back in an hour, I can show you then."

"What if I said 30 minutes?"

"I'd say 45 and we'd be good to go if there's no traffic."

"Do it in 40. I'll talk to you about going heavy at that time. Right now, I want your pedal to the metal on this."

"Rac, we haven't talked price. You know we have to do that. The Canadian dollar's in the toilet, man. There's a premium since your last shopping spree."

"Name it."

"Need 12."

"Ten even."

"Twelve. That's a markdown. This is like a legit dealer's piece, Rac. Really, you can't pass on this."

"Fine. I get the 12. You get the piece. Then we talk the heavy stuff."

He watches the front door of the parlour from a distance and sees Jacques return in his van approximately on time. The tattoo artist circles around and goes in by the back lane where he has a parking spot. The next time Raccoon spots him he's opening the shop again and flipping the card to the smiley face. Raccoon doesn't hurry. He keeps an eye on the premises, his other eye on the street.

A quiet day without traffic, vehicular or pedestrian, so assessing the risk is easier than usual. Nobody followed Jacques home.

The bell overhead jingles as he enters.

"Good day, sir, what can I do for you?" Jacques greets him.

Raccoon is okay with both the ruse and the civility. "Life's treating me good. You?"

"No complaints for the last half-hour or so."

When he first showed up, he was not expected. This time, the custom is to briefly talk in code to reassure each other that the previous arrangements are on track.

"I'll put you in the chair," Jacques says.

Raccoon goes past the curtain into the side alcove where Jacques can perform his artistry – with tattoos or weapons – in privacy and with equanimity. Rac is semi-prone in the client's lounge chair as Jacques opens his briefcase. Black, whistle-clean, not a speck of dust lies on the surface of the pistol.

Jacques frisks him gently, while he's lying down, hunting a wire.

He's clean.

"Target practice with a new piece is important," Raccoon stipulates.

"I agree, as long as you're talking after-purchase."

"I'm talking ammo. A beauty like this, I need to work it in. I'll need extra boxes."

"Whatever you require, Rac. Hey, I got some interesting stuff to show you. An undergarment holster. Think about it. You wear it around your gut. Walk the streets, you're like the Invisible Man. Not even a sweater on. A nice loose shirt and you're all set."

"Just the ammo for now, Jacques."

"No problem. You can't blame a businessman for trying."

Handling the weapon while he's by himself, Raccoon reconsiders the hidden holster. Without a car these days, he could use something like that. When the curtain opens again it's not the tattoo artist who's standing there. He's confronted by the men Jacques has ferried in the back of his van to have a word with him.

Chiclets and Sharpie.

"You are one hard motherfuck to pin down, Rac," Sharpie says. "Like I need a fucking appointment."

"Been busy, yeah."

Chiclets moves around behind the lounge chair where Raccoon can't see him, only the man's shadow where it falls across his own face and chest. The shadow reaches forward and removes the unloaded weapon from Raccoon's grip. No fighting this turn of events. Sharpie remains at an angle, too, forcing Rac to twist his neck to keep him in view. They're waiting for him to bolt, he assumes, so instead he stays perfectly still. He's feeling hollowed out. His blood has vacated his mind and chest to pool in his loins. Organs might gush out his rectum in the next moment.

He reminds himself to breathe.

"Whatcha been up to in the fast lane?"

"Hey, coincidence, I was planning to come see you guys."

"Is that why you're buying a piece? For your visit?"

He shifts his thinking from his brains to the wings on his heels. "Hey, you guys gave me a job to do, right? Right? I was thinking, better get that job done. Any concerns, they'll be void, know what I mean?"

"Explain it to me, Rac."

Until this moment, Sharpie has made no overt threat. Now, he takes a switchblade from his jeans pocket and snaps it open. A beautiful instrument. Lean and sharp. A shiv that keen would slice through Rac's innards like a surgeon's scalpel.

"I can tell," Raccoon says, "that you got your doubts, Sharpie. Don't. A man needs a plan, right? That's what I got. Taking off to Gatineau, playing the casino, that was my mistake. Everything went nuts, you know? Needed some time. To put things in the right perspective. That's why I'm back. To make up for that. As you can see, I'm here. I'm back."

"You like to talk, don't you, Rac? Words bust out of your mouth like diarrhea from a baby's butt."

"A man needs a plan, Sharpie. That's what I have for you."

"You want to pay me a visit. Part of your plan. First, you need Jacques to fence you a piece. Don't sound to me like a friendly visit. I'm taking precautions."

Raccoon can hear Chiclets chuckling behind him. He sounds very close.

"I need a gun to get Sykes! Sykes! Not you, not my friends! Not my business associates. That's my job, right? Get Sykes? That's why I asked for a Glock. Jacques offered me this other piece. I need it to finish the job, man. After that, with Sykes gone, I'd go see you then. You'd be more understanding, I think."

"The *flics* have him, Rac. He's unavailable right now."

"That's the reason! Why I can't wait, right? Mittens wanted him dead real quick. That's what you told me. No planning. No control. That's when things go south. They did, all the way south to fucking Antarctica, man, down there with the penguins. Polar fucking ice cap, man. I can still get the job done, Sharpie. I already made my first move."

"Coming here, huh?"

"What? No, no, this is my second move. My first move, I already talked to the wife."

Sharpie is picking at the dirt under his fingernails with the switchblade and looks over in the direction of Chiclets. Glad about that, Raccoon is guessing that he's provoked his interest at least.

"You're not married. Neither is Sykes."

"Not *my* wife. Cinq-Mars. *His* wife. You know. That cop's wife. I've set up a line of communication. Me to the cop, the ex-cop, the one Sykes is talking to."

"What fuck hole are you digging into now?"

"Sharpie, it's been on the news. Don't you tune in? That cop, he's—"

"I know what's on the fucking news! What the fuck are you talking about?"

"Sharpie, Sharpie, you gotta understand. I've got an *in*. I've got an *in* to Sykes. I been working it. Working an angle, man. I'm going to find him when he's out in the open. I swear to God. Then I'm going to powder him, man. Blow his fucking face off. You'll see, Sharpie. You'll be happy with me then. Mittens – he'll be happy with me then."

Sharpie takes a walk halfway around the lounge chair in one direction, then back again. He's wearing a smirk on his face that Raccoon does not appreciate.

"I have a different idea, Rac. Based on reality. I like to keep things real. I can't use a chainsaw in here – it'll disturb the neighbours, mess up Jacques's business reputation. In my vision of reality, Chiclets will strap you to the chair. Since I don't have a chainsaw, I'll use a regular knife to slice your balls off. How does that sound?"

"No, I—. That's—. That don't sound too good, Sharpie."

"No? Me, I kinda like the thought. Hey! You know what! Just had a better one! Chiclets, you're gonna love this."

"I love it already."

"You wanna hear this, Rac? I'll keep your balls where they are. You like that, right? I don't think Jacques wants your blood on his nice clean floor. I mean, he keeps everything germ-free in here. That's why I recommend him as a tattoo artist."

"Sounds, good," Rac says. "Keeping my balls on is good."

"I'll let you keep them. Instead, we'll tattoo them."

"No. Sharpie. Come on. No."

"Jacques won't do it. Too much skill. I could learn the trade, though. What do you think? Mind if I practice tattooing on your balls? I could draw a heart on the head of your dick, how about that? When we're done, I can tattoo fucking butterflies on your eyelids. How about that, Rac. You like the idea?"

"Not really. No. I don't like it."

"No? No? Why not?"

"Listen, I can get to Sykes."

"It's way too late for that. You screwed up. You let him go. You left him in bed and shot a cop instead. The hell were you thinking?"

He needs the wings on his heels to give him a thought, he needs to blurt something out, there's no time to even think. He has to say whatever jumps to mind and hope it makes sense. Raccoon asks, "Is Mittens pissed only about the second time, not the first?"

That provokes a silence in the room, then Sharpie demands, "Make sense to me."

"I gotta admit, at first, I thought it was a set-up. I find a dead cop. I'm holding a gun in my hands. I look fucking guilty. I mean, you wouldn't set me up! Not saying that. But that's what I was thinking. So later I'm thinking, Mittens hires me to shoot up the bank then hires me to go get Sykes. That shows he's willing to give a guy a second chance. Right? I only got three guys – well, two guys and a girl – the first time around. Sykes got away even though I shot him in the leg. Three out of four's not so bad when the fourth, he's also injured. I mean, it's a gunfight, man, fucking bullets flying everywhere. A real wild wester. Mittens fingers me to finish the job, right? Sends me to the hospital to gun Sykes down. No planning, and we come up against some pretty nasty complications, for fuck sake. You gotta understand. The main thing is, now I'm thinking, Mittens wants the job done and I got an in – an *in* – I'm talking to the wife, I'm in *communication*, man, you understand me? I can get to Sykes. I'll blow his fucking face off, man. Then everybody's happy. Mittens, especially."

Neither Sharpie nor the quiet Chiclets have anything to say. Sharpie is deep in thought, as evidenced by his steady pacing in front of their captive. He's like a prosecutor who's lost his train of thought yet continues to pace menacingly before a witness. Either he has no questions, or he has so many he can't sort through them quickly enough. Finally, he stands straight in front of Raccoon, looking down at him, and he moves his eyes slightly. That gesture causes Chiclets to reach around behind Raccoon and pin his shoulders to the lounge chair with his hands. Rac is exposed this way. He can kick, but if he does, it's likely he'll not breathe again. The strong hands on his shoulders have the effect of accelerating Raccoon's desperation and fear.

"Rac," Sharpie says, "just so I got this right—" and he glares down at Raccoon, aiming the tip of his knife between his eyeballs, about four inches away, and says, "*You* shot up the bank? *You* did?"

Rac tries to move his head, his flexibility limited by the hold Chiclets has on him. If he could shrug, he would, only he can't, so he says, "Yeah. I did, yeah. You didn't know?"

"You – fucking – shot up – *our* bank – killed *our* people – and now – and now – you want *what*? Fucking mercy? From me?"

"It was orders. From Mittens. I thought you knew. If I get an order from Mittens, I go fucking do it."

"You didn't tell us that at the gym, in our meeting."

"Course not. I'm not going to bring it up anywhere at any time. Lips are sealed, right? I just, you know, I just mention it here, that's all. I thought you knew. Sharpie, how come you didn't know?"

He sees his tormentor share more than a single glance with the man behind him. Either they know something that he's confirming or he's revealing something new to them. He doesn't know his next move.

"You bullshitting me, Rac? Tell me," Sharpie says in a tone that's calmer, more deliberate now. "Why the hell would Mittens want to shoot up his own bank? Were you supposed to steal the money?"

"Why would I do that? I wasn't supposed to touch the money. It's not mine. And I didn't. What's the matter with you? I mean, it's his money. Why would Mittens steal his own money?" Sow confusion, his instinct is to do exactly that. Confusion might keep him alive.

Chiclets finally says something. "Since when does Mittens talk to you, punk? He called you? You talked to him, one-on-one?"

"No. Of course not. He doesn't talk to me. He's in jail. He had an intermediary."

"An intermediary," Sharpie repeats, and scoffs. "Who's this fucking imposter, the Man on the Fucking Moon?" He shaves the air with his blade close to Rac's left eye.

"Not him, no."

"Who then?"

"You don't know?"

"That's why I'm asking. That's why you're answering."

"His daughter."

"Who?"

"You don't know her?"

"Mélanie?"

"So, you do know her."

"Mélanie."

"Her. She asked me to do it."

"Do what, exactly? I mean, fucking *exactly* what did she say?"

"Kill everybody," Raccoon says. He doesn't have to make this up. "In the bank. Make it quick and thorough. In and out."

"Quick and thorough. In and out," Sharpie echoes.

"Kill everybody," Rac says again.

Sharpie has backed away, to consider this news.

"Here's the thing," Raccoon starts in.

"Shut up a minute," Sharpie says. Chiclets takes his hands off the prisoner's shoulders. That's a relief. That Sharpie is thinking the matter over is an opening.

"Here's the thing," Raccoon tries again after a respectful pause. "I can get to Sykes. I can eliminate his presence off the face of the earth. Only I can do that. *Because I have an in.* I set up a line of communication."

Sharpie looks at him, almost with pity. "You're as dumb as a doughnut hole, aren't you, Rac?"

"Why say that? I'm not – I think on my feet. You said so yourself. You did, Sharpie."

"If Sykes didn't shoot up the bank, Rac, then what do I care if you kill him or not? He didn't do nothing to us. *You* shot up the bank. *You're* the one we want dead now. Do you see that? See how stupid you are, Rac? Please, figure that much out before you die."

"Mittens wants Sykes dead. You got to take that into account, right, Sharpie?"

Sharpie takes his time responding, then asks, "Why does he want him dead?"

"How should I know? You still got to take that into account."

"Maybe yes. Maybe no. I'll tattoo your balls anyway. Sketch a Harley."

"Something else. I can blow his face off. Sykes. His face. I got an in. But I can also get him out in the open. You know? Bring him in alive. I mean, do you know why Mittens wants him out of the picture? It's not for the bank shooting on account of he ordered that himself. Even if he didn't tell you. You'll be in the dark for all time if you're okay with that. But I can get him out alive. Bring him in here. Nobody else can. I can do that. I don't have to blow his face off, right? I mean, those guys – Mittens found out they were stealing from him, right? That's it, I bet. Didn't want to trouble you. Or he thinks you're involved with that so gets his daughter to call me.

Here's the thing. How about I bring him in alive, this guy Sykes? Does that change the picture? I mean, with respect to the tattoos on my balls here?"

Sharpie continues to stare at him, and Raccoon knows not to show his fear too much, except that he's got the trembles again, his fingers quivering. The switchblade button is clicked, and the blade vanishes into the handle, and Rac thinks he might have his life back.

"If you get him out alive that might explain things for everybody. We'll take you back to Clara's. Hold you there. Give us time to work this out. Yeah, your lucky day. You can get laid again. Or try. Heard you can't get it up anymore. Can't say I'm surprised, Rac, looking at you. Or it was Clara's fault. She's not so hot like she used to be, hey. By the way, you know whose side she's on? Yeah. Clara, she's always been our girl."

Leading him out, they pass by Jacques in the back room. Raccoon mutters to him, "Way to go. You lost your best customer."

"Don't give yourself too much credit, Rac," Sharpie advises him. "We provide way more business than you ever could."

Jacques, in fact, will drive the van as they take him over to Clara's place.

27. Simple and Pure

A high black edifice, the Parthenais Detention Centre casts an imposing shadow, one that traverses the rooftops of the surrounding low-rise community like a sundial's gnomon. SQ Headquarters occupy the lower floors. Jail cells on the upper levels afford stupendous views of the city, the river, and the bump of Mount Royal. Prisoners are free to appreciate the vistas as they sit in dread of court dates and sentencing.

Sandra would not permit her husband to travel to Parthenais without being in his company. The attending physician reluctantly complied, asserting that Émile was neither to walk nor drive. He should have no exercise beyond sitting up in a chair. Sandra insisted on enforcing the rules and drove him in. After her hubby has gone up to the top floors, she hunkers down in an outdoor parking lot munching a muffin, the windows of their Escalade open to summer air and traffic noise.

She wishes she could quell an anxiety seeping through her bloodstream after taking that call from a maniac.

Émile Cinq-Mars believes he's brought down two birds by tossing a single stone. He's left the hospital, a giant relief, and his wife is along as his escort – which helps keep her safe. In the aftermath of the call from Raccoon Rybachuk, he doesn't want her home alone until the fugitive has been apprehended.

Douglas Sykes is waiting in the interview room as he wheels in. Together again, they sit across a utilitarian table. Way up here in Jack's beanstalk, not far below the clouds, the windows are still heavily barred. Intimidating, that.

"Gloves off," Cinq-Mars warns him.

“Okay. What’s going on?”

“Your buddy Raccoon threatened me. I can live with it. I’m not sure he can. He also threatened my wife.”

Sykes’s head momentarily slumps in genuine dismay. “For the record, *buddy* isn’t the right word. Not sure what to call him.”

“Like I said, Douglas, the gloves are off. Me and you, we’re not going around the mulberry bush again.”

“What bush is that?”

“Don’t play the snitty smartass with me. You only pretend to be illiterate. You know as many nursery rhymes as the next kid down the block.”

“Not denying it, Émile. But that was not my point.”

Cinq-Mars waits for him to say what he obviously wants to get out. Sykes is trepidatious, though, as the man across from him appears to be in a brittle mood.

“Mulberries don’t grow on bushes, Émile. That’s all I’m saying.” Quickly, catching the other man’s expression, he offers up his palms in a form of surrender.

“Seriously?” Cinq-Mars asks him. He has never determined whether the man is an adversary or an associate. He’s never wanted to call him a stool pigeon, although there’s history to support the accusation, and he’s never wanted to call him a friend, although a degree of compatibility has been present between them. He does know that no other criminal has ever advised him that the mulberry is not a bush. “Go ahead. Explain.”

“Some say,” Sykes contends, “that back in time the rhyme said bramble bush. The alliteration was a tongue-twister, so it got changed to mulberry. Others say it was more about the Brits starting up a silk business. An enterprise that hit the skids. It went bust. The mulberry trees – *trees*, Émile, the ones the Brits were importing for silkworms to feed on – keeled over in the chilly English countryside.” Sykes sings the line, “‘*Here we go ’round the mulberry bush on a cold and frosty morning.'* A jolt of sarcasm, folks say. Makes sense to me."

Cinq-Mars leans back in his chair and a measure of the choler that burrowed through him earlier dissipates. He never thought that this would be the first question out of his mouth, yet asks, "What would've become of you, Douglas, if you didn't go down the road you travelled?"

Sykes has a look as though he's been sideswiped, that his inquisitor is touching on ground that ought to be out of bounds.

"Simple question," Cinq-Mars probes further. "No secret. You had potential and did nothing with it."

"It can cause a man pain, Émile, to think *woulda, coulda.* The greater the gap between a man's highest expectations for himself and the sorry result that followed, the bigger the hurt."

Cinq-Mars prolongs his stare.

The man offers back a worried shrug.

Cinq-Mars keeps staring until Sykes chooses to expand his answer.

"My mother," he begins, "had no great ambition for me. She wanted me to be a good man. That was about it. Missed that boat, hey? I used to tell her; she was aiming too low. I wanted to get up there in life. Yet everybody can see I got nowhere near her low bar. You don't have to be a total asshole, Émile, to point that out to me."

"She never thought of it as low."

"I get that now. I'm wiser now. She wanted me to be a teacher, Émile. Her dream. Not mine. Teach high school. She thought that would be the bees' knees, as she put it. Me, a nursemaid to the bratty masses. I wanted to be a philosopher, something dignified. You remember, Émile. You and me, we had big talks."

They exchanged a smile, which Cinq-Mars put into words. "That's not a real job, Douglas. Philosopher."

"Remind me about that, why don't you? Nobody's going to sit me on a rock on a hill with a shade tree over my head and say, 'Please, oh wise man, philosophise. Think out loud for us. Your cheque is in the mail.'"

"Noble," Cinq-Mars comments.

"What can I say? I knew nothing about the world until I got out there. OK, I read books. They helped. Books are good prep. The world, though, turned out different than I expected. Know why? It wasn't only because I tried, and failed, to ditch a man's feet. It wasn't only my fucking trauma like the shrinks say. And it wasn't only because the world is a shithole, which it is. I'll tell you why. Because *I* was different than I expected."

"I see why you wanted to be a philosopher. You're a natural."

"Go ahead. Make fun. See where that gets you."

Cinq-Mars can extend the discussion, he suffers from the inclination, except that matters have come to a head. He began by saying that he wasn't going to traipse around the mulberry bush with this man, yet that's precisely where he's been led. He reminds Douglas Sykes that Raccoon is on the run, and that his pal phoned his wife and spoke to her in a tone that conveyed an underlying threat. Now he wants nothing but answers.

"Raccoon saying that, doing that, being on the run. That's all bad."

"I'm not here to talk about him. We're going to talk about you, Douglas, and more importantly, you're going to talk. No more sitting on a hill philosophising. I want straight dope out of you."

"What can I say that hasn't been said?"

"What do you know? That's one thing. How do you know it? That's another. To be clear, I want nothing that goes around the mulberry bush on a cold and frosty morning."

"Life is hard, then you die." Raccoon's father had taught him that. Raccoon then passed his acquired wisdom on to his younger friend, Douglas Sykes. "Doesn't matter what creek you're pissing in." That was another burst of sacred lore passed down from father to son, then from friend to friend. "What counts, your stream should be pure gold. If it's red, you're dead. You wanna be golden."

The young Douglas thought it meant that, in life, your health counts more than anything. He was a philosopher that way. Raccoon took it to mean you had to be rich.

"That's the difference between me and you," Raccoon told him. "I know what's what. You think too much."

Sykes didn't argue.

All three went down to the railway tracks together. Father and son, and the son's loyal friend. In the woods, they raised ghosts to prance in the breeze and distract the engineer and brakemen. Both boys helped lash the man to the rails in advance of the train. Douglas cried. Raccoon told him to stop that. Mr. Rybachuk said he had to get the insurance for his family. Raccoon told Douglas they needed to do it for the money, so Raccoon and his mother could get a place of their own. Move out of Douglas's house, and Douglas Sykes wanted that, too. He wanted to have his own room back, instead of sharing, instead of having to listen to Raccoon's crazed talk half the night. He didn't want to hear about what he was going to do to some girl. Always something horrible, like making her take a crap in the woods while he watched. Mad stuff. He didn't want to hear it, and he went down to the railway tracks with the man who was determined to kill himself because the cancer was killing him anyway. "I shit and piss blood, kid. Red is dead." He was in serious agony. If the mob caught up to him they'd do worse than the cancer, this was the only way out. He'd finally make a big score, and he wanted to do that for his family. "I'm a goddamned saint," he claimed. Only it wasn't for his family; the boys just didn't know that yet.

"We tied him down, Émile. Tight like he wanted. We had to make this look like murder and take away the body parts because that proved it was murder, see. Not suicide."

Raccoon sat with his legs crossed at the base of the railway grade and when his father's head was sliced off by the locomotive it flipped into the air, then it tumbled down the grade and came to a stop right on Raccoon's lap. His father's dead eyes staring straight up at him. Blood leaking out. Even that boy who had a fetish for the macabre emitted a scream. He was the only one, though, who could hear himself. Douglas saw him screaming, the mouth agape, the neck reddening with the strain of it. The brakes on the train were screeching and the boxcars banging together as the engineer had either seen something or had felt the wheels lurch and had braked hard. The ferocious clamour of the train muffled out any sound that emitted from Raccoon's throat. And then the boy looked up to see where his father's hands had landed.

On the other side of the tracks, young Douglas glimpsed the two feet spin away, then shut his eyes. He wanted to look no more. Still, a flash of blood was imprinted on his synapses, the feet in the air, his own life gagging in his throat. He kept his eyes shut as the boxcars battled and the brakes squealed as if the sounds were ringing right along his spine.

A long train can only stop slowly. When it finally stood still, creaking as it breathed and releasing air from the brakes like periodic sympathetic sighs, the locomotive was way in the distance beyond a bend, behind factory walls. The caboose was nowhere to be seen, far in the opposite distance.

The head and tail of a snake that had swallowed his world whole.

"Get me the shoes!"

The first words that Douglas Sykes heard in the abrupt silence of the motionless train was a command from Raccoon to fetch his father's shoes.

"What?" he asked back, feebly.

"Get me his shoes! Get the shoes off his feet!"

"What? Why?"

"I want them! Get them! Now, Douglas!"

He had to locate them on the crushed stone grade. All bloody where the ankle was severed. Blackened at the point of impact by the steel wheels as if they'd been scorched. Not a clean cut, a portion of the ankle crushed. In a daze, the boy tried to hold his gaze away as he untied the laces. He removed the shoes from the horrid feet.

"Put the socks in the shoes!" Raccoon called from the other side of the tracks. Looking under the train's carriage, Douglas could see his friend moving around. He didn't know what he was doing. He didn't want to know.

He didn't question why he wanted the socks, or why he wanted the shoes.

Between them, the body of the man. Headless. Without hands. Without feet.

"Throw them to me!" Raccoon commanded. The boy was down on all fours and watching him now. When Douglas threw the first shoe, it hit the inside of the far rail and landed next to the bloody torso. He picked up the second shoe and threw it more accurately this time. It went under the train and across the tracks and Raccoon retrieved it. Then, after crawling under the boxcar next to his dead dad, Raccoon confiscated the first shoe. "Now pick up his feet and get out of here."

Douglas had not brought along a bag. He had not honestly believed this would happen. He suddenly knew that he couldn't walk down the street with a man's foot in each hand, so he tucked them under his shirt, against his skin.

"That's not what you told me the first time," Cinq-Mars interrupted.

"Okay, so I'm telling you now. You want the truth or not?"

"Go on."

He had to get a move on. In both directions, he spotted railway personnel – they looked like tiny men, being so far away – coming down the tracks, searching for whatever they might have run over.

They were hoping for a dog. They had stopped the train, though, because they expected a suicide, and so walked slowly, not wanting to arrive where they were going. Not wanting to see what they must see.

A block away, he went down an alley and plucked a sack from a garbage bin, which once held 50 pounds of potatoes, and a plastic bag that he emptied of debris, and walked away with two human feet in the bag and the bag in the sack slung over his shoulder. He now had to find somewhere to ditch his cargo. All that he ended up doing was wandering, until a cop ordered him to stop.

That cop would vouch for him, over time, and help get him off. He was never sure why. He didn't think the cop knew why either. After that, some talk arose about a debt owed. That part of the deal he understood.

He didn't pay the debt. Not immediately. After he was free of the cops and the courts, he ran. People in his district looked at him as though he was a madman; he couldn't stay home. He said goodbye to his mother and when she cried, he asked her not to. He was crying himself. He said he'd write. She pleaded for him not to go. He again promised that he'd write, as if that solved everything. Douglas Sykes stood on a highway's shoulder and stuck out his thumb. He could scarcely believe it when the first car stopped. He was on his way. He wanted the world to take him on, to consume him. "Chew me up and spit me out." He issued that challenge, even as he ran to get into the car. He didn't know why he made that demand, and he didn't believe that the world would do that, neither chew him up nor spit him out, but it did. Only as it was happening did he begin to understand what it meant.

On the road, he was amazed and at times alarmed by the kindness of strangers. People fed him indiscriminately. They gave him odd jobs – at a motel, in a restaurant, cutting grass or washing pots – and paid him fairly. They drove him where they were going, and they also drove him out of their way. He was often suspicious with no need to be and distrusting which was sometimes justified. In a town in northern Alberta, the town clerk paid for a room in a house and gave him a food voucher for the local restaurant. He ate so much he created a scene. Some folks wanted him gone. The local cop, not the brightest bulb, called him a transient. He didn't know what that was, had never heard the term, and couldn't agree or disagree when the cops posed the question. "Are you a transient?" A sinful thing to be one, apparently. Other citizens stuck up for him. He volunteered to help pour cement for a new church. A few folks were coming over to his side; others still wanted him gone. They were poor enough, they said, without paying his bills. When a travelling carnival came to town he was hired on, then he left with them. He had both aroused contempt and received hospitality; he could not believe how people locked horns over the issue of whether feeding a homeless runaway kid was proper.

He'd been hungry when first he arrived in that town.

He knew what it meant to be hungry and didn't like it one bit.

Hunger made him emotionally weak, he found out. It broke him down.

The carnival, a job that started as a lark, turned grim. The work was physically demanding; he revelled in that; unfortunately, some people proved to be mean-spirited. And worse. His boss went from town-to-town seducing underage girls, and sometimes when they were less than willing or hesitant he forced himself on them. The man expected Douglas Sykes to help him out in certain situations. The boy knew where associations of that nature would lead, so took the coins he'd cosseted and lit out on his own again.

In northern British Columbia, he was sleeping in a culvert when he was befriended by a collection of ex-cons. They were rounded up and conscripted to fight a forest fire and he didn't mind being a ground-pounder for the summer. He found that he enjoyed outdoor work and didn't mind when the weathers or conditions were harsh. He felt alive then, and strangely untroubled. When the fires were put out, he had money in the bank, and in his jeans, too, until he got rolled in Prince George and stabbed in the belly. He healed up in the hospital, then went on welfare while he got his strength back, then returned to the bar scene even though he was underage. One evening, he spotted his attacker playing a game of shuffleboard. He waited for closing. Followed the man back to his hovel hotel. Called to him just as he reached the door. The man asked who was there. He couldn't make out the boy's face in the dark, the street lights at his back. Rather than answer him, Douglas Sykes slashed his belly. Nothing more, and something less, than what had been done to him, and how his victim had howled. He awoke the dead. The outcry alerted a couple of cops napping in their patrol car. The chase was on. Ill-equipped for a life of crime Sykes was still holding the bloody knife when the cops ran him down. Weapon in hand, he wasn't slipping this charge, and got eight months. The judge considered the victim in passing sentence; he wasn't worth much in the mind of the court. Sykes served 11 weeks only and going out the gate, returning to the sun of freedom, the last guard to have contact with him gave him a mighty swift kick in the ass.

That was unwarranted, he believed.

He never got over the bitterness of that.

From prison, he had written to his mom. Told her he was doing "amazing." She told Émile Cinq-Mars that her boy was doing fine, he was fighting forest fires, travelling through the countryside, gaining experience. Cinq-Mars had been trying to track him down. The policeman had access to records, though, and found out where her son was living. A short while later, the mother passed on, and Cinq-Mars, anonymously, arranged for the news to be conveyed to the prisoner.

Douglas Sykes decided, getting out, that he wasn't cut out for the real world. He went home. Only it didn't feel like home anymore. He visited his mother's gravesite. That was important to him. Then he found work picking worms. That ended in disaster.

He got off again on another accusation of murder. His old friend Raccoon was ecstatic. He didn't know how the kid did it. He was a genius! Douglas Sykes didn't think so, and left town again. This time he chose not to hitchhike. He took a bus and ended up in Vancouver, on the coast, as far from home as he could go. Big city, big mountains, big sea. A nude beach, even. He drifted into an alternative lifestyle. Did drugs. He had more sex than he imagined possible. The people he was meeting read books, too, like him, and talked about movies, which he learned to do. He got a job at the post office by lying about his criminal past. He said he didn't have one. He was right to think that no one would check. He was beginning to imagine a future, a life. He was rounded up during a demonstration in which he was nothing more than an interested bystander gazing at the pretty girls and then the cops pulled his sheet on him. He and a detective discussed a variety of topics. Sykes shrugged him off, and the judge shrugged off the bogus charge. He'd been identified, and lost his job, although he wasn't sure how that happened. A good guess: the detective brought up his record with the post office. Shortly after that he was identified again, this time by a couple of guys who'd met him on the inside. They had a couple of beers together. Caught up. Went out back and did a little dope. Shared a few laughs. Stole a car on their way home.

Another stint in prison and this time he got a letter from Raccoon that was forwarded from his old address. Raccoon was asking where the hell he was because he was out in Vancouver himself and wanted to see him, except he never seemed to be home. He let him know where he was. Suddenly, Douglas Sykes was granted favours on the inside, night and day, and when he got out he was offered a job as a broom in a strip club.

"What's a broom?" Cinq-Mars asks.

"I cleaned up."

"Literally?"

"Literally. The dust, the puke, the people. Not all bouncers had brains. When a bouncer didn't have a head on his shoulders, I was his head. I told him when to jump. I told him when to chill. That way, I kept the place clean and kept the peace, too. Mostly – this is how come I kept the job for so long – I took care of the girls."

"Meaning?"

"Protected them. Saved them from harm. We even started a book club. Sort of. I'd read books then paraphrase the story for them. Sometimes I improved on the original. Kept the ladies entertained that way."

"You weren't pimping."

"Accused of. But not pimping, no. Not for one fucking second. I let them tip me when that was fair. You know, after mopping up puke in their dressing room. Or rousting out a drunk from a girl's face. I never took a dime from a girl otherwise and not once did I set anyone up. Guys would ask if I could make a recommendation, you know? I told them, they were on their own. If that didn't work, I'd point to a real pimp. Just because it's on my record, pimping, doesn't mean it happened. That's bogus."

"I didn't see that on your record."

"Oh. Right. That got expunged."

Detectives in Vancouver and detectives in Montreal took out a claim on him. The Vancouver cops expunged a few matters. He was gang-connected, in a minor way. Positioned. In a club. Around the players. He picked things up. He talked to the girls. He knew stuff. He'd spill. Occasionally. That's all he had to do. All that was expected of him. Spill. If not, he'd get more pimp time in the pen. That was the deal.

"I owe it all to you, Émile."

"I didn't sic any bark dogs on your heels."

"Wasn't sure how deep your fist went up my rectum, Émile. Up to the elbow. Up to the shoulder. Though I never could tell if it was your fist."

"Wasn't me."

"I didn't want to think so. Your people, though. Your firm."

"Montreal cops?"

"Yep. Montreal."

"Why?"

"You don't know? Biker boys party in Vancouver. They move people in and out. Vancouver alerted Montreal cops who figured I could hear things out there that might not be spoken out loud back home. Then a Vancouver badge figured that if I could do that for cops back east, why not contribute to the local economy while I'm at it?"

"So, you were a stool pigeon, so to speak."

"I was a rat trapped in a rat hole. This is news to you? The years went by, Émile. That's it. The years went by. But, hey, about my good potential. I tried. Three times, I started up a business. My tough luck. Three times I had an enterprise fell flat."

"What kind of businesses?" Cinq-Mars asked. The man keeps surprising him.

"First one, a tiny corner store type thing. Lost my shirt."

"How come?"

"My biker pals showed up on their Harleys. You know, to show support. After that, the neighbourhood moms and dads and their kids stayed clear. That was a bummer."

"Did you go back to being a broom after that?"

"The job was available. Next business, I thought I'd work with what I had going for me, you know. Opened up a specialty clothing store."

"What specialty?"

"Hooker clothes. Stripper costumes. That sort of thing. Even, get this, pimp duds."

"Sounds like a winning scheme to me."

"That's what I thought. Trouble is, I had too many friends. I thought that was a plus. I was expecting to sell to my friends, but they expected discounts and giveaways. They expected credit. They didn't expect to ever pay off their credit. I went under."

"Strike two."

"My final swing-and-a-miss was a bar. Had to finagle that one due to my criminal record, so officially I wasn't on the books, and unofficially I got swindled by my so-called silent partners. They weren't all that silent when they put a gun to my head."

"Your biker pals couldn't help?"

"My biker pals put a gun to my head. When it came to business, we weren't pals anymore. It was fine with them though if I went back to work at the strip club."

"Gotcha."

"I got screwed. That happens in business. I packed it in after that."

"Speaking of after that, did you stay out of trouble or were you just getting away with stuff? Your record is lean."

"Both. I never went looking for trouble, Émile. Some of it found me. I was living in rough company. This and that, sometimes for the dough, sometimes for the excitement, or to prove my value, you know. Sometimes out of despair. I'm serious. Don't matter if you don't believe me. I liked to tell the shrinks in the can – who I gotta say, were very fond of me, they liked working on me, I was a challenge or at least more articulate than the average joe-con – anyway, what was I saying?"

"You'd tell the shrinks in the can."

"Right. Sometimes I committed a robbery, or fenced stolen goods, out of pure and simple despair. Either that or pure and simple depression. A dark cloud comes over me and I know I'm doing wrong. I didn't hurt people. I want you to know that. I didn't play with guns or intimidate or cause damage. Not even property damage. All in all, I've been a pretty damn straight upright citizen, for a criminal. That's why I don't deserve to go down for these murders. Wasn't me. Not my way of being."

Émile does a short wheel-around within the confines of the small room. "Let me dial this back a bit. You implied that Raccoon had something to do with you being protected inside the pen, then getting you the job on the outside. He used his gang connections. Is that a fact or speculation?"

"He took the credit, yeah. Told me so, anyway. Said he put in a good word for me with the Hells and that word travelled out to Matsqui Institution to give me a free ride. I did not complain, I'm willing to say. I owed, of course, after that. I worked an honest payback job in one Hells bar or another. You could say I was trusted, within a strict limit. But yeah. I heard stuff. I learned stuff. Most of it I kept to myself. I was not stupid. Never wanted to be caught out. That would not be an acceptable demise, if you know what I mean. Friends of mine got blindfolded and made to kneel for their final prayers and got a swift bullet in the back of the head. Merely for overstepping. I didn't overstep as far as the Hells could see. Sometimes my Vancouver cop pushed me. I pushed back. I told him, 'I'll tell you what I tell you, you won't get nothing more. If that's not good enough, take a long jog around Stanley Park, or feed the pigeons, just don't come bother me.' Won that one usually. Not always. A dangerous life, Émile. I had friends, and the girls to look after and a few looked after me, now and then. We were kind to one another, let's put it that way. I had my books to read. In my own way, I was sitting on a rock on a mountaintop under a shade tree and contemplating the universe. I had become what I wanted to be, a fucking philosopher. With an income to boot. Time went by and the hell with it, I survived. Not many would've. Not many could've. Not many can say they did."

Cinq-Mars works to get past the fact that he likes this guy. Always has.

"This is what we know, Douglas," he tells him. "Somewhere down the line, you pissed off the Hells. They want you dead. They sent the wrong man to kill you. Consequently, you're still alive. Good for you. They sent that man back again to kill you twice. You're still alive. But a cop is dead. Let's say Raccoon did it. He has since threatened my wife and me. I'm supposed to get him off, that's what he says, because I got you off back in the day. Twice. I'm the miracle worker. That's what he expects from me now. Miracles are not my stock-and-trade. I'm retired, and when I did have a stock-and-trade it was incarcerating felons. That's what I plan to do here. Tell me, straight up, what did you do, or what do you know, that the Hells so badly want you dead?"

"If it is the Hells."

"It's the Hells. Or someone in the Hells."

"Like Mittens."

"Like Mittens, if you want to go with that. Why do you? What do you know, Douglas? Who did you tell it to? Why are you a walking dead man on this green earth?"

Cinq-Mars counts the man's frustration as genuine. He considers that he's blind or deaf to his own knowledge. He needs to cajole, and threaten, and coax, and tweak whatever secrets are hidden within him to leak out.

"I swear, Émile, I haven't been telling anything to anybody lately. Call Vancouver. I'll give you the cop's name. He'll tell you he hasn't worked me in a long time."

"What about Montreal cops?"

"They forgot I existed. You're not the only cop who retired."

"What are you doing here, Douglas? In Montreal, I mean. Why did you come back?"

"I'm done with the life. Packing it in. Retiring. It's not only cops who get to do that, though it looks like you're no better at it than me. Here's the difference. In my business, with my connections, I'm obliged to get away from where I was if I'm packing it in. I needed a place to go. Why not back home? Where else?"

"You can afford to retire?"

"Émile, I'm sorry to break it to you: Nobody who works in a strip club doesn't make money. I've always been frugal. No fast cars. No slow ones either. I've put a few dimes aside. One reason I stayed so long. I needed a dream. I dreamed. This is it. I'm back here to sit on a rock and read books and chat to people of average intelligence. I just want to live the life I was supposed to live all along. What better place than here, where I'm from? You can name some other dusty old town but look at me. Look. I don't fit in. Not fucking anywhere."

He had to keep him on point, keep scratching away. "Okay. Let's say I believe you. You haven't told anybody anything. You haven't betrayed or gone behind anybody's back. You're totally in the clear on that. Still. Bad folks want you dead. They go to extremes to take care of that business. They kill other people to make it look as though you're not the target. Why? Why is it so important to have you dead?"

“Émile, I fucking told you. I don’t know.”

“I accept that.”

Sykes is surprised. “Are we done here, then?”

“I accept that you don’t know. I don’t accept that there’s nothing. Definitely, you know something you shouldn’t. You didn’t pass it on. You didn’t put it up for trade. Most likely, you didn’t even pay attention. Someone else has, though. I could be wrong, but staying in Vancouver, it seems you were safe. Nobody cared. Coming back here set somebody off. You may know something that other people *know* you know, even if you yourself are unaware of your own secret knowledge. Follow my drift?”

Sykes does catch his gist, and sighs. He gives himself a head scratch, literally, as though that might free up his brain cells to be more revealing.

“What did you overhear? That you kept to yourself? That you then forgot because you didn’t rank it as vitally important? As anything worthwhile.”

He seems about to throw him off again, as he might toss off a heavy blanket, as though his exasperation is about to implode. He slams both fists against the tabletop and curses, loudly, on the brink of being out of control. Then he stops. His expression flat, he stares straight back at Cinq-Mars.

A notion dawns.

Then he says, “Oh shit. Was that it?”

“Tell me,” Cinq-Mars encourages him.

“Oh shit. Émile, that’s it. I wasn’t going to tell anybody. I didn’t give a damn about it. Yeah, it concerns Montreal Hells, but I was in Vancouver. What did I care? I don’t deal with Montreal. I mean, this is about a year, year-and-a-half ago. It went dormant, not that I gave it much thought at the time. Just people showing off a little bravado. Being self-important. That’s what I thought. Could be I was wrong if you consider the source.”

"What source?"

"I didn't pass nothing on."

"You moved to Montreal. Whatever you're talking about, did it have anything to do with Montreal?"

Sykes both shrugs and nods, a contradiction. "Yes and no," he explains. "The Hells are planning to take over the Maritime provinces. New Brunswick, Nova Scotia, P.E.I. They want to control the east coast ports."

Cinq-Mars demonstrates that he's not impressed. "That's documented, Douglas. From what I hear, they've already amalgamated a few satellite gangs, brought them into the fold under their control."

"Yeah. I heard that, too. It's gone smoothly so far, right?"

"They're doing well. It's worrisome, to say the least."

"It might not be smooth sailing the whole way through."

"Go on."

"What I heard. Part of the plan means to eliminate a few people once they're in control."

"And you didn't think that that was worth mentioning to anyone?"

"You never want to talk about stuff like that. You only want to forget it. Émile, I'm not working with Montreal. I never worked to take down the Hells. The occasional drug bust. I could fix it to never look like the intel came from me. The occasional heist. The cops could intercept, make it look accidental. That paved my way through life, Émile. Kept me out of the can most years. I even went into the can once in a blue moon to make myself look good. I mean, bad. I had the right friends inside. I was reasonably secure. Somebody says that this and that full-patch will go down, my skin crawls. I don't want to know. It's too dangerous. Not part of my pay scale. I forget about it. I never heard nothing. I'm good at that, now that I think about it."

"Did this guy name names?"

"Names were named. I'm not connected with the east. They meant nothing to me."

"You remember these names?"

"Nicknames. I can pull up a few. If someone ran down a list, a bell might ring in my head."

"Who do you remember? Take a stab at it. Hold on. I want to write this down. If you do remember, I don't want to forget."

Cinq-Mars knocks on the door to put in a request for a pad and pen. While he's waiting, he studies Douglas Sykes. The man appears to be fretting, more than usual.

"What's wrong?"

"You're not into miracles. That's too bad. If I turn on the Hells, I'll need a miracle."

"Cross that bridge later. It's not in front of us yet."

"Speak for yourself."

"Somebody already thinks you crossed them. Or that you might."

The paper and pen arrive. Cinq-Mars swings the door shut and wheels himself back to the table, although he prefers to write on his lap. "Go ahead," he instructs.

Five names in all. Brew. Tapeworm. Shutterbug. Chiclets. And Sharpie.

"These five were to get whacked? You're not connected here at all, are you?" Cinq-Mars asked him.

"Barely. Émile, the people out west, when I announced my retirement, they cleared me to come back east. Everything was above board. I mean, I was only a broom for God's sake. I'm not a security risk."

"People here, they heard you were coming."

"Yeah. Those eastern guys, I know nothing about them. I reported in, to keep myself in the clear. I think that's all the names. I guess my memory isn't shot yet."

"Douglas, two of these names are local. Not eastern. Local. This is serious and very smelly manure you're standing in right now."

"Local? No, I thought they were east."

"You overheard a hit on *local* Hells. *By* local Hells. Douglas, what were the circumstances? How was it you were eavesdropping on such a key talk? Did they say anything to you? Warn you?"

"No, I was napping. In a booth, in the club. Before we opened. I'd been cleaning up. I often had a nap before the girls came in and the place opened. They sat down in the next booth over. No, I think it was two over. Here's the thing. They didn't see me. They left before I got up. If somebody saw me get up later, I didn't notice. Anyway, I wasn't pressed at all. I just thought, that was interesting and forgot about it."

"I'll ask you again. Who was the source? Who was running his mouth in Vancouver?"

For some reason, Douglas Sykes is shaking his head.

"Not a guy," he explains. "That's why I thought it was only self-importance. Nothing more than bar talk."

"A woman? A moll?"

"Not exactly."

"What, exactly?"

"Mittens. His daughter. Her name, I forget."

"Mélanie," Cinq-Mars tells him. "Holy shit, Douglas."

"Yeah," he agrees. "Yeah. I didn't realize. I thought they were talking about east coast bikers. A few get whacked, who cares? I didn't think the talk was about their own people, too."

28. Mouse and Cat

Sergeant-Detective William Mathers returns to his desk downtown amid a rash of ribbing.

"Bill, hey. Heard somebody kidnapped you. Jay-sus. Who the hell would pay a ransom to get you back?"

"Worse than kidnapped," another cop qualified. "Abducted."

"There's a difference?"

"You bet. In a kidnapping somebody expects a ransom. Abducted means nobody will buy you back. A sniff-dog finds your bones in a ditch."

His colleagues assert that he's been lost to the dark side, up *nord*; they belong to the southern hemisphere of the police department, *sud*. Although the repartee is light, everyone's aware that a cop's life has been lost; Mathers is working the case and if anyone can do anything to help, Bill need only ask.

He wants the complete file on Raccoon Rybachuk.

At lightning speed, it's on his desk.

An item strikes him as trenchant: The man has a weakness for the lure of casinos. Mathers orders security to be notified and provided with a photo at the local hotspot. Knowing that the industriousness of security officers is forever hit-and-miss, he also orders a pair of uniforms onto the premises in plainclothes. He hopes they won't lose too much off their pay cheques loitering near the slots.

Should Raccoon fail to resist a roulette wheel, he'll be nabbed.

Next is a list of known associates. Mostly bikers and other aromatic felons. Mathers divvies up the list to have each beastly ex-con observed in his natural habitat. One name he peels off for himself. As a *sud* detective, he monitored the hook-and-ladder crowd – the second storey guys and their fences; the purse snatchers; the pickpockets; the muggers; the corner store stickup nits, the jiffy car thieves and dope dealers – anybody looking to climb the ladder of success to become gang-worthy by developing a hook. They all get scrutinized on his daily watchlist. He knows who hangs out where and when and how they operate. The pimps and stragglers, the grifters and bone-breakers, the pushers and gunsmiths, the fraud artists and counterfeiters, the cheaters and molesters: they dwell upon his patch of concrete. And here, on Raccoon's rap sheet, a detective penciled in the name of Clara Kendrick. Formerly a biker's moll, she has lived a life of woe. A reformed druggie, the last Mathers heard. He knows the lady, has both arrested her and on occasion dissolved her resistance to use her to procure information. He transcribes the scribbles in the margin: a detective looking in on Raccoon five years earlier jotted down that the object of his reconnaissance was enjoying a fling with one Clara Kendrick.

He orders her file. A connection to Raccoon is annotated there as well.

That gives him a thought and he asks for a check on the man's previous girlfriends. Only two additional names arise. One is currently in residence at Joliette, a women's penitentiary, the other decamped to Halifax. That leaves only Clara. Further romance in his life either never happened or was never recorded. Ruminating about Raccoon on the run, Mathers can imagine him seeking any port in a storm. He might consider Clara Kendrick a safe harbour.

Bill Mathers hits the streets.

A simple thing to do. Observe her residence. He strikes the mother lode on his very first pass. Hells Angels come and go from her modest digs. The easy part of his reconnaissance drifts into becoming a bore. His stakeout is amid the bustle of students and workers, businesspeople and hookers along Ste. Catherine Street East. He has places to eat – for hot dogs, poutine – and doorways to slouch in when the car becomes uncomfortable in the warmth of the day. Traffic's incessant, so it's easy to hide, be lost in the parade. His continuous presence may be a risk, but the ever-changing crowd will help him to go unnoticed.

Clara emerges, after 90 minutes have slipped by. Bill Mathers follows her.

She leads him into an Asian grocery. In an aisle adjacent to the udon noodles, he approaches her.

"Clara Kendrick. What do you know? Fancy bumping into you here."

He detects her fear of an indiscretion discovered.

"You again," Clara remarks. She continues shopping, selecting a package of flat noodles to deposit in the store's handbasket that she carries looped over a forearm.

"Good to see you, too."

"Detective – I got nothing."

"I'm out shopping, Clara. For soya sauce."

"Trust me, I been a good daddy's girl. I got nothing for you."

"I should take your word? We gave that up a decade ago."

"Mathers, what do you want?"

She tries to move down the aisle. Stepping ahead of her, he blocks her passage without making it seem so.

"What?" she asks again, trying in vain not to show her irritation. She's inclined to back up and go around the other way. "I thought you were shopping."

"I want Raccoon."

"Do I care? I never seen him in months. Years. Why do you want him?"

"Which is it? Months or years?"

"I don't know. Christ. I think I spotted him on the street two months ago. Okay? Something like that. He didn't look too healthy. He walked on by."

"Two months ago. Good. Then if I put a listening device in your apartment I won't hear him snore."

"No. Of course not. Somebody else, from time to time. Not Rac. We're done. I mean like since forever."

"I noticed the Hells going in and out. They snore, too, I guess."

That she was now in trouble rocked her a moment. She glanced around, finding nowhere to run. Nowhere, even, to turn. He'd backed her up against a shelf laden with varieties of red and white miso pastes. "What do you want?"

"Clara, you're the last person who needs to go down for this."

"Go down for what?"

"Don't play dumb. A cop is dead. Like you said, you're a good girl now. Why hook your veins on Raccoon's yellow piss?"

Her silence does not signify that she's fighting him, nor that she's caving in.

"I need Raccoon," Mathers states. "I prefer no serious loss of life to get him. How many Hells Angels are in your apartment? Sketch the rooms for me, the weapons there, a best time to strike. Also, yeah, tell me what they're doing. I can keep you out of it, but don't think about squiggling free. A dead cop, remember. From that, there's no exit out of this."

Her expression and body language reveal that she knows what he's saying.

"Confirm for me that Raccoon's inside. Just a quick nod will do."

She returns the slightest of nods.

"Now describe for me, Clara, his status."

She picks up the package of noodles already in her basket, weighs it in her left hand, then puts it back down. She looks up at Mathers, then away. She tells him, "Slow torture. They're wailing on him."

"Okay," Mathers said. "Is he talking yet?"

"About?"

"Anything."

"I think he's holding his own." She delivers a surprise. "You gotta save him."

"Draw me a map."

"What about me?"

"Give nothing away, the slate stays clean. We won't finger you for this. No worries. Keep your head down when the time comes. How long does he have?"

"I don't know why they're keeping him alive. They don't seem to want him dead. They want something out of him. Don't ask me what. They're prolonging his life until they get what they want. The fucker's stubborn. He's still breathing."

29. Bolts and Nuts

Émile and Sandra dine out in the city. He mixes business with the pleasure of her company, making a few calls and receiving two follow-up rings. Sandra doesn't mind too much, although patrons within the restaurant are miffed. She's tempted to snap at them. That Émile is coming around to a semblance of full health, notwithstanding the wheelchair, protects her from the pique of others. That he's rediscovering his appetite has her thinking they should dine out more often. Steer him clear of hospital grub.

"Should we get a room?" Her suggestion is not meant to evoke a romantic overlay to dinner. In his condition, a sorry laugh. She gathered from the snippets of phone conversations that he has more work to do in town, and she wants to spare him the travel.

"Sounds good. We can find toothbrushes. I've got a penitentiary visit this evening, then Bill Mathers wants me for a return trip to Parthenais."

"You have a *what* this evening?" She heard him the first time, but wants it explained. And justified. He is supposed to do nothing more physically demanding than sitting.

"Penitentiary visit."

"Émile, really? Tonight?"

"It's being arranged. I need to talk to the head of the Hells Angels."

"Now you're scaring me."

"Mittens, that's the bad guy's moniker. I think because he loved his cat. Or because he strangled it, one of the two."

He doesn't get a rise out of her. Instead, she challenges him. "Is it wise to see him while you're, you know, compromised?"

"What does that mean?"

"In a wheelchair. Not permitted *under any circumstances* to budge from it."

"Yeah, actually," he tells her, "it can work to my advantage. I don't want him to think of himself as a prisoner. Which he is. Or as subservient to me. Which he is. I'd rather be weak. Let him think he's strong by comparison. That might kickstart a process."

"What 'process?'" Sandra asks, dreading that this may turn into a dangerous saga.

"I need a better hand to play before I negotiate. But I need him to consider that a negotiation might work for him. Soften him up that way. It's a reason to go in at night. Less businesslike. Bordering on convivial."

On the table between them, a small candle flickers in a metallic bowl. The couple typically order different meals, then share; tonight, both opted for the Arctic char, now reduced to its skeletal scraps. A waiter clears the table and takes their coffee order. No dessert. Lights throughout the intimate room have been dimmed. Sandra can understand why patrons were annoyed to have someone on a mobile phone – the ambiance is meant to remove diners from the world of business and responsibilities. They've not been in the restaurant before, and she's not sure that she's spent time in this neighbourhood of restaurants and youthful street life. Émile called it Mile End.

"In daylight hours," he explains, "Mittens dwells in the lap of luxury. Or so he lets on. He's convinced outsiders that he has a palatial suite. What's really happened: he occupies a common room for prisoners that he confiscated by dint of his authority. That arrangement suits our side, the police side, as much as it does him. He doesn't know that. At night, he's put back in his plebeian cell, where he sleeps among the degenerates and the muddled, and the good-hearted/bad-hearted guys, too, same as the other felons. That's where I want to meet him. In his cold cruel cell. Not on his throne.

In his humble station where he can't lord it over me. At the same time, I want to present myself as weakened – compromised, as you say. It's a form of gamesmanship. Even though he's stuck in prison, he wields significant power. At the same time, he's an impotent prisoner. I'll play his circumstances against him: the impotent man of power stuck behind bars yet receiving guests."

Despite his calm, she's certain Émile's gambit is dangerous.

"I should charge admission, the way you cops keep showing up," Mittens says. "Some of you guys should move in."

"There's been other cops? What did they want?"

Émile Cinq-Mars wheels himself more deeply into the narrow cell; a guard slides the barred door shut behind him. The man's boot heels echo as he departs. The ex-cop is now locked in with a notorious killer and gang leader, protected by a mere buzzer in his lap. Two buttons are on the buzzer, one to call for his retrieval, the other to signal panic. He and Mittens have jousted face-to-face before, although neither knows the other well. Cinq-Mars never counted himself as a policeman who went after the gangs, despite circumstances playing out that way. After he'd dented their organization, the massive police operation that followed led to the arrest of more than 150 bikers and over 100 convictions were secured. After that, a joint task force went after a Hells/Mafia coalition and took down the surviving top people in both groups, disrupting their plans to jointly take over the east coast. That ambition is known to be ongoing, although the Mafia side of the partnership has recently been decapitated and Mittens is in prison for killing prison guards in the hopes of intimidating the judiciary. Subsequently, he's been charged for conspiring with his daughter to vanquish a rival. Despite all that, the drive to take over the Canadian east coast is heating up once more, and Cinq-Mars needs to insert himself into that fray to achieve what he needs. To succeed, he requires nothing less than another miracle, if he's going to again save the life of Douglas Sykes.

Mittens looks spruced up. A swarthy man, his wide-set eyes seem off his face when anyone glances at him too quickly. Buggy-eyed that way. The hair has thinned now that he's in his 50s, yet he has full coverage, his coif in the modern style: short, spiked upward, stiffened by gel. He's clean-shaven, and a faint waft in the air goes beyond deodorant to a scented oil. A little touch, Cinq-Mars suspects, behind each ear.

A new trend for convicts.

Otherwise, he sports the requisite forearm and bicep tattoos and, despite regulations, an earring.

"Minor shit," he replies to Émile's question about police visits. A lie. "Some days, life's a fucking armpit. What's up? You can't come during my regular business hours?"

"I'll be noticed. This late, wheeling down a dark corridor, I'm Mr. Anonymous. That might be better for everyone."

"That's how come you're whispering?"

"Ears listen in."

Mittens widens his buggy eyes. "Comes back to the same old fucking rule-of-law, Cinq-Mars. What do you want? Didn't you retire? That means you're not arresting me on some screwy charge. I don't know nothing more than that, which ain't much."

"This is one of the of the most curious puzzles I have ever been asked to unravel, Monsieur Grégoire."

"What puzzle? Look, call me Mittens. I'll call you Cinq-Mars."

He's pleased. In theory, using the nickname puts him at a disadvantage. If Mittens was subjected to an interrogation, the nickname would not be used. Cops would either be formal and address him as Monsieur, or they'd be antagonistic and call him by his last name only. They might be falsely friendly and call him Freddy or be confrontational and invent their own vulgar names for him. They would not deploy the familiarity of his nickname, which elevates and substantiates his status.

In this circumstance, Mittens is demanding exactly that consideration, and Cinq-Mars, for his own reasons, obliges. "Tell me, Mittens, did you order the hit on your own bank? If you tell me you didn't, then I'll ask other people about it. Friends of yours, for instance. Did you order the hit on your own bank? If so, why?"

As gambits go, this one is more audacious than it is risky. Cinq-Mars is convinced that Mittens ordered a hit on his own money-counting unit as a way to kill Douglas Sykes while making the action look as though it had been precipitated by an external assassin. He wanted no one inside his organization to imagine that he was embarking on his own plan or murdering his own people. He certainly did not want them to know why he was doing whatever he was doing. Audacious, though, for Cinq-Mars to bring it up, because he's approaching Mittens straight through the main door of the house he lives in and prying it wide open.

"Strange question, Detective," Mittens notes. He returns his look, less defiant than curious. More respectful than apprehensive.

"We live in peculiar times, Mittens. Don't you think so?"

"Sure. Why not? You're in here asking me to confess to ordering the murder of —. I don't know. You tell me how many people?"

"Four. Two more the next day."

"Six murders ordered altogether, is that right? How many got whacked?"

"Three on day one. One more the next."

"Six murders ordered," Mittens exults, a fat grin on his face, "four happened. Two less than advertised. I rest my case. I'd never be that sloppy. Of course, if I was that sloppy, I wouldn't admit it."

Cinq-Mars gives his chin a meditative rub. He turns only one side of his chair backwards, changing the angle between himself and Mittens. They're no longer square to each other. "I take it, then, that it's okay with you if I ask Sharpie if he knows what you did."

"What's it to me? Sharpie's been up against bullshitting cops before."

"Even when his name is on the list?"

"What list?" The man continues to exhibit no concern.

"I'm referring to the one that goes along with your scheme to take over the maritime provinces. Certain people need to go down, right? Be eliminated? That's customary, nothing unusual there. Surprising, though, isn't it, that Sharpie is on the list to be one of them? Chiclets, too."

Mittens scrunches up his face, not as though these speculations annoy him, rather that they are so remarkably irrelevant to the time of day.

"Cop talk," Mittens says. "Sharpie won't buy it. Neither do I."

He's cool under pressure. Cinq-Mars will give him that much.

"You're right. Who needs him? Who needs to bother Sharpie when Douglas Sykes can put your daughter away for conspiracy to commit?"

"Who?" Mittens asks. The key for Cinq-Mars is a virtually imperceptible delay in the other man's response, as though the prisoner took a moment to weigh and self-direct his options. To Cinq-Mars, his reaction feels studied. A false and rickety scaffolding.

"Douglas. Sykes. I know you know the man."

"Heard of him, yeah, that's all. A punk. Out of Vancouver? That guy?"

"Originally from here. Then Vancouver. Now he's back. He's the one. He's under my protection as we speak."

"Wait a minute. Sykes? Isn't he up for the murder rap? He's the one who did it, shot those people. What does Sharpie have to do with him? Never mind my daughter. Never mind me. Why are you talking to me about that punk? I got nothing to do with him. If you're accusing me of ordering him to shoot up my own bank, check yourself into the psych ward, Cinq-Mars. Retirement has fucked you over."

"It gives me more time to think, actually. From my hospital bed. I'm sane, by the way."

"Fooled me. Hey, you want a beer?"

"You can order beer?"

"If you don't mind a paper cup. Life is tough inside the joint, you know? On the outside, I drink straight from the bottle, then smash the bottle if that's my mood. In here, it's bad behaviour. I'm told it's unacceptable."

"I'm good, thanks. No beer." He's let him know that he's suitably impressed with Mittens' lifestyle on the inside.

"I don't know much about this Sykes guy. He doesn't work for me. Did he shoot up the bank? If he says I ordered it, he's off his nut. What are you here for? You want me to confess to something I never did? If you're not a cop no more, what's it to you? I don't get this."

"Mmm," Cinq-Mars murmurs, coming to the crux of the matter, "this is about rumours and hearsay, mostly."

"Like I give a fart. I admit, I don't mind the interruption to my routine. It's okay with me. But this is going nowhere."

"Rumour has it," Cinq-Mars forges on, "that a certain person, a lone gunman, might be talking about more or less what I'm talking about to anybody who might be listening. He might have no choice. You might be connected to that guy. We believe he's done work for you in the past."

"You pulled in a blabbermouth gunman. I care why?"

"You care because we didn't pull him in. He's not under our protection. We're not the people holding him."

The comment has gained the biker's interest. "Who has him, this guy?"

Cinq-Mars doesn't reply, and instead holds a hand to the centre of his chest and closes his eyes rather tightly.

"Don't kick off on me, Cinq-Mars. Not in here. I don't need the grief."

The former cop holds his position and does not respond.

"Hear what I say. Go outside to die if you have to. Not in my cell."

The former policeman comes around. He takes a deeper breath. His eyes flicker, then open again, his hand relaxes on the arm of his wheelchair. "I'm fine," he says.

"How much am I supposed to care? What happened to you anyhow?"

"Walked into a stray bullet. Didn't look where I was going."

"You dumb fuck. I bet that bullet was no stray."

"Possibly not."

"What happened to the shooter? I like wannabe cop killers. Except your guy failed."

"Very mysteriously, he vanished."

Mittens takes a second to consider what that might mean. "Watch yourself, Cinq-Mars. You might end up on this side of the wall permanently. You don't want to do life in here. Won't be no free ride for you."

"That's why I'm here."

"Meaning what? You're checking out the accommodations?"

"I'm interested in your power to give a man a free ride."

"Tough for a cop."

"For anybody. You got that power, though, right? You can see it gets done?"

"Some people have no brains. No accounting for what they do."

"But otherwise?"

"Otherwise, yeah. A guy can get a free ride if I say so. Tough for a cop, like I said."

"I'm not thinking that way."

"I know. You're a priest. A fucking saint. So they say."

Cinq-Mars pauses again and seems to focus on his own breathing. When he speaks, he continues the whispered modulation they've adopted, except it now sounds as though it's the best that he can manage.

"Mull it over, Mittens. If you haven't figured it out yet, I'm looking for an equitable solution to our mutual problems. One that keeps everybody happy."

"Happy is fucking overrated. I don't bother with it at all."

"Still. Like I said. He's out there. That lone gunman. He's in the wrong hands. How does that affect your will to live?"

"If I was you, I wouldn't worry about it for a minute. If you want to put that chip on the table, then that's different."

"What chip? How is it different?"

"I believe I can get you a name. An address might be in the cards. If you put that chip on the table, we can see what you got. Compare it to what I got."

Cinq-Mars clears his throat. His gentle hacking sounds fragile, as if he worries he'll hurt himself. He holds his chest again. "One step ahead of you, Mittens. That doesn't happen often. It must've happened in the past, though, since you're in here. We already have his name. We even have an address. What's going down, so to speak, is going down right now. That's the main reason I'm visiting off-hours. I can let you know what's happening, but it's too late for you to tip anybody off if for some reason you don't approve. But I think you'll approve."

Mittens nods. Cinq-Mars detects a buoyancy to his disposition that was absent only moments ago. He's coming around to his way of thinking. He's been whispering his responses, but now his voice goes way under his own breath. "Good to hear. Come back if you got something to talk about. When you have a chip to put on the table."

Cinq-Mars wheels back a few inches, then lines himself up for the cell door. His voice is also very low as he speaks over his shoulder to the man behind him. "Be ready to barter, Mittens, if I come back. No wiggle room on this one. Not with a dead cop. Get ready to sharpen a pencil."

"Don't mention my pencil."

Cinq-Mars spins the chair then, facing Mittens, but ignores the attempt at vulgar humour. "For my own personal satisfaction—"

"That don't interest me at all."

"Did you kill the cat, or was it a pet?"

Mittens returns his stare, confused. He declines to answer.

Cinq-Mars presses his buzzer, once, for three seconds, to signal that he's safe but wants out. He hears the electronic locks on the steel gate at the end of the corridor fire off, then the gate noisily grates open. The guard arrives, unlocks, and slides open the steel door for Cinq-Mars to drive his chair through.

"Cinq-Mars," Mittens says, and in the corridor the ex-cop turns his chair around to face him.

Rather than speak, Mittens puts his two fists side-by-side, twists, then breaks them apart, holding the head of an imaginary cat in one hand, the body in the other.

"Myth," Cinq-Mars says back to him, his voice incrementally stronger now. "I break down myth to arrive at the truth. It's what I do."

The gang boss flicks his hands open, to convey throwing the carcass and head away.

"Don't kid me," Cinq-Mars says. "You loved that cat. I bet it purred on your shoulder. I'll see you soon."

"Not if you croak first."

Cinq-Mars permits the guard to wheel him down the corridor.

30. Sinners and Saints

Sergeant-Detective Bill Mathers assumed command of the operation. Working in his own district, he handpicked fellow *sud* officers and invited along *nord* detective Léon Doucet as a courtesy. Mathers instructed him to stand by on the perimeter and let *sud* officers take the lead. Once their man was in custody, Doucet could provide a critical contribution. He told him what he had in mind. Doucet gave his consent; his enthusiasm guarded.

At dusk, they moved to side streets near their quarry. Reconnaissance had not alerted them to any exceptional level of security on the part of the Hells Angels. The bikers had Raccoon Rybachuk under their control, unaware that anyone else wanted to emulsify him in a Petri dish.

Nearby streets were designed for the horse-and-buggy era: narrow and congested in modern times. Homes jostle cheek-by-jowl without yards, the units stacked in twos and threes. Finding a parking space is a daily frustration, and the cops won't announce their presence by arriving in marked cars or by nudging unmarked units alongside hydrates. They circle the blocks until they find a spot, even when it's at a distance.

The trickier aspect will be remembering where the hell they parked.

Each pair of officers splits up, then each man moves toward the premises on his own. Mathers circles around, cuts back, checks out the territory, absorbs the lay of the land. Text messages share the obvious: a rear fire escape offers a way in and includes a landing where the stairs run under the rear windows. Judging by Clara's map of the apartment, Raccoon is being held in the room off the end of the fire escape, right where it turns to go up to the next level. He's strapped to a chair, she said. Often left alone to recuperate.

For reasons of their own, the Hells are keeping him alive. The police must count on an opportune moment, silently cut out a circle of glass, open the window latch, pry up the second-storey window while leaning way out, step across a void, enter, and haul out Raccoon before his ghost knows he's gone.

They don't go heavy. They don't bother with a warrant. Unofficially they are responding to a life in danger, thwarting a kidnapping. To arrive with a warrant would mean emerging with a train wreck of legal considerations. Raccoon would be safe from the Hells but also protected from the cops, which they don't want. If it comes up, this will be pitched as a rescue mission initiated by an anonymous informant. They want to grab him for their own benefit. Before the legal system protects him, they'd prefer to replicate the situation he's in now, but on their own terms.

The cops want to replace the Hells as his captors.

At the outset, they'll be gentler than the bikers. After that, given that he's accused of killing a policeman, no promises.

A dicey caper all around.

As are all kidnappings.

A lamp stands lonely in a corner, providing gloomy illumination. Duct tape binds Raccoon to a kitchen chair. Occasionally, he jerks his head, then his chin slumps down. His face is pulpy, bloody, smashed. Next to him, seated and leaning forward to speak in hushed tones, the man known as Sharpie consoles him in his plight.

"If we decide to shoot you, Rac, we'll shoot you. Cutting your legs off makes too much noise. We're not cutting out your tongue, either. Wiggle it around in your mouth, Rac. Feel that? It's still there. You need your tongue to tell us everything. Hey, Rac, did you notice? Your balls swing free. Should I send in Clara to give you a lap dance? She can rub them for you, remind you they're still hanging.

You can find out if you can still get it up, if you still got stuff to live for, right?"

Sharpie wipes saliva from his mouth, swallows, then continues. "Rac, listen up, you never came to us. You never came to me. You never said, 'Sharpie, we need to talk.' Nope. You took off instead. Tried to fix things – you say, anyhow – tried to fix things by yourself. Never a good plan. That's why I had you punched up, Rac. It's not personal. The worst is over. Maybe it's not *all* over, hey, but the worst. You'll heal up, Rac. Not like if we took your legs off, hey? Or only one. Hard as fuck to grow another leg. Anyhow, you're going to tell me what you know, Rac. Leave nothing out."

Sharpie leans closer, causing Raccoon to flinch back. The man whispers in his ear. He says, "Rac, Rackie. I'll hold off tattooing your balls, okay? But come clean, spit out everything you know, otherwise a Harley in technicolour on each side. I'm an amateur with needles. Won't be pretty, all that blood, dripping off your balls. Not to mention the screaming. I don't want to think about it, and I'm not you. Don't make me take it that far."

He steps away from him, and adds, "Rac, we got pepperoni and Hawaiian coming in. You hungry? Want a slice? Which you want? One of each?"

Raccoon's head lolls slowly from side to side. He states no preference.

"Even with a concussion, you still gotta eat," Sharpie remarks.

Pizza will arrive soon. It's time for Sharpie to go eat. Then he'll be back.

Cops congregate in the alley behind Clara's apartment. Tall wooden fences shelter the skimpy backyards which aren't used for anything more than sheltering garbage cans and recycling bins, and the cops huddle close to these, out of view from the upper windows. Both uniforms and plainclothes officers have changed into duds suitable for tradespeople and manual workers. They still look like cops. Mathers thinks so. He's irritated in the way that his former boss used to get irritated. "Cops acquire," Émile used to say, "cop skin, cop attitude, a cop's way of standing still and doing nothing like only a cop can do." Bill Mathers won't go that far, although he's glad his associates have gathered under cover of darkness. Daylight would surely give them away.

On Ste. Catherine Street East, a camera that's focused on the front of the building keeps rolling from within an empty parked car. Everyone arriving or departing Clara's place is being observed at the station house in real time, their presence recorded. As well, two trusted uniforms are on the beat. They pretend to be interested in preserving the peace, when really they're monitoring the doorway. If the Hells get wind of the action and try to break Raccoon out the front door, or flee without him, the policemen stand ready to intervene. Earlier, the same two cops sauntered down the back alley and made a pretense of ticketing a parked car. The car carries tools and even a couple of heavy weapons in its trunk. The ticket on the windshield is to appease any neighbours who might object to its illegal presence.

Mathers chose each member of his team for his physical prowess. One guy is super strong. Two are tall – long limbs may come in handy. Everyone is lithe, except for Mathers himself. He's the liability among them in terms of his athleticism. Too late to tone up now.

The strongest, Reggie, supports the tallest, Ariel, on his shoulders. Ariel pulls the bottom section of the fire escape to ground level, then the others climb up. As they go, Mathers notices how it is they can dress as manual workers but look like cops – they're wearing sneakers. Nikes with neon stripes.

He could just shoot them.

Mathers, though, wears street shoes with slippery soles and regrets the choice.

The fire escape zigzags up the back of the building. The men go only to the second floor, then down to the far end of the platform where Mathers confronts his first dilemma.

From below, the space between the end of the platform and the window they'll need to enter seemed to be a gap they could negotiate. Up high, looking down, that gap is a canyon. A tall wooden fence, each plank cut to a sharp peak, will impale anyone who falls. Lovely.

The window is far enough beyond the end of the railing that Mathers can't see inside to confirm if the abducted man is alone, or in there at all. He climbs over the railing, leans way out, and stretches a mirror across to help him peer inside.

Raccoon is on his lonesome.

Mathers pulls himself back to the railing. "Okay," he says. "Let's move."

"Move?" Ariel, the tallest one, objects. "Are we monkeys? Do we live in trees?"

Reggie, the muscular detective, elaborates on the theme. "I don't do my own stunts. I need a stunt double. Call me once he's done."

The banter hides a nervousness. This is not a typical action. They're not breaking down a door and going in guns raised. That's risky enough, and here they've dispensed with the luxury of vests to suit the physical challenges. They still face the prospect of being interrupted by armed killers. Mathers gets all that. Fear is legitimate, and the humour both masks their foreboding and acknowledges the danger.

"Move," Mathers says, quietly, softly, with respect. What he means is: *Take care*.

Wearing a tether, the officer leans far over from the platform railing. He makes a circular incision with a glass cutter. The strongest man in their group has a tenacious grip on him. A suction cup pulls the glass away, and the strong man hauls the other man back. Tools and glass are tucked away in a small kitbag. Ariel, the tallest one, leans way over again, reaching through the hole he's created, and springs the metal latch, which requires the full reach of his six-foot-four-inch range. Unlatched, the window is still difficult to budge. The officer has scant purchase on the outside; it feels painted into place. A heavy pounding may break the seal between window and frame – yet also alert their enemies.

Bill Mathers needs to figure this out quickly.

He wants to know who's left-handed. One guy raises his right hand, looks at it, then switches to his left. André. He gets to wear the tether and lean out above the spears in the fence below him while another officer maintains a hold on him. He stretches his right hand onto the outer cement sill, supports his weight there, then with his left repeatedly wedges a screwdriver between the window and the frame, working his way up, down, and across the bottom. Pokey, slow work. He must not make a sound.

Reggie, the strong man, is nearby, crouched on the fire escape grate under a window. Mathers brings him forward; he needs the power of his hands. After André does his job, without success, the stronger man sees if he can't force the window up. It's difficult to acquire proper purchase, especially for his large digits. He grunts and manages to raise an edge. He starts working on the opposite side. The left-hander with the screwdriver comes back into play when they're stuck again, then the man with the big hands takes over once more. The window yields an inch, then a fraction more. Reggie bullies the gap to two inches when suddenly it springs open completely and he almost smashes through the glass. Mathers turns away. He can't look. When he turns back, he's informed that the window sash is broken, that there's nothing to prevent the window from slamming shut again. Spread-eagled across the void, André keeps a foot in the gap while somebody thinks of something.

They've got wire cutters, they've brought tools: Mathers tells a cop to go downstairs and break off somebody's car radio antenna. In the spur of the moment, it's all he can think of.

The man hopping to it is Marcel. He forgets the protocol they've established. Going by one of the windows that overlooks the fire escape, he forgets to duck. Upright, he looks directly into the surprised face of a person inside. They've been discovered. Fortunately for their gambit, it's Clara who's staring back. He ducks, way too late, then heads down the fire escape to the lane below. Everyone is still, waiting to learn what Clara will do. If she plans to betray them, now would be the time.

Marcel returns with two lengthy antennae from older cars. Two drivers will be making insurance claims in the morning. The cops use the antennae to prop open the window, both on the near side, then Ariel stands on the top rail of the fire escape and stretches to put a foot on the window ledge, grips the edge of the window frame, then pulls himself over and leaps across at the same moment.

He makes it. He slips into the room. Gives back a thumbs-up.

He stays by the window to help the next officer across.

Four men pile into the room.

Bill Mathers really hates his choice of footwear now.

The first assignment belongs to Ariel. He withdraws his pistol and aims it at the room's door. If a Hells turns the knob on the other side, a bullet will fire straight through the door above his head. Which should remind him to knock.

Mathers checks on Raccoon. Clara warned him that the man would not be in great shape. He's worse than her warning foretold. His face pulverized; he's barely conscious and not coherent. Ribs have cracked and his breathing sounds impeded. Hauling him out will be difficult as Raccoon won't be able to help his own cause. He certainly won't be leaping across from the windowsill to the fire escape's railing. Another executive decision is vital. "Hold it," Mathers commands. "Stop."

The man who was slicing the duct tape binding the prisoner to the chair stops.

"Keep him strapped in. We'll take him out in the chair, like this."

Once over the surprise, his peers agree that that's an option. Still, it won't be easy.

"We can abort," André puts forward.

Mathers thinks about it. He doesn't want to push his men beyond their capabilities, or beyond their inclinations.

"I say we try to get him out."

Each man exchanges an affirmative nod. They're in.

Reggie, the muscle in the group, returns to the fire escape and informs the two officers there about the situation. Mathers, Marcel, and Ariel stay behind. Mathers is grateful that he brought along an exceptionally strong man as they begin to wedge Raccoon in his chair through the window. They balance him on the ledge, the sill taking his weight. Now it gets tough. As they take a breather to figure out the next move, one of the two antennae slips its moorings, springs upward, and falls to the ground outside. The second one buckles, and the window rams down on Raccoon's chest like a guillotine. Mathers lifts the window again and holds it open. The other two can barely sustain his weight on the ledge. His centre of gravity has shifted further outside. The heavyset man on the fire escape leans across, gets a grip, one hand on the railing, one on the chair. The prisoner may be more secure now, although everyone is trapped in limbo. They can't move him without precipitating a fall. If he doesn't impale himself on the fence he'll survive, but the resulting racket as he wails will reveal their caper.

On his count, Mathers coaches his men to nudge the prisoner an inch at a time sideways along the sill. With a pair of officers clutching the belt of the strongest cop, who holds the railing with one hand, the chair is released to his grip. Raccoon falls, the cop bends in half himself, yet holds on – one hand to the railing, one to the chair. The other two officers lean over the fire escape railing, one managing to grip a foot, the other a chair leg. Straining with the effort, they pull him up a little, then each man gets a second hand on the chair. On the count of three, a superhuman effort jerks him up to where a leg of the chair catches on the fire escape, supporting a portion of the weight.

They are now stuck in terms of their manoeuvrability. They have neither the strength nor the leverage to pull him higher. One officer has begun to flag. Those leaning out the window are no help. The entire mission is doomed yet they cannot retreat. They cannot undo what has been done, nor can they proceed. Let him drop, the only option, hope he survives. In his current condition, he won't. Once he falls, they'll extract their pistols and badges and try to explain this disaster away.

Mathers is at a loss. He must dream up something, *quickly*!

At the moment when nothing more can possibly go wrong, something does. Upside down, Raccoon regains a degree of consciousness. Imperiled in mid-air, he kicks, moans, makes gurgling noises, and hyperventilates.

"*Calm down*!" Mathers whispers hoarsely, to no avail.

"We need a rope!" the exceptionally muscular cop states.

"We don't have any fucking rope!" taunts the cop who's flagging. He's loud.

"Don't let go!"

"Don't you let go!"

"We gotta let go!"

"Hang on!" Mathers insists.

"Not for much longer! Fuck this. Fuck!"

"Use the clothesline!"

The latter direction is a new voice in their talk. Those who can, turn to look down the platform on the fire escape. It's Clara. She's stuck her head out the kitchen window. She has a point. A clothesline travels from the opposite end of the fire escape to a telephone pole in the lane. The man most in danger of flagging releases his grip to go and cut the clothesline free, while the other two take up the additional weight. The pair under siege vocalize their discomfort, groaning. Their faces reflect the strain. Those in the window both urge them on and warn Raccoon to shut the hell up. The line is retrieved, a loop drawn around Raccoon's chair once, twice, then a third time. The feebler man heaves. That relieves the pain the other two are experiencing, although it doesn't budge their man. He knows he's doomed.

Mathers then, with the lines around Raccoon, figures it's relatively safe for him to come back across to the fire escape. He sinks his fingernails into the brickwork and takes an enormous step across the void to land a foot on the railing. Damn his slippery soles! He relies purely on momentum, not grip, and lands by crashing onto the fire escape. Not pretty, and way too loud, but he makes it, face down on the grate.

Everybody waits to hear who noticed.

Clara shuts her window. She's done her bit.

Mathers takes up the strain on the line's tail while the other cop holds onto the opposite bitter end. By standing on the railing again, he can loop the line over a stair above them. Then the feeble man does the same. When he stands on the railing he has no wall beside him and balances like a tightrope walker. He releases the weight on his line to get it up and over a grill in the steps above him, and in that split second Raccoon descends a notch and hollers. He nearly unravels from their hold and all but loses his mind.

They wait again, listening.

They figure Raccoon must sound like another manic voice from the crazy streets to anyone who's inside. No one has rushed out.

They almost wish the Hells would show up. They can use their help.

Now, when Mathers and other cops endeavour to haul Raccoon up, they keep their gains, an advantage to their improvised pulley system. A wheel would be better than the sharp edge of a metal step, but it works, if slowly. Once he's higher, the strong man can do his thing. A better grip improves his leverage to where he's pulled over the railing onto the platform.

Raccoon still doesn't know what's going on.

The last man inside must evacuate the room with no one handy to hold open the window. At first, he fails. They pass him the line to tie around himself. The other end is looped over a bar on the fire escape. The cop is expected to hang on and swing out into the open air as the window bangs down shut behind him. Before he goes, he withdraws his pistol – there's a hand on the door inside. Someone – Clara? – must have called that person back inside the body of the house. The door never opens and the cop on the window ledge holds his bullet. He re-holsters, then falls away and swings under the platform the others stand upon. The line holds and is long enough that they can lower him down safely from there to negotiate the sharpened tops of the fence.

Two guys start down the fire escape lugging Raccoon in the chair while Mathers goes on ahead. Slow work. By the time they get their captive to the ground, Mathers is driving into the alley. Getting Raccoon in his chair through the rear door doesn't work. In a trice, Mathers elects to open the trunk. Dunked on his side, chair and man fit in.

"Don't shut it! Don't shut it!" Raccoon pleads, suddenly comprehensible.

They shut it.

The other cops are dismissed. Thanks will come later. They assume that Mathers is headed to Parthenais to book the cop killer. Instead, he heads out and is almost on his own. Only Léon Doucet, who's been standing by, who's been alerted by phone and has not been a part of the operation, trails along behind. Rather than head east and south, they drive north, the long way up to PDQ 33. Doucet opens the back door to the station while Mathers opens the trunk, and together they carry the man they've rescued under the light of the moon and street lamps halfway across the parking lot and into the station house. They're hoping to go in unseen and enter the elevator unnoticed. On the second floor, however, a cop and a felon join them. Both men look at the bloody and beaten face of the man who sits in a chair, bound in duct tape.

Not a common sight.

Mathers says, "He thought he could clam up. Guess what?"

A faint smirk passes across the face of the other man in custody. When he and his arresting officer step off at the next floor, Léon Doucet says, "Guaranteed. He'll be more compliant now."

"Our good deed for the day."

Half the top floor is vacant for the night. Under the red glow of an exit lamp, they convey Raccoon down the hallway. Doucet gets out his keys; they enter the main office area and proceed around a corner to a private interrogation room. Same place where they interviewed Douglas Sykes.

Now it's Raccoon's turn to talk to them.

They switch on the bright overheads.

The few words the man speaks make no sense.

"I'll call Cinq-Mars," Mathers says.

"Is he coming in?"

“I’ll tell him not to bother. Not tonight. This guy’s in no shape to talk. I don’t want him to die on us. We need to get a medic in here.”

“I don’t want to lose him.”

“I know a guy. We also need to photograph him, to show how he arrived, without us laying a hand on him.”

Doucet concurs. He stares at the beaten Raccoon whose head is lolling around. “You’d think he’d be more grateful,” he says.

“He’s too out of it.”

Mathers is wrong. A murmur from the beaten man draws them closer to him. Both men lean in. Through the blood in his mouth and the confusion in his head, they hear him say, quite distinctly, “Thanks.”

That bodes well for the morning when their interrogation shall begin in earnest.

PART FOUR

ENTER AND BREAK

31. Socks and Shoes

They could not interview their prisoner until the following afternoon.

The physician who Mathers corralled, a retired man, was willing to keep his mouth shut, but insisted that Raccoon receive immediate hospital treatment. They removed him from the station house strapped to a gurney; an ambulance ferried him to Emergency. Weary, the cops made calls, assigned guards and went home. Late the next morning, Raccoon was returned to the interrogation room, but by then they had to give him lunch.

Cinq-Mars appreciates each delay. He's not been feeling well, although he's improving by the time he arrives at PDQ 33. Not chipper, but good to go.

A new delay arises. Sergeant-Detective Léon Doucet insists on entering the interrogation room first, and alone. Mathers has seen Doucet in action, but Cinq-Mars decides to give him the benefit of the doubt. "If he wanted to go in *after* we're done, I'd be more worried. Ahead of time, we'll see the effect."

"Pound on him now, who would notice the difference?"

"Let's see what happens. If it's loud we'll intervene."

Nervously, they wait.

"Émile, have you seen these?" Mathers picks up a coffee mug. "Spill-proof. You can interview a suspect and drink hot coffee at the same time."

Cinq-Mars's facial expression appears to question his lineage.

Doucet looms over the prisoner. He has a few points he wants to make clear. "Freeing you took some doing. You owe us, big time. We can take you back there, dump you on Clara's doorstep, ring the bell to make sure you're noticed. Our prerogative. Now, Raccoon, show me where it hurts the most."

"What?"

"Where do you hurt, Raccoon? Show me."

He indicates his swollen right eye socket – the eye itself nearly shut.

"Not there," Doucet guides him. "Where else?"

Apparently, his neck is sore.

"Lower," the detective instructs him.

The cracked ribs.

"Good," Doucet lets him know. "Here? Right here?" He presses his palm on the sore spot. The man flinches. "Good. Ask to speak to a lawyer, this is where I land my best shots. Nothing personal. Or, I make it personal. We'll see. Do we understand each other, cop killer? We've got medical collaboration that your ribs were busted in already, so nothing I do can be proven. The Hells did it, everybody agrees on that. After I bust your ribs again, we leave you outside the Hells clubhouse. How can I do that, you ask? You're a cop killer, Rac! I'm a cop. How can I *not* do that? Call your lawyer, arrange to meet outside the Hells clubhouse. Does your shyster have a brain? The smart ones won't rush down there. You may have to cool your jets. Any questions, Raccoon?"

He has none.

"No lawyer?"

"Don't know one," Raccoon tells him. "Don't want to know any. Hate them."

"Keep it that way. I'll be listening. My fist. Your ribs. Got that?"

Raccoon nods again. He has little choice regarding these arrangements.

Cinq-Mars has not been privy to the conversation as he replaces Léon Doucet in the room. He's successfully lobbied to do this on his own. He knows what the man expects. Pummelled to pulp, badgered for hours, he's caught between the cops who have him and the Hells Angels who want him back. He's screwed and adrift, while escape is the last option on his mind. He expects the cops to burrow into the shooting at the biker's bank, and he expects to be pinned to the mattress about shooting the cop in the hospital. Cinq-Mars intends to take his time with that; he's looking for a result that goes beyond the inevitable convictions for murder. He wants to avoid being bogged down in the obvious: the man committed murder, he's going to prison, that's the easy part. Retired, he doesn't have to worry about that stuff. Gazing down his imperious nose at Raccoon, he asks instead, "What happened, Mr. Rubbachuk, between you and Douglas Sykes on the 14th green, the night you were picking worms?"

A gamble. Douglas never confirmed that Raccoon was there. Yet he believes that if Raccoon had *not* been there, Douglas might be more forthcoming about the night. He takes Douglas at his word, that he did not do the crime. If he stabbed that boy on the golf course, why wait for the police to show up, or phone Cinq-Mars? How could he have pled his innocence so calmly and with such conviction? Probably – not conclusively – he didn't do it. Yet Douglas always held something back about that night. Given that the events are ancient history, the only reason to hold something back now is because the ancient story reflects on the current situation, and the current situation involves the man sitting directly across the table from Émile. In any case, Raccoon fails to deflect the question properly, and Cinq-Mars gathers that he's guessed correctly.

"You want that one pinned on me, too?"

"Why would I? It's a closed case. Nobody cares about it now if anybody cared back then. I'm not a cop these days. You can own up to what happened, Mr Rubbachuk. Nothing comes back on you."

A different scenario than the usual threat and intimidation.

Tentatively, Raccoon admits, "Just helping a brother out." Then he says, "Rybachuk."

He did, then, kill the boy on the 14th green. Beneficial to establish the history. The larger issues relate to why it happened, the details, and what ramifications flow from that murder into the present time.

Having hooked him, he asks, "Mr Rybachuk, how old were you when you went bald?"

"Bald? Why ask me that? I don't know."

Unofficially, Raccoon admitted to committing murder as a young man. How that information deserves to be juxtaposed with his receding hairline is beyond his comprehension. An old technique: keep a talker off-guard and what he says will be less controlled, generally more truthful. Another technique, used in combination: manoeuvre a suspect into saying what's true about his life, and he'll keep saying the truth for longer than he intends. He'll voluntarily delay the lies, hold them in abeyance. Truth can become its own spell: once a man is under it, he may not shake free as quickly as he desires. Raccoon's baldness cannot be hidden. He can put a hat on, but he cannot deny his shiny crown.

"Twenties?" Cinq-Mars coaxes him. "Thirties? Forties? Some guys, it's the 50s. You?"

Raccoon reaches a hand up and caresses his dome before answering, as though to verify that it's true. "Early 40s, I guess. It went fast, my hair. Late 40s, gone."

"Funny thing, male pattern baldness. Pretty much men only. Imagine if women had the look."

Raccoon imagines exactly that; it gives him a laugh. Laughter hurts his ribs. When his light chuckling subsides, he says, "Yeah." The first fun-thought he's enjoyed in a couple of days. He's warming to his inquisitor.

"You phoned my wife. Why'd you do that?"

"Sorry. I— desperate, you know. You always got Douglas off."

"You want me to get you off. That's never been my job."

"Too late now, anyway. For me. For him, too, looks like."

"Did you think you owed him, back when you were kids?"

Raccoon doesn't ask for an explanation. He works the question through, and concludes, "Nah. I didn't owe nothing."

"Not even for your dad?"

He takes longer to reply, then elects to maintain his position. "Why would I owe him?"

"You guys lived together. Like brothers. Your two moms were in the same house."

He nods.

"I met your mother."

That surprises him once again. "I did not know that."

"She tried to stab me with a kitchen knife."

The burble of laughter that springs from him seems tinged with pride. As though he'd like to say, "That's my ma." Instead, he says, "Sorry about that."

"No problem. I guess she had her difficulties in life."

"Yeah. Well."

He's not going to add anything about that unhappy recollection.

"Why the shoes, Mr. Rubba – sorry, *Ryba*chuk? Why retrieve your father's shoes?"

The man's gaze goes up to the ceiling, as though travelling a distance, or through time. He knows now that Cinq-Mars is in possession of the details. When he speaks, he seems in a different place, working something through that he's not considered before.

"I never wanted his shoes. But his head – it rolled down the grade into my hands. I can't explain it. Suddenly, I don't know, I wanted something that wasn't his head or his hands. I just, suddenly, needed his shoes. I wore them. Later. They fit."

That sounded *mad*.

"My dad said once," he recalls upon further reflection, and Cinq-Mars appreciates the insight, "that I could never walk in his shoes. That hurt me when he said that. Could be I wanted to prove him wrong."

Also mad, but it made sense.

"What did you do with the body parts, afterwards?"

"I brought a bag with me. To hide it in the woods near the ghosts. I was supposed to take the ghosts away, too, part of my job, but I never did. I put the head and the hands in the bag and ditched it temporarily. But Douglas got arrested and I got scared shitless. I dropped everything except the shoes into the forms for an apartment building. Next day, soon as they poured the concrete, everything got hid forever. I learned. Think ahead. You got to plan.

Douglas, he didn't plan. That's why he got caught."

"He was a smart kid, though."

"He had no sense sometimes. Like, why did he stay on the golf course and wait for the cops? He was smart but that was stupid."

"He didn't run. He did that before, though. He ran. He learned from that."

"If you say so. I say stupid."

"Didn't run after you killed the cop, either."

He's not keen on that statement. His response is curious, though. No denial. Something was more important to him than defending himself. "Did Douglas say that?"

"Say what? That he didn't run?"

"That I killed the cop."

"Of course not. He's like a brother to you, right?"

Cinq-Mars lets that settle and reside under the man's skin.

"Do you think Douglas owed you?" he asks very quietly.

"What? When? No. Why?"

"I'm trying to see the whole picture, Mr. Rubbachuk."

"Call me Raccoon, if you can't say my name right."

"Thank you. I will. Douglas gets roughed up on the golf course. You go out there with him the next night. A guy pestering him gets a knife in the chest. Your knife, I presume. Like I said, you can talk about it, nobody's coming down on you for that. I'm thinking big picture here: Why would you stick a knife in another boy's chest in defence of Douglas Sykes unless you believed that Douglas owed you?"

"That makes no sense."

"Why not?"

"If I *owed* him, I'd do him a solid. Not if he owed me."

"A solid," Cinq-Mars repeated. "That's modern talk, isn't it? I hate that kind of talk."

"What would you call it then?"

"You did a friend a favour."

"Fine. Why would *I* do *him* a favour if *he* owed *me*?"

"To make it clear, once and for all, that he owed you. To put him even deeper in your debt."

"I don't get that. I don't get you at all."

"Raccoon, he helped you kill your dad."

"Newsflash. My dad killed himself."

"With your help! And Douglas helped you."

"You know that?"

"I do. I got Douglas off after he was caught with your dad's feet. At that point, he could have given you both up. Your dad for committing suicide. You, for your part in it."

"He should've." Strange, how that bitterness leaks out.

"Except, he owed you. You think that way because you took the head and the hands away. All he had to do was unload the feet. He got off easy, first with the feet and then with me. You were on the side of the tracks with the head. That's what he never experienced. Your dad's head in your lap. That's what you took on for your brother. He owed you for that. All he got was the feet and then he got off. You got the head, and you took your daddy's shoes – you took them, I think, to force Douglas to pick up the bare feet, to freak him out like you were freaked out by your daddy's head rolling into your lap. Right off the bat, you wanted him to suffer like you were suffering. Ever since, you've been one half-baked cookie. Am I right?"

"I dunno." He seems abruptly distant.

"You're pissed about that, too. Douglas comes back from wandering the world, free as a bird, while you're stuck pursuing a life of crime with a darkness in your head that never leaves you. You go out to the golf course with him and kill the boy messing with him. That drives home the point that he owes you, because you lost your life that day on the tracks, and now he owes you because he got off easy. He really owes you. I'm not saying it's logical. More like it's psychological. I'm wondering out loud if you think that that's what was going on inside your head. Deep down. I'm not judging you. You were only a screwed-up kid, right?"

Raccoon is looking away, trying to elude this. "I don't know what you're on about, mister."

"It's simple. You wanted your brother to see where you were at. You were broken. You were a tormented kid before that, nobody can blame you. A dad like yours. A mom in rough shape herself. Then your dad's head plops into your lap, the eyes staring up at you. What a wretched misery. All you wanted, years later out on the links, was to show your brother how far you'd fallen, what a disaster your life had been, so he'd join you down there in that hellhole forever. Just like you wanted him to pick up the bare feet. Then you made him take off not only the shoes, but the socks, too. You asked for the shoes to torture your brother. You wanted him to be in your hellhole with you. Not necessarily consciously, but does that sound about right to you?"

The man seems to consider the proposition.

"That's what happened," Cinq-Mars continues. "Then you established your bond. You made it official. I'm surprised you didn't swear a blood oath. Cut your fingers, press them together. Or did you? You whisper to him: *Pretend you don't know me. When we're around the same people, act like we're strangers.* Because you're the bad dude, he's the good. You look after him. But you look after him in your own way, so he will honour you. His friendship, his brotherhood with you, that's what holds you up. He never betrayed you. That holds you up. So, you hold him up. That's what's important to you in this world."

Raccoon is not about to deny it.

"It's my wife's theory, by the way. I should give her the credit."

Sharing that confidence is another revelation. It brings him back. "How's that?"

"She figured that no one has ever supported your friendship, your bond. People would say to Douglas, get rid of that guy, lose that fuck-up, stay away from him, he's bad news. But Douglas never betrayed you. He still hasn't. He could go down for murder one and not give you up."

"Think so?"

"That's one hell of a brother you have there."

A curiosity is aroused behind his eyes. He tries to look away; always his gaze returns to Cinq-Mars.

"You've done a lot for each other. Back and forth. He's been a faithful bro. You have, too. Do you want him to go down for you now? That's what I'm asking."

Cinq-Mars has accomplished what he intended. The whole of the man's life swirls inside him. They've barely touched on the recent violence, yet it's the full range of the man's life and the full range of his bond with Douglas Sykes that he wants to stir up, mixing it into the current calamity, to make all of it one and the same.

"What I'm hearing," Raccoon says. An odd diction for him. He's off his usual stump, internally. "You want to get Douglas off again."

The bitterness of that experience. That it's always Douglas who gets off. That his pal is always the one who escapes the brunt of the blame and the damage done.

"That's the idea. This time, you can get a piece of that pie. What do you say?"

"What do you mean?" For him, hope is a difficult concept to grasp.

"That's why you called my wife. To get off. Don't let me down now. Don't tell me you've changed your mind."

"Yeah, I want to get off."

"I mean. You killed a cop. You're not walking on that charge. You know that."

"Prison for me is a death sentence. You know that. Not a quick one neither."

"That's why I'm in the room with you, here and now. I'm a retired cop. I'm not supposed to be in here. But you threatened my wife. Gives me a certain cachet within the department, you know? They'll give me some slack to deal with you any way I want, since you're a dead man walking anyhow. Everybody knows that if things don't go our way we can just turn you back over to the Hells."

"Jesus, man, are you going to help me or not?"

"That depends. Are you going to admit to killing that police officer or not? You will go to prison for that. The key to the cell door gets thrown away. Life. Your life. No way around it. But here's the plan. There's a way for you to be safe in jail. You can live out your days in there. We can work that out together."

"The Hells won't keep me alive."

"Mittens might, if he wants to. I can see to it that he'll want to."

"Really? No way. That's crazy talk."

"You're forgetting something."

"What?"

"Mittens wanted Douglas dead in the first place. Instead, you kept him alive. I can award you for that. For the cop, you go to prison for life. For saving Douglas, you get looked after on the inside. Mittens will see to it. Remember, he wanted Douglas dead in the first place. And I know why. That *why* is your ticket to longevity."

Cinq-Mars can feel what it is that Raccoon is experiencing. It's what he was missing back when he found himself on death's door. A sense of reconfiguration, something vaguely transformative, not so much a rising to the light, although he'd been expecting that, rather, the sense of a shine emanating outside and within, and in this instance within the space between them. Cinq-Mars is being stirred by an experience and can't positively identify what it might mean. He can only acknowledge its effect on him, its presence. He's also dizzy. He's thinking that he had better leave the room or he might faint again, he might fall over.

"Okay," Raccoon says. "What happens next?"

"You trust me," Cinq-Mars informs him.

"Oh, sure. Why not? What does that mean anyhow?"

"You write out your confession. Fully and completely."

"That figures. Then I'm fucked. What comes after?"

"I talk to Mittens. See if he wants you alive or dead, or just ripped apart. I'll let you know how it goes. Don't look at me that way. You expected a better deal? It's the best one you'll ever get in this world. It's the only one that might work out for you."

The man sighs.

"Like I said," Cinq-Mars repeats. "Trust me."

32. Mercy and Goodness

"You look like you belong in a morgue," Mittens remarks as he sits down.

"You look like you belong exactly where you are," Cinq-Mars retaliates.

The retired policeman chose a different venue for his return visit to the penitentiary. They meet in the visitor's dock, a glass barrier between them. A disinterested guard stands in the background, but no one else is present.

"I've seen guys like you," Mittens taunts him. "Into biker boys. Leather turns you on. Sorry if you got the wrong idea. I only do chicks."

"Not lately, you don't."

"No? The newspapers say I get regular conjugal. Do you, Cinq-Mars? I can arrange for a con to blow you. Hope you don't mind if he has warts on his tongue."

"Don't be rude. I am not in the mood."

"Like I give a shit about your mood," Mittens goes on. "Entertain me, Cinq-Mars. Bring me a cake with a file inside – or fuck the fuck off."

"Another time."

"I prefer vanilla to chocolate." He wears an idiot grin.

Cinq-Mars explains his presence and purpose in detail. He knows what Douglas Sykes knows; he has Mittens and his daughter up against a stone wall, plotting against their own people. "You've killed your own before, Mittens. How did that work out for you?"

Not well. The Hells split apart and a new gang, the Rock Machine, formed. Their battle for turf resulted in 150 bombs and as many murders, and eventually the incarceration of most members in both gangs.

"You got chips on the table, Detective? Don't come back without 'em, I told you."

"Your hired gun is in our hands now."

That quietens him down. "Good to know," Mittens acknowledges.

"Sharpie and company worked him over. You're going to have trouble in that direction."

"Nice of you to take sides."

"Don't think that way. I asked you to be ready to negotiate."

"What am I selling?" Mittens asks.

"Douglas Sykes will live as a free man on the outside. Raccoon Rybachuk will dwell as a free man on the inside. They both get left alone."

"What am I buying? I hope you're planning on giving me the east coast. It's all I want for Christmas."

"Don't kid me. You know what's at stake here. As far as the coast goes, you can take it the old-fashioned way. Nothing gift-wrapped. You have a list of people you want eliminated. If anyone on that list dies, we'll know who did it and we'll start with that advantage. That's your problem, not ours." He clears his throat as he shifts gears. "Mélanie's involvement becomes a clean slate from this point looking back. Anything after today, going forward, that's her problem. I have other options, so choose now and accept the whole hog. Go back on your word, I go back on mine. We'll have Sykes's testimony recorded, written out, signed and sealed by a judge. Mélanie goes down if Sykes goes down, and she also goes down if Raccoon goes down. Both of you, father and daughter, go down together if this leaks out. The courts will be one thing, but your associates will be another problem for you. For as long as I'm in this room, I'm offering our silence. One more threat: if you don't come through, your son gets our full attention. Kiss his medium security days *adios*. And we take away your

Castle Pen. But here's a carrot. Come through, I'll give you a new prison guard."

"I like the one I got. Gives me no trouble. Brings me beer."

"Mittens, he's a Mountie. He knows stuff, too. You'll want us to keep that quiet, too. You don't want your people to find out you've been cosy with a Mountie. What you don't want them to hear, they'll hear. So, choose."

He doesn't have to think about it.

"Sounds smart," he says.

"Question is, can you deliver your end?"

That takes another level of thought. "Douglas Sykes on the outside, I see no problem. Move him off the map. Out of sight, out of mind. Once the word goes down to leave him be, people will. Raccoon on the inside, that's tricky. Put him in Port-Cartier. Don't let him say it's too far, that nobody will visit. All true, and it's cold outside in winter, but it's a super-max, he's safer in there. My order to keep him secure shouldn't be no problem. You keep our enemies out of there anyway, so that helps."

It's not publicly acknowledged, but Cinq-Mars is aware that the prison discriminates against one gang to keep the warring parties separated.

"You've got problems in this," Cinq-Mars mentions. "Sharpie worked over Raccoon who doesn't strike me as the silent-hero type."

"Sharpie, his pal Chiclets, they had Raccoon by the neck twice. Twice. Twice. Are you hearing this? Twice they let him get away. How is that possible? How can that go by without there's an appropriate change to how things work? Starting with a change in personnel."

"Your lookout, not mine. The rest of this doesn't go away," Cinq-Mars cautions him. "Accidents happen. If they do, that falls hard on you. Before I die, before you die, after we both die, this goes on."

"Mélanie has a charge up."

"That stays put. Imagine, though, if we brought a busload of conspiracy charges against her, how the one she has now will look. As is, we stay quiet, she'll be out before she gets too comfortable on the inside. Be a good life lesson for her, nothing more."

Mittens mulls everything over. "That true? My guard's a Mountie?"

"Out the front door as we speak. He chose not to say goodbye."

"Fucker. Okay. This is skintight between us. You're protecting my family. If you don't, nobody can protect yours. Understood?"

"You don't want to go there."

"Neither do you. Nobody needs to go no place. Pull your end. I'll pull mine."

"Done."

Mittens stands. He rises and leaves. The guard opens the door for him and escorts him out. Cinq-Mars watches him go, then wheels back to the door behind him. He presses the buzzer to be released. The atmosphere of the prison may be undermining his equilibrium; he's not feeling himself. He feels way off.

33. After and Before

Hectic in summer, Crescent Street in downtown Montreal is a mecca for revellers. The noise is constant, the glimmering sashay of limbs a continuous motion. Restaurants and bars keep the flow churning, as tourists and students, business folk and shoppers nibble and imbibe. Émile Cinq-Mars is hell-bent on an Irish pub. Hurley's.

His wife enters the pub ahead of him, seeking assistance. Even if Émile walks in under his own steam, she'd prefer if someone carried in the chair for her. She locates Bill Mathers sitting with the man she met at the hospital, Douglas Sykes, on the subterranean level, pints on their tabletop. Bill is rising but the other man elbows him out of the way. He wants the job. Sykes goes out and bounces Émile Cinq-Mars down the steps in his chair.

Sandra kisses her husband goodbye and warns Bill not to overwork her man. If needed, she's on her cell. Then she's off to visit a friend.

Cinq-Mars orders a beer. When in Rome… order Guinness.

"Here we are," he says. "Two cops and a thug."

"Thug!" Douglas Sykes challenges him.

"You prefer two-bit hood?"

"We're a couple of wounded warriors," Sykes remarks.

Indicating his old partner, Cinq-Mars announces, "You owe your life to this man."

Although they've been sitting together a short while already, Sykes pulls out his right hand from under the tabletop and offers it to Mathers. "Raccoon does, too, I heard. Let me thank you from the both of us."

"Freeing Raccoon freed you. Domino effect," Cinq-Mars explains.

"Good to know. Forgive me if I don't see how it puts me in the clear, Émile."

"About that," Mathers interrupts. "Story's up on the radio. This morning, over breakfast, both Sharpie and Chiclets went to their final reward. A hail of bullets put them facedown in their scrambled eggs."

Cinq-Mars nods. He'd been expecting news like that. "Who takes over?"

"We suspect a thug known as Pinkeye," Mathers attests. "Know him?"

"Met him," Cinq-Mars recalls. "What about you, Douglas?"

"He wears pink shirts. That's about all I know. He's come up in the world."

"The heir apparent, as far as we can surmise," Mathers confirms.

"Loyal to Mittens," Cinq-Mars states.

"Very. He's the one who sent me in," Sykes reveals.

"Sent you in where?"

"To the biker's bank. I reported to Pinkeye when I got back to Montreal. Let him know I was done. One *thug*, as you want to call us, to another, only this thug's retired. He could've cared less. When he got back to me later, I was surprised. He was short-handed, he said. He asked me to fill in as security at a bank. I'd be relieved late in the day. Worst case, I'd be bored out of my tree. That's what he told me."

"The man's no prophet," Mathers opines.

"You were set up," Cinq-Mars confirms. "You must've been shocked when Raccoon walked in."

"Shocked. Scared. He announced that he was my relief. Then he went into the back room and shot the little guy, Frank Bardi. Sweet enough kid."

"Cold."

"Totally. He came out of the room. We were stunned, and locked in, too. Nowhere to run. But I was thinking that it was one and done. He was here to kill one man and had done that. It was over. Then he said, "Sorry," and shot the other guy. Took that guy's gun off him. Gave me a look. I think I said his name or something. Up until then we didn't acknowledge we knew each other. Always the plan with us. We hadn't seen each other; now he's asking how I've been. Told him I just got back from the west, so he wouldn't be offended that I hadn't called. The whole time, the woman was down on her knees with her eyes closed. Praying, I think. Tears on her cheeks. She's shaking. Rac hardly looked at her. *Didn't* look at her. Shot her twice. I figured I'm dead, too."

Cinq-Mars closes his eyes a moment, allows a fleeting dizzy spell to travel through him, then pass. He's felt better. When he looks up again, he says, "Go on."

"He tells me to run. He'll shoot me in the leg. It'll hurt, he says, but it's the only way. He'll use the other guy's gun, he says. I don't ask why. Like I care which gun. This is so wack. I'm saying, how can I run if you shoot me in the leg? He says, 'You got to think fast. Be quick on your feet.' I wanted to argue that he wasn't thinking at all, but, you know, he's the one with the weapons."

"Then he shot you."

"Not yet. He said, 'I'm supposed to blow your head off, Douglas. It's you I'm here for. The rest, they're collateral, to make it look good.' Three people dead because of me, Émile, and I have no clue why. This makes no sense. I ran, like I was told to do. On my way out the back door he shot me. I got up, kept going. I'm in a state of pure terror at that moment. Totally freaked. He followed me, to throw stuff away – like a gun, I think. Then he went back inside. Could be he had a car out front."

"Jesus," Bill Mathers says. Then, in deference to his former partner's Catholicism, tacks on, "Sorry."

"Yeah," Cinq-Mars agrees. "Jesus."

They sit and drink beer.

Cinq-Mars turns his glass on the table as a notion revolves in his head. "If Pinkeye's in charge now, he'll bring order to the lawless. Not saying that's good or bad. Just bound to be one or the other."

"I'll pass it on," Mathers mentions.

"If you say it's from me, not many will listen."

"You might be surprised."

"Mmm." Cinq-Mars takes a good swig of his beer. Properly served at room temperature, on this hot day, it's refreshing. "Bill, say it's from you. Make it your opinion. That won't hurt you."

Mathers thinks about it, then concurs. "Okay. I will."

"Douglas," Cinq-Mars carries on. "A changing of the guard brings us around to you."

The man waits to hear his fate in the world. "I guess you got that figured out."

"We have options. What do you think, Bill? Is it time that this guy properly fulfils his lifelong mission to be a police informant?"

"I've been a police informant, Émile."

"Not in this city."

"How soon we forget."

"That was mainly to help yourself out. Why else do you think you can walk the streets of Montreal and have a beer in a pub? Although I wouldn't push your luck in that regard."

"Not sure that I have anything to offer." The man appears glum.

"If you're not a snitch, what else will you do? Oh, right. I forget. You've lived off the avails. You're independently wealthy."

"I did not live off the avails. I put honest coin aside, that's all. I can stay afloat."

"Define a stool pigeon for me, Bill."

Mathers recites the Cinq-Mars credo, that a stool pigeon is the bad luck feathered friend who attracts other birds only to be gunned down in the crossfire. "Life expectancy – remarkably brief. Never to flap a wing again."

"Hear that, Douglas? You've done well for yourself by living this long. You must have something going on."

"Cops," Sykes says. He's pissed. "You can never let a man reform, can you? You gotta keep working him, bleeding him, making him pay."

"Reform?" Cinq-Mars taunts him. "Who? You? You expect me to believe all your stories, swallow them whole, send you out into the world with an ice cream cone in one hand, dice in the other. Roll them. See what happens. I'd have to believe in you to do that, Douglas. I'd have to believe in a man who attracts murder to his side like some men attract mosquitoes. What's in your blood that so many die around you?"

Sykes has nothing to say to that, he's too busy suppressing his rage.

Mathers puts in, "A lot of people die around you, too, Émile."

"You sound like my wife."

"If the shoe fits."

"This is a man who worked as the broom in a biker's bar," Cinq-Mars insists. "Who knows what he swept under the rug? A friend to strippers and hookers, he read them bedtime stories. Every so often he got busted and went to jail, near as I can tell for the hell of it. Yeah," Cinq-Mars says, and takes his gaze off Mathers and lowers it onto Douglas Sykes, "I can believe in this guy. I've got no problem with that."

Another moment or two is required, as Sykes had fallen for the ruse hook, line, and sinker, and now it dawns on him that they have artfully played him for a fish.

"Your face," Cinq-Mars remarks.

"Never mind my face. You dickheads. I'm a man in jeopardy, you don't know that?"

"Ever meet a lowlife with this man's vocab?" Cinq-Mars asks Mathers.

"Can't say I have."

"Up yours, the both."

"You're wrong, Douglas. I can make fun of you until the cows come home because you're not in jeopardy. Mittens has given you a free pass. Did I not mention? As of this morning, his adversaries are deceased. Raccoon, as I told you, will be pleading out and transferring to the prison in Port-Cartier, where *he* gets a free pass, too. The question is, what are you going to do while you're recovering from your wounds? You're ahead of me, in that regard. What I'm thinking is, you can come out to the farm while we're recovering. Help out. Contemplate your future from there."

"You're kidding me." Although he says that, it's obvious he's hoping otherwise.

"Not this time. You can sleep in the barn with the other animals."

Sykes agrees to that. "Beats a cellblock."

"This time, he *is* kidding you," Mathers cautions him. "Not about the farm. The part about the barn."

Cinq-Mars disagrees. "No, I'm not. He sleeps in the barn."

Mathers is startled, and processes that news. He glances at Sykes, who says, "He's not kidding." Mathers shrugs. Then, with a movement of his chin, Cinq-Mars nods to Sykes to let his old partner in on the truth. "Yeah, he's kidding. Like a good slave, I get to sleep in the big house."

Taken in, Mathers accepts being the fool on that one. They share a chuckle, and simultaneously each man reaches for his glass. They drink to their good health.

"Émile," Sykes says, and enfolds his forearms on the edge of the table and leans forward, indicating that he wants to be serious now, "Sharpie and Chiclets are dead. How does that square me with Mittens, namely, take care of what I know?"

"Sacred rule. It's been borne out in the past when broken. Hells don't believe in killing their own. He'll pin today's murders on somebody else. If I was in the Rock Machine, I'd watch my back. What Mittens does not want anyone to know is that he planned this, that it's only about his own diminished power. Your knowledge is your passport for evermore."

Sykes juts his chin from side to side, a contemplation. "I called on you, looking for a miracle. You pulled it off. Mind explaining how? Mittens, I understand. But Rac?"

Cinq-Mars settles more deeply into his chair. "There's good reason why a magician won't reveal his tricks. People think they want to know how a trick is done, but as soon as they find out it's no longer magic for them. Just a trick. The magician is disparaged, his craft is not admired, even though he's very good at what he does, even though he's faithful to his art." He takes up his beer, sips and requests some leeway. "Permit me to go off on a diversion."

Both Cinq-Mars and Douglas Sykes are sidetracked by Bill Mathers, who has burst into a low laugh on his own. "What?" Sykes asks him.

"In my entire life, I have never had a beer with this man when he doesn't go off on a diversion. Go ahead, Émile. Don't mind me. I'm all ears."

"I can have you shot."

"No, you can't."

"I can do it myself."

"But you won't."

Cinq-Mars looks at Sykes, to see if he will acquiesce as well.

Sykes has something to say about their exchange. "Remember the old days, Émile? We had some crazy talks. I was a kid. I realize it only now: You weren't much older. We thought we could take the world by storm. We chatted about life, remember? The universe. Everything. I know you were leading me on, hoping to pry stuff out of me, but I was leading you on, too. Those crazy talks kept me alive. They gave me hope if that makes sense."

Cinq-Mars smiles, appreciating both the compliment and the memory. "You see, Bill, they have value, my diversions."

Mathers puts a hand in the air, to deflect his impatience. "Like I said, I'm all ears."

"I wanted to point out – and Bill, please, don't cringe – science is showing us how the trick of creation was accomplished. To a tiny degree, anyway. Consequently, folks dismiss the magician. Creation is still a damn good trick, but because we understand the Big Bang and what came right after, and because of that we have an inkling of what particles do in particle accelerators and we're into quantum. We have physics on the brain is what I'm saying. My point is, just because we comprehend a little about the *how* of creation, that doesn't mean we can do it ourselves. That doesn't mean it's not a helluva trick. So, to my point, the myths and metaphors in various cultures were good ones. They didn't give away the trick, how it was done, but they celebrated the mystery of life and that of the cosmos. For instance, I've never believed that somebody collected a couple of penguins from Antarctica and put them aboard Noah's Ark. Still, it's not beyond the realm that some guy named Noah collected farm animals germane to his existence to spare them from a flood. More importantly, the message embedded in the myth, the takeaway lesson, is that people are responsible for the whole of the planet. That's how I understand it anyway. We're responsible for all the world's creatures and creations, for the environment that sustains us all. And isn't that a notion from way back in time that was way before its time? As a metaphor, as a myth, it's stood the test. More valid than ever today, since we can stick every animal's DNA in a suitcase, but back in time it also served a purpose. I mean, imagine if God said to a caveman, E=mc squared, do you think that *that* would have withstood the test of time? Or lasted a single generation? Or even an hour? I say no. The average person still doesn't understand the theory, what would any cave-dweller do with it back then? No, a good story, a good metaphor, a strong mythology that appeals to the imagination, that's a way to interpret the world and keep us yearning, going forward forever. Revealing the intricacies of the trick has to await its time."

"Okay," Douglas Sykes says. Puzzled. "Whatever you're on about."

Mathers's agreement is also tentative. "Sure. Okay."

Cinq-Mars explains. "Raccoon held to his own mythology, namely that Douglas is his brother. He was an abused, distorted, unbalanced child, off his nut, who got into huge trouble that he could not handle. He went down a drain hole. He got flushed. In that sewer, he could not survive, but survive he did, in large measure because he had something to hold onto. Not Douglas, per se, but the *mythology* of Douglas. He had a brother-like person in his life who would never betray him. He needed that. He may have known that at its heart it wasn't true, in whole or even in part. Which is why he wanted to keep it a secret. He could hold onto it that way, as a secret, he could be devoted to the idea that way, as a secret. It could be permanent because it was never exposed to the light of day. He could think to himself, *Douglas will never betray me, and I will never betray Douglas.* And *that*, that was the light within him. The fact of the matter is, it's a light that still shines. It will carry him through the rest of his days, and that's why you, *Dougie*, are walking the streets a free man and drinking a pint in a pub with two cops."

"Okay. But. Why are you calling me Dougie?"

"Because *Douglas* is your own myth. We need to play with our myths now and then to understand them better and to appreciate them more. Look, if we said to Raccoon way back when, at that terrible time, 'Confess to helping your dad die' or 'Confess to killing that boy on the golf course. Douglas will like it if you do. It might spare him a life as a criminal,' that whole idea would never have flown. It had no legs. It would never have stood up and walked down the block. Today, on the other hand, we can say to him, 'Help Douglas out. Please, save him, and he'll save you. The two of you, like brothers, can save each other.' Like any good magician, we won't show Raccoon our tricks. He's safe, he's secure, and as far as he's concerned that's a *bona fide* miracle. Let's give him that, because he can live off that and let's give him the respect he's due for caring enough about you, Douglas, to make a sacrifice. Don't remind him that he was only saving his own skin. That won't get him anywhere. Let him think that he did it for his brother. That might keep him alive."

"You're saying," Douglas Sykes winds up the subject, "that the thought of me and him as sort-of-like-brothers kept him alive, down through the years."

"It gave him a sense that he was human, too, underneath his mess. Even, in a way, that he mattered to someone because in his head he mattered to you. You never gave him up, and he held onto that. It reconfirms his own worth. He gets something back from it, and I wouldn't take it away from him. It doesn't matter to me that it's only a fabrication, a personal myth."

Sykes appears saddened by this ebb and flow. The three men drink quietly, each to their own thoughts. Eventually, Douglas asks, "When can I see him?"

Cinq-Mars is adamant on this point. "You can't. Not without exposing him to the riff-raff. We have his protection as an order from on high, but he still has to make his way among the others. When they see that he's protected, other cons will lay off him. But if they see that you're on the loose and a free bird, questions will be asked. Like, how you got off. *Isn't he the guy who shot those folks?*

And shot a cop, too? They'll not think well of you, walking free, less of him for knowing you. Stories get around. Suspicion mounts. Raccoon understands the situation. When you're both quite old, and people forget, there might be an opportunity to pay him a visit. With that in mind, you don't need a new identity, Douglas, but you do need to start over."

"Yeah, well, what else is new? I've been looking to do that most of my life."

Cinq-Mars is nodding. "Now you can. Sandra is looking forward to having you out to the farm. As she said, 'It will be nice to have a man around the house for a change.' I think she means, instead of an invalid, but I have my doubts."

The three of them enjoy a laugh again, this time at Émile's expense, and it's a signal that the serious turn to their discussion has concluded.

"Do you have cows on this farm of yours? I could milk cows."

"Horses. They kick strangers if you try to milk them. Just so you know."

"That's fine. I'll be a cowboy. If I turn bad again, I'll rustle cattle."

"Sounds like a plan."

As they finish their beers, Douglas Sykes looks concerned. "Émile? What's going on? You're not looking so good."

Cinq-Mars closes his eyes, holds up a hand. After a moment, he offers, "This, too, will pass. It's nothing. Comes and goes. I'm dizzy though. Maybe, ah, sure, ah, Bill? Call Sandra. I could go home now. Hey. My work here is done."

Mathers is now concerned as well.

"Home, Émile, or the hospital?"

"Yeah. Yeah. This isn't exactly like before. Hospital. The nearest one. Call Sandra later."

"Ambulance?" Sykes asks Mathers.

"My car's outside. I have a siren. It'll be quicker."

"Let's go."

On the sidewalk outside the pub, amid the swirl of pedestrians and traffic, while Mathers pops a revolving light on the top of his car and creates space to get out of his spot with a quick buzz on his siren, Douglas Sykes drags Émile Cinq-Mars up the stairs in his wheelchair to the sidewalk. There, he kneels beside him. They clutch hands.

"Hang on, old bugger," Sykes tells him.

"You, too," Cinq-Mars says. "I'm counting on you."

"Be quiet for once in your life. Take it easy."

He takes his advice. He cannot do much more.

Mathers pulls up beyond the parked cars and rushes to them. He and Sykes lift the wheelchair high up to clear the bumpers of the vehicles at the curb. Émile Cinq-Mars is riding high for a moment, lifted above the throng and breaking through shadows cast by buildings into a slice of sunlight. They ease him down to the pavement, wheel him around the car and slide him into the front passenger seat. Douglas Sykes collapses the wheelchair and shoves it ahead of him into the back seat while Mathers hurries to squeeze behind the wheel again.

Doors slam.

Siren on, bright cherry flashing, the car bullies its way through traffic. At the end of the block, it veers right and tears off at a clip.

Once again, a race is on.

The end.